WHERE THE BOYS ARE

Books by William J. Mann

Novels

THE MEN FROM THE BOYS

THE BIOGRAPH GIRL

WHERE THE BOYS ARE

Nonfiction

WISECRACKER:
The Life and Times of William Haines,
Hollywood's First Openly Gay Star

BEHIND THE SCREEN:
How Gays and Lesbians
Shaped Hollywood 1910–1969

KENSINGTON BOOKS are published by

Kensington Publishing Corp.
850 Third Avenue
New York, NY 10022

Library of Congress Card Catalogue Number: 2002112656
ISBN 0-7582-0326-8

First Printing: May 2003
10 9 8 7 6 5 4 3 2 1

Printed in the United States of America

WHERE
THE
BOYS ARE

WILLIAM J. MANN

KENSINGTON BOOKS
http://www.kensingtonbooks.com

For Tim, Victor, and
the boys on the dance floor

ACKNOWLEDGMENTS

Thanks to my most wonderfully supportive editor, John Scognamiglio; to my industrious agent, Malaga Baldi; to Shirl Roccapriore and Laura Shabott; and to Tim Huber, my first and best critic.

I enjoy hearing from readers. You can reach me through my Web site, www.williamjmann.com.

Our lives are better left to chance—I could have missed the pain.
But I'd of had to miss the dance.

—Rockell, "The Dance,"
lyrics by Tony Arata

New Year's Eve 1999, New York City

Jeff

Across the dance floor, some guy's squirting Windex in his mouth.

"Now I've seen *every*thing," Henry says, all eyes and attitude.

I just shake my head. "Believe me, Henry. You have *not* seen everything."

For here on the dance floor, nothing quite makes sense in the way it does in the world beyond. Here the ludicrous becomes the sublime. Dress in spandex and sequins and funny little hats. Ingest substances not intended for human consumption. Stick your tongue down the throat of a beautiful stranger. Take off your pants and dance in your underwear. That's just the way things are.

"Still," Henry's sputtering, shaking his head, "the things some people will *do* for a fucking high. I mean, *Windex—*"

"Henry." I place my palms against his sweaty chest and press my face close to his. Eyes to eyes, nose to nose. *"No talking on the dance floor."*

It's my rule, and he knows it, even if he conveniently forgets it whenever he want to start gabbing. Henry's one of the chatty types. You know the kind I mean. The ones who insist on telling you, right in the middle of an awesome Rosabel club anthem remix, all about their new job or the size of the penis on their last trick or—worst of all—how tonight's DJ *just really sucks*: "Can you believe how he's mixing in all this trancey stuff with all this high-energy disco diva blah blah blah blah blah."

Dance! We're here to dance!

That's why *I* come, anyway: to escape, to forget, to get swallowed up by a moist cocoon of four hundred men with the music spinning me higher and higher until it's taken control, slipping past my defenses like the fingers of a stranger trespassing beneath the waistband of my underwear.

That happens, too. One more example of the way things are.

"Oh, shit, Jeff," Henry says. "He saw me looking."

I roll my eyes. "Who?"

"The Windex queen!"

A few feet away, to the giddy disgust of the boys around him, the tall blond guy is pumping the bright-blue liquid down his throat. But his eyes have locked onto Henry's, and he's now sidling our way, his lanky body easily angling around the huddles of boyflesh.

"Jeff, you've gotta hide me!" Henry yelps.

I just laugh. "Didn't I teach you to fight your own battles, buddy?"

"How you boys doin' tonight?" the Windex queen purrs, holding aloft his bottle like a prize. "Wanta get *really* twisted?"

I give the guy the once-over. A dyed blond, skinny and shapeless, with tiny little buds for nipples, one of which is pierced with a small gold ring.

"Thanks," I tell him, "but we're as twisted as we want to be."

"You boys are no fun," he says, pouting, moving on to his next victims. Henry leans into me and breathes a sigh of relief.

"Do you think that really *is* Windex?

"Henry," I remind him, "no talking on the dance floor."

Okay. So maybe you think I'm coming across a little overweening here. I don't mean to be. Really, I don't. Oh, I'm sure in the course of this you're going to hear people say that I'm self-absorbed, arrogant, selfish. They said it last time, they'll say it again. But it's just that I've come here to dance, to close out the rest of the world for a night, to forget what I want so much to forget. Is that so wrong? So much to ask? I have no patience for dance floor vaudeville.

And maybe tonight I'm a little more impatient that usual. You see, it's getting close to midnight, and Lloyd still hasn't shown.

"Forgive me if I use my voice again, Jeff," Henry says, drawing close. "But are you starting to think that Lloyd isn't coming?"

"He's still got time," I insist.

Henry snorts. "And you're *still* convinced he's going to tell you he wants to move back in with you?"

Here's something you need to know about Henry: he's my best friend and I love him and he's terrific and all that, but he can be a total *nag*. I think somewhere down deep, Henry would like us to be more than just friends, and the idea of my ex-lover and me moving back in together probably unnerves him a little bit. So I just smile. "Well, we'll just have to wait and see," I suggest sweetly, "won't we, Henry?"

He just smirks and goes silent. Finally.

We both fall into the music. It's awesome tonight, being New Year's and all. The Ecstasy is sending warm shivers thoughout my body. I reach over and run my hands down Henry's torso, tweaking his nipples as I pass.

He opens his eyes. "Just because you're rolling, Jeff O'Brien, is no excuse to hit on your sister."

I pull in close. "You *know* you want me," I tease.

Henry pushes me away. "What I *want*," he insists, "is to be in Miami. *Brent* is in Miami, and you can be sure he'll tell us *all* about it."

Okay, a few more notes on Henry. I created this monster. Yes, I admit it. I take full responsibility for what he's become. Henry Weiner was once a good boy who never had more than a couple of Heinekens at happy hour, whose idea of a big Saturday night out was watching retro Cyndi Lauper videos at Luxor with a couple of pals until midnight. He was one of those nameless, faceless guys you see on the sidelines of clubs, standing with their cocktails, watching the world pass them by. He was a 120-pound insurance-company geek on the fast track to corporate paralysis when I met him, enticing him to take off his shirt and step into the limelight. I'll never forget the look of sheer wonderment on his face as he slipped in between Brent Whitehead and me on the dance floor. Now Henry weighs in at 185, has a hard-won six-pack of abs and a star-burst tattoo around his navel. Now it's *very* important to Henry to keep pace with the other boys—especially Brent, circuit boy extraordinaire, who makes sure he's at every important party around the nation and whose primary goal in life is to get a photo of his sweaty torso into the pages of *Circuit Noize* magazine.

I look over at Henry with mock sympathy. "Now, now, buddy, we were just in Miami last month for the White Party. Let's not become *complete* stereotypes, shall we?"

He sniffs. "All I know is, it's *warm* in Miami, and we froze our butts off on Tenth Avenue tonight."

"Hey, *you're* the one that nixed the cab."

He shakes his finger at me. Literally. Like some old schoolmarm. "And well I *did*. After paying a hundred bucks to get in here tonight—not to mention what I had to fork over for the X—I wasn't paying out any more cash than I had to."

I lace my fingers behind Henry's back and pull him close, crotch to crotch. "So what happened to it?" I purr into his ear. "Ecstasy is supposed to give you a love for all mankind."

Henry smiles. Our faces are close enough that I can smell the Altoid in his mouth. In moments like these I can tell he wants to kiss me. Or me to kiss him. I can feel my dick swell against him despite myself.

"I'm just not independently wealthy like you," Henry needles. "And besides, it's the *millennium*, Jeff. I'm always going to remember where I was when the twentieth century turned over into the twenty-first—and here I am, in *New York* of all places, where I could be any time, any year, any century." He pouts. "And Victor Calderone is spinning in Miami. You *love* Victor Calderone, Jeff."

"Junior's doing a fine job here."

Henry smirks. "So long as the power doesn't shut off at midnight."

"Oh, don't start with the Y2K stuff." I hold my hands up. "How many gallons of water did you stockpile again?"

He ignores me. "At least in Miami we wouldn't freeze without power."

"Henry." I narrow my eyes at him. "*Read my lips.* Ix-nay on the dance floor talk." I grab him around the waist just as Junior mixes in "Unspeakable Joy" by Kim English.

Henry smiles nastily. "You know, maybe Lloyd got stuck in the thirteenth century and can't make it back to the twenty-first."

"Don't be snide, Henry."

Okay, time for a little more background. Lloyd—the guy I'm waiting for—the guy with whom I've spent the last eleven years of my life in a crazy back-and-forth *pas de deux*—had a first stop to make this evening before winding up here at Twilo. It was a past-life regression gathering at some lady's house on the Upper West Side. Now, *I* can make fun of Lloyd's New Agey-ness, but I will not tolerate others doing the same thing. Not even Henry.

"I'm not being—" Henry suddenly stops. "Oh, God, Jeff. He's coming back."

Two things at once: on my right, I spot the Windex queen approaching again, a tall flurry of arms with a mischievous gleam in his eyes, and on my left, beyond the perimeter of the dance floor, I catch a sudden flash of goatee and one well-rounded shoulder. *Lloyd.* He's quickly obscured again by the throng of manflesh, but I'm sure it was him.

"Come on," the Windex queen is saying. "Just one little baby squirt?"

I watch as the freak show pumps a dollop of the blue stuff into his mouth and swallows it, licking his lips. Henry makes a face in horror.

"Girl," I say, tapping a finger against his sticky, sinewy chest, "if you're drinking Windex, then I'm a straight boy from Jersey City."

At that moment, the crowd parts, not unlike the Red Sea, in fact, and I spot him again. *Lloyd*. Our eyes connect. He waves when he sees me. God, how beautiful he looks. I quickly slip around the Windex queen to push into the throng of flesh.

"What's the matter?" the guy asks, mock-innocently. "Was it something I *did?*"

Henry frowns. "It's not you," he says, raising his voice so I can hear. "It's his ex-lover, with whom he's expecting a roses-and-champagne reconciliation at midnight so they can fade out together behind the end credits and live happily ever after."

So let Henry be snide and sarcastic. That's what sisters do best, isn't it? Well, screw him. I'm not sure I still believe in happy ever-afters, given everything that's happened in the last five years, but right now, spotting Lloyd across the dance floor, all that matters is that he's *here*.

Lloyd

Even before I see him fully, I know it's Jeff. That's just the way it is with us. We have this uncanny way of finding each other, of connecting across great distances. Even during the time we were apart, if I would have a dream about him one night, he was sure to call the next morning. Don't laugh. I *believe* in such things as psychic connections, soul mates, partners with whom you travel from life to life. How else to explain Jeff and me? It's not as if we're much alike. He actually *enjoys* these places with their smoke and sweat and stink and drugs. So call it whatever you want, but there *is* something bigger than the two of us that keeps us together. There *has* to be.

"Hey!" Jeff pushes his way out of the snake pit of the dance floor.

I can't help laughing at the image. "You look like one of those devil kids emerging from the cornfield."

Jeff's eyes widen and he raises his arms like a monster. *"The Cheeldren of the Corn,"* he intones ominously, then breaks into a broad

grin. We both laugh and fall into each other's arms. It's one of our favorite bad movies, watched on a rainy day in Provincetown, a pan of
brownies rapidly disappearing between us.

We kiss. Lots of tongue and lips. I determine pretty quickly that Jeff
is on X. His torso is sticky and wet. I'm shirtless, too, having adhered to
the unwritten but widely observed policy of shirt removal moments
after checking one's coat, but unlike Jeff—who no doubt has already
been here for a while, slipping and sliding across countless boys on the
dance floor—I have yet to break into a sweat.

"You look great, Cat," I tell him. And he does—better all the time, it
seems. Jeff's always been good-looking—dark hair, classic features—but
now he's bigger, broader, more cut. He's spent a lot of time at the gym
over the past several years. And why not? He's had nothing else to do
and hasn't needed to worry about money the way he used to. Besides, I
think the gym, like his clubbing, is a way for him to escape. To forget.
Jeff spends a lot of energy forgetting.

"You, too, Dog," he tells me. "You look great, too." We kiss again.

Our old nicknames flow easily. In fact, everything's been surprisingly
easy these past few months, almost impossibly so. We stand there pec to
pec, chin to chin, arms wrapped around each other's waists. We're the
same height, so we're able to stare into each other's eyes until we both,
at the same time, let loose with a grin. That's been happening a lot:
whenever we look into each other's eyes for any length of time, we just
can't hold back the smile.

"I'm really glad you got here before midnight," Jeff says softly, holding my face in his hands.

I wink at him. "With twenty minutes to spare, too."

"I never doubted you for an instant."

Okay, so he probably did, but it's sweet of him to pretend. He kisses
me passionately for a moment, then pulls back to gaze into my eyes
again.

I smile wryly. "How much X did you do, Jeff?"

"Just one bump." He gets edgy, a little defensive—not what I want or
what I intended. "You said you trusted me. You know I don't get sloppy
anymore."

I nod. "I know, Jeff. I just worry that a little X—"

"Can lead to more? Please, Lloyd." He kisses me. "I'm okay. Just expressive. You said I *needed* to be more expressive."

A point of order here: Jeff was once *very* expressive about things,
without the need of any drug. I remember, when we lived together we'd
have fights about the laundry, in which he'd kick the basket of clothes

all the way down the stairs. Once, fed up with bill collectors, he tossed a ceramic dog his grandmother had given him across the room, where it shattered into a dozen pieces and left him heartbroken. I then painstakingly glued it back together for him as best I could.

Jeff never used drugs in those days. The emotion was real, heartfelt. The old Jeff used to cry over episodes of *Laverne and Shirley*—whenever Laverne would realize what a schmuck she'd been and how happy she really was living with Shirley in a basement apartment in Milwaukee, and then the two of them would start singing "High Hopes" as the camera panned up and out through the window. Jeff would be over there blubbering on the couch, and I was never quite sure if I wanted to laugh or cry along with him.

Then things happened. All the stuff he's been trying so hard to forget. He started doing drugs—and the *nasty* ones: crystal and GHB—and he shut down, reined in all those emotions. I hardly knew him. The Jeff I'd lived with for six years hadn't been afraid to let his feelings show. He might not have always known what they meant, but he let them flow. This new Jeff was as tight as a drum. It was a bad time. I worried he'd overdose. But he refused any contact with me or any of his old friends.

Then he just quit. He called me one day, out of the blue, saying he was giving it all up. And for the first time in three years, he acknowledged why he'd turned to drugs. It was grief. About Javitz—our friend, our mentor, who'd had the audacity to die one night when Jeff wasn't there. That was Javitz for you: always audacious.

Just how Jeff had managed his epiphany, I wasn't sure, and he hasn't talked about it. I just worry that even a single bump of Ecstacy might lead him back, push him over the edge to that dark place again. But I've promised to trust him. If we're rebuilding whatever it was we lost, I have to have faith in him. I have to believe in Jeff.

"Lloyd," he's saying, kissing me again, "I want you to know something. I don't ever want to celebrate another New Year's Eve without you."

I smile. That much emotion alone is worth the price of admission. For three New Year's Eves we were apart, and I missed him terribly every single year. Once New Year's Eve had been a tradition for us: Jeff, me, Javitz, and our cat, Mr. Tompkins. Times Square would be on the television set, and a couple of bottles of champagne would disappear rapidly. The picture of domestic tranquility.

Except, of course, it wasn't, at least not toward the end. I admit it was me who stirred the pot, upset the apple cart, whatever cliché you want to use. I was a dog pacing the parameters of my pen, filled with a wanderlust I couldn't explain. My karma in this life has always been about traveling, on journeys both within and without, and I had begun to question my confinement. I had no doubt that Jeff was my soul mate. Yet my own soul was yearning to see what else there might be out there for me.

Okay, so I sound a bit highfalutin. I don't mean to be. I can laugh at my cosmic quests as much as anyone. But it was heartfelt and honest. I loved Jeff, but it had all settled into something way too easy, far too predictable. So I left him. That's what it boiled down to: I left him. I said we ought to try living apart and moved out. For a while we tried to maintain a facade of togetherness, but it couldn't sustain itself.

Especially after Javitz died. Everything—all of our trials over the past few years—always comes back to that.

Jeff has taken my hand and moved us back toward the dance floor. He has a way of doing that: bringing me out of my head and back into the world. Is there any wonder why I missed him so?

"I don't want to leave Henry alone out there too long," Jeff explains. "You know how he gets."

I smile. "I know how *you* get standing around when the music is this good."

I wish I could predict how he'll react to the news I want to share with him. He's changed so much in the way he responds to things. I don't know whether he'll be happy for me, or angry, or hurt, or indifferent. And *when* should I tell him? Certainly not on the dance floor. Jeff hates it when people try to talk to him on the dance floor.

We push through the crowd, Jeff leading me by the hand. He turns all at once and says: "By the way, I think I know what you want to talk about."

"You *do?*" I shout over the music.

He just nods and grins, continuing to lead the way.

But how can he know? How did he find out?

God, I hope it's going to be all right. I hope this will only bring us closer, not pull us apart yet again.

I close my eyes as we take our place. How I wish Javitz were here. Javitz would've known how to handle it. Javitz—brilliant, irresistible, impossible—knew how to handle *anything*. Me . . . well, I'll let you be the judge of that.

Henry

I'm dancing with Shane when Jeff and Lloyd return to the dance floor.

Shane, the Windex queen.

"*Weeeeell,*" Shane says, bending his long body down to greet Lloyd. "Yet another cutie." He waves the blue bottle in Lloyd's face. "Want some?"

This is where my own fun comes in. "Go ahead, try it," I quip, looking over at Jeff and licking my lips. "It's yummy."

Jeff narrows his eyes at me. "Your lips are blue."

"*Are* they?" I ask innocently. I grin and look up at Shane. "Gimme another shot, baby."

The lanky one complies, squirting a strong dose down my throat. Jeff and Lloyd watch, wide-eyed. "*Sooo* tasty," I tell them, giggling.

"You're crazy," Lloyd snaps. He looks at Jeff, aghast. "I've *told* you, Jeff. People lose all *sense* out here! The things they'll do, just for a fucking high—"

"Lighten up, Marge," Shane chides. He thrusts the bottle under Lloyd's nose. "Gatorade."

I crack up laughing. I love seeing Jeff and Lloyd flummoxed. Between them, they think they have the answers for the whole world. To fool them, to put one over on them, is pure heaven.

Jeff huffs. "I *knew* it wasn't Windex."

"A good gimmick," Lloyd admits, laughing now himself.

Shane shrugs, looking askance at all three of us. "You gotta have a gimmick out here if you don't have bodies like you boys."

Bodies like you boys. It still boggles my mind sometimes to be grouped in with the beautiful boys. I just grab a hold of Jeff and we form a sandwich with Lloyd in the middle. I lick the back of Lloyd's neck. The X makes me do it. The drug is sending warm shivers all throughout my body.

Bodies like you boys.

Can I just tell you how *fucking awesome* it is to hear that? For it wasn't all that long ago that I'd felt like Shane: an observer, not a participant—an exile from the world of beauty.

Allow me to introduce myself. I'm Henry Weiner, age twenty-eight. I'm not sure what Jeff has already told you, but don't trust everything he says. He's probably said that I'm in love with him or something. Jeff can be the most conceited, most infuriating, most *incorrigible* person in the entire world. He can also be the sweetest, most charming, most caring, most compassionate—oh, forget it. You'll only start thinking that I *am* in love with him.

See, Jeff's my sister. We do everything together. Everything but have sex. Sure, we get gropey on the dance floor, but that's only because of the X. No other reason. I could very easily have gone to Miami with Brent, but Jeff wanted to come to New York, and hey, sisters stick together. I knew all along there was a very large probability that he'd hook up with Lloyd and leave me on my own. I'm okay with that. Really, I am. Okay, so maybe for a few moments there I actually allowed myself to hope that Lloyd wasn't showing up. But he did. Of *course* he did.

It's not that I don't like Lloyd, or that I mind him joining us. I *like* Lloyd. Really, I do. It's impossible not to like Lloyd. It's just that he's been around increasingly often these days, ever since he and Jeff reconnected last September. I remember the day Jeff told me that he'd seen Lloyd and they'd had sex and everything was, like, coming together. I told him *great*. I was *happy* for him.

Really, I was.

It's just that now every time I turn around, there's Lloyd. Jeff and I will be at Delux or over at the Galleria Mall in Cambridge, and suddenly Lloyd will just show up, and that's that. The two of them start mooning and cooing at each other and calling each other those stupid animal names. Okay, *what*ever. They were lovers for a long time, and I can do the math. They'll soon be moving back in with each other, if Jeff's right in his prediction of what Lloyd wants to talk about tonight. Jeff feigns ambivalence about it all, but I can see the truth. He wants Lloyd back *bad*. He *wants* to live together again. I can always see the truth with Jeff. I can see things he can't even see himself sometimes.

I know I'm coming across like I resent Lloyd. Okay, so maybe I do. A little. But I don't dislike him. Yes, he can be a bit lofty at times, a bit high-handedly spiritual, as if he alone understands the fate of the world—both this one *and* the next. But you know what? His presumption is truly tempered by a genuine compassion. Here's an example. It's five minutes to midnight and Jeff has managed to pull Lloyd off by himself, and suddenly I'm dancing alone. So what does Lloyd do? He opens up a space between him and Jeff and draws me in. Now *that's* a kind gesture. He didn't *have* to do it. *Jeff* certainly wouldn't have initiated it.

But, in truth, I wasn't really dancing alone. I was dancing with Shane, and now *he's* the one who remains unattached as the midnight hour draws close.

"You guys," I say, surprised at the sudden pang of guilt I feel. Maybe I'm remembering another guy who once danced alone, apart from the beautiful boys, and not so long ago. "This is Shane. He's from Boston, too."

"You *are?*" Jeff asks. "Then how come we don't know you?"

Shane makes a face. "'Cuz boys like you never know boys like me."

"Oh, come on, join in," Lloyd says, opening up a space between himself and me. Shane twinkles, wiggling his tall lanky self in between, careful not to drop that damn bottle of Windex.

Plastic champagne glasses and a bottle make the rounds. We break free of our little daisy chain but remain with our arms around each other's waists, watching as the countdown ticks off the last few seconds of the century. Weird, huh? The twenty-first century. It seems so . . . so *Jetsons*. Like we'll all head out of here and instead of hailing cabs we'll strap on our jet packs and zoom up into the night.

Five, four, three . . .

I look over at Jeff and Lloyd, who've pulled back a little, with eyes only for each other. I vow to myself that next year I won't be alone, that I'll be welcoming in the New Year the way they are. Together.

Happy New Year!!!!!!!!

The lights don't go out. Everybody around me starts jumping and hugging each other. Some stranger kisses me, tasting like cigarettes. When I look around, I can't spot Jeff or Lloyd in all the commotion, so I settle for an embrace and a quick kiss with Shane.

"Where'd your friends go?" he asks.

I laugh. "Who knows? They're supposed to be having an 'important talk' tonight." I can't help being a little sarcastic.

Shane snorts. "Not very nice of them to not even say Happy New Year."

I just shrug. "You learn to put up with things."

"Look," Shane says, leveling his eyes down at me. "I'm just gonna lay it on the line with you."

I look up at him quizzically.

"I find you way hot," Shane tells me. "And I don't want to spend the first night of the new millennium alone. Any chance you're going to come back with me to my hotel and fuck my brains out?"

I laugh awkwardly. "Well, I admire your direct approach."

Shane smirks. "I'm just a little emboldened by the chemicals. I came with a bunch of losers who didn't even stay till midnight." He pulls in close. "I don't often have a chance to make it with studs like you, so I'm just putting it out there. What do you say?"

I'm dumfounded. "Shane, I'm not really—"

"Attracted to me?" He laughs. "Of course you're not. If it hadn't been for that Windex bottle, you'd never have even *noticed* me." He leans down even closer. "But I'll *pay* you. What do you say to *that?*"

I gulp. Really, I frigging *gulp*. Wouldn't you?

"You're fucked," is all I can manage to say. He laughs then, and I laugh back.

Was he serious? I don't want to know. So I use Jeff's line. "Hey," I tell him. "No talking on the dance floor."

All I want to do is get away from him. I mean, here's some freak offering to *pay* me to have sex with him. Meanwhile, Jeff and Lloyd are nowhere to be found. Thank God I have the key to the hotel room. I look around, desperate to shake Shane and find some A&F to go home with—you know, A&F, for Abercrombie and Fitch. It's Brent's term for young, smooth, lean, cute boy. That's not such a lofty goal, is it? I can *do* it. I'm hot enough. Hey, Shane would have even *paid* for the chance.

I don't often have a chance to make it with studs like you.

Boggles my mind, I tell you.

"Hey, buddy."

I turn. It's Jeff. I breathe a silent sigh of relief.

"I lost you at New Year's," he says.

"Yeah, I looked for you," I tell him.

"Happy New Century," Jeff says, giving me one of those smiles that just turn me into mush. He pulls me tightly to him. I catch Shane's eye over Jeff's shoulder and grin. *See? He didn't forget me.*

"Happy New Century to you, too, Jeff," I say, and I'm surprised at how thick with emotion my voice is. The X, I guess. It can really dry out your mouth.

Lloyd taps me on the shoulder. "Actually, Happy New Millennium," he says, and kisses me on the lips.

I smile. "Actually, I've heard it's not until *next* year that the millennium begins."

"I don't know, buddy," Jeff says, sliding in behind me and wrapping his arms around my waist. "This feels like the beginning of a whole new ball game to me."

I don't want to ponder too hard just what he means by that. Has Lloyd told him he's moving back to Boston? Are they really moving in together? I close my mind down and let the X take me for a ride. A new mix begins breaking out of the old. The energy of the house pulses even higher.

"What *is* this?" I shout to Jeff. It's a little game we play: guess the song before it starts, a gay name-that-tune. "I think I recognize it, but I'm not sure."

It's a Thunderpuss remix of Sister Sledge's disco classic "We Are Family." Jeff pegs it, of course. He always does. I laugh, feeling all horny and happy and hilarious, and it isn't just the X. I even pull Shane back into our little group.

"I got all my sisters with me!" I sing out. Shane begins squirting Gatorade in time with the beat.

The crowd goes wild.

Jeff

It doesn't get much better than this. This is it—the heart, the soul, the center of gravity. This is where I come alive. This is what saved me. This is what brought me back. I love it all. I love the heat; I love the sweat; I love the steam that rises from a huddle of torsos grinding together. I love the way the music can transform even the most jaded muscleboy into Patti Lupone on a balcony. I love the silly banter, the sloppy tongues, the roaming hands. I love these boys who surround me, this manflesh that pulses and throbs and breathes as one.

There's a moment out here on the dance floor that rarely fails to find me: a moment of transcendence, when it's no longer a sea of disparate individuals but one big collective soul of queer humanity. Lost in the music, it isn't the drugs but a far more intrinsic high that takes hold of my mind and my body. I feel connected to every man on the dance floor, to every man who has ever been here, and to all who are still to come.

"Aw, man, someone just cut a fart," Lloyd groans.

"It wasn't me," I say quickly.

"Or me," Henry adds.

"Don't look at me!" Shane bristles.

Okay, so the dance floor can have its downsides. It can *stink*. People cut farts. Poppers reek. And it can get a little slimy, with beer and vodka spilled on the floor or down the back of your pants. Occasionally, some idiot has been know to puke right there in front of you just as you're about to spin off into lala land with Hex Hector's remix of Whitney Houston's "I Will Always Love You." But you learn to disregard these things. For where else are you really so part of everything around you, so connected?

So now for a little background on me. There was a period of time where I had a little bit of a problem. Nothing I couldn't handle. I proved that. I didn't need detox or anything to get over it. One day I simply looked across the dance floor and caught eyes with some guy. What I saw wasn't pretty. He was looking back at me, but I knew right away we weren't cruising each other. There was no love in his eyes. Just a hardness so fierce and shiny that I could see myself reflected from across the floor. My hand went instinctively to my jaw, and I felt how hard and clenched it was. Just like his.

The truth was plain, at least to me. Our girlfriend Tina had overstayed her welcome at our house. Oh, she was handy to have around when the place needed a good cleaning, and she certainly kept me going from one after-hours to another, but I'd seen too many guys end up in the trash because of her, and I was suddenly determined that wouldn't be me. I'm not sure the guy I was looking at ever came to that same conclusion, but I did. Then and there, and just like that. I get impatient with guys who are so trapped by crystal that they can't stop. They can't even *see* it. Don't they understand that it's a real buzz-crusher when you watch somebody overdose on the dance floor? Lloyd says I'm being hard, that addiction is an illness, with no blame to place. Maybe that's so. But that was the last time I ever did crystal, and I've kept Henry as far away from it as I can.

"All those people who died of AIDS," I told him, my voice harder and angrier than I meant it to be, "didn't die just so we could all fuck it up some other way."

"Do you want to talk to me about Javitz, Jeff?" Henry asked. "Is that what this is all about? You never talk about Javitz to me."

Man, Henry can be such a nag. Talking is *so* overrated. When things got bad a few years ago, I found my answers on the dance floor. They say the "circuit" is over, passé—that it's a phenomenon whose time has peaked and passed. Maybe so, but explain then the thousands who still show up for the White Party or the throngs of shirtless muscle boys who clog the streets of Provincetown at Fourth of July. *Something's* still happening. Call it what you want, but there's a whole subculture of gay men out there just waiting to dance their asses off for a weekend, to forget all their problems and turn whatever city they're in *queer* for the duration.

I laugh now to remember how convinced I was that my life was all over, that gay life ended at thirty. I was too old, I thought, for the youth-obsessed gay culture, and besides, I was alone and adrift, having just lost my lover and my best friend. But the guys on the circuit aren't twinks. "Circuit Boy" is a misnomer, for most of the guys I know are in their thirties like me. The rest range in age from late twenties to mid-for-ties. Most of us share the same cultural references. When dance remixes of old pop standards start to play, we know all the words: "If You Could Read My Mind." "I Say A Little Prayer." "California Dreaming." When a drag queen takes a shot at originality, showing up as Ann-Margret or Bea Arthur instead of the ubiquitous Liza or Barbra, we recognize them. When somebody makes a joke about Karen Carpenter or Jo on *The Facts of Life,* we get the punchline. Most of the guys I've gotten to know on the circuit have *lived.* They know about struggle, about heart-break, about love and loss and death. They've survived a lot over the last couple decades. One whole hell of a lot. They've got a few wrinkles around the eyes, and I've come to find that sexy.

Trite as it might sound, these are my people. Inspired suddenly, I break free of our little group, dancing on my own, my hands held up shoulder height, my body moving to the music. Anywhere else—say, dancing alone in front of a mirror—I would have looked absurd. But here—*here*—it's hot. It's sublime. I'm lost inside the music.

I feel Lloyd's arms snake around my waist, his lips on my ear.

"Did you really do only one bump?"

"Yes," I assure him. "Don't worry."

"I worry."

I turn around and kiss him. "That's why I love you. But I have no in-tention of ending up a GHB on the side of some dance floor in Detroit."

"GHB?"

"Girl Hardly Breathing."

Lloyd, smiles. "You make me laugh, Cat." His face gets serious. "Can we talk now?"

"After this song."

All right. So I'm putting it off. I'm both anticipating and dreading the talk. Look, I'm sure it's going to be a proposal to move back in together again—to go back to the way things once were. In the back of my mind, I suppose, I've always kept alive the hope that such an occurrence might happen. Maybe that's why the boyfriends over the past couple of years have never lasted very long. They were all fleeting, obviously mis-matched: a Russian flight attendant, a college boy from Missouri, a leather daddy who wanted to put me in a sling. I was just waiting for what, in my heart of hearts, felt like an eventuality. Getting back with Lloyd.

But it's not as if we had any precedent to follow, any charted path. Coming out of two decades of plague, so much of gay literature and gay

movies and gay magazine articles has focused on *losing* one's lover, not
holding on to them. In keeping the flame burning for Lloyd, then, I've
had no blueprint, no game plan. It's only been a dream, a hope, a trust.

Still, if it comes to pass and we somehow find the course to follow,
having Lloyd back will definitely shake up my life, and I have to admit
to some ambivalence about it. I've gotten used to the way I live now.
And I'm not exactly having a bad time. With Lloyd back, what will happen to those impromptu online hookups that lead to quickies at two
A.M. on my living room floor? And how about my circuit schedule? I
know Lloyd isn't exactly thrilled with my jet set routine from Palm
Springs to Chicago to Miami to Toronto. Yeah, my life will definitely get
some shaking up.

I open my eyes. I discover it's not Lloyd I'm pressing up against,
chest-to-chest. It's some other guy, a blond hunk with incredible pecs, an
awesome taper, and abs that look like speed bumps. *Hello, baby.* His
eyes are burning into mine, so intense that I have to literally blink back
from his gaze. The guy would be totally perfect except for one thing:
he's what Brent would call profoundly "R. C." *Rhythmically challenged.* He moves like a marionette whose operator has rheumatoid
arthritis.

"Sup," says R. C.

I smile. Stiff or not, the guy's abs are definitely lickable. "Sup with
you?" I ask back.

"Jeff." Lloyd is suddenly behind me again, his lips in my ear and his
arms encircling my waist. "Can we talk?"

I turn fast, pressing myself into Lloyd's torso, a little embarrassed, as
if he'd caught me in the act of something.

"Yeah," I say quickly. "Let's move over to where we can hear ourselves think."

I take his hand. I don't know why suddenly it all feels so scary. But it
does. In moments like these, I always think about Javitz. Usually I do
my best *not* to think about Javitz. But whenever I get scared or confused, suddenly he's right there—*right there,* but of course, not really.
That's the fucking problem.

I guess this is the point where I'm supposed to fill you in about Javitz
and tell you why he mattered and how he figures into the story. Those of
you who never met him need to know why this guy still has such a hold
over me and why his death makes me run away from emotion and all
that. Well, forget it. I'm not going there. Not tonight. I'm here to have
fun, to forget. You'll just have to find out from somebody else.

Lloyd

I can see all the thoughts going through Jeff's head. I can see him getting guarded and defensive, which only makes me all the more anxious to tell him what I need to say. As we head off the dance floor, I know he's thinking about Javitz—or, more accurately, trying *not* to think about Javitz. I also know he's not going to tell you more than that. So I guess it falls to me.

You see, Jeff dealt with his grief over Javitz's death by diving head-first into hedonism. I think a lot of guys on the circuit have done that. It will probably come as no surprise to you that I dislike the circuit. I attended enough parties in my twenties to know what I'm talking about. Looking around me as we leave the dance floor, I see so many wounded souls. We're the despised gay tribe, after all, and our wounds run very deep. It's why gay men seek so many sexual partners, I believe, and why they take drugs, and why they bulk up—becoming as big as the bullies on the playground, so big and strong (they subconsciously believe) that no basher or virus can ever touch them.

I don't mean to use the word *they* as if I'm separate from the rest of the gay population. I don't want to come across that way, though I admit that at times I do feel outside gay culture. The only reason I'm here in this cesspool tonight is because of Jeff. I want out as soon as possible, away from this collective denial of what makes us whole. It's just not part of the way I live. Where Jeff and so many others have dealt with their pain and grief by indulging in sex, drugs, and disco, I took the other route: I became celibate. After Javitz's death, my celibacy became a fast of my soul, a cleansing of my spirit, an honoring of what we had all been through together. I found refuge in Provincetown, a place Javitz had loved, sitting in quiet contemplation on the breakwater, listening to the wind and looking at the stars.

Some background here on me. I've always believed our souls have paths. Maybe not the soul nor the path that my father, a Lutheran minister back in Iowa, taught his congregation about. But in some ways it's the same thing: we come from somewhere, we make certain choices in this life, and then we go somewhere else. I was raised on a farm, where I slopped pigs and slaughtered chickens and watched the cows give birth to calves, and I discerned early a pattern to life. It's about finding your fate, your purpose, your place in the cycle. Each life that we live in succession is founded on what we did (or did not do) in the last. I grew up with a fear of getting stuck, of missing my turn, of being trapped on the farm, a chicken with my neck never far from the block. I've always questioned my place, chafed at limitations. The last of twelve kids, I was the only one to go to college, to leap into unknown territory. My siblings never ventured more than a few blocks from Mom and Dad, and all are now happily settled with kids and chickens and pigs of their own. And as much as they try, my parents can never quite figure out just what their son the "doctor of philosophy" *does* for a living.

Sometimes I had a hard time with it, too.

You see, about a year before Javitz died, I quit my high-paying, high-stress job as coordinator of a crisis program for a major Boston hospital. It came on the heels of all sorts of shake-ups, not least my decision to live apart from Jeff. I moved to Provincetown with the hope and the prayer that I could find something else to do with my life, to get back on the path I was certain I'd lost. But my disconnection to my life only got worse after Javitz died. There had to be *more,* I told myself; there had to be life beyond the walls of grief. Passion had long been my holy grail: where could I find it so that it wouldn't again slip away, where it might settle into the integral fabric of my life?

That's when this dream first took hold—the dream I want to share with Jeff now. That's why I wish so fervently that Javitz were here—*physically* here—here and now, in this stinky, sweaty club, so I could *feel* him, touch his greatness, partake of his profound wisdom. *Am I doing the right thing?* I want to ask. *Is all this crazy?*

"I've made a decision," I tell Jeff when we finally find a space away from the madness of the dance floor. "I wanted to wait to tell you until tonight because I thought the new year would be perfect to talk about it. It's a new start for me. A new beginning."

Jeff raises his eyebrow but he says nothing.

"I'm going to buy a house," I say quickly. "A guest house. A bed-and-breakfast. In Provincetown. With Eva."

There. All the pertinent info is out. And Jeff's face shows no change in expression. I wait for the reaction, but there is none.

Had he even heard me?

Jeff

I heard him. I just can't remember who the fuck Eva is.

"We decided for sure tonight," Lloyd's continuing. "We looked at the place last week. It needs a little work, but it's really in great shape. In some ways this is a tribute to Javitz. You know, it's the money he left me, and he loved Provincetown so—"

"You're buying a bed-and-breakfast?" I ask slowly. *"That's* what you wanted to talk with me about?"

Lloyd tries to smile. "Yeah."

I blink once, twice. "And you're buying it with . . . *Eva?*"

"Yeah."

I shake my head, trying to comprehend. "This is the woman you met at the seminar? The lady with the house on the Upper West Side who was having the past-life regression party tonight? The party you wanted Henry and me to come to?"

Lloyd nods.

I'm flabbergasted. "Since *when* have you wanted to run a bed-and-breakfast?"

Lloyd looks a little embarrassed. "Well, actually, I hadn't really thought of it before, until Eva started talking about it. But it just seemed prefect. You know how aimless I've been since Javitz died. You know how I've wanted to do something new, take some new chances. This feels like it could be it.

"So you'd be—*staying*—in Provincetown."

The weight of what he's saying finally settles down on me, like a heavy, wet blanket.

"Yes, Jeff," he say. "Eva and I would live at the guest house as well as run it."

I struggle for words. "And you've know her, what? A *month?*"

"Three months, Jeff." Lloyd is acting defensive, and I can tell he doesn't enjoy it. I know how much Lloyd hates being put on the defensive.

But I don't feel particularly sensitive to his issues at the moment. "Lloyd," I say, "running a bed-and-breakfast isn't easy."

His cheeks flush. "Do you think I think it *is?*"

"I don't know *what* you think. I certainly didn't know you wanted to run a guest house."

Lloyd glares over at me. "I'm sharing *good news* here with you, Jeff. This is *good news.*"

I shrug. "If you see it that way."

I see the anger boil up behind his eyes. My calmness is infuriating him. I think he'd have preferred that I threw something. Or stalked off in a snit the way I used to.

"I know what you're thinking, Jeff," Lloyd snaps. "You think I'm just going off on another flight of fancy. Like you thought when I moved to Provincetown. I *know* you, Jeff. I know you think I'm *blundering* into something, with someone I don't know, that I haven't thought it through. You think I'm still floundering, not knowing what to do with my life. I know how you think, Jeff. Do you give me no credit at all?"

I'm watching him calmly. "Lloyd, I think you're maybe putting some words into my mouth."

"Isn't that what you think?"

"I don't know what I think. Okay, yes, I do. I think you are blundering into something, but if you want to blunder, go right ahead. I want to dance."

"Is dancing really more important than talking to me?"

I sneer. "I paid good money to dance. We can talk anytime."

"You know what, Jeff?" he sputters. "If you can't be supportive, then just don't say anything, okay?"

He storms off. I just stand there, shaking my head.

What the fuck just happened? Funny how your whole perspective can suddenly shift, become something entirely different, in just a matter of seconds. In my mind I'd already been rearranging my closet to accommodate Lloyd's clothes. But Lloyd isn't moving back to Boston. How stupid of me to think he would. Like he's ever been able to make a commitment to me. Ten minutes ago I was pretending to be ambivalent about the whole idea. Now I feel nothing but a shattering disappointment.

All I want to do is get back out there on the dance floor and forget the whole thing. At the moment I don't care where Lloyd has gone. I just need to dance.

Henry

I turn around and there's Jeff.

"I need to talk to you," he says. He glances over at Shane, who hasn't left my side. Not for a moment. "You'll excuse us for a moment, I trust?"

Shane turns his hands up toward the ceiling. "Certainly. One of those mysterious huddles the beautiful boys are always having. What was it this time? A little snort of Miss Tina?"

Jeff ignores him and pulls me by the arm off to the other side of the dance floor. He looks me straight in the eyes.

"Lloyd is buying a guest house," he tells me. "A bed-and-breakfast."

"Jeff, I'm a little too twisted to play non sequiturs with you."

"*Listen* to me, Henry. He's buying it with that woman. Since when has he ever wanted to buy a *guest house?*"

"What woman?" I ask.

"The one he wanted us to go see tonight and get sent back to the Dark Ages with."

I laugh. "Well, a bed-and-breakfast might be a fun thing to do."

Jeff scoffs. "Get a *grip*, Henry. It's a shit-load of work. You ask any of the guest-house owners in Provincetown. What's Lloyd want *that* for?"

"I don't know. Maybe you should ask *him.*"

"I couldn't. He stormed off in a huff when I didn't jump up and down and shout 'Yippee!' "

I fold my arms across my chest. "And the reason you didn't, Jeff, is because you were hoping he'd move back in with you in Boston. Admit it."

Jeff scoffs again. "He can do what he likes." God, I hate when Jeff's disingenuous. He thinks he's fooling people, but he's just so obvious. He sniffs, "I just think he's in over his head. He doesn't realize all the work it's going to be."

"Look, Jeff." I get up close to him so that our eyes are no more than a few inches apart. "You read *my* lips for a change. You want things to be the way they used to be with Lloyd. Admit it. Make it easier on everybody."

Jeff sighs. His eyes can't lie, not so close to mine. I step back, suddenly uncomfortable with our proximity.

"Well, it's a moot point now," he says.

"Go find him before he leaves," I tell him. "You will be miserable to be around if the two of you have a fight."

He sighs.

I give him a shove. "*Go.* Work it out. And if you're going to leave with him, at least come back and say good-bye."

Suddenly, Shane is hovering over us. "Are you through plotting to take over the world and exile all of us uglies to Antarctica?"

"Excuse me," I snap, annoyed, "but we're talking here."

Shane winks and withdraws a few feet.

Jeff can't resist a smile. "I think the Windex queen is hot for you, Henry."

I roll my eyes. "Jeff, he offered to *pay* me."

"*Pay you?*"

"*Shhhhh.* Yes. Pay me."

Jeff looks stunned. "*You?* He wants to pay *you?*"

I make a face at him. "You don't have to act like it's so incomprehensible."

Jeff laughs. "So you gonna *let* him?"

I suddenly can't answer. I just keep looking back and forth between Jeff and Shane, surprised by how much the idea fascinates me. After all, Jeff and Lloyd are in the midst of one of their *things*—I sure can't count on *them* being around the rest of the night. And I don't particularly relish the idea of being alone on the first night of the new millennium, either.

Jeff's acting distracted again. "You're right, buddy," he says, looking back into the crowd. "I *should* go find Lloyd."

"Then go."

He turns to leave, then spins back. He pulls me to him, embracing me tightly. "Just be careful, buddy, okay?" he looks at me intently. "I love you, you know."

I feel my throat tighten.

See why he's my best friend?

I watch as he heads shoulder-first into the throng. I take a long breath, keeping my eyes on him until he's disappeared. I'm not even aware of Shane stealthily moving back beside me.

"So how about it?" he whispers in my ear.

I look up at him. He's not *that* bad-looking. Ordinary. The way I used to be, before Jeff.

"Let's dance," I say, taking Shane's hand and leading him back onto the dance floor.

Lloyd

I find myself standing in the line snaking out of the men's room, my arms folded across my chest and a black cloud hanging over my head. Why the fuck isn't the line moving? All these vapid boys doing their fucking drugs in the fucking toilet stalls and none of the rest of us able to take a pee.

Then I laugh. I let out a long breath and realize I don't really have to pee, that heading here had been merely an excuse, a place to go after walking away from Jeff.

I shake my head. I had behaved exactly the way Jeff used to. And *he'd* acted like me, standing there all calm and psychoanalytic. He had learned the game all too well.

I turn around to find him. I'll apologize. I'll admit that maybe there was some truth to the questions he raised, and ask if he'll help me look at them. You see, I *want* Jeff to be a part of this. *That's* how I should've presented it. *That's* how I should have led off. *I'd like you to help me with a project . . .*

But Jeff isn't where I'd left him. He's slipped back into the writhing mass of bodies.

I sigh, not wanting to wade out there again. Suddenly behind me I feel hot breath and a pair of hands. "Hey, sexy," someone whispers in my ear.

Some drunk guy is grabbing my ass. I can smell the alcohol and cigarettes even without looking around at him. God, how I hate these places. I shake the guy off and take a deep breath. I fight my way back onto the dance floor to find Jeff.

It doesn't take me long. He's looking for me, too.

"Jeff, I'm sorry," I say.

He smiles. "Me, too."

I put my arms around his neck and kiss him. The dance floor must be 110 degrees. Steam rises between us.

"I guess I was just feeling a little sensitive," I say. "Jeff, I want you to be a part of this. I really want your support."

He's nodding. "I know you've been wanting to find something new, Lloyd. I was just a little surprised, that's all." He gives me a smile. "I'll support you in whatever you choose."

"That means so much for me to hear."

I kiss his neck. I can feel my dick getting harder, even without any X to goad me on. I run my hands down Jeff's arms, felling their hardness, the curve of his biceps, the solid horseshoe of his tris. I want to make love to Jeff tonight. I want to consummate this moment, ensure that our reconciliation is real.

"How much longer do you want to stay?" I whisper in Jeff's ear.

"A while," he says, and immediately I pick up on the distance.

I pull closer. "I was hoping now that the clock had struck, we could go celebrate on our own. . . ."

Jeff smiles tightly. "Well, I'm having fun here."

I move my head back so that I can look at him. "Jeff, you know I came here just to see you. You know I don't like hanging out in these places very long."

"Maybe if you just gave it a chance, Lloyd."

"I don't like being mauled by strangers. I don't like the drugs."

"Why is that all you see?"

"Jeff, I only came here to be with you."

"I understand that, Lloyd." He gives me a smile that seems sincere, but I've known him long enough to recognize it's anything but. "And I'm appreciative you came so we could be together at midnight. But if you want to go, I understand."

I try to keep contact with him, but Jeff closes his eyes, leaning back and moving to the music. I know what he's doing. He might not throw fits anymore, but he's still pissed. He's learned how to say he's sorry but not how to *live* it.

Damn him. Maybe I *had* brought it up wrong, but that was no reason to wash four months of progress down the drain. Well, I know one thing: I'm not going to stick around and play that game. I'm not going to *beg* him to come back to Eva's with me. I'm also not going to stay in this stink-hole much longer.

"Then I'm going to go, Jeff," I tell him.

Jeff opens his eyes and smiles. "Okay."

I glare at him. "I'll see you later, then."

"Yeah," Jeff says. "Happy New Year, Lloyd."

Our eyes hold a moment.

"Happy New Year, Jeff."

I turn to leave. I look back once. Jeff's looking at me. I see his struggle, but he's not going to back down. I don't fully understand why, but, as stubborn as I know he can be, I'm not going to stay here and try to find out. I just mouth the words: "I love you."

He pretends he doesn't see me.

Then I turn and force my way out, headfirst.

Jeff

I watch as Lloyd leaves the club. I can't literally see him, of course, but I can imagine him clearly enough: putting his shirt back on, reclaiming his coat, tying his scarf, pulling on his gloves, heading outside, hailing a cab, ringing the doorbell at Eva's—no, I figure, she gave him a key.

She'll greet him with a cup of hot cocoa, and they'll curl up on her Upper West Side couch and talk the rest of the night. What kind of drapes they'll buy for their new home. What kind of china. Whether they'll replace the carpet. How soon in the spring they can plant geraniums in the window boxes.

"Sup."

I turn. It's the R. C. boy again, still barely dancing, still looking incredibly lickable.

I feel a smile stretch across my face despite myself. "Sup with *you?*"

"Not too much."

Bad answer, I think. Guy's not quick on his feet, literally or figuratively. A good answer would have been "Interest rates" or "The spaceship Mir, at least for now" or, best of all, "My dick." But all R. C. manages is: "Not too much."

Still, he has incredible abs. I reach out and slide my palm down his stomach. Yep, *just* like speed bumps. Hard and round. "What's your name?" I ask.

"Anthony."

"Anthony." I've learned the key to remembering tricks' names is to repeat them as soon as they're first said. Even a couple of times for good measure. "Well, Anthony," I say, "I'm Jeff."

"Hey, Jeff."

Anthony reaches out to shake my hand. *Such a straight boy,* I think. I take his hand and pump it heartily, like a straight boy's supposed to do.

I spy Henry and Shane dancing nearby. "You know Henry and the Windex queen here?" I ask, elbowing toward them.

"Good to meet you," Anthony says.

"It's *true,*" Shane says. "You boys are drawn together like magnets. Like the swallows to Capristrano or something." He stands back to appraise Anthony, feeling his shoulders. He looks back at me, shuddering dramatically.

I laugh. I skillfully bring Anthony back from Shane's clutches, moving in close to him. "You from New York?" I ask.

"For the time being," Anthony says. "I'm looking for a job."

I eye him. "You rolling?"

"What's that? A kind of dance?"

"Hoo boy," I sigh. "I know. How about if you just kiss me and we can stop talking?"

Anthony beams. "Sure."

He's a little awkward with the tongue, but I can overlook that.

Anthony tastes yummy, and his shoulders and his back and his butt are certainly worth exploring.

So let Lloyd have his cocoa and his guest house and his little past-life bride. It's a new millennium. I can find my own way.

Henry

The night ends for all of us soon after that.

"Just for the hell of it," I ask, as Shane hails a cab. It's cold, *very* cold, and I zip my leather jacket all the way up to my throat, watching the steam escape from my mouth. "What *would* you have paid me?"

Shane laughs as the cab pulls up to us. "How much are you worth?"

"I'm not sure."

We slide into the backseat of the cab. The warmth is enveloping. We push down close together into the hard naugahyde of the seat. Shane gives the driver the address of his hotel. I figure it's safer to go back there; Jeff has disappeared with that hunky Anthony guy and I don't want to walk in on them going at it.

"If you were *really* escorting, honey," Shane's telling me, "you could get two hundred fifty easily here in New York. In Boston maybe two hundred."

"A night?"

"Sweetie, an *hour!*"

"*Two hundred dollars an hour!* How do *you* know?"

Shane scrunches up his face. "Don't tell me you've never looked in that back section of *Next* before. No, wait. Of *course* you haven't. Why *would* you, with *that* face and *that* body?"

"Shane, I have the same insecurities as anybody—"

But he's not listening. "I admit it," he's saying. "I've hired escorts. I've paid two hundred dollars to lay beside an Adonis for an hour. *You*, however, are the first one who's ever come willingly."

Adonis. By implication, he just called me an Adonis. Such talk can still rattle my brain. I look up at Shane, realizing he's totally serious.

He would've paid two hundred dollars just to suck my dick.

I think about my credit card balances. About my student loans. My car payments. That Prada suit in Neiman-Marcus.

"Here we are," Shane barks. The driver pulls over to the curb. I reach into my jacket to pull out some cash, but Shane holds up his hand. "Allow *me*, gorgeous. Believe me, it's an honor."

I open the door and push myself back out into the cold night. I feel a little numb, not quite able to imagine myself in this particular situation. I watch in silence as Shane slams the door of the cab and the cabby pulls off down the street.

"Now," Shane says, staring down at me, "it's just you and me."

"Yeah," I reply, and my voice sounds thick and unfamiliar to my ears. "Just you and me."

Shane shivers dramatically. "You're even more spectacular away from all that smoke and fog."

All at once I kiss him. Just push myself up on my toes and kiss him hard, taking Shane by surprise. After a couple of seconds, he responds wholeheartedly, kissing me back with lots of tongue and moans and interjections of just how lucky he is to have found someone as stunning as me.

It turns out to be the very best sex I've ever had.

Somewhere in the Night

Lloyd

So what's your impression of all of us so far? Think we're pretty fucked up? Or just like everybody else, trying to untangle all the karmas and dramas and unexpected twists of our lives?

Let me tell you a little story. I talked to my parents earlier tonight. I called them on my cell phone when I first got into the city, wanting to wish them a happy New Year. And my mother says, two minutes into the conversation, "Lloyd, you're thirty-five years old. It's time you *settled down.*" I hadn't yet told her about the guest house, and now there was *no way* I was bringing it up. She and my father had finally accepted that I was gay and making a life with Jeff when I suddenly up and left him—a move they're still puzzling over. Telling them about the guest house would only further muddy the waters. I just said, like I always say, "I don't believe in settling down."

Parents are always telling their kids to "settle down," no matter how old we are. They start when we're just three or four, whenever we laugh too hard or get a little too rough with our toys. "Settle down," they scold. Then we're fifteen and we bring home a few Cs on our report cards and they say, "You need to *settle down* and get to work." They've got us scared to *move.*

Jeff used to be big into "settling down." He was the one who got all cozy and domestic when we lived together. It was perhaps inevitable that I left, because we had gotten too "settled down"—too exactly what my parents had always told me to be.

Now I find our positions switched. I'm talking with Eva about the colors we'll paint the living room and picking out matching wallpaper while Jeff is out there, still exploring, still partying, still as far from set-tled down as one can be. I'm certain that it took no more than forty-five seconds, *tops,* for Jeff to set his sights on somebody else after I left the bar. I know him so well.

There's not much I *don't* know about Jeff O'Brien. He can be the most self-absorbed asshole and the most compassionate friend you'll ever meet. He can spend all day rolling around in the mud with his five-year-old nephew, not caring who sees, but he also has the inseam of every pair of jeans specially tailored to make his butt look more perky. I mean, can you think of anything more self-indulgent? Yet when I'm feel-ing sick, it's Jeff I want to take care of me. There's nobody better at bringing in soup, tucking in blankets, changing cold cloths, and just generally being warm and nurturing and comforting than Jeff.

But Jeff's changed. I know deep down he's still the same guy I fell in love with over a decade ago, but our old friends don't seem to recognize him anymore. He heads off to Seattle and Cincinnati and Toronto and even Sydney, Australia, for every party, every dance, every whitewater rafting trip, and every gay ski weekend he can find. He doesn't see much of these old friends anymore, the ones who were with us through the whole long process of Javitz's dying. Instead, he's surrounded himself with new friends, most of whom I don't care for. I like Henry, but the others seem merely accessories, pretty boys with designer drugs and de-signer muscles who don't challenge, don't provoke, don't confront.

And Jeff is *not* going to admit *why* he prefers them. He's *not* going to talk about Javitz, no matter how hard you push, so I guess it's up to me yet again. You *do* need to know about Javitz to understand everything else. So . . . where do I start?

We once had a friend named David Mark Javitz. Everybody always called him by his last name. He died of AIDS. Do you remember AIDS? It's really not such an outrageous question. Javitz would be so pissed off to see how everyone seems to have forgotten about AIDS these days. It hasn't been four years since he died, yet already the world seems so dif-ferent. To those boys on the dance floor tonight, the world of AIDS seems as foreign and unfamiliar as Zaire or Antarctica or the surface of Mars. Or maybe it's not so unfamiliar. Maybe they just like to pretend it is. The way Jeff does.

Javitz died just as most people were starting to live, just as the new drugs came in, just as a powerful hurricane was rushing up the arm of Cape Cod. It sent winds so fierce along the finger of Provincetown that the old oak on Commercial Street that had been growing since 1875 was finally felled. In the morning, the town awoke bewildered and bewailing, and Javitz's body was taken out of his house on a stretcher by the coroner in the middle of a driving rain.

Yes, Javitz would be pissed to see how people have forgotten about AIDS.

And *is* pissed, I'm sure, because I believe he's still here, just in a different form. Before he died, he promised he'd come back to me, and he *has*. Okay, so it's been in dreams, but maybe that's the best he can do. Jeff says he doesn't even dream of Javitz. I feel sorry for him. I would go crazy without my dreams.

Although we weren't sexual with Javitz, in every other way we were, in fact, lovers. Sure, it was Jeff and I who lived together with our cat and celebrated our anniversaries and hung our Christmas stockings side by side on the mantle. But Javitz was, from the start, an integral part of our union. Straight people just never got it, and a lot of gay folk had trouble with it, too. The three of us were fused together, a family—but, as we always added, even more than what family usually means for straights.

How do I explain who Javitz was to us? He was teacher, he was mentor. He got us angry, got us inspired, got us out onto the streets shouting about how the government had blood on its hands. Oh, we were such earnest young boys then, so ready to fight. Our anger was righteous and indignant, and Javitz had been proud of us. Javitz taught us that gayness meant opportunity, that it was a gift which allowed us to rethink the old paradigms that had proved so unsuccessful for straights—like marriage and monogamy. He infused in us the radical notion that queers weren't just *equal* to heteros but, in a way, actually *superior*: at least we had a leg up over easy, conventional definitions. We could forge something *new*, something that worked better—more honestly—than what straight culture had created.

Javitz had been one prickly, political queen, but he'd also represented the one solid thing in my life, the one person who was always there, one hundred percent. Unconditional love he'd promised, and Javitz had delivered. The most important thing he taught Jeff and me was that friendships and relationships didn't need labels or definitions or limitations; what mattered was the love, and how unconditionally it was shared.

Every summer for six years we rented a place in Provincetown. We became a familiar sight walking together down Commercial Street, shoulder to shoulder to shoulder, Javitz always in the middle, slightly taller than Jeff and me. The gossips wagged their tongues over our three-way friendship, our age difference (Javitz was more than ten years older than Jeff and I), and the nonmonogamy we all so prized. Many were known to wonder: "What do the three of them *do* together in that house? Are the two younger ones his boy-slaves? Or is he just their sugar daddy?"

Sitting on our summer deck, Javitz had sighed dramatically. "How to disentangle the myths of age?" he asked, waving his cigarette in the night air.

Jeff had responded in kind: "How to explain to a world fixated on the paradigm of two the power of *three?*"

Those were the discussions we had, late into the night. I laugh now at our pomposity. How we enjoyed hearing the sound of our voices in the stillness of a Provincetown night. But that's who we were. A family—audacious, maybe, but constant, a fact that nourished me.

The images are there, at the flick of a switch in my mind. Javitz on the back of a motorcycle, riding sidesaddle, being dropped off at seven A.M. by a trick on his way to work. "Who do you think you are," I had scolded him only half-mockingly, "worrying us all night?"

Javitz simply shook his long black hair, his curly ringlets still wet from a shower at the biker's house. "I've never ridden on the back of a motorcycle before," he gushed. "I felt like Nancy Sinatra in *The Wild Angels.*"

"Who *is* this man?" more than one trick asked both Jeff and me, as they woke up to be greeted by a thin, long-haired older man with a platter of raspberry croissants and coffee. We didn't even try to explain. How could we try? There were no words. No way to adequately describe who Javitz was to us. Friend, lover, family. We broke the rules, the three of us.

And then there were two.

He died just as the hurricane roared up Cape Cod. I was with him. Jeff wasn't. See, that's a large part of the reason why he can't talk about Javitz. He carries some guilt about that, I know. I'd called him around ten o'clock the night before to say that I thought he ought come to Provincetown, that Javitz was fading fast. But the weather forecast was ominous; we were all bracing for the strongest hurricane to hit the Cape in years. Jeff considered it and told me he'd leave first thing in the morning—but by morning, of course, Javitz was dead.

In truth, it wasn't Javitz's literal death that was the hardest thing to deal with. You see, Javitz had died with dementia, and in some ways, I had as little opportunity as Jeff to say good-bye. Dementia had been Javitz's worst nightmare, the one thing he prayed he'd never get. "Give me pneumocystis; make me go blind; cover me with lesions; just don't give me dementia." His intellect had been his most treasured attribute. People sought Javitz out for his wisdom. They came to him when their lives were a mess or they stood at some crossroads, unsure of which way to go. Javitz always knew what to advise. He could see through bullshit. And he died unable to counsel, unable to impart any last words or offer any insight into what was happening, to him or to us. He was just a docile little boy confined to his bed, eating his chocolate bars, smudging them all over his face and hands.

It was only after his death that I realized why, on a karmic level, Javitz had died with dementia. Javitz, who'd spent his life taking care of others, who'd grown up with a cold, distant mother, was at long last the child surrounded by love. Finally it was our turn to give back as unconditionally to him as he'd given to us.

And his intellect, his mind—it was the one thing he had to learn to surrender, the last attachment to this life that he had to give up, just as he had given up his faith in the old ways and gone on to chart a whole new course. By letting go of his mind, which had held him so firmly rooted to this plane of existence, he could at last take that one final leap into the unknown.

I like to believe that Javitz died with all of his karma fulfilled. It's selfish of me to wish he were still here, to help me through mine.

But I do.

Jeff

Okay, so I suppose Lloyd has told you some stuff about Javitz. That should do you for a while. Don't expect me to follow suit, getting all introspective and touchy-feely, with all that talk about karma and the wounds of the despised gay tribe. I've got other things to attend to. Chief among them is what's-his-name, R. C. Boy, and his skin is just about the sweetest thing I've tasted in ages.

Still, I'm fuming. Like I should have expected anything *different* from Lloyd, Mr. I-can-talk-a-good-game-but-I-won't-walk-the-walk. He's still the same commitmentphobe he's always been. Isn't he the same guy who walked out on me, the one who *left* me—who even in our six years of cohabitation always held back the promise of forever. The whole time, I lived on tiptoes, waiting for the curtain to be rung down. What a fool I was to have even *considered* trusting him again.

So stop thinking about it!

"Come here, Anthony." I lift his shirt, exposing his abs. I run my tongue from his navel down the wispy happy trail of blond hair that leads to his dick.

But I can't stop thinking. What *really* gets me is that I was falling *right back* into the same old pattern. I really was. I was going right back to the place where I used to be, which is, *waiting for Lloyd to walk out on me*. I'd vowed never to go back there. But I did. Did I *ever*.

Six years. That's how long Lloyd and I were together. Actually, we lasted a year more after that, but we lived apart, and then finally it just flickered out, like a flame at the end of a wick, struggling against the wax. Neither of us made any kind of an announcement. We just wandered off our separate ways, and that's how it's been these last three years. Then suddenly last September, Lloyd called out of the blue, saying he was in Boston and asking if he could stop by to see our cat, Mr. Tompkins. I said sure. He showed up, we had sex, and that just started the whole ball rolling again. So to speak.

Okay, so I jumped to conclusions when Lloyd said he wanted to talk about something, but it wasn't all that illogical a leap. I know the house he's renting in Provincetown has been sold, that he has to move out by spring. I'm well aware that his attempts at starting a new career on the Cape have yielded only mixed results. Add those two facts to the reality that, since that September day, things have been going really fabulously between us, and see what you get. We laugh like old times. We cook meals together like old times. We watch old movies like old times and visit my sister and my nephew like—well, not like old times, because my nephew hadn't been born back then. But little Jeffy, who's kind of like my unofficial kid because his dad's a no-good bum in jail, took to Lloyd really fast. So it's actually pretty logical that I'd assume Lloyd wanted to take that next step: move back in together and pick up where we'd left off.

What a joke. I can hear Javitz laughing at me from wherever he is. And no, I'm not going to talk about him. I have abs to lick.

Henry

Don't judge him, okay? Jeff, I mean. I'm sure he's coming across as guarded and defensive and self-absorbed. That's what everyone thinks at first. But there's so much more to Jeff O'Brien than meets the eye. Just promise me you'll give him a chance, okay?

See, I owe so much to Jeff. Early on he went through my closet and tossed out every Izod shirt and pair of Wrangler jeans I owned. He took me to his hairstylist and got me a decent do. He held my hand as I got my tattoo. He introduced me to books by Andrew Holleran and Ethan Mordden, and every single Bette Davis movie at the video store. At the gym, he pushed me on, goading me into two, three, four or more reps, teaching me to curl, to crunch, to load creatine. I might be seven years younger than he is, but I take inspiration from Jeff's stamina, his endurance, his commitment. He's at the gym faithfully five times a week, with one day set aside for cardio training. Because of Jeff, I didn't give up after a few weeks, the way I'd always done every time I'd tried working out before. Jeff helped me realize my long-cherished dream of having the body I'd always wanted but despaired of ever achieving.

So any claim to fabulousness I owe to Jeff O'Brien. Henry David Weiner, at his core, is *not* fabulous. I was the skinny runt always chosen last for the basketball team in gym class. I'm the nebbish claims manager of a stodgy Boston insurance firm, the gay nerd overlooked for years by the muscle boys on the dance floor. Now suddenly I'm dancing side by side with the A-listers—with *Jeff O'Brien,* whom I'd admired for years without him ever knowing it. Without him ever knowing *me.*

I will never, ever forget the night when Jeff first invited me into a daisy chain with him and Brent. It was three years ago on the dance floor at Buzz. I couldn't believe my luck. I had finally worked up the nerve to dance beside Jeff and a gaggle of other pretty boys, but I was barely moving, just standing there, bouncing up and down slightly on the balls of my feet. I watched the boys beside me as if they weren't really there, as if they were part of a movie: no minds, no selves—just bodies, and glorious bodies at that. At one point, Jeff's eyes met mine—I could tell automatically he wasn't as wasted as the others were—and he smiled. He actually *smiled* at me. I will never, ever forget how Jeff looked in that moment: so aglow, so magical, so beautiful. He *smiled* at me and beckoned for me to join in, and so I slipped in between him and Brent, feeling as if I'd just won the Publisher's Clearing House Sweepstakes. Jeff kissed me, and Brent slipped his hands down the front of my pants. Honest to God, Cinderella at the ball never had it better.

Am I sounding too goopy? I just can't help it. I was just dazzled, and I admit I felt like such a hot shit when the friends I'd come to the bar with stood on the sidelines with their mouths agape. I never looked back, either. I have no idea what's become of those guys. Maybe they're still there, on the edge of the dance floor, watching me, the way we'd once watched Jeff and Brent.

And no, I wasn't disappointed when Jeff went home with someone else that night, for I hadn't dared to allow myself to dream *that* far—but still I lay awake smelling Jeff on my hands and my chest, reliving again and again the moment when he had reached over and slipped my shirt off over my head. Never before had I taken my shirt off in a club. It was a moment of sublime power, of exhilaration beyond all my wildest dreams. I had danced in the midst of gods, and the world hadn't spun off its axis. No one turned to stare, to point. Then and there I determined I would attain a body like theirs, and in a rush of emotion I turned to ask Jeff where he worked out.

"Mike's Gym," he told me.

"If I join, will you help me?" The excitement was breaking through my usual reserve.

"I'm no trainer," he cautioned me.

"But maybe you can just give me some hints. Some encouragement."

"Hint number one," Jeff told me. "Don't talk so much on the dance floor."

We never slept together, not even after my body did indeed begin filling out, bulking up, molding itself under Jeff's guidance and encouragement. But Jeff's attention was constant. "You can be anything you want to be, Henry," he said. "You've got a lot to offer, more than you realize. Stop selling yourself short."

We became friends, *sisters*. He took me with him to clubs, introduced me to the whole circuit scene. I remember how excited I was the first time Jeff took me to Rise, the after-hours club in Boston, as his own personal guest. I'd heard about the club but never had the opportunity—or the courage—to go. Jeff gave me the courage I'd always lacked.

I did my first hit of X with Jeff. When someone else gave me some K and I found myself in utter terror floating above my body, it was Jeff who found me, brought me down, and sat with me until I emerged from the K-hole.

"You have to be careful with drugs, Henry," Jeff told me later.

"I did too much?"

"Rule number one: never take anything from someone you don't know."

I shivered. "I don't want to do drugs unless I'm with you, Jeff."

Of course, there were those who right away assumed I was in love with Jeff. Brent still insists that's the case. Once I got so pissed off by his smug insistence that I actually threw a martini in his face.

Okay, so maybe early on I did have a little crush, but sisters last longer than boyfriends. Jeff's always told me that. And until Lloyd came back into the picture, it always proved true. I was there to offer counsel as a series of boyfriends came and went from Jeff's bedroom. I never liked any of them very much, and neither did Jeff, as it turned out. There was Alexei, that Russian flight attendant, who got way too possessive; and Randy, that college kid, who was far too needy; and Zed, that leather guy from San Francisco, who wanted to hang Jeff from a rope and light a match under his toes. I'd counseled him pretty quickly to give *that* one the hook.

We do that for each other. We take care of each other. Before I got my contacts—Jeff had advised me that eyeglasses in a club were definitely not cool, unless they were yellow sunglasses—I would make lots of mistakes zeroing in on guys. "Henry, don't waste your time," Jeff would warn. "He's a Monet."

"A what?"

I can still see Jeff's smirk. "What, a little too cultural a reference for you, buddy? A *Monet*. As in the *paintings*, duh? Looks all put together from a distance, but when you get up close, it doesn't look like much of anything."

Jeff makes me laugh. See, I'd never be here without him. Shane can offer to pay me all he wants, but the money should rightfully go to Jeff. Go ahead and think whatever you want about what I feel toward Jeff. I owe him my world.

New Year's Morning, The Upper West Side

Lloyd

Eva greets me with a mug of hot cocoa. Its warmth feels good in my cold hands, even better down my throat. She sits beside me on her living room couch and watches me drink. "Happy New Year, Lloyd," she says.

Thank God for her. I tell her about the experience with Jeff, and she listens, present and attentive. Unlike Jeff, she's listening to me—not running her own agenda and issues in her head, just waiting for her chance to speak.

"Until that point, it had all been going so well," I tell her. "But now it just feels like it did before. This game of pulling closer, then pulling back. I don't want to play that game anymore with him."

"I imagine it must make you terribly weary."

I nod. "Jeff can be impossible at times."

"Well, it must be a little hard for him to understand," Eva offers.

I scoff. "Understand what? The guest house?"

She smiles. "Do you think, Lloyd, that maybe, just maybe, he was hoping you were going to move back to Boston?"

I take another sip of cocoa. I guess I'd already wondered that myself. I just shake my head. "I gave him no reason to think so," I say defensively. And I hate feeling defensive.

Eva's eyes well up. She's a very empathetic person. That's why I love her, and why I think you will, too. "That poor boy," she says. "Oh, of *course*, I can understand how he's feeling. If that's what he'd been hoping for, and then here you are, moving in with *me* instead . . ." She looks as if the tears will come any second. "That poor, poor boy."

I let out a long sigh. "I wouldn't spend too much time feeling sorry for Jeff, Eva. I can assure you his mind is *not* on our guest house at the moment."

"No matter what he's doing to forget," Eva says, "I'm sure somewhere he's hurting inside, and I feel badly about that."

Eva's a good woman. Kind, compassionate, wise. She reminds me of Javitz, actually. Always there with a ready ear, solid insight, and unconditional support.

Let me give you an example. I knew Eva was somebody I wanted in my life—that I could enter into a partnership with—when I watched her with one of the guys she takes care of as a volunteer for an AIDS service agency. The miracle cures haven't worked for this guy. Alex has about four T cells and weighs about ninety pounds—a stark reminder that the plague isn't over—but so far he's managed to still live on his own and make his own life. Except that he needs help getting groceries and things like that, for which Eva is only too glad to volunteer. I watched her with him, and she was *perfect:* warm, interested, nurturing, but never condescending. She fixed his meals, kidded with him about his hair, gently massaged lotion into his feet until he drifted off to sleep. "I admit I dote on him," she told me. "When I look at Alex, I don't see a wasted, dying man. I see the man he was and still is: handsome, witty, talented. If he wasn't gay, I just might well fall in love with him, virus and all."

Eva Horner is fifty years old. She's a widow, still grieving her husband. In her youth, I imagine, she was very pretty. Even now she's got large brown doe eyes, strawberry blond hair, and a scattering of freckles across her cheeks that belie her half-century of life. Yet she seems to do her best to conceal her attractiveness, pulling her hair back severely in a bun, keeping her large breasts shrouded in loose, heavy sweaters or smocks. Those oversized mammaries are an anomaly: everything else about her is tiny, petite, delicate. She stands just four feet ten, with hands as small and delicate as a girl's. She smiles easily but shyly, always with a hint of embarrassment, as if she didn't feel she deserved to be having such a good time.

I know that I make her smile. Until meeting me, she was as adrift as I was: unsure of her next move, still trapped in her own prison of grief. Her volunteer work was a bold leap back into the world for her, a move from which I took inspiration. She doesn't have to work: she admits that she came from money, and then her husband left her fairly well off on top of that. She lives in opulent splendor—three bedrooms upstairs, a downstairs den, a parlor and full pantry—but it was a jail cell for her nonetheless. Before I met her, I'd never known anyone in New York who had an apartment bigger than my closet in Provincetown. But her wealth never bought her happiness or a respite from her grief.

"It's only by living that you can really live," she said to me one night—a simple, almost banal statement, but one that made me look over at her in wonder. We've had many such moments like that, moments of insight that have startled me and encouraged me back on my road to wellness. "It's only through connection with another person that one understands why we're here," she said another time, a truth that might have been uttered by Javitz himself.

She's struggled with finding connection all her life. Her mother died when she was very young, and she was raised by a series of nannies. She craved the love of her distant but adoring father, a diplomat in the Eisenhower and Nixon administrations who was forever flying around the world. Often months would go by before Eva would see him again. "He never failed to bring me home a beautiful doll from Japan or a dress from France," she said. "How happy I would be to see him. As a little girl, I'd climb into his bed and stay there with him all night. The nannies always thought it wasn't proper, but I was just so glad to see him, and he me." His portrait hangs in her living room, a somber, gray-haired man I have a hard time imagining showing any warmth. "That's how I picture Daddy when I think of him now," she said. "In oils. I saw that portrait more often in my childhood than I ever saw the real man."

Her greatest disappointment in life, she's told me, is that she and Steven never had any children. "I guess in the old days they would have called me barren," she said. But ultimately she thinks it was probably for the best, given the truth she discovered about the man she had married.

"You know, Eva," I say, setting down my mug of cocoa, "I felt bad leaving you to go to the bar tonight when I realized you'd be alone. You told me you were having a gathering, that there would be other people, everybody doing past-life regressions. But it was just you and me."

She looks a little uncomfortable. "Well, I had thought Jeff might come with you, and your other friend—Henry, isn't it? And the friends I invited all canceled at the last minute."

"Oh." I'm not quite sure what to make of that. Eva's spoken of other friends but rarely gives any names. The only people she seems to spend time with are Alex, her AIDS buddy, and her late husband's lawyer, Tyrone, who, Eva blushingly has admitted, is in love with her.

"Don't worry about me, Lloyd," she says suddenly. "I'm good all by myself. Okay, so at midnight I had a little cry, remembering Steven, but it was good for me. I haven't cried in a while. It actually felt good."

I smile. "Javitz wanted so much to see the year 2000. I remember him saying when he was a kid he'd figured out how old he'd be in 2000 and thought fifty-two seemed so *old.*"

"To a kid, it would seem old. Not to me." She sighs. "It's *young.* Javitz should have seen 2000. So should have Steven."

We both sit in silence for a moment. "I want to tell Jeff about Steven, Eva," I tell her. "Do I have your permission?"

She reaches over and takes my hand. "Of *course.* It might make a difference for him, knowing that Steven was gay, and that he died of AIDS—"

Suddenly, she begins to cry. That happens with her. She'll be going along fine, and then all at once, *whammo!* Something kicks in and she remembers Steven and she starts to cry. I understand. It's sometimes like that for me with Javitz. I reach over and pull her close to me. Her tiny hands grip my shirt and hold on tight, like a frightened child clinging to her mother. I pat the back of her head.

"It's so silly," she says, breathing hard. "It's been almost five years since Steven died. And here I still am, breaking down at the slightest mention—"

"It's okay to cry. It's not good to put your grief in a box." I take her by the shoulders and bring her up so I can look down into her eyes. "That's what's so wrong with everything today. Because so many people got well so quickly, suddenly we're not supposed to show our grief anymore. We're not supposed to cry out and curse and agonize over the hundreds of thousands who weren't so lucky. It's like we're just supposed to stop talking about it. Like it was all a bad dream and it's over now." I laugh scornfully. "Well, fuck that. We haven't finished crying yet."

My little speech seems to impress her. I have that effect on her. She's always saying so, giving me credit for inspiring her and motivating her. But she's done the same for me. It's been Eva over the past few months who's gotten me talking about my grief, who's allowed me the space to share my stories about Javitz. Jeff sure as hell won't do that.

She takes both my hands in hers and looks me steadily in the eyes. "Tell me how he died again, Lloyd. Tell me the story."

The *story.* It feels good to tell it.

I let out a long breath and look out the window. There are more lights on in the city than usual, people still awake and celebrating the coming of the new millennium. Yes, I'll tell her the story. She takes power from hearing it. I take power from telling it.

"It was the night of the hurricane," I begin, the way I always begin. "I remember our neighbors buying plywood to nail across their large picture window that faced out onto the bay. People were staking trees and stockpiling water. Javitz had been declining for weeks and hadn't spoken in three days. That afternoon he began breathing heavily, laboriously. The active dying had begun."

I settle back into the couch. Eva sits close to me so that our shoulders are touching.

"As the evening went on, he seemed to grow increasingly agitated, as unsettled as the sky outside. When the first winds hit, he began making a low whine in his throat, and his hands were clenching and unclenching into bony fists. He was in a hospital bed by then, so it was difficult to comfort him. In his own bed, I could crawl in beside him and take him in my arms. But now there were those horrible aluminum guardrails separating us. I slid one down and managed to get in as close as I could. Outside, the wind slammed against the house. The shutters that I thought had been nailed down securely came loose and slapped madly against the windows. I worried the glass might break. We lost power. I lit candles and told Javitz not to be afraid."

I can't continue. Eva squeezes my hands. "I'm right here," she whispers.

I find my voice. "We had morphine. I knew I could put a few drops in his mouth and that it would calm him, but I also knew it would hasten his death. I told him what I was doing. We'd had so many talks over the years, I knew he'd want me to. I gave him the morphine and then sat down beside him again.

"And he did calm down. He was looking at me. All of a sudden, I remembered something he'd once said. 'Be with me at the end and tell me about the wind.' See, Javitz loved the wind. It was so perfect that he should die during a hurricane. So I took his hand and described the wind, how fierce it was, how powerful, and I told him that he was like that wind, just as strong, and that all he needed to do was become one with the wind and he'd be free."

My throat tightens but I continue. "I told him that I loved him, and he mouthed the words back to me. He hadn't been able to communicate in *days*, but he died saying those words. At that moment, I saw the life just disappear in his eyes, like a light switch turned off. I sat there staring at him, his lips still wrapped around his final words, his eyes still open. And suddenly there was such a wind outside, so tremendous that I thought the roof would come off. Tables fell over and a vase in the living room flew from the mantel and shattered against the floor. I thought the house was collapsing inwards, but it was only Javitz, finally released from this world." I pause, smiling. "Leave it to him to go out with a bang."

Eva's crying softly. So am I. "How I wish I had known him," she says. "Thank you for sharing that story with me. It means so much every time I hear it."

You need to understand how important it is to tell it. For three years I'd kept that story bottled inside. Jeff couldn't bear it, and neither could other friends. But it felt *good* to speak it. It felt *empowering* to remember it. Javitz would *want* me to remember it, and to tell it often. And with *passion*, with him as the star. I smile. Javitz always loved being the star.

And it took Eva, a woman he had never known, to become his most eager fan.

She seemed to sense, right from the start, my need to talk about Javitz, and she's continued to encourage me to do so. Even when I might not be thinking about him at the moment, she'll bring up his name, ask me to tell her something about Javitz. It's been the way to my heart. In the past three months, Eva's become the closest person to me on earth.

We met cute, as they say in the movies. At a seminar on psychic healing at New York's Open Center, I tripped over her purse and sent a row of metal chairs clanging down like dominoes. Horrified that everyone turned to glare, including the speaker, I sat down beside Eva with my cheeks burning. She offered me a Tic Tac, and a friendship was born.

I accompanied her that night for the first time to meet Alex. He'd wanted to attend the lecture himself, but had felt too weak. Eva bought a cassette for him and set it up where he could listen to it. When she inquired how he felt, Alex told her he was "taking baby steps back to life." She seemed to love that line, and repeated it to me on the way out for coffee later.

"That's me, too." she said. "My volunteering, going to the seminar— they're my own baby steps back to life."

Me, too, I realized. We talked for hours that night about grief, about how to live with it, even make friends with it. She said I inspired her with such talk; I told her she was the true inspiration. In the ensuing months, we attended many workshops together, and I saw her brighten, emerge from her shell of grief and despair. She told me that my friendship was a beacon of light to her, offering her a direction, a promise that life wasn't over.

And she's provided similar hope for me, too—especially a few nights ago, sitting in her living room, musing about the future, when she was suddenly struck with the idea of a guest house, and I jumped on it. "Let's do it, Lloyd!" she said. "You and me!"

Does it really seem so impulsive? It doesn't to me. It feels right. I think of Eva's strength, her compassion, her wisdom. People come into your life for a reason, I truly believe. This is fate. We're meant to do this together.

All at once, she stands. "Lloyd! Come with me!"

She takes me by the hand and leads me across the room. We climb the stairs to the second floor. "This was Steven's room," she says, opening a door at the far end of the hall. It's the one room of the house I've never seen. I look around. A canopy bed with a very gay white veil. In a silver frame hangs an enormous photograph of a flower's bright yellow stamen. I recognize it immediately as a Mapplethorpe original.

"You and Steven had your own rooms?" I ask, and immediately regret the question. Of *course* they did—at least for the last few years, after he told Eva he was gay.

"Yes," she says softly, looking down at the bed and patting the blue velvet comforter. "We thought it best." She takes a deep breath. "This is where he died. I sat here, in this chair, holding his hand."

She walks over to the closet and slides back the mirrored door. My jaw drops. There's an array of leather jackets, some with shiny chrome chains on the shoulders. Next to them are dozens of pairs of blue jeans, all neatly pressed and folded over hangers. I can't help but smile. Javitz pressed his jeans, too, and hung them up like that. The mark of a generation. Steven had been the same age as Javitz.

"I want you to have Steven's clothes," Eva says. "My goodness, all this beautiful leather just hanging here untouched. Steven loved leather. He had jackets, pants, shirts, chaps . . ." She reaches in and pulls out a pair of black motorcycle boots. "And the footwear! My word! You *did* say you were a size eight-and-a-half, didn't you?"

"Yes, but Eva, I couldn't just . . ."

She looks at me earnestly. "Of *course* you could. You're the exact same size as Steven. This will all fit you marvelously."

I smile. "That's very kind of you." I can't stop my smile from turning into a broad grin. "But Eva, you never told me Steven was a leather queen."

She laughs. "Oh, he wasn't into sadomasochism or anything." She's blushing. "He just liked how he looked in leather. See?"

She picks up a framed photograph from the bureau and hands it over to me. A dark-haired man with a walrus mustache in leather motorcycle jacket and cap, a harness and no shirt, chaps over his jeans.

"Very Tom of Finland," I observe. I noticed a cardboard box in the closet, a shiny flash of chrome from within. I bend down and extract a pair of handcuffs. "Not into S and M, huh?"

She looks down at the cuffs. "I've never gone through that box," she says in a small voice.

I feel suddenly uneasy standing there with Steven's photograph in one hand and his handcuffs in the other. I toss the cuffs back into the box and return the photo to Eva.

"Steven taught me a great deal," Eva says, carefully replacing the photograph back on the bureau. "When he told me he was gay, of course I told him he was free to go and find himself—and another man if he chose, someone with whom he could spend his life." She's gazing down at the picture but then turns quickly to focus again on me. "But he chose *not* to. He chose to stay with me. He *loved* me, Lloyd. He may have been gay, but he loved *me*."

"Of course he did, Eva," I reply gently.

"It was a great blessing, really, that Steven turned out to be gay. It meant no children, of course, but I learned so much about the human condition by getting to know Steven as a gay man. Oh, Lloyd, how I wish you could've known him."

"He sounds like a wonderful guy."

"Not any more wonderful than you." She beams at me. "Here. Try on this jacket."

"Oh, I don't know . . ."

"Don't be silly. It was his favorite." She pulls a heavy black coat off its hanger. Long fringe dangles from its sides. I hate it immediately but obediently slip my arms into its sleeves. I look ridiculous as I stare into the mirror, but it *does* fit. Perfectly.

"Well, pick out what you might want to take with you tomorrow," she tells me. "I'll have the rest shipped up to Provincetown."

She's trying to do something kind. These clothes mean a lot to her—such an intimate connection with Steven. Idly I pull open a drawer from the bureau. Steven's white brief underwear are still neatly folded there. I quickly shut the drawer. The man's been dead *five years*.

I look at myself again in the mirror and shiver. *She's been hanging on to his memory,* I tell myself. I'm a psychologist; I know this isn't healthy. But we all handle grief differently. By giving the clothes away she's taking an important step toward healing.

I replace the jacket on the hanger.

Somewhere in the interior of the house, a cuckoo clock heralds five A.M. "We should get some sleep," I say gently.

"I've just been too excited to sleep these days, ever since we decided to do this." She wraps her arms around herself. "This is *our* millennium, Lloyd. *Ours.*"

I smile at her.

She points out the window, where the purple sky is starting to fade into the first glow of dawn. "It's a whole new chance for us," she says. "Oh, Lloyd, I am just so *consumed* with passion for our project! Do you realize just how much you've offered me? How you've given me a life again—a life I never imagined I'd see? Can you possibly grasp how grateful I am, how *honored* I feel by your faith in me?"

"It's mutual, Eva," I tell her, and she suddenly rushes to embrace me. Her breasts wedge between us like large cantaloupes. She tucks her head under my chin against my chest.

You're thinking she's a bit dramatic. Okay, I'll grant you that. But see, I'm drawn to Eva for *precisely* that quality. I've been adrift, and the person once closest to me—Jeff—has made himself unavailable. Eva is demonstrative where Jeff is distant, and now, watching the sun come up, holding her in my arms and remembering how Jeff has pulled away *yet again,* I'm as glad to have her in my life as she's glad to have me.

"A penny for your thoughts," she says, looking up at me from our embrace.

I smile, a little sadly. "I was thinking of Jeff."

She pulls out of the embrace gently and walks back over to the window. She seems a little hurt. "Do you think he might want to live there eventually?" she asks, not looking at me. "Our guest house?"

I sigh. "Jeff doesn't share my passion for Provincetown, at least not since Javitz died. And besides, I just don't know where Jeff and I stand right now."

She turns to face me. "For me, Provincetown is the most exciting part of all." She's hugging herself again. It's a gesture she does often, I've noticed: a way of almost hiding her breasts. "Ever since Steven died, I've told myself that I wanted to leave the city and go somewhere where the air is pure, where there are long stretches of nothing but earth and air and sea, where I can find my soul."

It's uncanny how closely our paths have converged. That's exactly how I view Provincetown: that sandy peninsula where the land ends, crumbling into the sea. There I've found another way to live. I've become more aware of the sun and the stars and the wind than ever before in my life, reveling in the light that's like nowhere else on earth.

"We still haven't decided what we'll name our house," I say quietly.

"Nirvana," she announces, suddenly looking up at me with wide, eager eyes.

"Wow."

"It just came to me. What do you think?"

I consider it. It feels a bit extreme, but I trust moments like these. "Nirvana," I say, smiling. "Nirvana it will be."

New Year's Day, Chelsea

Jeff

"This way, boys."

Our waiter is a harried queen covered in glitter. Whatever he touches, like my shoulder, is left graced with a sprinkling of red and silver and green. A throng of gay men stands waiting for their tables, their eyes puffy, their cheeks shadowed with morning stubble. We pass through them, getting a whiff of the cold January air that still clings to their leather jackets and wool scarves. The poor waiter looks exhausted; he's probably been showing people to tables ever since the restaurant opened at six A.M. Now it's three-thirty in the afternoon, and we're all still looking for breakfast.

"Here you go." The waiter hands us each a menu and gestures toward a table near the kitchen. The smell of bacon snaps through the air. "I'll be back for your order in a minute." Glitter sprinkles onto the table as he flits off to seat the next people in line.

I take the seat next to the wall. Anthony sits opposite me, transfixed by the residue of glitter on the table. He presses his forefinger onto it, lifting his hand to show me. "Like sparkly snowflakes," he says, grinning like a little kid.

In the past twelve hours, I've discovered he's filled with a wonder rare among gay men, usually so worshipful of irony and cynicism. Anthony gets excited by little, ordinary things, like the way the exhaust fan in the bathroom quickly evaporates the steam on the mirror, or the sight of kids with a puppy on a leash. With undisguised glee he gazed into store windows, ginning at their moving Santas and elves. He laughed without affectation at the antics of a street vendor and his pet monkey.

He caught snowflakes on his tongue, something I would never, ever consider doing on the sidewalks of Manhattan.

Looking across the table at him now, I observe the deep dimples that indent his cheeks when he smiles—a precious little detail I'd failed to notice in the darkness of the night before. I can't help but smile myself as I watch him study his menu, his forehead scrunched up and his lips pursed in thought, as if choosing between eggs and pancakes were a life-or-death decision.

"So what's your last name, Anthony?" I ask, breaking the silence.

He replies something like "Sobby," without lifting his eyes from the menu.

"What?" I ask. "What ethnicity is that?"

His blue eyes peak over his menu. A few specks of glitter sparkle in his dirty-blond hair. "I think it's some kind of Middle Eastern," he says.

"*Middle Eastern?* You don't look very Middle Eastern to me. How do you spell it?"

"S-A-B-E."

"I see." I frown. "So are you adopted?"

"No. I don't think so, anyway. Why do you ask?"

I shrug. "It's just that . . . well, never mind."

Anthony sets his menu down, folding his hands on top of it. "Blueberry pancakes," he announces. "That sounds *awesome*. Do you think they use real blueberries?"

"Well, I imagine they might be frozen this time of year."

"*Still.*" He beams like a kid at an ice-cream shop. "So what do you do?"

Now, it might strike you as unusual that it's taken us this long to finally get around to exchanging such trivia as last names and occupations. But hey, we've been *busy*. Dancing, kissing, then going back to the apartment on Nineteenth Street where Anthony was crashing with a friend. I figured that was the best choice: the way Henry had been dancing with the Windex queen, it was pretty clear where things were going with him, and I did *not* want *Shane* walking in during an intimate moment between Anthony and me. So down to Nineteenth Street we'd walked, happily discovering Anthony's friend fast asleep with his door closed.

You're probably expecting me to describe an incredible sex scene here. Okay, I'll do my best. From the hollow of his throat down the line between his pectorals straight through his abs, I licked his honeysweet skin, following the treasure trail of blond hair that leads from his navel to his dick, which, when I pulled down his underwear, sprung up to point at the ceiling. A good-sized piece of meat, with a thick mushroom head, and no hair on his balls at all—natural, not shaved. I found his ass tight and hard, and Anthony was an eager bottom. For an hour we fucked on a mattress on the living room floor, and when it was over we drifted off to sleep with our cum drying between us.

How was that? Hot enough?

Yet all that aside, truth be told, the sex was just okay. Nothing spectacular. Maybe Anthony was just too inexperienced in knowing how and when to move, to give back, to take initiative. And maybe I was just tired and distracted. I found sleep welcome, and I'm pretty sure I dreamed of Lloyd, for I woke up thinking about him.

"At the moment," I say, bringing myself back to the present to answer Anthony's question, "I don't do anything." I smirk. "I'm independently wealthy, as they say."

"Wow," Anthony says, wide-eyed.

I set my menu down. "Have you no sense of irony, absolutely none at all?"

Anthony shrugs. "Guess not."

I smile. "How long have you been out?"

He seems suddenly defensive. "What do you mean? Out from where?"

"As gay." I feel a little impatient. "Out as *gay.*"

"Oh." Anthony does some calculations in his mind. "About six months, I guess."

"Well, then. *Six months.* That explains it."

"Explains what?"

The waiter has come back for our order. More glitter rains upon us. I order poached eggs on rye toast, no butter. Anthony asks for the blueberry pancakes and a side of fried eggs and bacon. How does he manage such abs with such fatty foods?

"Explains what?" Anthony asks again after the waiter has left.

"I don't know. It's just that you come across a little—oh, I don't know—*green.*"

He smiles. "Maybe that's because I am. Gay culture fascinates me, but I admit I feel a little out of it."

I study him. "How old are you?"

"Twenty-nine."

"So you're no kid. Why'd it take so long for you to come out?"

"I don't know. It just did."

I frown. "So what were doing with yourself all that time? Did you have a girlfriend?"

Anthony shakes his head. "I was just—by myself."

The waiter sets down two coffees. Both of us drink them black. I let the coffee revive me, feeling it settle down inside. Around me the faces of the people reflect their hangovers: the dull headache behind the eyes, the dry mouth, the lethargy. I'm grateful I did just the one bump and drank only one beer. I remember what it feels like to be sick and still be craving more of the substances that made you sick. How had I ever let myself get in so deep? Why do people do that to themselves?

I turn back to Anthony, not wanting to remember that time. "So what do you find so fascinating about gay culture?"

He beams. "Everything. I never imagined there was so much going on. All these parties all across the country. How awesome it is." He blushes a little. "I never realized how good-looking gay guys were, and how *friendly* everyone is. I think I thought gay life was just a bunch of drag queens. But it's really all these awesomely built guys. And everyone is so friendly. So embracing. I met this guy a couple of months ago who took me to the White Party in Miami—"

"You were there? So was I."

Anthony laughs. "Yeah, you and me and a couple thousand other guys. That's what was so *awesome*. All these *men*. And everyone was so friendly."

I don't doubt it. Circuit boys have reputations as being major attitude queens, unless of course you have speed bumps for abs like Anthony here. If you look like Anthony, a circuit event can be the most powerfully positive introduction to gay culture you could ever imagine. If you look like the Windex queen, however, it can send you scrambling back to your closet as fast as you can run. As much as I love the scene, I'm not blind to its realities. Yet Anthony's truth is as real as Shane's or anybody else's; I can't take that away from him.

"It's been incredible meeting people at parties," Anthony's continuing. "I've made so many friends so quickly. One of them is the guy I'm crashing with here." He pauses, seeming to consider something. "Though . . ."

"Though what?"

He sighs. "I think he's started liking me too much. Do you know what I mean?"

I smile empathically. "Oh, yes. I know exactly what you mean."

Anthony frowns. "He wanted me to stay in last night with him. To celebrate the New Year, just him and me. But I wanted to go out. I can't stand being inside, cooped up for too long. Especially in places as small as that apartment."

"A little claustrophobic, eh?"

"Yeah." He looks off at nothing in particular. "Actually, a *lot* claustrophobic." He looks back at me and continues. "I *had* to go out dancing; I just had to. So he went to bed early." He pauses, seeming to have arrived at some conclusion. "I don't think I should stay with him for much longer."

I nod. Ah, how the world turns. I think of that poor guy behind that closed door. He never came out the whole time we were there, but I'd seen his underwear in the bathroom and his toothbrush in the holder. There was a photograph on the refrigerator I assumed to be him: a typical circuit queen, torso shaved and chiseled, a gad of love beads around his neck. How many years ago had that been taken? Did he still look like that? I imagined him lying there in his room, listening to us fuck on the living room floor. Poor guy. Everyone's in their own little dramas, aren't they? Even as this faceless, nameless guy probably lay there *hating* me for "stealing" Anthony from him, there I was, screwing Anthony but never once really thinking about anyone but Lloyd.

This morning, I considered heading over to see Lloyd. I still had this Eva lady's address, after all, but by the time I was up and showered, I figured it was too late. I knew Lloyd was anxious to get back to the Cape, especially now that he has a closing to plan for and furniture to buy and a whole new fucking life to build.

But if I was looking for a distraction, I couldn't have found a better one. Waking up this morning, I looked over and there Anthony was, stretched out on the mattress wearing nothing but a pair of tight white 2(x)ist briefs, still sleeping like a baby, his perfectly sculpted chest rising and falling in sweet, soft breaths. Just why he'd put his briefs back on after we'd had sex, I wasn't sure, but it sure did make him look like a model on an underwear box.

So you can understand the impulse that led me to wake him up and initiate sex again—it was still just okay, not great—and then we showered together and headed out for breakfast. Anthony pulled on the same jeans he'd worn the night before, and the same socks. The stale odor of smoke and sweat still clung to them, but I figured it was all he had. At least he extracted clean underwear and a sweatshirt from a backpack on the floor.

I lean in toward him now. "Let me tell you something about gay culture, Anthony," I say. "It can be just as you experienced it. It can be awesome and empowering. It can also be cruel and shallow. You just have to learn how to navigate it."

He blinks his eyes a few times as if trying to understand. "Cruel and shallow? How do you mean?"

I sigh. "Come on. Are you really as innocent as all that?" I take another sip of coffee. "It's no different from straight culture. Beauty trumps wisdom. Youth triumphs over experience. It should be the other way around, but the human condition doesn't seem to allow it."

"So in other words," Anthony says, stroking his smooth face, his stubble hardly worth the bother of shaving, "I should enjoy my time at the ball because it ain't gonna last?"

Finally. A spark of insight. I laugh. "You got it, pal."

"Well, for now I think it's awesome." He smiles. "That feeling I got on the dance floor in Miami—it was like I was part of some great, big brotherhood or something. You don't know how long I've wanted that. To feel a *part* of something. To be . . . accepted, you know?" He blushes. "Does that sound really dumb?"

Actually, it sounds absolutely endearing. "I know what you mean," I say fondly. "That *is* part of the scene. Despite what everyone says, it's not just the drugs. There's definitely more than X bonding people on the dance floor."

"So then, what's the shallow part you're talking about?"

I laugh. "Anthony, I'm thirty-six years old. When my dad was this age, he had three kids to support. He got home at six o'clock every night and watched television until nine, then went to bed. On weekends he mowed the grass and fixed the roof. Any extra money was used to pay for our dental expenses or school clothes. And maybe once a year a trip down to Sound View Beach on the Connecticut coast."

I lean back in my chair and cross my arms over my chest. "Meanwhile, here's my life. I just reserved hotel space for Gay Days at Disney World in June. My friends and I are already planning what Speedos to bring so we can splash around with a couple hundred other guys in Typhoon Lagoon."

"Sounds like a lot of fun."

I shake my head in amusement. "That's just it. It *is*. Part of the appeal of the circuit scene—of gay male culture in general—is that it allows men to remain boys. I don't subscribe to the school of thought that says that's always such a bad thing. It's actually really wonderful, but there's a flip side to the Peter Pan syndrome, which is immaturity and irresponsibility. The fear of growing up, growing old."

"You talk like a writer," Anthony observes.

I feel my face flush. That speech is, in fact, part of an essay I've been writing in my head for over a year, but which I've never been able to get down onto paper. "Don't ever give me a soapbox," I say, "because I'll take it every time."

"No, *really.*" Anthony looks at me seriously. "I *like* talking to you, Jeff. You've really thought stuff through. I've never met anybody like you."

The waiter arrives with our breakfasts. Anthony licks his lips and rubs his hands together, salting his eggs heavily, breaking the yolks and spreading them all over the whites. He pours at least a cup of maple syrup over his pancakes. He eats ravenously. I watch him a minute before carefully starting myself.

"So tell me about being independently wealthy," Anthony says between bites, a dribble of syrup on his chin. "Do you come from money?"

"Oh, God, no." I practically choke on my rye toast. "Money is *definitely* not from where I come." I pause. I hate moments like these, but they always seem to work themselves into conversations whenever I meet someone new. They'll ask what I do, I'll say "nothing," and then they'll ask how it works. A logical progression of thought. Except that I don't want to get into the answer too deeply. "A friend died a few years ago," I explain. "He left me some money."

"Was this friend your lover?" Anthony asks softly.

I sigh. "Once, a long time ago." I hesitate. "But later . . . we evolved into something else . . . something beyond that. It's hard to describe what we were to each other. We were family, but even more than the way family is usually defined by straights."

"So you were close, then."

"Yeah." I smile at him warmly. "You can definitely say we were close."

Anthony opens his eyes wide. "Well, it must have been quite a lot of money he left you if you don't have to work."

"It *was* more than I expected," I admit.

Truth was, both Lloyd and I had been stunned by the total amount of Javitz's estate. For a working-class community-college professor, he'd socked away a good chunk of cash. Plus there was his annuity, not to mention the several life insurance plans of which he'd made us joint beneficiaries. Long had I dreamed of financial security, and Javitz had been privy to many hair-pulling moments when I'd dodged creditors' calls or torn up credit cards. But the irony of achieving such financial freedom at the cost of losing the greatest friend I've ever known is almost too much to bear. What good is financial security when your emotional ground is pulled out from under your feet?

"Actually," I admit, letting out a long breath, "the money won't last much longer. I *do* need to do something eventually. *Some* kind of work."

"And what kind of work would that be?"

I smile. I don't like talking about my writing, but it's preferable to talking about Javitz. "You've already hit on it," I tell him. "In a past life, I was a writer. A journalist. I worked for a newspaper and then went freelance. Did some writing on my own." I laugh, looking across the room at some indefinable point. "Once I actually thought I'd write something important. A novel or a screenplay or something grand like that."

"Maybe you still will."

"Yeah, and maybe Tom Cruise will come out of the closet." Time to move on to another topic, I decide. "And what do *you* do?" I ask. I love flipping the conversation around.

Anthony's finishing his eggs, wiping up the yolk with the remnants of his pancakes. He doesn't look up as he answers. "Nothing at the moment," he says, echoing me. "But I am *not* independently wealthy. Not anywhere *near* it."

I smile. I'm really beginning to feel some warmth toward this guy. I've always liked people without privilege. I've never much cared for middle-class guys whose daddies set them up with trust funds and bank accounts and credit cards. My weakness is always for guys like myself, from blue-collar families and working-class backgrounds.

"Where are you from?" I ask.

"Near Chicago." Anthony wipes his mouth with a napkin and tosses it onto his now-empty plate. "But I've moved around a lot since."

"Like where?"

Anthony averts his eyes. "Oh, too many places to get into."

I frown a little. "So what brought you to New York?"

He shrugs. "Same thing that brings anybody here, I guess. I thought maybe I could find something to do with myself, some kind of career."

"And what kind of career do you want?"

"Not sure."

I look at him. "Well, what did you do before you came here?"

"Odd jobs. Nothing for very long."

Okay, I think. *Is this guy being deliberately vague on details?* The old investigative journalist in me is starting to sense some stonewalling. So I ask, "Did you go to school for anything in particular?"

Anthony smiles. "Yeah. I got a degree. Just a two-year college, but it was a degree."

"A degree in what?" This is like pulling teeth.

"Office management."

"Well, that's something." I decide to leave the last piece of toast (too many carbs) and motion to the waiter, who quickly snatches up both our plates. "What about your family?" I ask. "Where are they?"

Anthony looks away from me. "I don't see my family anymore."

I study him. "Was it the gay thing? Coming out?"

He just shrugs.

"Well," I offer, "if it's any consolation, it took mine a while, too, but they've come around."

"Mine will *never* come around," Anthony says plainly. And *decisively*—as if it's as far as he'll go on the subject.

"Okay." I had zoned Javitz off-limits; he can do the same with his family. I take a sip of coffee. "So can you at least tell me where were you living before you came here?"

"Albany." Anthony drains the last of his coffee and waves the waiter away when he attempts to refill it.

"What did you do in Albany?"

"This and that. Nothing important. I was only there a very short time."

I raise my eyebrows and smile with a tinge of exasperation. "You are definitely coming across as a man of mystery, Anthony Sabe."

He smiles. "There's just not a lot to tell."

Oh, I imagine there *is*, that there's *much* more to Anthony than he's willing to admit. No one spends their entire twenties doing nothing of importance, moving from city to city, jumping from job to job . . .

Or maybe they did. I pause, considering my own myopia. I've always hung around with *achievers*: people with ambition, direction. Until my recent aimlessness, I myself had been fiercely driven to succeed. I consider that my own current situation might offer a clue in understanding Anthony. Maybe guys like him *do* exist; I've just never met one until now. Maybe our aimless energies attracted us to each other.

But *no*. There's something more going on than just that. Anthony might lack ambition and direction, but he's far too bright to have spent an entire decade as an adult that way. Anthony's no slacker, no vagabond. He's hiding something. Look at that body. It implies a gym membership somewhere, and those things cost money.

Aha! My eyes light up looking across the table at him. Maybe he'd been a *kept boy*. Sure, that's it. Wealthy older man pays Anthony's way all through his twenties. Then, on the cusp of thirty, he gets tossed out, replaced by some new, younger twink. Hadn't Anthony just said he'd been out six months? Maybe he didn't mean out as *gay*, but out as an *independent* gay man.

No, I think to myself, watching him fiddle with his coffee cup. That's not it, either. I narrow my eyes as I study the young man across the table. It may be a few years since I've done any actual investigative reporting, but my instincts are still as sharp as ever. I've always trusted those instincts, and rarely have they failed me. Anthony's not a liar. There's absolutely nothing disingenuous about him, nothing cagey. If he says he's only been out for six months, I should take him at his word.

Still, to go through your entire twenties without a relationship? There was no girlfriend, he said—

"Are you two finished?"

It's a woman, nosing over us, trying to get a jump on our table.

"Not quite," I tell her, keeping my eyes on Anthony.

I return to my thoughts. No girlfriend . . . but might there have been a *wife?* Anthony's transfixed again by the glitter on his hands. Denying a girlfriend isn't the same as lying about a wife. Is that it? Had he left a family behind? Were there kids, too? The image seems *very* incongruous, I have to admit: Anthony seems far too much like a kid himself to have any of his own.

I can't deny that my curiosity is piqued. Who *is* this guy?

Anthony looks up and smiles over at me. Damn, those dimples again.

"I like you, Jeff," he says.

I smile automatically in return. "You do? How come?"

"Well, you're awfully handsome, to start."

I wink. "I need a better answer than that."

"Okay. You're funny. And you ask a lot of questions. That means you're interested in other people, not just stuck on yourself."

I lean my chin on my hand. "Some would say otherwise, but go on."

"There are people who talk only about themselves—or worse, about nothing in particular." Anthony rolls his eyes. I listen carefully, for every statement might be a clue to who he is and where he's from. "You know what I mean? They'll talk about the weather or what's for dinner or the stupid television or who's got cigarettes. They never ask you anything about *you.* I like people who *really* ask you stuff. That's how I want to be. If I'm going to talk to you, I want to get to *know you.* There's so much more to somebody than just what they show outside."

The waiter comes by to ask if everything is okay. I assure him it is. He places the check down on the table and the woman is immediately back. "Are you finished *now?*" she asks.

I look at her, annoyed. She's about my age, pretty, with a chubby boyfriend in tow. "If it's okay with you," I tell her, "I'd like to have these last two sips of coffee that are left in my cup."

She snorts, turning back to her boyfriend. I hear "faggots" under her breath.

"Excuse me; I didn't hear you," I say, starting to stand, feeling the sudden pump of adrenalin.

"She didn't say anything," the boyfriend says meekly.

"What did she say, Jeff?" Anthony asks.

I settle back down. The anger subsides as quickly as it rose. The host seats the couple far away from us at the other side of the restaurant.

"Let's get out of here," I say.

"What did she say, Jeff?"

I'm just shaking my head. "No matter where you go, even here in fucking Chelsea, there's always someone ready to get down on fags."

"Did she call us that?"

"Forget it." Lloyd would be counseling me to send her love. But I can't help it. I hope she chokes on her bagel. "Let's just take a walk."

I open my wallet. Anthony offers to pay his share, but I won't let him, prompting him to sit back in his chair and beam over at me. I pull out a twenty and a ten from my money clip and wink.

"Let's go. I need to get some air."

Ninth Avenue is cold, but it feels good after being closed in with all those bodies. The dance floor is one thing; cramped cafés reeking of bacon grease and populated with snot-nosed homophobes are decidedly another. I take a long, deep breath. The first couple of blocks we walk in silence.

I'm not sure what will happen next. I kind of like this guy, and I have to admit I'm intrigued. I'd love to have more time to figure him out, to slowly extract his story bit by bit. It's what I loved most as a writer: interviewing people, discovering their experiences, their values, and sometimes, when I was lucky, their secrets.

But fate has deigned to merely cross our paths, nothing more. After all, Anthony's in New York, poised for some new life, and I'm heading back to Boston. I really can't afford to get involved with someone right now; the drama with Lloyd is way too complicated. Besides, I know from experience that spending more than a day with a trick can often have disastrous results. I still smart over how much I'd come to care for Eduardo, my summer love of five years ago. No, it's best just to shake hands with Anthony and walk away. Wish him good luck and a happy New Year, and quickly hop on the subway.

But neither Anthony nor I make any attempt to say good-bye. We walk leisurely, shoulder to shoulder, Anthony every once in a while catching snowflakes on his tongue. It makes me laugh.

Odd how Lloyd's name hasn't come up all day. After all, Anthony saw us together last night. What will I tell him if he asks? What *are* Lloyd and I to each other, anyway? Yesterday I would've given one answer; today I'm not sure. The last few months had seemed to suggest we were heading back together, but what about now? Has his news really changed so much for us? There was nothing in his words to suggest that he wanted to end our reconnection. In fact, he'd seemed to want it to continue. He said he wanted me to be a part of this with him. But it's as if a barrier had just been erected in the road and I can't go any further. It took me a while to open up and trust and spend time with Lloyd again. I wasn't keen on being hurt once more.

You see, for all the radical theorizing I'd learned practically at Javitz's knee, I have to admit there's always been a part of me that has wanted *exactly* what I said I didn't: that joint checking account, that Saturday night safety blanket, that cozy presumption that the person across the breakfast table from me will still be there when I turn seventy. Never had I found that with Lloyd: oh, the *trappings* of it, maybe, the illusion. But Lloyd had always chafed against too much commitment, too much domestic permanence.

Until Eva, that is. He can buy a house with Eva, but never with me.

Why should I trust that it's any different now? I try to imagine what it would be like. I'd schlepp myself down to Provincetown and help build their home together, and then Lloyd would turn to me someday and say, "Well, you know, I can't really commit to you." I'd walk in and find him with Drake—the guy he'd originally left me for—or somebody else, who he'd eventually leave, too, just as he had left Drake and me. What guarantees do I have that the past won't merely repeat itself?

"There are no guarantees in life, darling," Javitz always said. I laugh as I walk down Ninth Avenue, and Anthony looks over at me curiously. I've actually parroted the same words to Henry, many times, with the same weary inflection Javitz used to use, whenever Henry has started fretting about finding love and a husband. "No guarantees," I tell him, "just the eternal hope that what you're looking for is just around the corner."

Hope. Despite everything, it's still there, inside me. I can't deny that I still hope somehow, some way, Lloyd and I will be back together, finishing what we started. I just can't give up on him. I might be fearful, I might be wary, but I can't give up. Not yet. The memories of our life together have never receded as far as I might pretend. The thought of holding Lloyd in the breathing position, in my arms, in our bed late at night, safe from everything, together—that image is never very far from my consciousness. Sure, I've moved on; I have a life of my own now. But I'm drawn back, as ever. Drawn back to what Lloyd and I had, what we shared.

So I'll go down to Provincetown. I'll see the house. I'll meet Eva and give it a chance—

"Jeff?"

I look over at Anthony. I realize I've been lost in my own thoughts, and that Anthony has asked me a question.

"I'm sorry. I was . . ."

"In another world." Anthony smiles. We've stopped at the corner of Ninth and Fourteenth. "I was asking you if you always use a condom."

I laugh at the starkness of the question. "Well, yes," I tell him. I'd slipped one on both times I'd fucked him. "Why do you ask?"

"Well, you're the first guy I've been with who has."

I stare at him. "You mean, you've been going bareback for the last six months?"

He nods. "I guess that's being kind of risky, huh?"

"More than kind of." I sigh. How much should I say? I've just met this guy. We're about ready to part ways forever. I can't start pontificating to him. Besides, the issue is too complex.

"Look, Anthony," I say after a few moments' thought. "Just be informed, okay? You've just come out, you're learning your way. Do yourself a favor and get some HIV material and read up. Don't just bareback because some guy says it's okay." I hesitate. "And you might want to get tested."

He looks at me strangely. "That's the most anyone has ever said to me on the subject. Thanks, Jeff." He reaches over and kisses me on the cheek.

I blush a little. "Just take care of yourself."

"I wish you didn't have to go back to Boston."

I look at my watch. Okay. So here it is. The place where we say good-bye. "I'm supposed to meet Henry at Grand Central at six o'clock," I tell him.

Anthony frowns. "That's too bad, tonight being Saturday and all."

"Yeah, I know but—well, I promised my nephew I'd take him to the movies tomorrow. He's in Connecticut. He's five."

Anthony's frown turns into a smile. "You *are* a good guy," he says.

The thought of little Jeffy brightens my mood. My sister Ann Marie named her son after me, a tribute that moves me more with each passing year, watching the boy grow. I'm glad that Ann Marie decided not to marry the lout who'd fathered her son, and I'm thrilled to play substitute daddy as often as I can. We live two hours apart, but I get down to Connecticut every couple of weeks, taking Jeffy to the carnival or Mystic Aquarium or the *Pokemon* movie. This time Henry's going along. Jeffy's used to gay men. He's a good kid.

"So I may be green," Anthony's saying, folding his arms across his chest, "but I know enough that I gotta ask. Is Henry your boyfriend?"

Once more I laugh. "No, no, no, he's just my sister"—though even as the words are out of my mouth, I regret the "just." I know that sisters often last a lot longer than boyfriends. "But the guy with the goatee last night," I say. "Do you remember him?"

"Sure. The cute one with the nice green eyes you were slobbering over."

I blush, just a little. "It was the X. Anyway, we've been together, off and on, for many years."

Anthony nods. "So *he's* your boyfriend."

I stammer a little. "Right now I'm just not sure. We're . . ."

Anthony raises his eyebrows, waiting.

"We're—well, it's hard to describe—"

"Family," Anthony interjects. "You're family, but even more than the way family is usually defined by straights."

I smile. He remembered my words. It actually sort of touches me. But he's not done.

"You can't describe it, because there aren't words," he's saying. "You don't set limitations on each other, because you're always surpassing them. You don't let others tell you how you're supposed to be. You're true to yourselves and nobody else. You're just who you are."

"*Whoa.*" I do a double-take. "Where did all *that* come from?"

Anthony shrugs. "Just something I picked up."

"You are definitely *not* green," I say, breaking into a broad grin. "Forgive me for thinking so." I feel my dick stir again in my pants. Great abs, *and* a mind and heart, too. Who *is* this guy?

This could be dangerous, I tell myself. The old familiar quiver roils my belly.

Oh, yes. Dangerous, indeed.

Meanwhile, Uptown

Henry

Quite frankly, I'm still staggered by the sex. *Who knew?* The Windex queen got me off not once, not twice, but *three times*—the last about nine A.M., and only then did we fall asleep.

Even now, more than six hours later, I'm still a little shell-shocked, standing off to the side of the crowded store, watching Shane play with an enormous Slinky. A harried salesclerk finally asks him to put it down. Shane sticks his tongue out at him.

"You're gonna get us kicked out of here," I say, laughing.

"Believe me, I've been kicked out of a lot better than FAO Schwartz." Shane makes a face, considering something. "As well as a lot *worse*."

I look at my watch. "We still have a couple of hours before we have to meet Jeff."

Shane holds aloft a bride doll and inspects under her skirts. "Just as I thought. Not anatomically correct." He shifts his gaze over at me. "Are you sure Jeff's not going to mind driving me back to Boston? It sure beats buying another Amtrak ticket."

I take the doll from him and set it down. "Not if you don't mind seeing *Toy Story 2* with his five-year-old nephew."

Shane makes a queasy face. "I love kids. Especially with Swiss cheese and sauerkraut grilled on rye."

"You crack me up, Shane."

He moves in close. "I do more than *that* to you, baby."

I blush. Yes, it's true. Shane's biceps have no peaks, his gut is slightly squishy, his face so unremarkable that even a police sketch artist would have trouble capturing it—and still the sex had been awesome. *Awe-*

some! But as much as I might want to pat myself on the back for finally finding bliss with an average-looking guy instead of the body-beautiful circuit boys I've lusted after for years, I can't deny the *real* reason the sex with Shane was so good. It fed my own starving narcissism, a fact that both troubled and fascinated me. I mean, who *wouldn't* get off on it? There I was—*me*, Henry Weiner—being asked to stand on a hotel bed naked so that a guy could adore me. *Literally.* Down on his knees, worshipping me, telling me how sublime I was, how radiant, how muscular, looking up at me as if I were the naked Christ on the Cross—an analogy that would give my Jewish mother an apoplectic fit if she knew I was thinking it. But the truth remains: it was simply the most awesome, most intense, most mind-boggling sex I've ever had.

And to top it off, Shane had even been willing to *pay* me! Even afterward, he'd taken out a crumpled hundred-dollar bill from his jeans pocket and waved it in front of my face, saying, "You sure?"

He was only joking, I insist to myself, watching him now as he tries to open the pants of a GI Joe doll.

"So what do you want to do until we meet Jeff?" Shane's asking. He's given up trying to get a peek at the GI genitals. "Ride around in a cab so I can blow you in the backseat?"

I blush again, certain that the handsome father and adolescent son looking at a train set next to us have heard every word. I grab ahold of Shane's coat and pull him out of the store onto Fifth Avenue.

"What?" Shane asks, mock-innocently. "Something I said?"

Outside, a Salvation Army volunteer cheerlessly rings her bell. Who still gives after Christmas is over? The sidewalk is thronged with people returning holiday gifts, their faces muffled in upturned collars and scarves. Suddenly, Shane takes my leather-gloved hand in his. Oh, boy. This is the awkward part. This is the part of tricking that Jeff calls "the hard truth of the light of day," when you have to tell the guy it was fun but it's over now. My first reaction is to pull my hand away, but I don't want to hurt Shane's feelings. He's too nice a guy.

He squeezes my hand. *Oh, great,* I think. *What if he's falling for me? What do I say? The truth? You didn't make me hard, Shane. Your protestations of devotion did. You can't base a relationship on narcissism. And that's all it was, Shane. You feeding mine.*

Right. As if I could say *that* without feeling like a total shit.

I can't wait to talk about this with Jeff. Jeff would know how to handle things. He always does. No matter the experience, Jeff has already had it. "Stay away from two kinds of guys," he's counseled. "The ones who act like they're in love with you the next morning and the ones who act like they don't care in the slightest. They're both exactly the same." And, "Stay away from two kinds of drugs. Tina and Gina. They're not at all the same, except that they'll both destroy your life if you let them."

Jeff is probably the smartest guy I've ever known. I'm not *that* much younger than him, but sometimes I feel a whole generation removed, as if crammed into Jeff's head start of seven years is an entire lifetime of achievement and failure. The school of gay hard knocks.

"So are you guys going to the Blue Ball in Philly in three weeks?" Shane is swinging our hands between us, as if to show the entire avenue what he's caught. "I can't decide whether to go to that or to the Fireball in Chicago next month. Doing both seems a bit excessive. You know what I mean? I don't want to be like those tired circuit queens who blow all their vacation time hopping from one party to the next."

I smile with some amusement. "I think actually the next one we talked about was the Winter Party," I tell him.

"But of *course* the Winter Party. You *can't* skip Miami."

I laugh. "That's where I wanted to be *last* night. All our other friends were there. But Jeff and Lloyd had other ideas."

"Jeff and Lloyd," Shane repeats, as if trying out their names. Then suddenly, he breaks his grip with me. We've stopped in front of another dour Salvation Army bell-ringer. Shane's fishing into his jeans for a handful of coins. I watch him as he tosses them into the pail. They make a clanging sound, and the volunteer gives him a small, tired smile.

Quickly I try to hide my hand so Shane can't reclaim it. But he finds it without much effort and sticks it along with his into the deep pocket of his down parka.

"Anyway," he says, "as you were saying . . . ?"

I sigh. "I really wasn't saying much of anything."

"Yes, you were. About Jeff and Lloyd. So which one are you in love with?"

I balk, trying to stop our stride, but Shane won't let me. "I'm not in love with *either* of them," I insist. "They're my *sisters*. Especially Jeff."

"So it's him," Shane says, all superior-sounding.

I make a dismissive sound but am careful not to "doth protest too much" yet again. "Think whatever you choose to. But I'd never want to date Jeff."

"Not wanting to date him is different from not being in love with him."

I say nothing. I'm damned if I do and damned if I don't.

"Don't get pissy now, sweetheart." Shane lets out a hoot. "It was just obvious last night. The way you looked at him. The way you seemed to know exactly what was going on for him."

"We're sisters," I repeat.

"Have it your way, honey. Believe whatever you need to believe."

This guy is really pushing it now. I am *not* going to admit to a near-stranger, even one with whom I've just had the best sex of my life, that sure, once, a long time ago, before I'd met him, I'd had a "star-crush" on Jeff. I would see him at Buzz or Avalon or After Tea in Provincetown, and yeah, I thought he was cute, charismatic. But look. I see the way Jeff is with tricks. In and out by the next morning, if that long. If I'd tricked with him way back when, we wouldn't be friends today. I'm sure by now Jeff has already managed to untangle himself from Anthony, his phone number already conveniently "lost" on some sidewalk in Chelsea. The only man in the world for Jeff is Lloyd, no matter who else comes along.

"You're thinking about him right now," Shane says.

I huff, "I am not."

"Look, I understand," Shane says. "He's a hottie. Some would say very hot. But you know what? I think you're much hotter. *Much.*"

I laugh. "Okay, Shane, you don't have to still make with the flattery. You already got me into bed."

He looks down at me, knitting his brows. "I'm serious, Henry. You've got a much sexier look. Jeff looks like any tired old circuit boy. But there's an *edge* to you, Henry. One minute you look like an angel, the next a devil. It's very appealing."

I can feel myself blushing. "Whatever."

"And Jeff probably subtly encourages you to keep thinking of yourself as inferior to him. Guys like him need guys like you. They need acolytes. Disciples. But baby, you could outshine him if you just stepped out from his shadow."

I pull my hand free from Shane's pocket. "Look, Shane. Jeff's my best friend. You've got it wrong. He's *always* encouraging me. If not for Jeff, I'd still be like . . ." I struggle with the words.

"*Me?* Go ahead, Henry. Say it. You'd still be like me."

"I didn't mean that."

We walk the last block in silence, our hands scrunched down into our own pockets. Shane's wrong about Jeff. Okay, sometimes Jeff can be a little selfish, like when he'll leave me only moments after we've arrived at some club, to dance with some new hot guy, and then never showing up again all night. But he's always encouraging me to meet somebody, too, telling me I look good, building my ego.

Isn't he?

Yes, he is—at least, he used to be. I try to remember the last compliment Jeff paid me. I can't. Instead, all I can remember is his comment last night: "*You?* He wants to pay *you?*"

I don't like it when I start feeling this way. Brent says the only reason I haven't found a boyfriend yet is because of Jeff. I've dated a few guys, but nothing has lasted longer than a couple of months. Sometimes it seems pretty bizarre. I mean, here I am, constantly surrounded by hot guys and finally having achieved a hot body myself, and still I end up going home alone. There are times I wonder about the whole scene. Why do I traipse along with Jeff to the White Party and Hotlanta and the Russian River, only to never find a guy? Everybody assumes circuit parties are these hothouses of wild nonstop sex, but actually *hooking up* with somebody, I've discovered, is rare. If not for the groping on the dance floor, there wouldn't be very much physical contact at all. Everyone's either too tired, too wasted, or too scared of rejection to pair off.

Except Jeff, of course. Jeff always seems to bring some hottie back to the hotel room, leaving me to sit reading *Tales of the City* in the lobby until they're through—which sometimes means the next morning. But one makes sacrifices for sisters.

Even if—okay, I admit it—one sister usually does most of the sacrificing.

We've reached Grand Central. My heart suddenly softens toward Shane. "Let's go in and wait for them," I say. "I'll buy you a cup of coffee."

"Okeydokey," Shane agrees. We push through the doors, letting the warmth envelop us. We head toward one of the kiosks, where I buy two coffees. Shane thanks me. Suddenly, I feel it's the least I can do.

We drink our coffees sitting on the floor, our backs against the wall facing the central clock, where Jeff and I have plans to rendezvous. We watch silently as humanity crisscrosses in front of us, a thousand voices transformed into a buzzy chorus that echoes up into the vast dome of the station. Faces indistinguishable from each other, yet endlessly fascinating to watch. Why is that? Why do we never tire of watching people we don't know? I become transfixed by the crowds that rush back and forth.

Finally, I turn my face slightly toward my new friend. "Shane, I need to be honest with you," I say quietly.

"Why?" Shane replies, equally as soft. "You've only just met me. Can't we keep the fantasy going for just a little bit longer?"

"I don't want to hurt you," I tell him.

Shane smiles, leaning his head back against the wall and closing his eyes. "You've let my adoration go to your head, Henry. You presume way too much power." He lets out a long sigh.

"I just thought I should—"

"Let me down easy?" Shane keeps his eyes closed. "Look, Henry. I'm not in love with you. I'm not hoping for a romance when we get back to Boston. You filled a fantasy for me. That's it."

He opens his eyes but keeps them looking up at the dome. "I had another fantasy once. It was to have sex thirty thousand feet in the air in the lavatory of a jumbo jet. I fulfilled that one last year courtesy of American Airlines on the way back from the White Party in Palm Springs. I didn't fall in love with the flight attendant who sucked me off. I didn't ask him to move in with me. It was a fantasy fulfilled. That's all."

I'm quiet. "I see," I say at last. "Well, if that's all it was . . ."

"That's all it was."

I shrug. I feel a little hurt, strangely enough. I thought it had actually meant more to him. Whatever. "I guess it was a fantasy for me, too," I say. "Funny thing is, I never realized I *had* that particular fantasy. I never realized what a fucking narcissist I am."

Shane turns to look over at me. "Come *on*, Henry. To get that body in that shape you spend *many* hours a week in the gym. Hours you could spend reading, or delivering hot meals to shut-ins, or visiting your mother, or watching reruns of *Growing Pains,* eating whole cans of Pringles. Not that you *should* be doing any of those things, but one can't deny one's narcissism when one spends six, seven, *eight* hours a week pumping heavy weights for no other reason than to enlarge one's deltoids and pectorals—and watching oneself in a mirror as one does it."

I look at him defensively. "I'm *not* denying it, Shane. You've made me acknowledge my narcissism. I'm not sure it's something I like very much about myself, but you made me see it. So bully for you."

"Don't get touchy, Sallie Mae." Shane laughs out loud suddenly. "You think you're the only narcissist sitting here? I might not have your pecs or your biceps, but I have my own arsenal." He pats his backpack. "The Windex bottle. That got me quite a *bit* of attention, didn't it? In Palm Springs it was glow sticks. And I've just discovered Flame Wands that take the whole glow stick experience to a brand new level. I'm planning to debut them in Miami. They're like fucking *spotlights*. Wait till you see. I'll be able to turn the attention of the whole fucking dance floor on me. Don't you see, Henry? In a sea of gym clones, I stand out. I *make* myself stand out."

I look over at him. I'd never really thought of it that way before.

"I made *you* notice *me*," Shane says simply.

"That you did," I admit.

Shane sighs. "So don't worry about letting me down gently. I understood right from the start what this was all about. I'll be fine. I've got a whole bag of tricks I'm waiting to use."

I smile. I reach over and take Shane's hand back in mine. "You're okay, you know that, Shane?"

"Usually," he says. "Sometimes I forget. Remind me once in a while, okay?"

"Deal."

We sit that way for about twenty minutes, reverting back to silence, watching the crowds scamper and scuttle around us. The clock in the center keeps track of the seconds that pass.

At a quarter to six, promptly as we'd planned, I recognize Jeff among the throng. Funny how it happens: how suddenly, out of the indistinguishable blur, a familiar face can pop right out at you. I'm quickly on my feet, waving him down.

But Jeff isn't alone. Is it . . . Lloyd?

No. It's the guy he went home with. The one who couldn't dance—

"You remember Anthony?" Jeff's asking.

"Yeah," I say, giving him a look. "You remember Shane?"

I don't need ESP to hear the question both of us are asking: *What the fuck is going on here?*

"Shane was hoping for a ride up to Boston," I quickly explain.

Jeff looks from me over at Shane. "Henry *did* explain to you that we're crashing at my sister's in Connecticut tonight? And that tomorrow we're taking her five-year-old son to the movies?"

"I *adore* children," Shane insists grandly, looking up at us, still sitting on the floor.

"Well, okay, then," Jeff says, making a wry face. "Show him your Windex bottle. He'll love that."

Shane shrugs. "They all do."

It's my turn for questioning. "And Anthony?" I ask, turning to the fourth member of our little group. "*You* like kids, too?"

"Don't really know any," Anthony admits. "But Jeff says I'll like Boston." For the first time I notice a large backpack slung over Anthony's shoulder.

"Oh, *did* he, now?" I ask. "And I thought you had just moved to New York, Anthony."

Jeff blushes a little. "He did. But I told him it was easier to find a job in Boston."

"But wherever will you *stay?*" I ask Anthony, heavy with sarcasm. He smiles. "Jeff said I could crash with him."

"Jeff's got a good heart," I purr, putting my arm around my sister's shoulders. I whisper fiercely in his ear: "*What the fuck are you doing?*"

"We're gonna miss our train," Shane announces.

"Yeah, wouldn't want that," Jeff says, shrugging me off and hurrying toward the track. Anthony follows. Shane takes his time standing, unfolding his long form gradually, dusting off his jeans. I watch him.

"We came down as two and we're going back as four," I murmur, more to myself than anybody else.

Shane turns, winks, and blows a kiss. "We're off to see the Wizard, stud boy."

"Oy vey," I say, sounding like my mother. But that's how I feel, and "Oy vey" is all I can think to say. I just shake my head and follow the troops to the train.

A Week Later, Provincetown

Lloyd

"Really, Eva, I can't eat any more," I tell her, patting my gut, but she brings over another plate of waffles anyway.

She makes a face. "You haven't tried any with blueberries."

"The strawberries and bananas were plenty," I insist.

My little apartment is filled with the aromas of coffee and cinnamon, vanilla and maple syrup. Eva drove up from New York, rising at three A.M. to make the six-hour trip. When she got here, I was still asleep, not expecting her until noon. But she came early, she explained, because suddenly she'd been filled with the desire to cook me breakfast. And cook she had: eggs and waffles and fresh fruit and freshly whipped cream.

It's delicious, but it's thrown me seriously off schedule. "I'm going to be late meeting Jeff," I tell her. "I still have to shower and pick up the key from the realtor."

"Just one more waffle, *please?* I made so much batter. They'll go to waste."

I smile. "You eat it. All you've had is a banana."

She shakes her head. "I couldn't possibly. I'm too excited. To actually be *here*, in Provincetown, planning for our home . . ." She shivers.

She slips the waffle onto my plate. I sigh. "Okay, just half," I say. She beams, pouring a gob of syrup over the waffle and sprinkling a handful of blueberries on top.

I really *am* full but don't want to hurt her feelings. She's gone to so much effort, buying the fruit in New York last night because she knew nothing would be open here in town when she got here. She was so excited to do this, so filled with passion about our guest house. The energy is good.

And I'm hopeful that Jeff will come around, too. He agreed to come down today, and I arranged to show him the house even though we haven't yet closed. Our realtor was a friend of Javitz's, an artist who'd gotten sick about the same time Javitz had and who most of us thought would follow him to the great beyond. But Ernie's one of those Lazaruses you hear about, one of the lucky ones: near death one day, he suddenly rose and walked, courtesy of the new drug cocktails. Now the struggling painter is a highly successful Provincetown real estate agent, making a killing off the inflated property values in town.

I manage to eat about a quarter of the waffle before my stomach feels as if it will burst. I push my plate away and wipe my mouth with my napkin. "Really, Eva, that's the best I can do. It was fabulous, though. Beyond fabulous."

She smiles, looking as if she might cry for happiness. "I'm *so* glad you liked it."

I stand up. I have to get in the shower. It's ten-thirty, and Jeff's meeting me at the guest house by eleven. I don't want to be late. After that fiasco on New Year's Eve, I want this encounter to go smoothly.

Under the spray of the shower, I think about Jeff. There's something going on with him that concerns me. I called him New Year's Day on his cell phone, catching him at his sister's. I could hear little Jeffy playing in the background. I told Jeff that I wished we'd spent the night together, and he seemed to melt, admitting that he wished the same. I asked him to come to Provincetown; he agreed he would, even going so far as to say he'd consider spending the night.

That's when I asked to say hello to little Jeffy. "Tell him Unca Lloyd wants to say hi to him." Last Christmas, Jeff and I had loaded up a sackful of toys and dressed as identical Santas, driving down to Connecticut and surprising the boy. He'd been ecstatic.

But Jeff hesitated. "He's playing with somebody right now," he said. "I don't know if he'll come to the phone."

I assumed it was a little friend. But when I heard Jeffy say no, that he was too busy playing his computer game to talk to me, I heard *another* voice—an adult male voice—offer to wait until he got back. Still Jeffy refused to come to the phone. I asked Jeff who was playing with the boy.

"Um . . . his name in Anthony," Jeff said.

"Who's Anthony?"

He hesitated. "Some guy I met in New York."

I was stunned. "Why's he with you in Connecticut?"

"He . . . um . . . he's coming back to Boston with me. He wants to look for a job."

I didn't have to ask where he'd be staying. Remember what I said about Jeff and me? How we just seem to know things about each other? I knew in that moment that this Anthony person was going to be staying with Jeff, and it troubled me. It's not like Jeff to just invite a stranger to stay with him. Jeff was, in fact, *notorious* for preferring that tricks not spend the night. He didn't even care for *friends* crashing for more that a day or two on his couch. And here was this Anthony *moving in.*

I knew right away it was a reaction against me. Against the guest house. I had made a move that had appeared to exclude Jeff, and so he was taking similar action against me.

I was angry when I hung up the phone, pissed off by his childish game-playing. My anger, however, has evolved into concern over whether this Anthony is trustworthy, and concern over Jeff's state of mind. Had my news really been so devastating to him?

I determine that I'll get to the bottom of it today. I'll let him know how much I want his involvement. I'll introduce him to Eva. I'm sure he'll love her. Especially once he learns about Steven. I can still smell the cinnamon in the air, even through the closed bathroom door. How could Jeff *not* love her? How could anyone?

That's when I hear her sobbing.

Jeff

As Lloyd predicted, it's a house I've passed many times, a sturdy but undistinguished Cape on a side street a few blocks past the Ice House, overgrown with ivy, with a shingle out front that reads *SEABREEZE INN.*

A soft, steady snow has begun to fall, blanketing the town with three or four inches. There's no sound, only the occasional wail of the wind off the bay. I look at my watch. I'm a little early, but usually so is Lloyd.

I push my hands down deep into the pockets of my leather jacket, the snow collecting on my shoulders and the top of my woolen hat. I watch, nearly entranced, as the shingle swings silently back and forth. The peacefulness of the place offers me a clarity that I haven't had in days. I think about the stranger back home in Boston, sitting on my bed watching TV, flipping through the channels with the remote control. *What the fuck did I do?* I ask myself.

In the wind, I can hear Javitz's answer: *You asshole, you know precisely well what you did.*

A gust of wind seems to laugh at me. The way Javitz would, when I was being obtuse or stubborn. *Inviting a complete stranger to live with you,* he's telling me, *was an impulsive act, a passive-aggressive counterpunch to Lloyd. Who knows who that boy in your apartment really is? What could he be making off with, right at this very moment?*

But Anthony's no thief. I trust my instincts enough to know that. I saw how authentic he'd been with little Jeffy. Anyone who can play that well with a kid is definitely trustworthy. We'd all arrived from New York at my sister's house ready to do nothing but crash, the lateness and the drugs of the night before finally catching up with us. I sprawled out on Ann Marie's couch, Henry fell asleep in a chair, and the Windex queen propped himself in a corner and gabbed all night on his cell phone. Alone among us it had been Anthony to get down on the floor and play computer games with Jeffy. From under half-lidded eyes I observed that he let the kid win every time.

Yet in almost every other way, Anthony has remained a mystery. He still hasn't shared much more about himself than he had the first day. I asked him again about his family, but he simply restated they wanted nothing to do with him. I asked him again where he'd grown up, and he only repeated "outside Chicago." I asked him again if he'd ever had a relationship, and he said, for the third time, no. It's as if his life only began six months ago, when he'd stumbled into his first circuit party.

I look at my watch again. Ten minutes to eleven. I consider waiting in my car, but despite the cold, I'm enjoying the air and the light. I used to *love* spending time in Provincetown in the winter. There's something about the rawness and the wind that makes you feel right on the edge of life, as if you were pushing living to its limits. That was the reason Javitz has so loved it here. He was forever pushing limits, his and ours.

Damn it. See what happens? This is *precisely* why I don't come to Provincetown anymore. Because it makes me think of Javitz. Even more than during the hectic summer months, I can feel Javitz here in the winter. He's present in the wind he loved so much, in the taste of the brine in the air, in the uncanny light that reflects off the water in three directions. Even after four years, thinking of Javitz is still too hard for me to do.

God, I wish Lloyd would hurry up and get here.

The wind whipping in from the bay is getting colder. I consider standing on the wraparound front porch of the guest house; at least up there I'd be sheltered. But somehow I just don't feel right walking up the steps until Lloyd is with me.

It's not my house, after all.

I look around at the houses on the street, wishing in at least one I'd spy a light, a shade being lifted by a curious homeowner. But no one. The snow collects in window boxes, drifts up against front doors. Here Provincetown still looks the way it must have thirty, forty years ago. Weather-stung white clapboard houses with widows' walks, stone walls overgrown with sea grass. In the winter most of the places in this part of town are boarded up, their owners safe and warm in New York town houses, like the one Eva's leaving to move here.

What if this were our house? Mine and Lloyd's?

The shingle creaks in the wind. *SEABREEZE INN*—a sign I know will soon be changed to read *NIRVANA.*

What would we have named it, Lloyd and I? Would I have even agreed to such an idea? To run a guest house?

I'd never considered it. But then, he'd never asked me. The few innkeepers I know seem overworked and scattered. The workload is tremendous, the responsibility daunting. But I can't deny, standing here, watching the shingle sway in the wind, that I wish the place were mine. Mine and Lloyd's. It's hard even to remember now what it was like when we'd lived together. I have only fragments, memories like torn pages in my mind: watching the six o'clock local news cross-legged on the floor, balancing our dinners on our laps. Putting up the Christmas tree. Waking up on the edge of the bed at three in the morning, Lloyd's arms snaked around me. Faux-finishing the walls of the bathroom. Grocery shopping at the Star Market, always opening the bag of potato chips before we checked out. It's the silly, ordinary things I remember, little images and moments I'd never admit to cherishing as much as I do.

But in so many of those memories, Javitz is there, too. Topping the Christmas tree with a Star of David. Critiquing the color of the bathroom. Taking the half-eaten bag of chips away from us and finishing them off himself. Listening to us bicker, rolling his eyes and signaling when one of us went out of bounds.

"Shit," I say out loud, amazed at how quickly my thoughts go around to Javitz again, standing here.

It's eleven o'clock. Where the *fuck* is Lloyd?

Lloyd

"It's okay," I tell her. "It's okay."

Eva shudders in my arms. I'm very conscious of how precariously my towel is secured at my waist. I'd rushed out of the shower when I heard her crying. She was sitting at the kitchen table with her face in her hands, sobbing uncontrollably. "What's the matter?" I shouted, but she was unable to answer for several minutes. She just wept hysterically, as if she'd gotten a telegram giving her bad news.

But it's just a memory.

"It just came over me," she manages to say. "I thought of Steven. Of our life together. And here I am starting something new . . ."

"I know," I tell her, stooping down, one hand holding on to my towel to keep it in place. "Sometimes it does make you feel guilty in a way. How we're continuing our lives, moving on."

She grips my free hand. "You understand."

I look up at the clock. It's now a few minutes past eleven, and I still have to get the key. The guest house is in the East End, a good ten-minute walk from here. I'd ride my bike, but it's snowing pretty hard now. I'll make faster time on foot. Still, I'm going to be at least fifteen minutes late for Jeff—more if I have to console her much longer.

I try to head back into the bathroom to towel off, but she holds on to my hand. "I'm sorry to be such a burden," she says. "The tears—I never know when they might strike."

"Grief is an unpredictable thing," I say. "Look, Eva, I've got to hurry. Jeff is waiting."

"Of course," she says, but it still takes several more second before she releases her grip.

I hurriedly dress and pull on my hat and gloves. I give her one final embrace. She seems reluctant to let go, her tiny hands clinging to my wool sweater, her heavy breasts pressed up against my stomach. Finally, I have to take her by the shoulders and look down into her swollen eyes. I tell her to take a walk in the snow and clear her head, then to meet us at the guest house.

Thankfully, Ernie's not at the office when I arrive, so I won't have to engage in time-consuming small talk. His assistant hands me the key and I begin a fast trot down Commercial Street. The wind slaps my cheeks. I think about Eva's tears. They had come last week in New York as well. She had been sitting there on the couch, smiling as I called Jeff on my cell phone, but then, just as I was hanging up, she broke down in tears. A sudden memory of Steven, she explained as I consoled her, putting my arms around her and moving her head to my shoulder.

And now, tears once more.

I don't like playing psychologist with my friends. I can't be diagnosing them every time they act out or have a fit. But Eva's more than a friend: she's becoming family, and I'm planning a major life change with her. I tell myself that her little outbursts are signs of nothing more than a temporary adjustment disorder. A grief problem, maybe on the edge of depression. Nothing that can't be treated. Maybe I'll suggest an antidepressant, have her see someone. It's nothing that I need to be overly concerned about.

First impressions tell the truth: mine of Eva was one of *strength*. I remember how strong she was with Alex. How insightful she was about taking those baby steps back to life. How she had counseled me so sagely about my own grief, sitting up with me late into the night talking about life and love and death and loss. It's exhilarating to talk so openly about my grief, to have it understood and resonated, especially with how guarded Jeff has become. When I'm with Eva, I feel more heard and more appreciated than I've been in a long, long time.

I needn't worry that she isn't up to all this. Her strength inspires me. This is a woman who, when she discovered her husband's gayness, had not only accepted it but *embraced* it. Hadn't she cared for him lovingly during his final illness? How many women could have done that? Wouldn't most have thrown him out, viewing his sexuality as some kind of personal affront? How many could have sat at his bedside along with gay friends and lovers, all of them linking hands in Steven's final moments? It's an image of love and unity that brings tears to my eyes whenever Eva describes it to me.

That's what true family is.

"I loved Steven's gay friends," she told me that first day we'd met. "I even loved his lovers." It was right after I'd told her about the family that Jeff and Javitz and I had made, a family misunderstood by so many but which Eva seemed instinctively to appreciate. When she went on to describe the queer family she and Steven had constructed, it made sense. Our whole so-called coincidental meeting at the seminar suddenly seemed karmic. We were *destined* for this path together.

I trudge through the thickening snow remembering that night. We'd disclosed so much about ourselves right away. We'd gone out for coffee after visiting Alex, and within moments of sitting down in the booth I'd learned she was fifty years old, that she'd had a scare with breast cancer two years ago (the lump turned out to be benign) and that her husband had died of AIDS. We sat there for hours swapping stories, marveling over the synchronicities in our lives.

"This Jeff person you keep mentioning," she observed toward the end of the night. "Are you . . . lovers?"

I smiled. "We're a rather unconventional couple," I explained. "We were together for six years, then drifted apart after Javitz's death. Lately we've started to reconnect. I believe we're soul mates."

Look, I'm smart enough to recognize Eva is a little threatened by Jeff. I understand she's probably a little frightened about meeting him. Maybe that's why her nerves are on edge today. Hey, it's only natural. A little insecurity is to be expected. This is a big change she's making, after all. She's overhauling her life, uprooting herself from the world she's known for so long. She'll have to leave Alex, to whom she's become so attached. But she has the strength to do it. I'm confident of that.

And once Jeff gets to know her, I'm certain he'll love her. How could he not?

I see him standing there in the snow, looking up at the guest house. I run the last few yards. "Cat!" I shout. "Cat!"

Jeff

Lloyd flings his arms around me. His cheeks are flushed and his nose bright red. He looks adorable.

"I was beginning to worry," I say to him.

He sighs. "Eva just arrived. We were . . . talking. I'm sorry."

We kiss.

"It's bigger than I thought," I tell him. "The house."

Lloyd grips my hand through our gloves. "Come on," he says. "I can't wait to show it to you."

He leads me up the path to the front steps. He fumbles with the key, and the front door creaks open. Stepping across the threshold, we're careful to wipe the snow off our shoes. I look around. The previous owners have left behind much of the furniture, and despite the sudden whiff of mustiness, I have to admit, it doesn't look too bad. Tattered antiques, mostly, nothing too kitschy. A Victorian sofa, a Hepplewhite table, an ancient globe standing in the corner. I spin it gently. Ancient indeed: across much of Europe is still printed AUSTRO-HUNGARIAN EMPIRE.

"Let me turn up the heat," Lloyd says, adjusting the thermostat. The old furnace kicks into gear beneath us, exhaling a gust of warm air through the grate on the floor.

I walk over to the bookcase, running my fingers along the spines of the volumes. They're certainly an eclectic lot: T. S. Eliot. Fitzgerald. *Moby Dick*. Mary Heaton Vorse's *History of Provincetown*. Henry Beston's *The Outermost House*. A thick layer of dust suggests it's been a long time since any of these books have been read.

"Come on into the kitchen," Lloyd calls.

It's newly tiled, with a modern refrigerator, but the stove is an old black beauty. "Works perfectly," Lloyd says, opening the oven door. "Gas. Vintage 1935."

He struggles to bring more light into the place, hoisting the Venetian blinds as high as they can go, but the window is nearly covered outside with crosshatches of bare wisteria branches. "I think I'll cut those back," Lloyd says. "Bring more light into the kitchen. Eventually, I'd like to put another window in here. Really open it up."

I look over at him. I can see the excitement in his face, the glow in his eyes. It's been a long time since Lloyd has been so enthused by anything. I know he's spent the years since Javitz's death struggling to find a direction, trying to decide whether to continue hammering out a living as a psychologist or to do something entirely new. I didn't expect this—playing Bea Benaderet at Petticoat Junction—but I can't deny Lloyd's enthusiasm; and no matter what, it's good to see him so animated again.

"Come upstairs," Lloyd's beckoning, crooking a finger at me. "Wait'll you see the view."

The stairs are narrow and creaky. On the walls hang somber sepia photographs of ship captains and their wives: former inhabitants of the house? I pause briefly to study one pair. Why did they always look so *grim* in those days? Is it because they had to sit still so long for the camera that they couldn't hold a smile? Or were they just unhappy?

Lloyd's reached the top of the stairs. Somehow he bypassed an enormous, sticky cobweb that I walk straight through. "Shit," I curse. "Didn't they clean out this place before selling it?"

"Look, Jeff, in here," Lloyd calls, oblivious to my dilemma. He's entered a room off the top of the stairs. I follow, my fingers in my hair, certain that a nasty spider has landed there. It takes several seconds before I relax enough to look around.

The room is large, an old stone fireplace set into the far wall. A canopy bed stands in the center, a rolltop desk pushed up beneath a window. "This will be my room," Lloyd is telling me. He corrects himself. "*Our* room, Jeff, when you're here."

"It's a good size," I say, looking around, consciously noncommittal.

"The rooms on this side of the house have a water view," Lloyd says. "See?" He bends down, gesturing for me to follow. "If you look out that way and turn your head—no, farther, Jeff, this way—see? Beyond that house? You can see the bay."

I turn my neck nearly a hundred and eighty degrees, finally making out a glimpse of the water, angry with whitecaps. The wind howls suddenly through an eave of the house.

"You can sit here at this desk," Lloyd tells me. "You can write with a view of the bay."

I rub my neck. "Lloyd, it might be difficult working on my laptop with my neck twisted around like Linda Blair."

He smiles. "Don't be a wise-ass."

"I just don't want you to advertise water views and then get sued for truth in advertising."

He touches my face gently. "I want you to be a part of this, Jeff," he says, suddenly serious. "I want us to share this vision."

I look at him with equal seriousness. "Lloyd, it was never my dream to run a guest house. Neither did I know it was yours."

He shakes his head. "I didn't know either, Jeff. It just came to me. Can't you be at least a *little* excited for me?"

All the way down here I tried to prepare myself for this conversation. I want to give Lloyd a chance. I want to give this project a chance. I don't want to turn my back on him out of fear or pique the way I had on New Year's Eve. I'd been a shit. I admit that.

"It's just that you never even *talked* with me about this," I tell him. "That *hurt*, Lloyd."

He starts to reply but I cut him off. If I'm going to share my feelings, I'll have to do it fast, before they get all confused and jumbled and I change my mind.

"You know what it reminds me of, Lloyd? How quickly you decided to move out of our apartment when we lived together. You didn't talk to me about *that*, either. One day after six years, you just turned to me and announced you'd decided to move out."

He approaches me and takes my hands in his. "That was a long time ago, Jeff. Things are different now. I'm asking you to come down here, to spend time here. To *share* this with me."

I smile uncomfortably. "But it's not just you anymore. There's this . . . this woman."

"I think you'll understand all this better after you meet Eva."

I break free and move over to the window. The snow is turning the red rooftops white. "Lloyd," I say, trying to measure my words, "I know this is the eleventh hour. But—well—have you completely, *thoroughly* thought this through? I know you've struggled with what you want to do with your life. I know you were tired of playing healer and caretaker as a therapist, but here you are, making that role not only your job but now your *home*. You'll be living with it twenty-four-seven, three-hundred-sixty-five."

"But it's *different*, Jeff." His eyes plead with me to understand. "*Way* different than being a therapist. I'm meeting new people. Tending to a garden. Living here with the seasons. I know it will be hard work, but it's not hard work I mind. Hard work is good for the soul. This is a dream, a once-in-a-lifetime chance. Don't be sour on it, Jeff. Please."

I take a deep breath and then let it out slowly. "I'm sorry if I've seemed that way."

Lloyd takes my hands again. "I do believe that Javitz is with us on this, Jeff. He loved this town. We could put down roots here—"

"But *we're* not doing this, Lloyd. *You and Eva* are. Remember that."

He sighs. "Jeff, I can see you here, as a part of this. I can see you here, *writing* again."

"Oh, yeah?" I break free once more of his grip and walk across the room. "And what am I writing?"

"*Anything*, Jeff. I want you to write again. You say you worry about *me*. Well, I worry about you. It's been *two years* since you've had an article published."

"I don't need to worry about that anymore," I tell him. "Javitz made sure of that."

"Javitz didn't leave you that money so that you'd stop writing. He'd be *crushed* by that. Jeff, what happened to your dreams of writing a novel? Or a screenplay?"

My back stiffens. "Lloyd, I did not come down here to talk about my writing career." *Or lack thereof.* Suddenly, I want to go outside, get back into the cold air.

Lloyd stands in front of me. "Jeff, since Javitz died we've *both* been adrift. Neither of us has been able to get a handle on our dreams. I'm trying to do that here. Maybe you don't understand, but I don't understand you, either. These people you hang with. These circuit parties. The drugs."

"Don't *start*, Lloyd." I sigh impatiently.

"I know you said you only did one hit of Ecstasy on New Year's. I believe you. But one hit can lead to two. And you don't want to go back to being—"

"Lloyd, X is not crystal. It's not fucking GHB."

"There are studies that show Ecstasy can be lethal, Jeff."

I'm flabbergasted. "How did we get on this? I didn't come down to be lectured about drugs."

"I don't mean to lecture. But the circuit isn't healthy, Jeff—"

"Don't go there, Lloyd. You have no idea what you're talking about. You're reacting to what the media writes about the circuit. Just try coming with me some time and see for yourself."

Lloyd places his hands on my shoulders. "Jeff, I know you've got a good head. But how long has it been since you've seen our old friends? Melissa and Rose? Wendy and Chanel?"

I scoff. "All of them consumed with playing mommy to a series of Chinese babies. I'm sorry, I just got tired of sitting around going goo-goo all the time."

"Jeff, it's not just that—"

"Okay." Once more I pull myself free of Lloyd and move to a new spot across the room. "So I admit that since Javitz's death I've found some new friends. Maybe I *had* to. Maybe it was the only way for me. You grieved your way, Lloyd. You lived here among all of Javitz's old cronies. You spent your time in quiet contemplation with the universe. Well, your way has never been mine, Lloyd, and I'm not going to apologize for my way."

Impulsively I suddenly swirl around like a crazy Julie Andrews on top of a mountain. "Life is too fucking short not to dance," I say, louder than I intended. "Do you remember who said that, Lloyd? It was *Javitz*. Javitz would be dancing if he were alive. But he's gone, Jeff! He's gone and we're still here and I'm going to *fucking dance!*"

Lloyd covers his mouth as if he's just realized something.

"What?" I ask. "What is it?"

He shakes his head. "It's funny, that's all."

"What is?" I'm suspicious, defensive.

He smiles. "That's the first time you've ever really talked about your grief, and how you've handled it."

I just sigh.

Lloyd approaches me again. "It's a *good* thing, Jeff. Nobody talks about grief anymore. It's as if because of these new drugs, because so many people are living, we're all supposed to be *over* it, *done* with our grieving."

I hold firm. I will not cry. Not here, not now.

"It's like AIDS never happened," Lloyd is saying. "Or that it was something a long, long time ago, and now it's time to be moving on. It's like we're not supposed to bring it up anymore."

I struggle to find my voice. "If you speak it," I say hoarsely, "it might come back."

"But it's never left," Lloyd says.

I let out a sudden, irrepressible wail of anguish. "That's just it, Lloyd! That's why coming here, to Provincetown, is so fucking *hard*. I see him everywhere! There's not one place in this whole fucking town that doesn't hold a memory. I used to love going to the breakwater, but I can't anymore. Not even after all this time. Because I see him there. Maybe that comforts you, but it feels like *hell* to me. I don't want to feel Javitz in the wind! I want to feel him sitting in his chair and smell his fucking cigarettes and hear that croaky laugh of his."

Damn it, I've started to cry. Too late to stop now.

"I want to tell him how shitty I feel," I say, crumbling, "and I want him to make it go away." I can't stop the damn tears. They're like a god-damn broken faucet. "Only *he* could do that. You know that, Lloyd. Only *him.*"

I sit down on the bed and put my hands over my face.

Lloyd sits beside me and places his arm around my shoulders. "I *do* know, Jeff. I do." He kisses my forehead.

He does know. The only one who truly, truly does. None of my new friends knew Javitz. Maybe that's why I find it easier being with them over the old.

"You know what makes me crazy sometimes?" I whisper. "How Henry will come to me with stuff, the way I used to go to Javitz. Henry will come all confused and upset over some guy, or about something he read, or knotted up about something at work. And he'll want my take on it. As if I have all the answers."

Lloyd strokes my hair.

"But what's even crazier is that I *give* him answers, Lloyd. I stand there against the bar and I *talk, talk, talk*. I tell him this is the way it is, and all these boys, they fucking *listen* to me, Lloyd. I'm a goddamn fraud, but I get away with it." I make a bitter face. "Javitz must be laughing his ass off at me."

"Javitz isn't laughing at you, Jeff. I'm sure he's very proud." Lloyd lifts my chin to took into my eyes. "But he wouldn't want you to stop writing."

I look away. "It's too hard. It's just too hard. I just can't seem to get fired up by anything. In a way, I suppose, I envy you, Lloyd. Getting pumped up about this place. You have something to dream about again."

He touches my face. "Will you share it with me, Jeff? This dream? Will you at least try?"

I look at him. I look at his beautiful deepset green eyes and run my hand over the top of his close-cropped head. I smile. I remember the night we met, so long ago now. I remember how he took me back to his place and drew a bath for us, dotted with daisies. I remember how hard I fell in love with him, how the very thought of him filled up my entire self, sucked the air right out me. I'm about to say yes, yes, of *course* I'll try—and although I can't promise anything, it means the world to hear him ask. In that moment everything disappears: Javitz's death, my disappointment over Lloyd not moving back to Boston, even the worries about that stranger back in my apartment. I'm about to tell Lloyd that I love him, that more than anything else in the world I want to be with him, but before I can utter a single word, I'm cut off suddenly by a voice from downstairs:

"*Yooooooooo-hoooooooooooooooooo.*"

Lloyd

God, I hate when she does that.

"What *is* that?" Jeff asks, looking around for the source of the sound that echoes against the walls far more sharply than even the howling wind.

"It's just Eva," I say.

She's downstairs somewhere. Damn her timing. Why did she have to come in just at that moment? Finally, Jeff was opening up a little and—

"*Yoooooo-hooooooo!*"

I bound to the top of the stairwell. "Eva! *Please!* Stop that! We're here! Upstairs! We're coming down."

I turn and smile resignedly over at Jeff. I regret having to cut off our conversation. "We'll talk more later," I tell him. "Okay?"

He just shrugs.

"I've brought some dishes over," Eva's calling up to us. "Wait'll you see!"

We find her in the kitchen lifting them out of a cardboard box. I notice she's tracked snow across the tile floor.

"Eva," I ask, "should you be bringing stuff in yet? It's not officially ours for another few weeks."

"Oh, I know, but Ernie said it was okay if I brought up a few things from New York." She holds a plate up so we can see. There's some kind of a crest in the center. "These have been in my family for generations. Made in Dresden. My father's father brought them over in—"

"Uh, Eva, this is—"

Her eyes settle on Jeff. "Oh, my! Forgive me!" She sets the plate down and hurries over to embrace Jeff. "You must be Jeffrey," she gushes. She squeezes him tight, wrapping her arms around his torso and resting her head under his chin. He looks over at me with some surprise. "I have been wanting to meet you for *so* long."

Jeff tentatively pats her on the back. "It's nice to meet you, too, Eva."

She pulls back enough to look up at him. "Do you like the place? It matters to me, Jeff, that you feel at home here."

"Thanks," he says, clearly uncomfortable with the sudden intimacy.

I sense Jeff's discomfort. Eva's intensity is one of the reasons I love her, but Jeff is, after all, a born-and-raised Connecticut Yankee, and Yankees don't usually go for all that touchy-feely stuff, especially not at first meeting. I try to draw her away from him. "What do you think about eventually cutting out another window here, Eva?" I ask, moving across the kitchen.

Eva does let go, but she takes Jeff by the hand and leads him over to where I stand. "I think it's a splendid idea," she says. "Oh, yes. Just fill the house with light."

"My idea exactly," I agree.

Eva looks up at Jeff. "It's uncanny how Lloyd and I think alike," she tells him. "We're always finding little moments like that."

I see Jeff's eyes flicker away.

She drops his hand and returns to unpacking her plates. "I'm hopeful you and I might find some time to take a walk, Jeff. Just the two of us. To get to know each other."

I watch as Jeff smiles noncommittally.

Eva keeps chattering. "I'd love to cook both of you a big meal tonight. A celebration!"

She's trying hard to win him over. Too hard, probably. "Eva, you know my kitchen is so small," I offer. "Why don't we just get pizza from George's?"

She pouts. "But look what I was able to do for breakfast." She smiles over at Jeff. "I made Belgian waffles with fresh fruit this morning. They're Lloyd's favorite."

Jeff smiles back tightly. "I know."

She holds a plate against her bosom. It's that unconscious gesture of hiding her breasts I've noticed before. "You know, Jeff, my husband was gay," she announces. "I don't know if Lloyd told you. He was gay and he died of AIDS."

Jeff blinks a couple of times in response. I put my hands in front of my face.

"Yes, he was," Eva continues. "He taught me *all* about gay culture." She smiles to herself, remembering something, then returns to placing the dishes in the cupboard. She's talking fast, almost giddily. "Oh, my goodness, how many times we listened to Judy at Carnegie Hall. And watched *All About Eve*. That was Steven's favorite. And a favorite of yours and Lloyd's and Javitz's, right?"

Jeff looks over at me, then back at Eva. "One of them," he says.

"Oh, my, how Steven *loved* that movie. I do, too. I can see all the gay parallels. They're so obvious. Why doesn't *everyone* see them?"

Way too hard, I think.

"Do you know we watched *All About Eve* the night Steven died? Of course, he was clear-minded right to the end. Not like Javitz. Gosh, how cruel a fate was that? Javitz, so brilliant. To end up with dementia." She shudders.

Jeff turns and looks at me again. He seems incredulous. I just manage a helpless little grin.

"You know what?" Eva says suddenly, holding another plate against her bosom. "I *feel* him here."

"Javitz?" I ask.

"Actually, *both* of them. Javitz and Steven." She shivers. "They're *together*. Maybe they're even *lovers* in that other world. Oh, wouldn't that be wonderful!

I notice a nasty little grin cross Jeff's lips. I brace myself.

"I think I see them, too," he tells her. "They're standing right there, in fact—*behind you.*"

Eva lets out a little gasp, dropping the plate she's holding. It falls to the floor with a shattering crash.

"Oh, dear!" she cries.

Both Jeff and I are quickly down on our knees picking up the pieces. Nose-to-nose, our eyes meet and I shake my head at him.

"I'm awfully sorry," Jeff says as he hands her three small slivers of ceramic. "I didn't mean to startle you."

She smiles uncomfortably.

"I know these plates mean a lot to you," I say, dropping a few shards into the trash. I look over at Jeff. I hope he's satisfied with himself.

"No, please. It was just a plate." She sighs. "It's just a *thing*. An *object*. Right, Lloyd?"

We've had discussions about this. I've told her that I thought she was sometimes too attached to *things,* to material possessions. Eva grew up rich and sheltered, accustomed to the fineries of her class. I know Jeff's deep distrust of the rich; I'm hoping it won't prejudice him against her.

He does seem genuinely remorseful for his mischief. "Now you'll always be one plate short at dinner." He frowns. "I *am* sorry."

"No, don't be," Eva insists. "It's the first lesson of this house. Don't be attached." She looks to me for affirmation. I give it to her with a smile.

"Lloyd has taught me so much," Eva says fondly, looking over at Jeff. "I am so thrilled to be embarking on this journey. And I'm sure there will be many more lessons to learn."

She walks quickly across the kitchen floor to embrace me, just as she did Jeff earlier—tightly, with her head tucked underneath my chin. I see Jeff look away.

Jeff

It's probably a good thing it's *Lloyd* describing that scene for you, because—as over the top as I'm sure she comes across—I'd probably have done a whole hell of a lot *worse*. Because she *is* over the top—of Mount *Everest*. Oh, my God, that doesn't even *begin* to describe her. Over the top, off this planet—I mean certifiably *loony*. But shrewd! I can see that right off. She knows exactly what she's up against, dealing with me, and she's got her game plan *all mapped out*.

She wants to show me that she's Lloyd's partner now, not me.

So I agree to take the walk with her, after reluctantly posing for a quick photo in the snow in front of the house. "Say, 'If you please, pass the cheese!'" Eva instructs as she snaps a picture of Lloyd and me.

What a wacko.

"I'm going on ahead to return the key to the realtor," Lloyd says.

"Run along," Eva says, taking my arm. "Jeffrey and I are going to get to know each other." We walk out along the beach as the snow continues to fall.

"I was born in Connecticut just like you, Jeff," she tells me.

"Oh?" I raise an eyebrow. "Whereabouts?"

"Greenwich."

I smirk. Greenwich is *not* the same Connecticut I was born in. Greenwich is the Gold Coast. I was born in a little factory town outside Hartford.

"My father worked for the government," she tells me. "He was always traveling all over the world. I wanted nothing more than to be with him always, but our time together was always so brief. Were you close to *your* father, Jeff?"

I'm presuming Lloyd told her my father died a few years ago, and that I regret never having the chance to be fully authentic with him while he was still alive. That's what she wants me to say: she wants me to start disclosing the way she's been doing. Just spew out all our emotions and secrets and fears. But I'm being stubborn.

"I knew my father as well as possible," I say, ending the discussion. Or at least trying to.

"My father was devoted to me," she rambles on. "He would always bring me a doll from every country he visited. We would sleep in the same bed when he was home, until the time I was twelve. Do you think that improper, Jeff?"

I don't have any idea how I should respond. I just look at her.

She keeps talking. "Some people thought it was wrong. But my father was the kindest, gentlest . . ." She stops talking and looks out at the water. The snow is raising a cloud of mist over the beach. "I still miss him. Just like I still miss Steven. I don't think we ever stop missing those we've lost." She looks up at me with her big round eyes. "Is it hard for you, Jeff? Being here, in Provincetown, remembering Javitz?"

Her casual references to Javitz are beginning to bug me. She didn't know him. Okay, so maybe she can relate to his death since her husband also died of AIDS, but she knows *nothing* about Javitz's life. She knows *nothing* about his queer politics, his campy sense of humor, his delightfully twisted love of sex. She knows nothing of his suspicion of heteros. Javitz would've thought she was whacked.

"I'm fine, Eva." I look over at her. "If I seem distant, it's just because I'm cold."

She smiles. "Then maybe we can pop into a café. Let me buy you a cup of coffee."

Okay, so you're probably seeing her as really sweet, and me as a real prick. But this is her strategy. Win me over with kindness. Then it's off with my head. Then she can have Lloyd all to herself. You think I'm being too hard on her? You just watch. I'm *onto* her little game.

We take a table near the window in Fat Jack's. Her feet don't even reach the floor. She reminds me of a Munchkin. Or the Bride of Chucky.

"Jeff," she says after the waiter has taken our order, "I *meant* it when I said I want you to feel at home here."

I raise an eyebrow. "I've been coming to Provincetown for *twelve years.* I feel very at home here."

"Of course. But I meant at Nirvana. *Our* home."

She's made the reference to "their" home already a couple times. Don't think I'm not picking up on her subtle meaning.

"Thanks, Eva," I manage to say.

"No, seriously. I really, *really* mean it. I want you to know that you are always welcome."

The waiter places two coffees down in front of us. I drink mine black. Eva doesn't touch hers. She just sits there, hands folded over each other on the table, staring at me with those round button eyes of hers. She's so small it's almost creepy—except for those bazookas she tries to hide under her heavy wool sweater. She's so busty and short, it's a wonder she doesn't topple over face first when she walks down the street.

"So tell me about *you,*" she's saying.

"What's to tell?" I smile. "I'm sure Lloyd has told you that he's been hounding me to get writing again."

"I'm sure you're a *brilliant* writer," she says.

I took at her oddly. "Why are you so sure of that?"

"Just a hunch."

I sip my coffee. She still hasn't touched hers. Part of me wants to give in, to *be nice,* but I have the sense that if I open up even just a little, this lady will suck me up faster than a superpowered Hoover.

She fills up the dead air with her own voice. "There's so much to do, getting ready for this house," she blathers. "Permits and inspections and this and that. My head boggles sometimes. We have to go over to the bank today and open a joint checking account." She looks at me intently. "Did you and Lloyd ever have a joint checking account when you were together?"

Okay, I admit I'm on edge, maybe even *looking* for things to jump on, but there's *definitely* something behind her words. *"Did you and Lloyd ever have a joint checking account when you were together?"* The implication is that A, we no longer are, and B, Lloyd is with her, and C, their fucking joint checking account makes them a real couple. Because she surely knows damn well Lloyd and I never did have a joint checking account.

"You're running a *business*," I say, hoping that word forever dislodges the "our home" from her brain.

She seems, however, oblivious to my chagrin. She just goes on chattering, like Henry at a circuit party. "Well, I was just wondering how you'd suggest we *manage* it," she says. "You know, if Lloyd prefers to keep a running balance, or if he'd just rather someone else handle those things. I don't mind. I'm good with figures. I have a feeling Lloyd's more a big-picture kind of man, and that's okay, because I do best with details. That makes us a good pair, I guess. You need the big picture and you need the details and you need—"

"So how'd you find out your husband was gay?" I ask, interrupting her. "You catch him in bed with somebody?"

She seems stunned by the question. "No." She flushes. "He just told me."

I actually feel bad. It was an impulsive question, designed to shock, to shut her up. I soften. A little. "I'm sorry," I say. "I didn't mean to be so blunt."

"That's okay." She quickly recovers. "You know, Lloyd is so much like Steven. Steven was a big-picture man, too. And very spiritual, like Lloyd. You don't believe in all that, do you? Past-life regressions and psychic readings."

What has Lloyd told her? I pride myself on passing no judgment on Lloyd's more mystical hobbies. Sure, I might make fun of them from time to time, but I have an open mind. Why would she think I don't *believe?*

I start to tell her just that, but she's blabbing again. "I can understand skepticism," she says. "I was a skeptic, too, but Steven promised to communicate with me—and he *has*. Through Lloyd. Lloyd has taught me so much. I suppose that's why we're together now. He needed someone to share this path with him. It's something to be shared, the journey into spirit." She stops talking and looks over at me significantly, touching my hand. "Lloyd needed someone to *believe* in him."

Okay, here it is. She's crossed the line.

"Are you implying I *don't* believe in Lloyd?"

She seems unnerved by the question. "Oh, no! Not at all! No way was I implying that, Jeff! I was just talking about myself. I wasn't thinking about you."

I watch her for the rest of the time. She has exactly two sips of coffee. She talks only about Lloyd: about how much he's taught her and inspired her, how much he reminds her of Steven, how wonderful he is, how handsome. "And *gay,*" I want to add but don't. I just nod my head. All the way back to Lloyd's apartment she keeps chattering about him, about their future together.

"I'm still learning all of his likes and dislikes," she gushes, a school-girl enthralled by the dashing quarterback. "Do you know he likes ketchup and tomato sauce but *not* fresh tomatoes themselves? Isn't that *peculiar?*"

"Yes," I inform her. "I knew that."

But the only thing I find peculiar about Lloyd at this particular moment is the fact that he wants to share a house with *her.*

Lloyd

"You're going *back* to Boston?"

I can't believe what Jeff's just told me.

He nods. "The snow is getting heavier. I should get on the road before it really gets too bad to drive."

Eva's just left to move her car so the plow can get down the street. "It's *already* too bad," I argue. "Besides, we still have so much to talk about. We'd been making *progress.* And you promised you'd spend the night."

His eyes hold mine. "With Eva sleeping on the couch? The quarters are a little too tight for me, Lloyd."

I try to take his hands, but he won't let me. "Jeff, please don't go. I know she comes on a little thick—"

"This is *your* thing, Lloyd. Yours and hers. I don't belong here."

"Yes, you do . . ."

"No, I *don't.* The two of you have a lot of planning to do. Lots of decisions to make. You've got tile to pick out, checking accounts to open . . ."

My heart drops. I feel angry. "So what's waiting for you in Boston? Nothing but a trick on your couch."

Jeff narrows his eyes at me. "Better than some crazy straight lady."

"Jeff, *please.* Give her a chance."

"I *gave* her a chance. And she wasted no time in letting me know that I have no place here, that it's about you and her."

"You're being stubborn and defensive! She *told* you that she wanted you to feel at home here, Jeff!"

He spins on me. His eyes look crazy. For an instant it's the old Jeff in front of me, the one who threw fits, the one who didn't guard his emotions like the Crown jewels in the Tower of London.

"Can't you *see?*" he says, his voice rising. "That's just it! Her wanting me to feel at home. That implies *she* has the power to make me feel that way. Or *not*. Power that *you've* given her. Don't be so *dense*, Dr. Griffith! You understand power differentials! You talk about them in lectures. You counsel your clients about them."

I shake my head. *"You're* the one who's feeling powerless, Jeff."

He seems to calm down. The passion in his eyes dissipates right in front of me. "Maybe I am," he says. "Maybe I am, and I don't like the feeling. I felt that way once before, Lloyd. I felt pretty powerless when you walked out on me after six years because you were feeling discontent. That was a pretty awful feeling, and maybe I don't want to feel it again."

"Jeff, if you're still angry at me for that, you need to—"

"I need to make sure I don't let you do it again." He seems to suddenly stand taller, and his words are deliberate. "You say you want me to be a part of this, Lloyd. Yet I'm *not*. You never talked about it with me. You never asked *my* feelings. You bring in someone and expect that I'll love her. That we can recreate what we had with Javitz. Admit it, Lloyd. That's what you hoped for. That it was going to be you and me and Eva the way it had been with Javitz."

I just look at him, at a loss for words.

"Well, that's not fair to me *or* to her," Jeff says. "She's not Javitz." He draws close to me. "She's *in love with you,* Lloyd, and if you can't see that, then I think it's time for the doctor to heal himself."

He slips on his jacket and begins putting on his gloves.

"I love you, Lloyd, but I'm not going to risk getting hurt again."

"Jeff, I don't want you to leave." Suddenly, the idea of spending the night alone with Eva seems unbearable without Jeff at my side.

Then the front door suddenly opens and she stumbles back inside, trailing snow and slush across my floor.

"Would you *please* remember to wipe your shoes?" I snap.

"Oh, I'm sorry!" she exclaims, suddenly anxious and remorseful. She removes her boots and begins wiping up the snow with her gloves.

"Eva, leave it," I say, regretting my outburst and stooping down to assist her back up. "It's fine."

"I'm sorry. I wasn't thinking." She seems near tears. She looks from me over at Jeff. "Are you leaving?"

He nods. "I want to hit the road before it gets too slippery out there."

"Well," she says, and I marvel at how quickly she can transition her emotions. She takes Jeff's arm, looking up at him warmly and strolling with him toward the front door. "I want you to know you are welcome here *anytime*," she tells him. "Please know that, okay?"

He looks over at me. "Thanks," he says, and I can't miss the sarcasm, even if she apparently does. "How very kind of you to say so."

She holds his hands tightly and beams. "It has been *wonderful* meeting you, Jeff."

He turns and leaves. I don't even get to kiss him good-bye.

That Night, Boston's South End

Henry

"She's a *total* freak show," Jeff's telling me.

I try to balance the cordless phone between my shoulder and my ear as I unknot my tie, slipping it out from under my collar. The phone had been ringing as I walked through the door. "Worse than I imagined," Jeff's saying. *"Way* worse. Like *psycho killer* worse."

"Jeff," I interrupt, "can you hang on just a second? I'm getting another call."

I hear Jeff sigh. I know how much he despises being put on hold for call-waiting. But Shane had left a message for me at work saying he was going to call tonight about something *important.* . . .

"Hey, my sexy man," Shane breathes.

I laugh. "What's up?"

"Roundtrip to Philly just ninety-nine dollars."

"That's what you were calling to tell me?"

"The *Blue Ball,* sweetie. You said you couldn't afford to go."

I laugh again. "Shane, I'm not sure . . ."

"You're *not* going to wait four more months to show off that physique again, are you? Come on, stud. All those circuit boys dying to see you . . ."

"I'll think about it," I promise. "I've gotta go. I've got . . . someone on the other line."

"Who?"

"My mother. See ya."

I switch back to Jeff. "I'm *sorry.*"

"You know I hate that, Henry. I was ready to hang up."

"Jeff, I'm sorry." God, he can be *so* fucking entitled. Shane calls Jeff a diva, and he sure is acting the part now. "So finish telling me," I say. "I want to hear."

I unbuckle my pants and let them fall to the floor, pulling on a pair of sweats as Jeff goes on—and *on*—about how he thinks this is finally the end of him and Lloyd, that he must have been *crazy* to think they were getting back together, that this time Lloyd has *really* gone off the deep end with this crazy bitch, yada yada yada blah blah blah.

"Maybe you shouldn't give up yet," I counsel. "Maybe there's a reason for all this."

"Bullshit."

I stick my tongue out at him through the phone. He's really bugging me tonight. I hate how whenever *I* try to offer advice, Jeff says, "Bullshit." Had it been *him* saying the same thing to me—as he has *numerous* times—he would've expected me to thank him profusely for his insight and wisdom.

"The worst part of it is," Jeff's saying, "when I got home, Anthony had gone *out!* Can you believe it? Out on his own!"

I'm almost dumbfounded. "And what's wrong with *that?*"

He makes a sound in exasperation. "I don't know where the fuck he *is!* He just left a note: *'Hope you had a good time at the Cape. I'll be back later.'* That's it. Not where, not when."

"He needs to tell you *where?*"

"He doesn't know Boston!" Jeff lowers his voice. "And *Henry*. He took his backpack."

"So?"

"So he has his toothbrush in there and all that shit. I mean, is he coming back tonight? Tomorrow? Next week? What the fuck does 'later' mean?"

I'm reaching the end of my rope. I can't remember feeling this impatient with Jeff in a long time. Maybe Shane is right. Maybe I *am* too enmeshed with Jeff.

"Look," I say, trying to keep my voice level, "you told him you were going down to spend the night with Lloyd in Provincetown. Did you really expect him to sit at home hoping you'd change your mind and come back? Honestly, Jeff, sometimes you—"

"I gotta go." I can hear the petulance in his voice. I'm not being understanding enough. I'm not supporting him.

I sigh. "Now don't get mad at me."

"Henry, I've got to go."

"Okay, bye."

Dial tone.

I'm actually quite pleased with myself. I didn't buckle under the way I usually do, begging Jeff not to hang up, apologizing for my impatience and letting him ramble. And I don't feel guilty, either, as I usually do when I've said or done something to upset Jeff. I don't feel the need to call him back and check in and make sure he's okay and ask if maybe he wants me to come over. . . .

Okay. So maybe I do just a little bit. I put my hand on the phone for a second. Jeff's my best friend, and he's hurting—

"No," I say out loud. This time Jeff can just go through his dramas on his own. I have my own stuff to think about.

I sit down at my computer. Dinner can wait. There's something I've been thinking about all day, something I want to check. I log onto America Online.

"You've got mail," my computer chimes at me. There's a message from my mother *("Don't forget your Uncle Sol's birthday")*, two forwards from Jeff about how a Ralph Nader candidacy could give the White House to George W. Bush in November *("If that happens, it's like going back twenty years")*, and a quick note from Shane, obviously sent within the last few minutes: *"Let me just repeat myself. Roundtrip to Philly just $99. Tickets gotta be purchased by midnight tonight."*

I sign off. Sure, that's easy for Shane to say. I discovered the Windex queen is a fucking *architect,* making *six figures* a year. "Whatever," I grouse to myself.

Sitting next to my computer are this month's bills. My parents always warned me about spending beyond my means. Still, I went ahead and bought that black Jeep Wrangler after watching those bootleg copies of *Queer as Folk.* I love my Jeep, especially last summer tooling around off road in the dunes of Ptown. But with payments of three-hundred-plus a month, it's an expense I probably could've lived without. No one *needs* a car in Boston.

Here's the deal. I make a decent living, but I'm always short on cash. Even after six years at the same job, steadily advancing through the ranks, I've yet to really save any money. Of course, I tell my parents I have, even making up some fake mutual funds I claim to have invested in. Otherwise I'd get one of my father's famous lectures about how when *he* was thirty, he'd already made a killing in the stock market. He also had three kids and a mortgage. At least I don't have *that*—the kids *or* the mortgage.

I take a deep breath and sign on again, this time under my "slut name." Everyone I know has at least one slut name. Mine, like most, changes every couple of weeks. Currently my handle is MuslStudBoi4U, and my profile reads: *Hot, good-looking muscle stud, 5'10, 175, brown/brown, swarthy, muscular. If I'm online, it means I'm looking. If u ask for a pic, u send first.* I especially love that "swarthy" part.

I scroll down through the chat rooms. There it is, the one I'm looking for.

EscortsM4M.

It takes several tries but finally I get in. I've noticed these chat rooms before; they're always filled to capacity. No one is talking. I wait a few seconds, not sure what I mean to do by coming in here. I'd just been thinking about it all day. I glance at the screen names of others in the room: TopStud4Hire. StunningScort. XHndsmEscort. I check their profiles. A couple have links to personal Web sites. Hot photos and rates. Shane's right: Two hundred bucks an hour. Even more for outcalls. One claims to be a porn star and charges *three hundred fifty.* An hour! Even lawyers and psychologists I know don't get that much.

I sigh and click out of the room, entering into more familiar territory. BostonM4M.

Almost immediately: *Brrrnnnng.* An Instant Message. Some guy with a screen name of LeanMuslNBost. *Sup dude,* LeanMusl writes.

I type back: *Sup with u bro?*

I laugh to myself. Nobody talks this way in real life. At least none of us white South End gay boys who gather in this room every night at the same time. But it's the online lexicon. If someone instant-messaged me with, *Hello, how are you?* I'm not sure I'd respond.

Horny as hell, the guy writes back.

Me 2, I type in reply.

These chat rooms have replaced happy hours in the gay subculture. Sign on in the comfort of your own home and cruise the guys you would've met at the bar. I've never actually hooked up this way, of course, but I know plenty of guys who have. Jeff included.

My second phone line rings. I turn the phone over to check the caller-ID. It's Brent Whitehead. I groan. I haven't returned Brent's calls since I got back from New York. I've been dreading hearing about what a *fabulous* time he had in Miami. But I can't avoid him forever. I press the TALK button and say hello, cradling the phone between my ear and my shoulder as I type.

"*Ohhhhh,*" Brent says, hearing the unmistakable sound of Instant Messaging, "am I *interrupting* something?"

"No," I tell him. "Just the same old Wednesday night bullshit."

Like *anything* could've stopped Brent from talking. "So Miami was *fab*-u-lous," he's already saying. I roll my eyes. "We were *sooo* twisted, Henry. You should've *been* there. Very high PH factor. Highest I've seen in a long time."

Of *course* it was—and of *course* Brent would tell me so. Knowing PH stands for *potential husband*, I ask, "So didja find one?"

Brent's answer is exactly what I could've recited right along with him. "Well, I did a three-way with a couple of very hot boys from New Jersey, but I wasn't really in the mood to look for a husband."

"Uh-huh."

Brrrrrnnng. What r u into? It's LeanMusl, being persistent.

I smirk. I type back: *Safe sane and a little crazy. U?*

Brent hasn't stopped talking. "But it was *awesome*, Henry. Best party I've been to in a *long* time." I hear him exhale on his cigarette. "So did you get laid in New York?"

"Yes," I say. "As a matter of fact, I did."

"*Kewl.* What did he look like? Where was he from? How big was his dick?"

I think of Shane. Brent would so *totally* not understand. "Oh, I forget," I tell him.

"Too twisted, huh? I hear you there. You should have seen us in Miami. It was like a fucking alphabet soup. X, K, a little G. . . ." He exhales cigarette smoke again. "So why *did* you and Jeff go to New York, anyway? I mean, *everyone* was in Miami."

" 'Cuz of Lloyd, remember? We went to New York because Lloyd was there."

"Oh, *puh-lease.*" Brent makes a gagging sound. "Why don't those two just get *over* themselves and admit they're a *couple?* I can't *stand* it."

"They just don't want to be fenced in by definitions."

"*Whatever.* But that still doesn't explain why *you* went to New York, Henry. It can't be just because Jeff was going. Oh, wait! It *can* be! You *did* go just because Jeff was going!"

"Fuck you, Brent."

I hold the phone away from my ear as Brent cackles across the line.

Brrrrrnnng. Trade pics?

I type: *U send first.*

"But they *are* still sleeping around, aren't they?" Brent asks. "Jeff and Lloyd?"

"They've never been exclusive," I admit. "Why? You interested?"

"Well, not in *Jeff*. Been there, done that. Who *hasn't?*" Brent cackles again like a mad queen. No, not *like*—Brent *is* a mad queen. "It's *Lloyd* whose pants I'd like to get into. I'd do him in a *second.*"

"Yeah, you wish."

Brent snorts. "So what's this I hear, that Lloyd's buying some house with a woman?"

I'm stunned. "How'd you find *that* out?"

"Nothing gets past me, Henry. You should know that."

Brrrrrnnng. Sent. So where r u?

I type back: *SE. u?* I attach my pic to an E-mail and send it off.

"Henry, are you making a *date?*" Brent asks.

"Maybe."

"What's his screen name?"

"LeanMuslNBost. Hot profile."

Brent gags again. "Ewwwww. Done him. *Total* fake. He's lean, all right. As lean as Mama Cass before the ham sandwich."

Brrrrrnnng. Dorchester.

"I *mean* it, Henry. He's from Dorchester, right? I tell you, you're asking for trouble.

Brrrrrnnng. This is a new one. It's Shane. CircuitBoiUS. *Get my email?*

I type back: *Yes. I'm still thinking.*

TIME'S RUNNING OUT, Shane types back.

"I'm telling you, Henry, stay away from him."

Another message from Shane: *BTW, I saw what room you were in a minute ago. Bad Boy : -)*

How the fuck had he seen me? I was in the Escorts room for just a few *seconds.* Shane must have me on his buddy list. What is he, a fucking stalker?

"Henry, are you *listening* to me?" Brent's sounding very impatient.

"Yes, Brent, I am." I type back an explanation to Shane, saying I'd just gone in there to check it out, to see what was up.

"He's a *loser,* Henry," Brent's saying. "Have I ever steered you wrong?

"Yes. Many times. Especially when you're interested in the guy yourself."

I set my computer to MUTE. No use letting Brent know if I *do* end up meeting Mr. LeanMusl. I've just opened his pic, and he doesn't look half bad. Nice shoulders, sculpted pecs . . .

"*Trust* me. He is *not* someone I'm interested in." Brent laughs. "However, *speaking* of interests of mine, who's this *Anthony* guy who's living with Jeff?"

How the fuck Brent finds out these things amazes me. The South End is like goddamn Mayberry, for God's sake. Everybody seems to know everybody else's business. "Okay, Brent. *How* do you know about Anthony?"

Brent twitters. "I met him this morning at the T station. I was on my way to work. I saw this hottie sitting there, and so naturally I struck up a conversation."

I think it odd that Anthony was on the T that early in the morning. He must have headed out as soon as Jeff left for Provincetown. "Where was he going?" I ask, curious now myself.

"South Station. At least, that's where he got off."

A thought strikes me. Jeff said Anthony had taken his backpack with him. Maybe he was heading back to New York. Maybe he was skipping out on Jeff. At South Station. He could've hopped on a bus. . . .

No. I'm not going to go there. I am *not* going to rush to call Jeff and get all enmeshed in this. If it turns out that Anthony doesn't return, I'll give Jeff the information. Of course, Jeff will be pissed at me for not telling him sooner, but I'll just have to deal with that.

"So who *is* he?" Brent's insisting. "He is *so* cute."

"Anthony's cute," I admit, "but a total R. C."

"Oh. Well, like I always say, if they can't move on the dance floor, they can't move in bed." Brent giggles. "Though I'd be willing to give this one a chance to prove my theory wrong. He really *is* cute."

"I'm noticing a pattern here, Brent. First Lloyd, now Anthony. Do you go after *any* guy who's connected with Jeff?"

"Weiner, *I'm* not the one hung up on Jeff O'Brien."

"Fuck off, Brent."

I look down at my computer screen. Yes, LeanMuslNBost's pic is *definitely* hot. But why haven't I heard back from him? I sent my picture in return. Oh, wait. It's the old game of "I won't say you're cute until you say I'm cute first." I smile. Okay, I can be a big man. I type in: *Hot pic,* and send it off.

Brent's back to rambling on about Miami and the boys from New Jersey, giving me their AOL screen names so I can check their profiles. I don't even bother taking them down. I just wait to hear back from Mr. LeanMusle about *my* pic. But the seconds tick by and there's no reply.

Maybe he didn't like it. I feel a knot foolishly grip my stomach. I've been meaning to scan a better photo. This one's a shot from last summer on Fire Island and I had to crop Jeff out, though his arm still dangles over my right shoulder. It's hard getting a photo that really shows you to best advantage.

And who cares anyway about some stupid AOL fake?

Then I notice Shane had replied to me. With the sound turned off, I hadn't heard it come in. *Yeah whatever. Look, if u can't afford the flight to Philly, why not set up a new screen name? HotMuscleEscort. Easy couple hundred bucks.*

I don't respond.

I check to see if LeanMuslNBost got the pic. He did. He opened it a *full five minutes ago.* And now the fucker is signed off. Either he got bumped or he's a pic collector or . . . or—my back stiffens at the thought—he found someone he liked better. Someone *hotter.*

I sign off. AOL can be too much like the bars sometimes.

"Are you *listening* to me?" Brent says, as irritated as a bee in my ear.

"I gotta go. It's late and I gotta get up early."

"Yeah, me too. Gotta get our beauty rest. None of us are getting any younger, you know." He exhales smoke again. "Hey, you going to the Blue Ball in Philly in a couple weeks?"

I pause. "I'm considering it."

"Well, let me know. We could go down together. Ta-ta!"

I hang up the phone. I sit staring at my computer for several seconds. Then I sign back on under my main account. I click on "Create New Screen Names." I type one in. HotMuscleEscort. My finger hesitates before hitting "Confirm." I summon up the courage and do it.

Then a message appears that the name is already taken.

I laugh. "What the fuck was I even thinking?" I say out loud. I'm ready to sign off when I think I'll just try one other thing . . .

MuscleEscort4U.

It comes back *confirmed.*

I sit back in my chair. Wow. I sign on under my new name. I create a new profile and then click my way back into the Escorts chat room.

I forget all about dinner. I don't sign off until well past midnight.

The Next Day

Jeff

Anthony's in the shower. I won't ask him where he's been. It's none of my business. None at all.

"Hey, get down from there," I shout, clapping my hands.

Mr. Tompkins is trying to eat the flowers Anthony brought me. Sunflowers and day lilies. I move the vase from the coffee table to the top of the TV set and scold Mr. Tompkins. "You already weigh twenty-seven pounds," I say. "You gotta eat *everything?*"

The doorbell sounds. "Yeah?" I call over the intercom.

"It's Henry."

I buzz him in. In moments, Henry's at my door, wiping his feet on the mat. "I've got to talk to you," he says, all serious.

"What about?"

"Don't be mad at me for last night, Jeff."

"Whatever." I stretch, feigning indifference, and flop down on the couch.

Henry takes off his coat and hangs it over a rocking chair. He's still dressed from work, tweed jacket and striped tie. "I was just preoccupied. I know you were upset about..." He pauses, making a face. "Who's that in the shower?"

"Anthony."

"He came *back?*"

I look over at him. "Yeah, he came back. Why do you act so surprised?"

"No—no reason." Henry sits down opposite me. "Did he stay out all night?"

I nod, flicking on MTV with the remote control. "Yup. Got back about an hour ago."

It's now past seven-thirty. *All night and all day* Anthony was out. I hate myself for being upset about it. I have no right to be. I haven't even known the guy for a *week*. What's *really* screwy, though, is how much Anthony's absence bugged me in light of the fact that I'm sure *Lloyd and Eva* have been together every second. How fucked is *that?* I hate myself when I get this way.

"He didn't say where he'd been?" Henry's asking.

"Nope. But he brought me those flowers."

"They're nice." Henry smiles. "Well, he *is* your guest, after all. You don't want him just coming and going at all hours."

I look over at him. "That's right. I can be pissed about *that,* can't I? It's not like he's a roommate or anything. He's a *guest.*" It's as if Henry has just given me permission—a rationale—to be angry with Anthony. But somehow I just can't. I sigh. "No. I just need to let it go."

Henry nods. "It's really Lloyd you're upset about, Jeff."

"Please, Dr. Freud." I stretch my legs out, placing my head on the armrest of the couch. "Don't start."

"I just don't like to see you hurting."

"I'm *fine.*" I raise the volume on the TV set. Madonna's "Ray of Light" video. "So what do you want to talk to me about?"

Henry seems to struggle. "Jeff, do you remember how—well, re-member on New Year's when—well, when Shane . . ." He grunts. He stands, walks over, takes the remote out of my hand, and lowers the vol-ume. Then he crouches down beside me. "I don't want to be shouting."

I narrow my eyes at him. "What's going on, Henry?"

"I was online last night and—" The shower suddenly shuts off. Henry sighs. "I can't talk about this with Anthony around."

My brows knit. "What's Anthony got to do with it?"

"Nothing." Henry stands, returning to his chair across the room.

"So tell me later, then. He's getting ready so we can go to Club Cafe. Come with us."

Henry just sighs again. I shake my head. Henry can be so petulant at times. What is it *this* time? Some guy he's developed a crush on and is afraid to tell? Yet again, he comes to me for the answers. It's like I was telling Lloyd. They all come to me with their troubles, their heartaches. I laugh to myself. How did Javitz *stand* it? All these little boys coming to him with all their little problems?

Just then my own little problem places his hands on my shoulders. "Hey," Anthony says. He's emerged from the shower all steamy and glowing. His towel-dried blond hair sticks up at random. Around his waist he's wrapped a towel. The baby-fine white down across his stomach only helps delineate his abs.

"Hey, Henry," Anthony says, sitting on the armrest of the couch. He leaves one hand on my shoulder. I move my face so that my nose is close to Anthony's skin. God, he smells good.

"Hey, Anthony, how's it been?"

"Shhh," I command all at once. "Turn up the volume! I want to hear this."

Henry obeys. It's a public-service announcement against antigay violence with Judy Shepard, the mother of Matthew Shepard, the gay college kid who was bashed to death a few years ago. I've seen it before—an incredibly powerful piece. Kids shouting "Queer!" and "Faggot!" and Mrs. Shepard, unable to hold back her tears, asking people to *think*.

"She is so awesome to do this," Henry says.

I've never been gay-bashed. The worst I've suffered were the occasional taunts of "fag" in school and now, sometimes, late at night, coming out of a bar. You know what I'm talking about: cowards driving by in their cars shouting epithets out the window to impress their girlfriends. Every gay man alive has had the experience in some form. That's why the Matthew Shepard case struck such a chord. He could have been any one of us.

After the PSA ends, I look over at Henry. "Had you seen that before?"

"No," he replies in a small voice. "It's very powerful. Good for her for doing that."

It's only then that I notice Anthony has withdrawn his hand. "So what did *you* think?" I ask, looking up at him.

He's sitting rock-still, still staring at the TV set. He doesn't answer.

"Had you ever heard of Matthew Shepard?" I ask.

"No," Anthony says, finally looking down at me, like a marble statue coming to life. Some of the glow from the shower is gone. "I take it he was murdered."

"Yeah, by a couple of punks," Henry snaps. "Fucking self-repressed, self-loathing closet cases."

"That's usually the case," I say. The buzzer again.

"Who the fuck . . . ?" I stand and press the intercom. "Yeah?"

"Hi, Jeff. It's Brent Whitehead."

Henry is suddenly looming behind me. "Jeff, I'm sorry. I saw him on the T and I mentioned I was coming by here and that I figured we'd end up at Club Cafe. . . ."

I scowl at him. "You told *Brent Whitehead* to come by my house?"

Henry makes a face. "You can't just leave him standing down there, Jeff. It's *cold* out." I let out a long sigh and buzz Brent in.

You've probably gathered that I don't really care for Brent. You're correct. Despite his killer blues and bubble butt and the fact that, yes, we slept together a couple of years ago, I really don't like Brent. I went home with him from Buzz one Saturday night, but Brent proved useless, a blob, lost in a K-hole. Ever since, I've considered him much ado about nothing. Others might rave about his naturally chiseled looks—high cheekbones, prominent jaw, skin so naturally smooth it shines like marble (with none of that typical circuit-boy razor stubble on his chest)—but I buy none of it. To me, Brent's that particular type of gymboy whose body simply doesn't match the voice or the personality, whose muscles only belie the girl within. In another generation, Brent would never have become so buff. He'd have been a tea-and-china queen, with gold bracelets dangling from his wrist and too much cologne on his shirts, drinking mai-tais until he was a silly mess, an "auntie" before he was thirty-five. But the Circuit Era demands even aunties have biceps and traps, and so the gold bracelets of yore have been exchanged for henna tattoos, and the mai-tais for ketamine.

He comes upstairs, but I won't allow him to linger long in my apartment. He tries petting Mr. Tompkins, who promptly bites him, as he's wont to do with anyone except Lloyd or me. After that, I quickly orchestrate our exit for Club Cafe.

Brent's chattering about the Blue Ball and the Winter Party, directing all of his attention at Anthony. I do my best to ignore him. When I spot a guy I know coming at us from the opposite direction on Tremont Street, I latch on to him, glad for an opportunity to drown Brent out, even for a couple of minutes.

"Hey," I say, suddenly realizing I've forgotten the guy's name. Jack or Jake or Jacob or something. I stammer a little. "Hey. How are you?"

"Hey, Jeff," he says.

I've known him for years; we marched in a couple of ACT UP demos way back in the Eighties when marching was cool and we were young.

"What's going on?" I ask. "What have you been up to?"

"Oh, you know, keeping busy," Jack or Jake—or is it Joel?—says. He hands me a flier about a rally to be held at the State House in favor of gay marriage.

"Still the activist, huh?"

He nods. He's gone a little flabby since our ACT UP days. I try to remember: did I have sex with him? It's possible. It's quite possible.

"You want to join us?" I ask. "We're heading over to Club Cafe."

He rolls his eyes. "To watch Madonna videos? I don't think so."

Suddenly I remember his name. It's Jason, and we *did* sleep together, and we had a huge fight because he took one look at my video collection and launched into a tirade about gay culture. "What is this fascination with Bette Davis and Marilyn Monroe and all these dead movie actresses? Gay culture is so tiresome. Recycled hetero pablum, in my opinion."

I got defensive. "We've reclaimed it and made it our own."

"But it's not ours," Jason had said. "Once, gay people adored literary genius. Oscar Wilde. Edward Carpenter. Dorothy Parker. Now it's Cher. What a pitiful state gay culture has devolved into."

Oh, you can be sure I did not allow him to spend the night. I look at him now, with his sour expression and the joyless way in which he passes out fliers to people on the street.

"I haven't been to Club Cafe in ten years," he tells me, as if he's proud of the fact, as if it's some kind of achievement. Suddenly I find Brent's prattle infinitely preferable, and I get us away from Jason as quickly as I can manage.

"He's toxic," I tell Henry, settling myself at the bar so I can see the video screen, where Shania Twain is telling the boys they don't impress her much. "Why do some gay people hate gay culture so much?"

Henry shrugs.

"I mean, old Bette Davis films *speak* to something for us. Marilyn's story has relevance. Judy Garland, too. And so on, all the way up to Princess Diana. It's archetypal."

"Maybe they think it's stereotypical," Henry says.

"So what? Behind every stereotype, there's truth. Gay men *do* love old dead movie actresses. And larger-than-life divas. What's so wrong with that? Why do some gay people act like it's a bad thing?"

Henry doesn't appear to be listening to my rant. I remember that he wanted to talk to me about something. But now my attention is drawn back to Brent, who's cornered Anthony, talking at him intently only a few inches from his face. I can't hear what he's saying; the place is packed and the noise level is too loud. Many of the guys are still in their suits and ties, the grown-up costumes they wear in their offices downtown or in the Prudential Center. Brent's the only one not to loosen up, however, even after he starts getting trashed. His tie always remains

tight to his throat, the knot projecting from his tab collar almost per-
pendicular to the floor.

He's trying to regale Anthony with sloppy wit. I catch a snippet of
their conversation. "Now, don't believe what you hear about Boston
boys, Anthony. We don't *all* have attitudes."

"I know," Anthony says earnestly. "I've found everyone very
friendly."

"I'll *bet* you have," Brent says, eyeing him over his cosmopolitan.

I order a Rolling Rock. Brent's definitely hitting on Anthony, and
Anthony seems not to be objecting. He's listening to Brent's every word,
laughing at his every so-called joke. Oh, Brent can be dazzling, no doubt
about that. He holds some big job in some high-rise—I can never remember exactly what it is that Brent *does*—and he's always dressed real
sharp. But already he's starting to slur his words.

"You're seething," Henry says, leaning in toward me. "You're letting
Brent move right in on Anthony."

"I'm not seething," I say, watching Brent get closer and closer. Every
few seconds or so, he'll touch Anthony's chest, laughing at something.
"Anthony can do what he wants. Isn't that what you said?"

Henry shrugs, turning his back to them. "They look like a couple of
Ken dolls," he sniffs. "You know, Jeff, you really ought to put a time
limit on his stay with you."

It's my turn to shrug. "He intrigues me. There's a mystery underneath that boy. I don't buy his ingenue act."

Henry squints at me. "You think he's a schemer?"

"No. Not a schemer." I watch him interact with Brent. He seems
genuinely interested. As if he really wants to get to know Brent—all of
them, *anyone* he meets.

*I like people who really ask you stuff. That's how I want to be. If I'm
going to talk to you, I want to get to know you. There's so much more
to somebody than just what they show outside.*

Henry gives me one of those looks that indicate he's about to say
something profound. Or *try* to, anyway. "Are you sure you're just not
looking for a quick, easy replacement for Lloyd?"

"Henry, this is called happy hour. *Happy*. What part of that don't
you get?"

"You can't deny it, Jeff. I know you hoped—"

"I hoped for nothing. And if I did, I was an idiot." I take a sip of my
beer. "Lloyd and Eva are like *newlyweds*, Henry. I should just accept
that and move on."

"But you love him . . ."

"Sure. And he loves me." I look over again at Brent and Anthony. "But I'm not going to set myself up for disappointment again. It's time for me to realize it's never going to be the way I want it to be. It's time for me to move on with my life the way Lloyd is moving on with his."

Brent's leaning in over the bar to order new drinks for both himself and Anthony. Even in his suit pants, his butt looks round and hard, and his shoulders are impressive under his starched white shirt and suspenders. How did he ever get so pumped? I bet he does steroids. Anthony seems to take note of Brent's body, too.

Ah, so what? Why should I care if Anthony goes home with Brent?

"Jeff, you're seething," Henry repeats.

"I am *not* seething."

"Jeff, it's plain on your face. You're pissed Anthony hasn't walked away from him yet. I know you, Jeff O'Brien. Anthony was *yours*. You found him."

I smirk. "Henry, if I *pay* you, will you go away and stop bothering me?"

Henry flushes. "Jeff, that's what I need to talk to you about."

I finish the last of my beer. "So Shane still wants to give you cash? Take it, baby. *Take* the damn cash and get it over with."

Henry seems to struggle with what he wants to say. "Do you ever think about it?" he asks me, lowering his voice. "Be honest with me, Jeff."

"About what? Getting paid?" I laugh. "Who says I haven't been?"

"You liar."

"Once. It happened once." My mind flickers back to that day five years ago. I had no money back then, and the cash came as a surprise, the guy pressing it into my palm. I stared down at it in disbelief, then shrugged, folding it into my pocket. I used it to buy milk and bread on my way home. It came in handy. God, how Javitz had *loved* that story.

"Yeah," I say, smiling in spite of myself. "I discovered I could make money at what I'd been giving away for free."

"Exactly." Henry laughs. "How much did you get?"

"Twenty, just for getting sucked off."

Henry hoots. "*Twenty*! I could make *ten times* that much!"

"So do it."

I notice the look I get back from Henry. He isn't joking about this. We hold each other's gaze until I reach over and draw my buddy's face close to mine.

"This isn't Shane we're talking about, is it?" I whisper. Henry shakes his head. "Somebody *else* offered you money?"

Henry nods.

"Hoo boy. How'd that happen?"

"I created an escort screen name." The words rush out of Henry's mouth. "We talked online. I'm meeting him tomorrow at the Westin Hotel. He's some business traveler from Des Moines in Boston for the night."

It takes several seconds for me to absorb the information. Then I grip the back of Henry's neck and pull his face in even closer to mine. "Are you *crazy?*"

"Jeff, look—"

"You could get hacked up into a million pieces! You have no idea who this guy is!"

"Jeff, he's staying at the *Westin*, for God's sake! It's not like I'm meeting him at the Bates Motel."

I release my grip. "Henry, he could be a cop."

"He *isn't*. I asked him. If he was a cop, he'd have to say yes. You taught me that."

I frown. Yes, I did, and Javitz had taught me. It's a way to avoid entrapment at rest stops or at the dick dock in Provincetown. You ask the guy if he's a cop before you unzip your pants. He's got to tell you the truth. I assume it works online as well.

"Look, guys meet tricks online all the time," Henry's saying. "You've done it dozens of times. If I was standing here telling you I'd met a guy in the BostonM4M chat room and that I was going to hook up with him at his hotel, you'd be like, 'Go for it, Henry.' But just because of the exchange of money you suddenly think it's dangerous."

I order another beer. "But why are you doing this, Henry? Do you need the money that bad?"

"Actually, it can only help. This one guy in the Escort chat room said he made a thousand a week in his spare time. A *thousand a week!* And that's tax-free. Do you know what a thousand a week would do for my cash flow? Even four hundred a week—two tricks, two hours!"

I take a gulp of beer. "Henry, if you're that tight for cash, I can lend you some."

He smiles. "Underneath it all, you are a sweetheart, Jeff O'Brien. Don't ever let anyone say otherwise."

I scowl. "Who says otherwise?"

"Never mind."

I press my point. "But you're going to have to sleep with *trolls*, Henry. How will you get it up for some old fat guy?"

Now, don't get me wrong. I've had some great sex with old fat guys. But on command? Talk about performance anxiety.

"That's just *it,* Jeff. I put two key words in my profile. *Muscle worship.* Can you stand it? See, I don't have to touch them at all. I just lay there, let them do the work. There's a whole culture of guys out there who will *pay* to worship guys like us."

I pull back a little. "Whatever happened to the little Henry Weiner I met so long ago?"

He laughs. "Oh, I don't mean to sound so conceited. You're the only one I can talk to like this, Jeff."

"Well, it will keep you motivated to stay in shape anyway."

Henry smirks. "You know I can't have sex with anyone unless my body's perfect."

It's my line. He's right: there aren't many people we can talk to this way. It sounds fucked, and maybe it is, but it's how I feel. If I've been away from the gym for too long or if my love handles have gotten just a teensy bit too squishy, *Brad Pitt* couldn't get me into bed. It wouldn't matter what *he* looked like; what would stop me would be my own self-consciousness about what I looked like. Sad, yes, but true.

So I guess Henry's little enterprise might be doable, after all, providing it's *his* body that's the focus of attention.

"You're really going to do this, buddy?" I ask. "Sex for Money?"

"Yeah," he says. "I think I want to give it a try."

I shake my head, trying to clear it out. What's *happening* to the people closest to me? Lloyd buys a house with a woman; Henry turns into a prostitute.

"You know, Javitz would have loved you, Henry," I say, laughing. "Selling your body. How *scandalous.*"

Henry smiles at me. "You hardly ever mention Javitz. I wish you would, Jeff. I'd like to know more about him. It seems like you guys had an awesome friendship."

"We did." I can tell Henry realizes that's all I'll say on the subject. He just sighs.

Something makes me look around. Anthony and Brent have disappeared. I feel a stupid pang. Shit, how I hate getting attached to tricks. Never has it turned out well. Not once.

Ah, so what? There are dozens more, *hundreds* more, just like him. I could pick up one of these boys here tonight very easily. I could bring them back home with me.

But I'm not going to. I'm *tired* of it. Tired of that old game. I want something more, something I thought was possible—*imminent,* even—until Lloyd sprang his news on me. Sure, I could bring one of these boys back home, but I won't.

Because you know what? I *love* gay men. I look around at all the gay men in the bar. Pressed close together, their drinks in their hands, laughing and bitching and waving their hands to make their ridiculous points. I think of Jason, passing out his fliers, seemingly so committed to the advancement of his gay brothers. But he despises them. He hates the people he's supposedly trying to help. *What a pitiful state gay culture has devolved into.*

I won't deny the triviality of much of what goes on in places like this. A couple of weeks ago, two queens actually got into an argument over whether or not Cher had had a rib removed. I'm serious. That's what they were fighting about. One of them actually stormed off in tears. *In tears!* As if it *mattered* when kids were killing themselves in Roxbury over Nike sneakers. As if it mattered even if kids *weren't!*

Still, I love them. I love gay men. They're my *family*, the only family I've ever really known. I love them despite their silliness, their bitchiness, their maddening reverence for the superficial. Sometimes I even love them *for* such things. Last summer, on Fire Island, I overheard a bunch of gay guys talking among themselves. "Poor Kate Hepburn," one of them said. "She's the next to go." It was completely endearing. Once, over breakfast at Bickford's after some late-night partying, Henry had asked me, in *utter* seriousness, who I loved better—Cher or Madonna—and I, with equal solemnity, had paused to consider the profound implications of the question. Our waitress may not have literally rolled her eyes as she tore off our check and placed it on our table, but I felt her bemusement nonetheless. Henry and I looked at each other and cracked up.

I forgive gay culture its indulgences because they're sincere. I'm so tired of all this caterwauling and bitchery from the self-appointed critics of gay culture, who throw out words like *tedious* and *childish* and *trifling*. Sometimes gay people can be far more savaging of our own lives than any faultfinder of the religious right.

"I never want to become so ironic and detached from the culture that I sound bitter and resentful of those who aren't," I suddenly blurt out to Henry.

"Huh?"

"I'm just thinking out loud. Our worship of divas, our reverence of pop culture, our veneration of the ephemeral, our obsession with dreams—in our very celebration of the cursory, we are in fact often being far more genuine than those who pontificate endlessly on the weighty and profound."

"I guess so," Henry says, shrugging.

"Of *course* it's so. A gay man pining over the loss of a summer love can evoke the soul of a Shakespearean tragedy. There's a *realness* to gay men that gives the lie to our superficial veneer. It's the genuineness of *children,* passionate and honest in its sincerity."

"But can't our child*like*-ness become *childishness?*"

"I'm not denying that. But why must the pettiness of one be allowed to obscure the joy of the other?"

"Sounds like an article," Henry says, smirking. "You really ought to try writing it down, Jeff."

I sneer. "Don't go there, Henry."

"Okay. Then let's go to the Blue Ball in Philly instead."

I look over at him.

"You *love* Philly, Jeff. What do you say?"

I consider it. Why not? At that moment, being in the midst of a throng of shirtless gay men, their sweaty torsos pressed against mine, singing all the lyrics to a remixed Karen Carpenter song, seems mighty appealing.

"I e-mailed Rudy," Henry's telling me. "You remember that guy we met at the White Party last year? He said we could stay with him if we came to Philly."

"Hmm. Rudy. I do remember. Pretty eyes." I smile, leaning against the bar and lacing my fingers across my chest. I think about the small wooden box that I keep on my dresser, filled with little slips of papers and business cards, phone numbers, and E-mail addresses scrawled upon them. My extended gay family.

"It would be nice to see Rudy again," I say. "And Eliot and Oscar and Adam and Billy. They'll probably all be there."

"I'm sure they will be."

"You know," I say, feeling thoughtful, "they can blast circuit culture all they want, but there's a real brotherhood, isn't there? A real gay fraternity linked by E-mail."

"So that's a yes?" Henry asks.

Before I can answer definitively, however, Brent and Anthony are suddenly in front of us. "Well, well," I observe, making eye contact with Anthony. "The prodigal returns."

"Are you boys having fun?" Brent chirps. "I've just been introducing Anthony to *every*body. You can't keep him sheltered down there on Shawmut Ave now, Jeff. You've got to bring him up to the *good* side of Tremont Street once in a while."

"Hey," Henry says suddenly. "Check out this video. Have you seen it? Melissa Etheridge."

We all look up. I have indeed seen it before. "Scarecrow," I say. "Her tribute to Matthew Shepard."

"That's the guy who was killed, right?" Anthony asks.

"Yes," Henry says. "It's very powerful."

"Such a tragedy, wasn't it?" Brent asks. "And poor li'l Matthew was so *cute*, too."

I move my eyes from the video screen over to Anthony. He's watching intently. It's the same gray-faced concentration I noticed earlier, back at the apartment during the PSA.

Brent's still gabbing. "Those bastards who killed him should have *fried*."

"I don't know," Henry objects, looking over at him. "I've been thinking about them. Matthew's killers were probably gay, too. They just haven't been able to accept it."

"Most gay-bashers are," I say.

Henry nods. "They're fucking closet cases, but in a way, *they're* victims, too."

"Oh, spare me that bleeding heart liberal crap, Weiner," Brent says, shuddering.

"No, seriously," Henry insists, "*think* about it. What if Matthew Shepard's killers receive counseling or something in prison and then realize they're gay? Then what happens? Like they could ever be accepted by the gay community now."

"And why should they be?" Brent hisses. "They're *scum*. Did you *see* them on TV? *Scum*. Gay-bashers are *scum*, Henry. They should have been killed the same way they killed poor Matthew. Beaten and tied to a fence and left to die in the cold."

Henry looks aghast. "That would make us no better than them, Brent. What would that accomplish?"

I haven't taken my eyes off Anthony. He's listening to this exchange while looking back and forth at the video. Suddenly he senses my eyes on him and he looks over at me.

"You okay?" I ask him quietly, reaching over and touching his arm.

"It's just so sad," he replies, barely above a whisper.

Again my heart leaps out at this guy. No, he's *not* a schemer. Whatever mystery is wrapped around Anthony Sabe, it's not about scheming. It's about *sadness*. This kid has been through something *wicked*. No wonder he doesn't want to talk about his past.

"I say an eye for an eye," Brent's saying. "That's from *your* Bible, Henry. It was the *Christians* who got all soft and said turn the other cheek."

Henry's getting huffy. "Are you implying all Jews should be *for* the death penalty? I'm sorry, Brent, but that sounds a little anti-Semitic to me."

"Oh, Henry, *puh-lease.*"

I step in. "Stop it, children, or no milk and cookies before you go to bed."

"What do you think, Jeff?"

It's Anthony. Something in his voice causes us all to look over at him.

"What do *you* think should have happened to Matthew's killers?"

I sigh. Unlike Henry, I'm not one hundred percent always against the death penalty. But neither am I as barbaric as Brent. I know the death penalty is overused, especially in places like Texas, where that idiot governor who wants to be president seems to take sadistic glee in pulling the switch. I wrote an article about the death penalty once several years ago, and ended up nearly convinced that capital punishment should be abolished. But there are always cases so heinous—Oklahoma City, James Byrd being dragged to death along a dirt road, Matthew Shepard—that I feel nothing can quite balance out the scales of justice except the ultimate penalty.

"I feel sorry for them, I suppose," I say, after reflecting a second. "I think Henry's right. In some ways, they're as much victims of a homophobic society as anyone. But still, they killed an innocent kid."

"So should they have *died?*" Anthony persists.

I look at him. What is it behind his eyes? What does Matthew Shepard represent for him?

"I don't know," I admit. "In this case, the brutality of the crime—hey, maybe I'm just too emotionally connected to offer an unbiased opinion. The bottom line is, they killed one of us. I suppose I wouldn't have been sorry to see them fry."

I try to see the reaction in Anthony's eyes. But there is none. He just nods.

"Well," Brent announces, clearly tired of the conversation and the fact he's no longer the center of attention, "I suggested to Anthony we grab some Thai food. I haven't had any dinner. Any takers?"

"No thanks," Henry says. It's obvious he's had his fill of Brent for the night.

"Not me, either," I say. If Anthony's going home with Brent, I'm definitely not tagging along to watch it happen. "I'm just going to get a slice of pizza."

"Fine. You boys have it your way." Brent turns his back to us to face Anthony. "You'll *love* this place. It's—"

"Well," Anthony interrupts, "if Jeff's not going, I think I'll take a rain check." He smiles. "See, I was gone yesterday, and he and I really haven't had any time to catch up."

"Oh." Brent looks properly rebuffed.

I study Anthony closely. "Hey, if you want Thai, don't let me hold you back."

"I don't want Thai," he says decisively. "I want pizza."

My heart melts.

Okay, so I'm getting in too deep with yet another trick. I can see the flashing caution lights as well as anyone. But it's too late to turn back now.

Late That Night, Provincetown

Lloyd

I think it's Jeff. No one's been in my bed but Jeff for the past four years. But even asleep, I know there's something different.

The smell. Too sweet.

Perfume.

A woman's perfume . . .

I sit up in bed. Something has startled me awake. My breath is coming fast and hard, and I put my hand over my chest. My heart is racing. My studio apartment is dark. Only the moonlight offers any illumination, a soft blue tint. I took around. The first thing I realize is that I am not in my bed, but on the couch. *Right.* Eva. I let Eva sleep in the bed.

I squint through the darkness, trying to make her out, but it's impossible. Certainly she's there, asleep. It's so completely silent. I strain to hear her breathing, but there's nothing.

What woke me up? Was I having a dream?

Then I smell it again. Eva's perfume. Like lilacs.

Why *shouldn't* I be smelling it? It's a small apartment, and she's lying there asleep not six feet away. It must be on her clothes as well, hung carefully over a chair. It must be everywhere in this room.

I lie back down. But why does it seem stronger here, near my pillow?

I sit up again, swinging my legs off the couch and placing them on the floor. I stand, padding across the shag-carpeted floor to the bathroom. I pull the sliding door shut behind me and switch on the light. From the mirror, my eyes blink back at me. I pull down the front of my sweatpants and begin taking a pee, the sound of water hitting porcelain echoing through the quiet space. It momentarily stops me, causing my pee to dry up. It feels odd, a little too intimate, for Eva to be lying there just a few feet away, listening to me pee.

Stop it, Lloyd, I scold myself. *She's fast asleep. And anyway, who cares?*

I resume peeing. When I've finished, I rinse off my hands and quickly shut off the light. Stepping back outside the bathroom, I hear a small voice.

"Lloyd."

"Sorry," I whisper. "Didn't mean to wake you."

"I wasn't asleep," she says.

I can barely make her out in the moonlight. I stand at the foot of the bed, trying to fasten my eyes on her. She remains a dim figure, every once in a while shifting in the darkness, a flash of white sheet catching the moon.

"I haven't been asleep at all," she says softly. "Would you turn on the light for just a second?"

Part of me doesn't want to. Some unexplainable, ridiculous part of me feels safer in the dark. *Good God, Lloyd, what am I scared of? What was I dreaming that's gotten me so edgy?* I reach up and pull the string for the overhead lamp.

Her eyes are big, looking up at me. They don't even blink from the sudden brightness of the lamp. She lies there in my bed, her hair loose and down around her neck, her pink shift falling off one shoulder. For the first time, she seems unconcerned with trying to hide her bosom. A deep cleavage reveals itself as she sits up. She positions herself on her arms behind her. It looks as if she's presenting her breasts as gifts.

I take a step backward. "Are you—okay?"

Her voice is dreamy. "I just can't stop thinking about all we're doing. How similar our paths are. How much synchronicity there is between us."

"Eva, go to steep. We can talk about all this in the morning."

"It's impossible to sleep, Lloyd. I've just been lying here, so many thoughts going through my head . . ."

"You think too much."

"Please, Lloyd. Sit beside me a second."

I hesitate. "I'd rather stand here," I tell her.

She starts to cry. "Do you know there was never anyone for me but Steven? Not before, not after. Even after he told me he was gay. I never wanted anyone else." She covers her face with her hands and falls back on her pillows.

Oh, God. I approach the bed and look down at her.

"I'm sorry to be crying again, Lloyd. Really I am."

"The grieving process is never really over, Eva," I tell her. "It's okay to cry."

I'm trying to be supportive. Trying to show sympathy. I really am. But you know what? For the first time, I feel a little manipulated by her tears. I'm tired of comforting her. All I really want to do is get back into bed and turn off the light.

She moves her hands away from her face. "I know. Thank you, Lloyd. Thank you for being here."

She reaches across the bed and takes one of my hands. She holds it to her face. She kisses it. She doesn't let go.

"Let's try to get some rest," I say. "You've got a long ride ahead of you tomorrow back to New York."

She still hasn't released my hand. She's turning it now so that my palm is face down over her face. She kisses the soft fleshy spot beside my thumb. Her eyes look up at me from between my fingers. "Lloyd . . ." she murmurs softly.

I pull my hand away. I say nothing more. I just walk back toward the couch, reaching up to grasp the cord for the overhead lamp. Then, in the last second before the light goes out, I notice a long hair on my pillow. It's curled in a big inverted S. My mouth goes dry. Even without thinking about it, I run my hand over my own buzzed dome.

For the rest of the night, my pillow remains on the floor.

A Few Nights Later,
The Westin Hotel

Henry

W*hat the fuck am I doing?*

I stand in the hotel lobby listening to the steady rushing sound of the indoor waterfall.

Jeff's right, I think. *The guy could be a cop. There could be a whole fucking squadron waiting for me up there. To arrest me, toss me in jail. It would make all the papers.*

MALE ESCORT ARRESTED IN WESTIN HOTEL STING OPERATION.

What would my mother say?

"A nice Jewish boy like you, Henry Weiner." That's what she'd say. "A nice Jewish boy like you. A common hustler. A whore. A tramp!"

I pull out my Chapstick from my jacket pocket and run it over my dry lips.

I am *a whore. I'm* whoring *myself. I'm selling my body.*

There's no denying it, not now, not as I stand here waiting to go upstairs to some stranger's room and take off my clothes and receive cash for doing so. There's no denying what I'm about to do, nor is there any use in denying that the idea turns me on. Already my dick is swelling in my Calvin Kleins. Forty minutes I'd spent obsessing over which underwear showed me off to best advantage. I want to make sure the guy gets his money's worth.

Two hundred bucks. Two hundred fucking bucks.

"Henry!"

Oh, shit. It's Shane. Of all people. The damn Westin Hotel is smack-dab between the T station and Copley Square. If you take the skywalk, you have to pass through the lobby, and on cold nights like this, *every-*

body takes the skywalk. But of all the people to run into, it has to be Shane.

"So I'm glad you reserved those tickets to Philly," he says. "*Knew* you would. Though I *was* hoping you wouldn't drag Jeff along. You've got to learn you can do stuff on your own." He bends down to give me a quick peck on the lips. "So, wanta grab some dinner? I've just got off work and I am *starved.*"

Shane's still in his office garb. Plaid suit and a smiley-face tie, all wrapped in a long gray flannel overcoat. But it's my clothes that suddenly seem to draw the most attention. Shane pulls back a bit, studying me, his brows knitting together and his lips pursing in interest.

"Well, look at *you* in your studly motorcycle jacket. And your jeans sure couldn't be any tighter." He lifts my jacket to peek in under my arm. I try to protest, but he's too quick and too tall. "And what a hunk-a-hunk muscle shirt . . ." His face lights up. "*Henry.* What are you doing in this *hotel?*"

I can feel myself blush. "I'm just stopping by to see a friend who's in town."

"Who is he? *Tom of Finland?*" Shane shakes his head, grinning from ear to ear as the truth dawns on him. "Henry! You're here as an escort! You took my advice!"

"Shhhhh!!!" I glance quickly around. "You trying to get me *arrested?*"

"Oh, you *stud!* I'm so *proud* of you! How *enterprising*!" He gives me a quick hug. "Oh, my God, tell me *everything!*"

"Shane, I've got to go. I'll be late." I look around again. "I'll talk to you later."

"Oh, no. You don't think I'm going anywhere, do you?" He folds his arms across his chest. "Dinner can wait. I'm going to sit right here in this lobby and wait for you to come downstairs so you can give me all the details." He quickly spots a chair and settles his tall frame into it. "I'm assuming it's just a standard hour session. It's not an overnighter, is it? Because then I'd have to run over to Au Bon Pain for a turkey sandwich—"

"Shane, will you *please* be quiet?" I sigh. "I'll be down in an hour."

He grows misty-eyed. "I feel like a mother watching her baby trot off to school for the first time."

I ignore him and head off toward the elevator. Truth be told, somehow, having Shane waiting in the lobby makes me feel a little less anxious. By now the horniness has become paramount, and as the elevator doors slide shut anyone who looked could tell I'm circumcised right through my tight jeans.

Walking down the hall to the guy's room, I even kind of swagger, like a goddamn porn star or something. *Hey, man, Jeff Stryker here. You want this big dick, dontcha? You want to get down on your knees and—*

Here's the room. I gulp. The bravado vanishes. *What the fuck am I doing?*

I rap on the door.

My initial thought when the guy appears is that I must have gotten the room number wrong. First of all, he says, "You must be Brick," and I momentarily forget that's the alias I'm using. Second, the guy is a tubby little gnome with a shiny bald head. He'd described himself as average, dignified, with just a receding hairline. I imagined an august college professor, not one of the Keebler elves.

"Uh," I say, standing in the doorway. So much for studly entrances.

"Oh, Brick, you are everything you said and *more*," the guy says, taking me by the arm and almost pulling me inside, quickly closing the door behind us.

I blink a few times. He's no more than five feet and almost as wide. When he smiles, I can't shake the impression of a Halloween pumpkin. His big ears are bright red.

"Oh, my, my, my," he says. "Take off your coat, Brick."

I swallow and do as he instructs. He throws my coat over the back of a chair.

The man beams. "Such muscles. I *looooove* muscles." He reaches over and lifts a plate of fruit from a side table. "I had room service send us up something to eat. I thought maybe you hadn't had your dinner. Would you like a strawberry?"

Something about the image of this little man standing there offering me a strawberry makes me want to both laugh and cry. "Thank you," I say, and accept one from him, popping it into my mouth.

"Yes, yes, indeed. You are beautiful. Please sit down."

I oblige. The man approaches me and runs his small, cold hands up along the length of my upper arm. "Such firm biceps. Such amazing triceps. Will you flex for me?"

I do as I'm told, feeling very self-conscious. The man holds a hand to his heart.

"Oh," he says, as if he might faint. "My name is Vernon, by the way."

I feel like crying again. *Vernon.* Knowing his name touches me. This little guy has a home somewhere, and a mother, and maybe a dog. . . .

"Would you like another strawberry, Brick?" Vernon's asking me. "A piece of melon?"

"No, no, thank you," I manage to say. "And my name . . . my *real* name is Henry."

I don't know why I tell him that. It just comes over me; I just blurt it out. He approaches me again. Our faces are almost level now that I'm sitting down. Vernon seems to study me, to look into each and every pore on my face. "Henry," he finally says. "Do you allow kissing?"

I look into the little man's eyes. They're blue. Bright blue.

That's the great thing, Jeff. I don't have to touch them. They just do me.

Vernon's eyes look at me with all the wonder of a kid at Christmas. "Sure," I say.

And so we kiss. At first Vernon just kisses me, his little tongue squiggling its way into my mouth. Then I begin kissing him back. I put my hand behind the man's head and pull him in tight.

I want to make sure he gets what he's paying for.

Two Weeks Later, Philadelphia, The Blue Ball

Jeff

"Shane, if you put that in my eyes again, I will break it over your head."

I'm crotch to crotch with Anthony in the middle of the dance floor. Shane has just unveiled his latest gimmick: a laser with all the power of a goddamn police searchlight. Normally I wouldn't be such a bitch, but the X is finally loosening Anthony up, and he's talking a little about himself. He even mentioned his father. Then along comes Shane to shine the sheen, and Anthony clams up instantly.

"Well, isn't *she* a pet all of a sudden?" Shane gripes to Henry. I know the lingo. *Pet. Poor edgy thing.*

"Hey, Jeff, X is supposed to make you happy," Henry calls over. "What part of *happy* don't you understand?"

"Listen, Happy Hooker, I'm going to report *you* to the IRS." He makes a face as I rest my forehead against Anthony's, looking into his eyes. "So . . . you were saying?"

Anthony smiles dazedly. "I thought you didn't like to talk on the dance floor."

"Usually it's a hard-and-fast rule." I kiss the tip of his nose. "But you said something about your father. It's the first time you've ever mentioned either of your parents."

Anthony closes his eyes. "It's not worth telling. He was an asshole."

"Was?"

"Hey. What's this song?"

I scowl. "Don't change the subject."

"I think it's a diva vocal."

I sigh, laughing. We've been waiting for one for a while. The music is awesome, but there's no denying the sudden blast of power that happens on the dance floor when the DJ suddenly slides in a remix of Madonna or Celine or Whitney, or even something from one of the lesser-known circuit divas, the "Triple A's" I call them: Amber, Anastacia, or Abigail. This one actually turns out to be Taylor Dayne, one of my all-time fave divas of the Eighties. *"I'm naked without you!"* I sing out, grabbing Anthony by the waist and grinding into him.

We've been feeling celebratory ever since Anthony's HIV test came back negative. He'd been worrying ever since I talked to him about barebacking, so I took him over to Fenway to be tested. As his blood was drawn, he'd broken into a cold sweat, his face draining of color, as if the full weight of the Russian Roulette he'd been playing for the past several months had finally hit him. During the next few days we had major conversations, about the science, the ethics, and the politics of AIDS. Talk about feeling like Javitz! I found myself playing the wise old elder: "It comes down to responsibility. To others and to yourself." Blah blah blah. I couldn't wait to just move past it all, to hop on the plane and get here, to forget how anxious I, too, had become, waiting to find out Anthony's results. I'm honestly not sure what I would have done— how I would have proceeded—had it not come back negative. I can't even begin to think about it. Thankfully, I don't have to. I can just have fun.

And Philly's a fun city. Small like Boston, with the same higher-than-expected ratio of cute guys—especially surprising given Philly's proximity to New York. You'd think the big city would've drained off more of the A-listers. But Philly's jumping with them. Still, I only have eyes for Anthony.

We flew down as a little posse: Henry, Anthony, Shane, Brent, and I. Brent, of course, annoyed the shit out of me when he started pushing buttons on his cell phone as soon as we'd arrived, trying to get some crystal. "All he's doing is reserving his place in line at the detox center," I told Anthony.

"I've never done crystal," he said. "I was going to try it in Miami, but then the guy I was with said he couldn't get any."

"Stay away from that stuff," I insisted to him. "I've *been* there. I saw what was happening to myself."

"What?"

"I was getting hard. Brittle." I laughed. "And I don't need any help in that department."

"But they say you get such an awesome feeling—"

"Anthony, I'm telling you. Don't go there."

"But you *tried* it, Jeff. I never have."

I gripped him by the shoulders. "Listen to me, Anthony. You just tested negative. Be glad of that. Be glad you're alive and healthy. Tina would just mess all that up."

He sighed, nodding. "Okay, Jeff. If you say I shouldn't, I won't."

I smiled. He was learning his lessons well.

The welcome party on Friday night was okay, but it was the overnight party at ShamBlue that really rocked. Brent, thankfully, disappeared with a couple of devoted Tina fans from across the river in Jersey. Meanwhile, Shane was a hit, delighting the crowd with his laser guns, strapped to his hips in holsters. He looked like Gary Cooper suddenly gone gay in *High Noon*.

As we planned, we crashed at our E-mail buddy Rudy's house on Spruce Street. I blushed to spy a Polaroid of myself on Rudy's refrigerator, secured by a Judy Garland magnet. It was from the White Party, and I had my arms around Rudy, both of us shirtless and sweaty. I looked pretty twisted; I sure don't remember that photo being taken.

But if Rudy had thought this might be round two for us, he was mistaken. As pretty as I still found his eyes and his body, it's *Anthony* who's commanded all of my attention. As distractions go—since Henry still keeps insisting that's all Anthony is to me, a distraction from Lloyd—he certainly is distracting. We slept in each other's arms on the floor until nearly four this afternoon. Henry and Shane shared Rudy's couch. Once, when they thought we were asleep, I heard them going at it. I just laughed to myself. If Anthony was *my* distraction, then what was Shane to Henry?

When we all had finally roused ourselves, I insisted we eat some bananas and protein bars, and filled everyone's sports bottle with water. Henry complained that we'd be pissing for hours, but to survive a circuit weekend, you have to be savvy. You've got to keep nourished and well hydrated. I also took a long, hot shower, giving my chest and torso a good close shave for tonight's party. Lloyd likes me better with some hair on my chest, but it tends to obscure the definition of my pecs and abs. Go ahead and call me self-absorbed if you want: I've worked *hard* for that definition. And besides, Lloyd's preferences are not necessarily high on my list right now, even if I do keep thinking of him at the most unexpected moments all weekend.

Later, pumping up at the Twelfth Street Gym, Anthony must have picked up on something. "Do you wish Lloyd was here, Jeff?" he asked.

He was spotting me as I bench-pressed my max weight, two hundred pounds. I looked up at him from under the bar. "Lloyd never comes to circuit parties," I told him.

Anthony just shrugged as I proceeded to do eight reps, stepping in to help me with the ninth and tenth. I let the barbell clang back into place and sat up. I could see Lloyd wasn't the only thing making Anthony anxious.

"Why do you keep looking over your shoulder?" I asked.

"I'm worried about Brent. Where is he? We haven't heard from him since we got here."

"If he's not here at the gym for his party pump," I reasoned, "he's *really* twisted."

That's when some guy walking by made an obnoxious comment about all the circuit queens taking over "his" gym.

"Excuse me?" I asked, going from zero to six thousand on the anger scale in the space of a microsecond.

The guy shrank back but still managed to give me a sneer. "What's the matter? Roid rage?"

"I don't take steroids," I snarled.

The guy sniffed. "You guys come down here and just take over. Every goddamn restaurant, every fucking cafe. It's the height of winter, but guys are walking out of the gym without their shirts on."

"And what's so wrong with that?" I asked. "Why are you so offended?"

The guy just huffed off.

Brent never did show up, and all night Anthony's kept an eye out for him. I've come to realize that's just the way Anthony is: fiercely protective of anybody who comes within his sphere. He's truly as compassionate as he is sexy. The other day in Boston, his eyes had misted up when he saw a dead cat in the road. I found his tears endearing. I could see how Anthony might become much more than simply a distraction—if it weren't for the fact that he continues to disappear for one night a week, and that he still refuses to talk of his past.

"*Na-ked,*" he's chanting now, along with Taylor Dayne. "*Na-ked!*"

I keep my arms tightly around his waist. There's one other thing that hasn't changed about Anthony as well: he still can't dance. Janet Reno could manage better than he can.

Some guy sidles up beside us. "You two make a fabulous couple," he says.

"Hey! Thanks!" Anthony's face lights up.

I smile, too, but instantly wish the guy hadn't said it. It's what people used to say when they saw Lloyd and me together—and now suddenly Lloyd's right here again, squeezed down into the infinitesimally small space between Anthony and me. *Damn*. And I was doing so well. I hadn't thought of Lloyd in over an hour.

"I love small-waisted guys," the guy-with-the-compliments is continuing. "Awesome abs, too, dude." He actually has the audacity to run his hand down Anthony's stomach. Anthony doesn't flinch or push him away. He just grins.

The guy's obviously hoping for a three-way. He punches both hands against my chest in that primal gesture that gay men use on the dance floor: sizing up the meat, inspecting the merchandise, a tribal mating ritual. But I'm not interested. Suddenly I want Anthony all to myself. I maneuver my back to the intruder, putting Anthony out of his reach. The guy's hot enough, but he's wearing one of those heavy chain-link necklaces that are *so* last year. So *two* years ago, even.

Packing to head here to Philly, I laughed when I opened my top drawer. It looked like a dragnet through partyland: love beads, freedom rings, ticket stubs, whistles, pacifiers, glow sticks, armbands—even the same clunky chain-link necklace the guy's wearing. Even as I bought the damn thing, I knew it would eventually end up there, along with the rest of the debris. But I can't bear to part with any of it. Each of the trinkets holds some memory. Javitz bought me the leather armband. The whistles hail from the days of Doc Martens boots and sideburns down to my jaw when we marched through the streets with Javitz shouting until our voices were hoarse. More embarrassing are the kitschy freedom rings I wore in my very first Gay Pride parade in Boston. The love beads date from the summer of '91 or '92, when Lloyd and I spent nearly an hour trying them on together, picking out complimentary colors.

I was staring down into the drawer when Anthony had appeared over my shoulder. I laughed and tried to close the drawer quickly, but he asked to see what was inside. I stepped back, letting him look. He reached in, lifting out the flotsam and jetsam of my life as if he were running his hands through buried treasure. He treated the trinkets with reverence, and even though he said nothing, I'd already become adept at reading his emotions. *This could have been my stuff,* Anthony was thinking. *I could have experienced all of this too if I hadn't come out so late.*

So why *hadn't* he?

It's been almost a month now since Anthony came into my life, and still my hunky houseguest remains an enigma. He's like a character in some sci-fi movie who's just hatched out of a pod or thawed out from a hundred-year sleep. It's as if he'd come to life on some mad doctor's table—no childhood, no history, no family, no past.

He's taken a job with a local florist, delivering arrangements on foot to customers in the South End and Back Bay. He's getting paid under the table, which he prefers. He gives me a few dollars toward food and assures me he'll soon start looking for a place of his own. But I'm not pressuring him to leave. Okay, so Henry's right. Although I miss my privacy, Anthony's presence means I don't have to think about Lloyd, about the fact that our phone calls have diminished, or that neither of us has made any plans to visit the other.

Still, Anthony hasn't made the move to sharing my bed. I just can't go that far. He sleeps on the couch. No rule has been made about it; he just seems to sense that I prefer it that way. After sex, he shyly says good night and retreats to his spot in the living room. I never make the offer for him to stay, and he never asks.

Yet while he hasn't learned much rhythm on the dance floor, I have to admit that Anthony *has* been making progress in other areas. The sex is definitely getting better. I've noticed he copies little things I do, like the tongue in the ear or the slapping of the dick against the face. Either Anthony was telling the truth and he *really* never had gay sex before a few months ago, or he's had very *boring* gay sex. When I press for details, he still insists there just isn't much to tell. There's been no one. He's been alone.

I just don't buy it. I didn't that first day we talked and I still don't. One just doesn't live almost thirty years without *some* relationship. Certainly not when one looks like Anthony.

Finally, however, I've found a clue. At least what *might* be a clue. Three days ago, while Anthony was still asleep, I'd looked into his wallet. He usually keeps it zipped up in his backpack, and I vowed to myself I wouldn't snoop. But this time the wallet was on the floor between the living room and the bathroom. He must have dropped it. Lloyd says there are no coincidences or accidents. Everything happens for a reason. That's what I told myself as I picked it up. It fell open, and I couldn't resist. Honest, that's what happened. I chalked it up to the universe giving me permission to pry.

Inside, there was no driver's license, which I'd known about: Anthony had told me that since he'd always lived in cities with good public transportation, he'd let his license lapse. Instead, he had a New York State nondriver identification card, complete with what looked to be a recent photo. There wasn't much info on the card, just his date of birth—September 30, 1970—and an address, the same Nineteenth Street apartment in Chelsea where we'd spent New Year's Eve. He'd told me he'd only been there a few weeks, but clearly he must have considered putting down roots if he went for this card. That changed, I figured, once the guy started "liking him too much." Weren't those his words?

I didn't know what else Anthony's wallet might reveal, but I looked inside. There were a ten, two ones, and three business cards: the florist's, one from a local coffee shop with three purchases punched through it (with ten, you get a free cup), and Brent's. *Eeew.* He must have given it to Anthony and said, "Call me." I had to steel my hand against involuntarily pulling it out and tearing it up.

But that was it. Nothing else.

Except . . .

At first I thought it was a credit card. But as I slipped it out from an inside slot, I saw it was a laminated newspaper photograph. The photo of a man about my age: handsome, smiling, and obviously gay. Not queeny or anything like that, but there are some guys you can just *tell.* I can't describe it, and it wouldn't hold up as proof for a demanding editor, but I can always make out *something* in the smile, the eyes, or the haircut. This guy was smiling a little too girly, a little too sassily, and his hair was foofy in the way no straight man would wear it. Too combed. Too perfect. Very eighties, in fact, and he was wearing a shirt and narrow tie, vintage 1985. It looked like a corporate headshot. The caption under the picture read: *Robert Riley.*

I flipped it over. The photo had indeed been cut out of a newspaper, for there was a section of an article on the back. It read like gibberish, with the beginning and the end of the column cut off, but I considered the words as *evidence*—the way I'd once considered evidence as a journalist. What information might these words, as mangled as they were, reveal?

You can always learn *something,* even if it's merely learning what a particular piece of evidence *doesn't* tell you. I studied the words carefully. From what I could deduce, the article on the back was about oil prices, and it contained the end of a quote from someone named "Herrington." I also took note of the typeface. It seemed familiar, although it wasn't the *Globe* or the *Herald* or the *New York Times.*

I replaced the wallet on the floor where I'd found it. By the time I got out of the shower, Anthony was awake and the wallet nowhere to be seen. I made no mention of the photograph. How *could* I, without admitting I'd snooped? But later that day, I hauled out my almanac and discovered John S. Herrington had been secretary of energy under Ronald Reagan from 1985 to 1989. That meant the photograph likely dated from that period. It fit with the guy's clothes and hairstyle. So that means Anthony would've been between the ages of fifteen and nineteen at the time it was taken.

Who was Robert Riley? It's a question that's been haunting me these last few days. I'm barely listening to Taylor Dayne, not even dancing very hard, just staring over into Anthony's eyes. He suddenly reaches over and begins kissing me. I kiss him back.

"You want some more water?" Anthony asks, pulling his lips free.

The old Ecstasy dry-mouth. I reach around and withdraw the bottle I stuffed down into the back pocket of my jeans. It's nearly empty.

"Yeah," I say. Anthony gives me one more sloppy kiss and heads off through the throng to the bar.

I took over at Henry. "Wanta take a break?"

He nods, following me off the dance floor while Shane glowers. "All he has to do is snap his fingers and there you go," he bitches. Neither of us pays him any mind.

Still, Henry looks concerned about something. "Should we be at all worried that we haven't seen Brent in over twenty-four hours now?" he asks as we find a piece of wall to lean against.

"Nah."

Henry raises his eyebrows. "You think he's okay, then?"

I sneer. "I think he's probably lying in a ditch somewhere in a coma. But *worry?* I don't think so."

Henry smirks. "Jeff O'Brien, you will feel *so* guilty if that turns out to be true."

I dismiss him with a wave of my hand. "So what do you think about Anthony's dancing? Is there a school somewhere for rhythmically challenged gay boys?"

Henry shakes that damn finger at me again. "That boy is in love with you, Jeff. I can see it happening."

I sigh, wiping my forehead with the tank top I wore into the club but which has been pushed down into the back of my jeans for most of my time here.

"You just let it happen," Henry's scolding. "You knew it would, and you let it happen. Just like you did with that kid from Missouri. And Alexei, the flight attendant."

I shrug. "Ooops, I did it again."

He stands with arms akimbo. "Listen, Britney, you're acting pretty smitten yourself."

"Okay, Henry." I roll my eyes, tired of this. "Lecture's over."

He meets my glare, nose to nose. "Look, Jeff. I like Anthony. But you still don't know anything about him. Besides, there's that little matter of that guy down in Provincetown . . ."

"Who I haven't heard from in almost *two weeks.*" I pull away. "I guess he's too busy out buying drapes."

"Maybe *you* should call him. Did you send any flowers or anything when they closed on the house?"

I look at him askance. "Why are you turning into Miss Manners all of a sudden?"

"I just worry about you."

I laugh out loud. "This from the guy who's a corporate honcho by day and a streetwalker by night."

Henry crosses his arms over his chest. "I do *not* walk the streets."

"No. Just the highways and byways of cyberspace."

"Is this your way of telling me you're worried about *me,* too?" Henry smiles. "Aw, Jeff. You're such a *doll.*" He reaches over and kisses my check. "But I'm fine."

I harrumph. "Guess *you've* been too busy to call me, too. I left you *three* messages this week and you didn't call me back until we were getting ready to fly down here."

"I'm sorry. I've been working late."

"At which job?"

Henry makes a face at me. "I'm not telling you *anything* anymore about what I'm doing. Not a word. Because you just broadcast it to everybody."

I put my arm around his neck and lock his head in a choke hold. "Henry, how many times have you done this escort thing now? Tell me the truth."

"Let me go, Jeff."

"*Tell* me."

"Five. I've done it five times."

"*Five times in three weeks!*" I laugh. "What's the matter? Can't make it an even six?"

"Thought I'd save *something* for this weekend." He grimaces, looking around. "Though it looks like the same old pattern. Everybody's too twisted to have sex except on the dance floor."

"There's always Shane."

Henry gives me a look. "You know what I think it is, Jeff? Shane actually shed some light on this for me. He says two attractive guys sometimes don't hook up with each other because each is waiting for the other to cruise him *first*."

"That's fucked, Henry," I say.

"Well, it makes sense to me. I'm starting to think it's true what they say about circuit boys. They're all a bunch of narcissistic posers."

I scoff. "Are *you,* Henry? Am I?"

"Sometimes, yes." He shrugs. "I'm getting tired of the circuit. It's the same old thing all the time."

"You're the one who wanted to come here," I remind him.

"I know, I know." He sighs. "But I'm sick of these boys twisted out of their minds. Like Brent. I mean, he didn't come here to dance or have fun. He came to get fucked up. That's all. You know, there was an article in some gay paper that said the circuit scene could be as damaging to gay men as the religious right—"

"Henry! What the fuck has gotten into you?"

He pouts. "I'm just tired of it all. I want something more."

"Look, Brent annoys the shit out of me, too," I admit. "He's the poster boy for all the critics of the club scene, *exactly* what they rail against: a self-absorbed substance abuser who masks his lack of self-esteem with chemicals, who mindlessly makes his donation to AIDS Action or GMAC and then gets so twisted he's willing to do anything." That was for sure: the night I brought him home he would've let me fuck him without a condom if I'd been into barebacking. "But to say he's as bad as Pat Robertson or Jerry Falwell," I say, shaking my head. "That's *fucked,* Henry."

"All I know is, I'm tired of bullshit. I think that's why the escorting thing is such a rush for me. The guys are right there, no games. They put what they want right out on the table."

I lean in close again. "Look, I *do* worry about you, buddy. I know the escorting is a real trip for you, and it's way hot and everything you've told me sounds cool, but there's just so much that could happen. Your job, your reputation, not to mention getting ripped off by—"

"Hey, it's *Celine,*" Henry says, recognizing the mix. "Let's dance."

I frown. "You're doing exactly what you accuse me of doing. Avoiding the topic."

Henry smirks. "And I'll say exactly what you always say. *We're here to dance.*" He grabs my hands. "Come on, Jeff. It's *Celine.*"

"I want you to *feeeeed* me," I sing, using our own special lyrics to the skinny diva's song.

Back in the middle of the crowd, we fall into a group of friends. We form a little huddle, Henry and Eliot and Oscar and Adam and Billy and

Rudy and I, swaying to the music, pawing each other's chests. I feel that surge of brotherhood, of connection. Narcissistic posers? Right now Eliot's passing out bracelets he made for all of us, with our names spelled out in little beads. I picture him stringing them all on his kitchen table back in San Diego in advance of this weekend. At the White Party he gave us all customized visors, with our names and home cities stitched onto the front. I watch as Rudy tells Eliot he loves him, and they lock in an embrace.

Okay, I'm not discounting the alphabet soup of G, K, T, or X that may be contributing to this happy little lovefest, but the connection is nonetheless real. Eliot slips my bracelet over my wrist and I kiss him. We might not be intimate friends, knowing all of our secrets and hopes and fears, but we're *family* nonetheless: part of that big extended gay family that has sustained me over the last few years, with the sense of belonging that comes with it, a feeling of being part of something bigger than yourself. Community exists only where you make it. I think about how events like these transform the places where they're held: the middle of the desert, the Olympic Stadium in Montreal, the streets of Philadelphia. The guy in the gym was right: we *do* take over a place. We turn them queer for a weekend: the restaurants, the subways, the gyms, the parks. I laugh when I read the phrase "gay community" to describe the gay population as a whole—a necessary fiction, I suppose, to empower a movement. But here's where community is *real*: here in our little huddle, the seven of us exchanging bracelets and sloppy kisses.

Narcissistic posers? My friends here have been called a lot worse, actually. Drug abusers. Misogynists. Immature children. Murderers, even, because of their supposed cavalier spread of the AIDS virus through unsafe sex. I watch Eliot's face as he slips his little gift over the last wrist. I watch Henry embrace him, kiss him on the lips. I think about the time I slept with Eliot: how he labored to roll that condom over my cock, how I lost my erection in the process, and how we ended up just falling asleep in each other's arms. "This is the best part anyway," he said to me.

The best part.

Look, of course there are guys like Brent, who has been known to have crystal blown up his ass. Of course there's unsafe sex and bad drugs and attitude queens, and probably even within this little huddle there have been moments of transgression. I remember once how Billy freaked out, having been fucked bareback at one party. Billy's already got HIV, but he worried about new infection, and how much of a risk he'd been to the guy who topped him. He searched in vain for him the entire rest of the weekend, constantly on the lookout. "What are you going to say to him?" I wanted to know, but he had no clue. He just wanted to find him. The guilt Billy assumed, appropriate or not, eventually led him to leave early that weekend. He just couldn't have fun after that. Even now I'll occasionally see him glance around, scanning the crowd for the face of the man he still carries in his mind.

There are consciences here. There are souls here. Like anywhere else, there is good and there is bad, but never is it as starkly delineated as some critics would describe. All I know is that these are the people—all of them, even the ones I don't know—with whom I feel most at home.

I listen to the soulful lyrics of Mary Griffin mixing into the trance we've been dancing to. *"I wish I could keep you all of my life . . . this is my moment . . . this is my perfect moment with you . . ."*

Yes, yes indeed. This is my moment. I am part of this, part of the now, part of what's happening and pulsing and marking our lives. It may be a celebration of the ephemeral, but at least I'm experiencing it. Jason, the activist back home in Boston, and the angry guy here in the gym: will they ever feel they missed out? I don't know. I just know Javitz is gone, his dance stopped in midstep. This moment is *mine*, and I'm savoring it.

Anthony spots us then and waves. He comes bearing gifts: a dozen bottles of water pressed up against his glistening chest. The boys dive upon him, and Anthony laughs heartily as he doles them out, a sexy young Santa Claus. I spot the gleam in his eyes. There's no hiding how truly happy he is here among us all. As if he's found a place at last. A home. Somewhere he finally belongs. I understand the sentiment, but not the longing behind it. I found a home here after Javitz's death, after my world had been turned upside down and all its contents shaken out—but what brought *Anthony* here? What did all this replace?

"Thank you, Jeff," he whispers. "Thank you for bringing me here."

We kiss. I vow then and there to find out the mystery behind Anthony Sabe.

Meanwhile, at Nirvana

Lloyd

Eva's a little tipsy. No, more than a little.

"I useta be Snow White, but I drifted," she purrs, standing up on a dining room chair, hand on hip, her other hand pushing at her hair. She's a miniature Mae West in an oversized red-and-blue ski sweater.

"It's not the *men* in my life that count, it's the *life* in my men. *Ooooooooh!*"

Ty and I nearly slide under the table laughing. I actually can't catch my breath. I've never seen her like this. She's *hysterical*. Who knew?

"*Frankie and Johnnie were lovers,*" she sings, going into a whole Westian routine. She's dead-on. Uncanny, even. I wish Jeff could see this. Jeff *loves* Mae West.

Ty leans in close to me. "She used to do this for all the queens who'd come visit Steven," he whispers. I notice he lets his hand remain on my knee.

I smile. Many times has Eva told me that she thought Ty, her late husband's friend and lawyer, was in love with her. But when he arrived this morning in Provincetown, stepping out of his Lexus in his Prada suit and Versace sunglasses, I knew instantly that he was gay.

"Goodness, madam," Ty's saying now, feeding her lines, "what beautiful diamonds you're wearing."

"Goodness had nothing to do with it, dearie," she shoots right back. She steps up onto the dining room table and sashays across it, swinging her hips left to right.

"Ba-boom, ba-boom, ba-boom, ba-boom!" Ty shouts, keeping in

time with her swings, just as I'm certain he'd done countless of times to the delight of her husband's gay friends.

She stops in front of me. "*Ohhh*. I always *did* like a man in uniform, and that one fits you just grand."

"This old thing?" I laugh, pulling on my UMass sweatshirt.

"Why don't you come up some time 'n' see me? I'm home ev'ry evenin'. *Ooooh.*"

"Ba-boom, ba-boom, ba-boom, ba-boom!" Ty shouts out again as she swings hard and fast back down the table. I howl.

"I'm going to have to handcuff you," Ty calls to her, another obviously well rehearsed line.

"Mustcha really?" she answers, on the spot and ready. "You know, I wasn't born with 'em."

Ty can hardly keep from laughing. "Many men would have been safer if you had," he manages to say.

"I dunno," she says, considering. "Hands ain't ev'rythin'."

Back to swinging the hips down the table. "Ba-boom, ba-boom, ba—"

"*Yaaaaaaaaaaaa!!!*"

I'm not sure what happened. One second she's up there parading down the table; the next she's gone. Ty is leaping out of his chair.

She'd walked right off the edge!

"Are you all right?" Ty's shouting.

I run around to the other side of the table. Eva is sitting up, rubbing her ass.

"Eva, are you hurt?" I ask.

"Well, nobody can ever say I didn't fall for ya," she quips, still in character.

We all break up laughing, rolling on the floor. Ty falls over me, and I think it might be deliberate. Eva is nearly under the sofa.

"Hey!" she exclaims. "Look!"

She pulls a small, crude wooden figure of the Buddha from under the couch. She hands it to me. Something about the face makes me smile.

"It looks almost handmade," I say, "as if somebody whittled it from a piece of wood." I glance over at Eva. "It's a good omen. A gift from the house."

"Let's fill the house with Buddhas!" she says. "All kinds of Buddhas!"

I hand the figure back to her. "Maybe we could paint this one. Bring it to life."

"Maybe it's time for another bottle of wine," Ty says, refilling my wineglass.

That's how the night goes. Empty bottles of wine stack up beside the trash. By the time the grandfather clock in the hallway chimes two, I'm on the floor shoulder to shoulder with Ty, leaning up against the couch. Eva is spread out above us, the Buddha on her chest. We're passing around a joint. Good stuff. A perfect way to celebrate our first weekend in the house.

I have a nice, solid buzz. Nothing that impairs my thought process, just a nice, relaxing, contented feeling—a relief after the weeks of frenzied packing and unpacking, anxious transfers of money, and seemingly endless documents to sign. In between, we made probably two dozen trips down to Orleans or Hyannis to buy those household necessities we couldn't find in Provincetown: shower rings, silk sheets, plush towels, coffeemakers for every room. "If we're going to do this," I insisted, "we should do it right."

The days passed by in a blur, and I realized this morning I hadn't called Jeff in nearly a week. But he hadn't called me, either. It works both ways. He didn't even send flowers on the day we closed.

"I never dreamed I'd be starting over like this," Eva says, mellow now, handing the joint down to Ty. "Did you?"

He takes a hit. "Not like this, Eva," he says after exhaling the smoke in a long, languid breath. "Not like this."

Her hand rests on top of my head. "Well, if it wasn't for this young man here, I might still be a widow living all alone in New York."

"Well, you're a still widow," I say a bit dreamily, taking the joint from Ty. "There's nothing I can do about that."

There's a silence. I didn't mean for it to sound snotty. I meant it funny, but no one laughs. Was it insensitive? I hope Eva didn't take it that way. Maybe I'm just feeling paranoid from the pot. Jeff always says I have a tendency to get that way when I mix pot and wine.

"Oh, by the way, Eva," Ty tells her, "Alex was in the hospital. A throat infection. He's out now, doing better."

Alex. The guy with AIDS to whom she'd been so devoted. The one she saw every day, the one she said she loved.

"I'm glad," Eva says, looking away. "That he's doing better, I mean."

A few weeks ago, I asked her if leaving Alex would be difficult, and she said of *course* it would, but that she'd stay in touch, that she'd travel down to New York often to see him. But apparently she *hasn't* been in touch, not if she didn't know he'd been in (and out of) the hospital. Curious.

There are, in fact, lots of curious things about her.

Ever since that night in my old apartment—the night something had woken me up and I'd discovered Eva awake and she'd kissed my hand—sometimes I feel a little weird around her. Oh, I *love* Eva; I really do. It's not weird enough for me to back out of the deal. But I'm a trained psychologist, after all: I can't help diagnosing people. It's not fair, really; I don't like doing this with friends. I don't want to start assigning them pathologies or suggesting meds.

But Jeff's words have come to haunt me: *She's in love with you, Lloyd, and if you can't see that, then I think it's time for the doctor to heal himself.*

I insist to myself that she's not *in love* with me. Maybe a little *infatuated.* That's all it is. Infatuation. It isn't *love*—not that kind of love, anyway—and she'll see that, if she hasn't already. It's just a little crush, brought on by her grief over Steven and the sudden transformation we've made together. It's nothing she won't be able to work through. Maybe I ought to suggest a therapist she could see here in town. There are some really good ones in Provincetown, who know how to work with grief and depression.

Because, in truth, I worry. Just a little. The intimacy Eva sometimes presumes with me can make me distinctly uncomfortable. There are times she does indeed talk as if we're a couple. At Sears in Hyannis the other day, she giggled to the clerk in the appliance department, "We still have to decide which one of us will do the laundry"—a simple enough statement, perhaps, but the clerk looked over at us as if we were married, a fifty-year-old lady and a thirty-something husband. And just now: *If it wasn't for this young man, I'd still be a widow.*

Well, you still are! I suddenly want to shout. *You still are a widow!*

It's just a manifestation of her grief. Grief can make even the most stable, the most insightful, the most introspective people behave in ways aberrant to their true selves.

And there's another thing, too: that sleeping with the father bit. She made it sound so sweet and innocent, but a grown man sharing a bed with a nine-, ten-, eleven-year-old girl? Yes, the more I think about it, the more I feel I ought to recommend that she see someone—

"A half-dollar for your thoughts." Ty's hand is on my knee again. Our eyes meet.

"Just buzzing," I say softly.

He smiles. Eva's hand on my head and Ty's on my knee. Okay, let's make things even *more* awkward, shall we?

So I admit I find Ty attractive. He's very handsome, very debonair, very sure of himself. I've always been partial to men with a little silver in their hair. It's hard to imagine Ty pining after Eva, as she's insisted he's been doing for years since Steven's death. It's hard to see him pining after *any* woman, in fact, with his three gold rings studded with emeralds, his turquoise silk scarf, his solid onyx cufflinks. Yet despite the trappings, he's not effeminate, just sophisticated, cosmopolitan, in the ways guys used to be back in the forties and the fifties. His skin is a deep, shiny cocoa, his eyes a startling brown-gold. I can't pretend I don't want to see him naked.

Maybe it's because for the past several years before Jeff and I reconnected, I was celibate—part of my grief and healing process—and then suddenly there was a rush of sex with Jeff for a period of several months. But now there's been nothing, not since Christmas. There's a *hunger* to my horniness, the way I feel when I skip breakfast and lunch and then become ravenous by dinner. When Ty stands, walking in front of us out to the hallway to check his messages on his cell phone, I can't resist checking out his butt. High and hard. My desire becomes a physical thing. I have to wrestle it down.

I turn suddenly, locking eyes with Eva on the couch. She's caught me looking.

"Another hit, Lloyd?" she asks softly, holding out the joint.

"No, thanks." I feel my face flush.

She stubs the roach out in an ashtray. "He hides it well, don't you think?"

I stand up, brushing off my pants, trying to cover my erection. "Hides what?"

Eva smiles. "His feelings for me."

I shake my head down at her. "Eva, that man is as queer as I am."

She yawns and stretches. "Maybe. Maybe not."

"What do you mean?"

She smiles enigmatically. "Nothing. Just—well, didn't you once say human sexuality is a complex thing? That gay and straight are merely constructs?"

"I didn't say that. Javitz did. I merely repeated it to you."

"Well, I've been thinking about it. I think it's very true. I think it's true about Tyrone, and I think it's true about you, too."

I frown. "You're trashed, Eva. If it's true for us, why not for you? Maybe you just haven't found the right woman."

"Maybe I haven't. Maybe *you* haven't, either. Maybe Tyrone hasn't." She giggles, covering her mouth. "And maybe he *has.*"

Ty's come back into the room. He narrows his eyes at us. "What are you two conspiring about in here?"

"Just deciding what color to paint this room," Eva tells him, sitting up now on the couch. "I think blue. What do you think?"

How well she covers up. How fast on her feet. She stands, extinguishing the candles we'd lit hours ago at dinner, now burned down to tiny stubs. It's been a long day. A good day, bottom line. Ty answered a thousand questions about business law. Eva cooked us an excellent meal of wild mushrooms, risotto, and gingered string beans, and the bottles of wine Ty brought from a vineyard in upstate New York had been fabulous.

"Tyrone," Eva says, "your room's all made up. If you need anything, just whistle, okay?"

"Will do, love."

"You know how to whistle, don't you?" she purrs, back in character. "Just put your lips together and blow."

"Wrong diva," I correct her. "That's Lauren Bacall."

She kisses Ty, then approaches me. "I know my divas, sweetheart," she assures me.

We kiss briefly on the lips. "You were very entertaining tonight," I tell her, patting her cheek.

"Ohhhh," she purrs. "I always do mah best work at night."

She moves off, puttering around in the kitchen. She seems reluctant to go to bed. She washes wineglasses, puts dishes away, wipes down the counters. She's clearly waiting until she's sure Tyrone and I are also going upstairs—*alone*, to our *separate* rooms. A couple of times, Ty and I exchange those looks—those looks any gay man can recognize, looks that say, *Okay, how are we going to manage this?* There's something unspoken about our flirtation: *Eva shouldn't know about it.*

Finally, after watching her practically rearrange the entire kitchen cupboards, I conclude sleeping with Ty is going to be impossible, at least for tonight, and that we may as well just surrender to the inevitable. Eva's not going to go to bed, no matter *how* tired she gets, until she's sure both of us are alone in our own quarters. So I say good night, climb the stairs, and close my door behind me.

Once I'm alone, as always happens, I think about Jeff.

Unbuttoning my shirt, I look out at the sky. The moon is full. I murmur a spontaneous prayer for Jeff, wherever he is. People do strange things under full moons. This is the weekend of that party down in Philadelphia. Damn circuit craziness.

There's a soft knock at my door. I open it to see Ty standing there.

"I hope you don't find me bold and brazen," he whispers.

I feel the grin spread across my face. "I like bold and brazen men," I say, stepping aside so Ty can come in.

We kiss. I feel the strength of the man's body. I let my hands fall to his incredible ass. "We should be quiet," Ty whispers. "I don't think Eva would deal well with this."

"I don't think so, either."

We kiss again.

"She's funny like that, you know," Ty says, close to my ear. "When Steven was alive—"

I put my hand up to his mouth. "You probably shouldn't tell me anything."

He looks at me. "I only thought you might want my opinion."

"Opinion of what?"

"Eva."

I make a face. "What do you mean?"

He sighs. "Lloyd, I was tremendously encouraged to see her breaking out of her shell, doing her volunteer work after being a recluse for so long. I thought it was good, healthy." He pauses. "But don't you think it odd how she didn't want to talk about Alex?"

I do, but something keeps me from admitting it to Ty. "I imagine she's feeling a little guilty about leaving him behind," I say. "I'm sure she'll make it a point to get down and see him soon."

"Maybe. Maybe not." Ty takes my hands in his. "But I've been watching her with you, and I'm reminded of the days with Steven, and I wonder how much she's told you."

I shake my head. "Whatever it is you're thinking she needs to tell me, we need to let her do it on her own. I owe her that much. We shouldn't talk about her, not without her present, not about things she should tell me herself."

Ty looks surprised. "It's just that I think you should know—"

"No. It's not fair."

"Maybe, but—"

I put my hand back up to his lips.

He shrugs. "Okay, Lloyd. Whatever you want."

"I want you to kiss me," I tell him.

Ty smiles. "You referred to a partner a couple times tonight. *Jeff.* This is cool, then?"

I look at him. "There are probably a hundred reasons why we shouldn't do this, Ty. Are you going to recite them all?"

"I'll quit talking," he says.

"Good."

I kiss him hard. He responds. I unbutton his shirt, slipping my hands across his hard, smooth chest. He bites my neck. It feels incredible. We make love, falling onto my bed with a passion that fills my entire being. My hunger is being satiated. I bite his nipples, and he grabs at my sheets and growls. He takes my dick into his mouth. I let out a sound of shattering relief.

Not until the sun is coming up does Ty go back to his room. And it's only after I watch him gently close his door that I smell the coffee brewing downstairs. At first, I don't think anything of it.

Then I remember something.

We don't have an automatic coffeemaker.

Somebody has to be downstairs brewing it.

Eva is up. And I know somehow that she never went to bed.

Valentine's Day, the Red Roof Inn

Henry

This one has a foot-and-shoe fetish. He told me so on the phone. I have no idea what to expect.

I check my watch. It's three minutes to four. Three minutes to show-time. Only briefly do I reflect on the irony of the date, on the fact that here I am, sitting in the parking lot of some motel, on Valentine's Day. Here I am, selling myself to a stranger, while all over the world sweethearts are opening boxes of candy and popping bottles of champagne.

I laugh a little to myself. In a few months I'll be twenty-nine years old. I've never had a boyfriend last longer than a few months. My record-holder is Sean, an Irish boy with red hair from South Boston, who'd stuck around for four months and sixteen days. Sean's pubes felt like a Brillo pad, and he had a disgusting addiction to Cheetos. His lips glowed a perpetual orange. After polishing off a bag, he had the rankest breath I've ever encountered. I wonder briefly how Sean is celebrating Valentine's Day, then conclude I really don't really care.

I pop a mint into my mouth and step out of my Jeep, lifting a heavy black traveling case from the backseat. I don't feet lonely, or depressed, or sorry for myself—not with my dick already lengthening down the leg of my jeans. Not with the prospect of some guy paying me big bucks just for the privilege of being with me.

The guy told me he'd be in room 215. The motel is U-shaped, with an outdoor staircase leading up to the second floor, where the rooms are accessed off a wraparound landing. An elderly couple passes me on my way up the steps, the wife looking at me oddly. And why not? My jeans are practically spray-painted on, I wear a silver latex tank top under my leather jacket, and just *what,* she must be thinking, is in this *case?*

I can hardly suppress a smile. This is all just so totally unlike me. At least, so unlike Henry Weiner, insurance claims specialist, who just this morning sat glassy-eyed through his weekly staff meeting, attired in his usual tweed sportcoat and Bass Weejuns. Every five or six minutes I looked at my watch, chewing idly on my pencil as my supervisor droned on about projected earnings. When it came time for me to give my weekly report, I straightened my papers against the table, cleared my throat, and read off my figures in my usual efficient monotone. To my coworkers, I'm a reliable, competent, even skilled claims manager, whose drab clothing and serious demeanor merely reflect a studious commitment to my work.

Or rather, that's what they *think* it reflects. But there's another Henry Weiner, and you don't have to scratch too deep to find him. This is the Henry Weiner who, as a horny teenager, regularly swiped *Blueboy* and *Honcho* magazines from the drugstore in my hometown of West Springfield, Massachusetts. I'd read them with a flashlight under my covers late at night, jacking off one, two, *three times* before falling asleep. This is the Henry Weiner who, as a University of Massachusetts student, was one of the loudest and most flamboyant members of my campus gay group, whose first sex with another guy was outside and in broad daylight, behind the student union. This is the Henry Weiner my coworkers don't know. This is the Henry Weiner who takes chances. This is the Henry Weiner who had closed himself down, hidden himself under a guise of respectability—read, *geekiness*—until Jeff O'Brien rescued me and set me free.

Few at my job suspect this other side. A few months ago, I brought a hip young secretary out to Avalon with me on Sunday night. Veronica's a real fag hag. "I just know you've got muscles under that jacket, don't you, Henry?" she'd gushed. I suggested she find out for herself on Sunday night. She agreed, and found out a lot more than that—though none of our other coworkers would believe her tales when she got back to work on Monday. She'd been astounded watching me on the dance floor with Jeff and Brent and the other shirtless boys, the transformation almost too drastic for her to comprehend. For the rest of the week, all Veronica could do was stare at me in my cubicle as I demurely processed claim forms.

If she thought that was drastic, she should see me now. I laugh to myself as I head for room 215, lugging the traveling case at my side. I feel my dick swell almost to its full size.

I rap on the door. A good, hearty *man's* rap, no girly knock-knock. The door is opened by a man in his sixties: gray hair, glasses, thin, in white collar shirt and beige polyester slacks. He stands in his socks, about eye-level with me.

"Hank?" the man asks breathlessly.

I nod. I'd ditched the "Brick"—it just sounded too funny, making me want to crack up every time anybody referred to me that way. Instead I chose "Hank." It's a derivative of Henry, after all: my grandfather had always called me Hank, much to my mother's dismay. As a boy, I'd never liked "Hank"; it sounded too much like "wank" or the sound you made when you blew your nose. But now it seems absolutely *perfect*: still a part of myself, but different. Manlier. Studlier.

"And you must be Gilbert," I say.

The man nods, stepping aside to let me in. The room is standard motel fare: two full-sized beds against the wall, separated by a small table with a phone and a clock. On the opposite wall is a desk and a small bureau, above which hangs a large mirror. I set the case down on the floor.

"Oh, your pictures don't do you justice," Gilbert says, falling to his knees. "You are a god, sir! Thank you for allowing me to lick your boots!"

They're Jeff's. Old Doc Martens from his ACT UP days.

"And you *did* bring the others, too, sir?" the man asks without looking up.

"Open that bag," I command.

The man crawls over and unzips the case with his teeth. A nice little touch; I should've ordered him to do it that way. I do my best to stifle a laugh.

"Oh, *thank you,* sir!" The man lifts a pair of beige work boots out of the case. They're Shane's. He told me he wears them to shovel snow. Shane has a size-twelve foot, and Gilbert had wanted the *biggest* shoe size I could find, even if my own foot was nine and a half.

There are other goodies in the case. Dirty sneakers. Dirty socks. A pair of aviator boots (also Jeff's) with the zipper up the side. A pair of shiny patent-leather tuxedo shoes which I've owned since high school, not worn since my senior prom. And finally, my Bass Weejuns from work. Gilbert had even wanted *those*.

He kisses and caresses every single pair. "I want to worship your feet and your shoes, sir!" He presses a Weejun to his face, sniffing the inside.

I fold my arms across my chest. "Yes, you will worship your master's feet and shoes."

"Yes, sir. Oh, *yes,* sir!" Gilbert goes back to licking my boots.

I can't resist the smile that stretches across my face. My eyes move around the room. On the table, ten crisp new twenties are fanned out. I love it when clients leave the money in plain sight. It's such a turn-on. I spot the man's keys next to the cash. On the key ring I discern a Star Market value card, just like the one I have myself.

I sit down on the edge of the bed. I watch the back of Gilbert's head as he licks my boots. I imagine him buying TV dinners and frozen pizzas and kitty litter for his cat. I don't know if he even has a cat, but somehow I imagine he does. In our brief phone conversation, he'd told me he was a retired appliance salesman. Where had he worked? I wonder. Sears? Or possibly his own little shop, in one of those working-class towns of central Massachusetts. Maybe he'd been Gil the Appliance Man, the Washing Machine Guy, the Stove-and-Refrigerator King. Housewives from Gardner to Fitchburg knew they could count on Gil!

I smile to myself. Why does this happen, every time? Why do I always imagine scenarios for every guy I meet? I wonder if all escorts do that, or if eventually they become so jaded every guy looks the same.

It's been with such remarkable ease that I've fallen into the escort routine. All so excruciatingly simple. My AOL profile had led to an on-line escort bulletin board with my own Web site, complete with several photos. Most nights now when I get home from work, I sign on, click my way into an escort chat room, then go about making dinner, doing laundry, watching TV. The ring of instant messages brings me back to the computer, and I'll either tell pic collectors to buzz off or I'll make a connection. Legitimate guys get my cell phone number, and we arrange our dates over the phone, sometimes for that evening, more often a day or two in advance. I'm insistent that I only make out-calls, for I remain uncomfortable about letting anyone into my space.

Most of the guys meet me in hotels or motels, but a few take their chances and invite me to their homes. I shy away from any South End addresses, fearful I'll end up hired by someone I know or recognize. I prefer guys from the suburbs, because I know practically no one out there. In the past few weeks I've traveled out to Woburn and Melrose and as far north as Methuen. A few inevitably turn out to be no-shows, but most come through. In all, I've made twenty-five hundred dollars, including tips—and every cent tax-free, with no overhead except for the gas in my Jeep.

Jeff just laughs. "It doesn't gross you out to see big rolls of flesh?" he asked. "Saggy tits? Little pink dicks that can't get hard?"

It *is* odd, I have to admit that. On the dance floor, if a guy has even a little bit of a fleshy overhang, I never took twice at him. *Maybe that's why you haven't found a boyfriend,* I think now, scolding myself. But as an escort, it doesn't matter what they look like. It only matters what *I* took like.

I can't explain it. There's just something *happening* for me, meeting these men and having sex with them. Every one of my clients seems so exquisitely *satisfied* when we're done, many tucking an extra twenty or fifty or even a *hundred* into my back pocket. I've started getting repeat calls. Business, as they say, is *booming*.

That's it. *That's* what turns me on to this whole enterprise. I'm not only good at what I do, but I *enjoy* doing it. For the first time in my life, I really *like* my work.

Gilbert has by now removed my boots and my socks and is busy cleaning between my toes with his tongue. "That's it, slave," I say. "That is your purpose in life. To service my feet."

I lean back on my elbows on the motel bed. How did I learn it? How do I know just what to say? *Instinct.* I just fall into it naturally, as if I were *born* to do it.

I can feel Gilbert's warm, slippery tongue slide between and around my toes. It feels awesome. No circuit boy ever gave me a toe-sucking job like this.

"Master, please put on *these* shoes now."

I lean my head forward to see what Gilbert is offering. Shane's work boots. I nod and the man slips them on my feet. They feel enormous.

"Walk in them, *please,* sir! "

I oblige. The boots are so big, they nearly fall off my feet. I feel like Donald Duck flapping around the room. I can't help but let out a laugh.

"Tell me how *big* those feet are, sir, *please!*"

"Size—twel—" I have to cover my mouth to keep from hysterics.

"Please don't laugh, sir," Gilbert says, momentarily reminding me who's paying the bill here.

"I'm not laughing, slave." I hide my amusement and summon Hank's butch voice. "They are size *twelve,* you puny runt!"

The man seems near faint. "Oh, they are *bigger* even than that," Gilbert says, jacking himself now, looking intently at the oversized shoes. *"They are even bigger than that!"*

I catch his drift. "Yes!" I bark. "They are size fourteen! No, *fifteen!"*

"Ohhhhh!"

The man falls to the ground, his mouth eagerly lapping at Shane's scuffed boots. I picture Shane wearing them, shoveling snow off the sidewalk in front of his house.

"Size-*sixteen!*" I intone.

"Ohhh, yes!"

"Size—*twenty!*"

"Ahhhhhhhhhhhhhhh!!!" The man screams as if he'd been shot in the heart. He falls over onto his side, cum dribbling over his fist.

He doesn't move. For a moment I worry he's had a heart attack, that he's dead. What would I *do?* But then he opens his eyes and looks gratefully up at me.

"Oh, *thank* you, sir," Gilbert says, nearly in tears. "Thank you!"

I smile. Ah, yes. One more satisfied customer.

I love this job.

Meanwhile, Back in the South End

Jeff

"He's gotten even fatter since Christmas," Lloyd says. "Jeff, this *can't* be a good thing."

I just smile over at the sight of them, our twenty-seven-pound cat curled up in Lloyd's lap on the couch. "You remember what the vet said," I remind him. "'Just let him live.'"

Lloyd grimaces. "She said *live*, not *explode*."

Surprised to see Lloyd at my place? So am I. So is Mr. Tompkins. He immediately went for Lloyd's lap, settling down and purring loudly, like the rattling motor of an old refrigerator. He's missed him. Last fall, when Lloyd was coming by more frequently, Mr. Tompkins would always plop himself down in front of the door after he left, awaiting his return. He'd stay there for hours, despite my attempts to move him—which, at twenty-seven pounds, isn't easy. Finally he'd give up, and for the past few months he's been particularly surly. The only thing I can conclude is that he misses Lloyd something fierce.

See, Mr. Tompkins isn't known to be the friendliest cat, except to Lloyd and me. He was notoriously jealous of Javitz, leaping at him from countertops. Now far too obese for such sport, he settles for chomping down on Henry's hand whenever he attempts to pet him, which isn't often anymore, to say the least. To our friends, Mr. Tompkins is the Hellspawn, but we call him our baby; and now Baby is purring, fast asleep, in Daddy's lap.

"I want to get a cat for us in Provincetown," Eva chirps, standing awkwardly in the middle of the room, watching the reunion between Lloyd and Mr. Tompkins.

Yes, she's here, too. Which *doesn't* surprise you, you say. Me, either. I'm trying to be pleasant, even accepting one of those choke holds from her that she calls hugs. But she's such a little imp, like some annoying creature out of Sid & Marty Kroft. Every other word out of her mouth is "we." *We did this* and *we're buying that* and *we have so much to do* and *we're just having so much fun setting up our new life together as husband and wife.*

Okay, so maybe not that last one, but that's what she means. It's her way of reminding me that *she's* in my place now, and I'd better not forget it. She's stuck so close to Lloyd ever since they got here that she actually seems jealous of the cat.

"No, Eva," Lloyd is saying, shaking his head. "I've *explained* that to you. We can't get a cat. Guests might be allergic."

She shrugs and looks over at me. "I keep forgetting about the guests."

Of course she does. *Of course!* She isn't in this for some quaint little bed-and-breakfast experience. She's in it to play house with Lloyd. *Why can't he see that?*

And why does it upset me so? I've accepted that it's his choice, that the hopes and the dreams I allowed myself to embrace last fall just won't be happening. Lloyd and I are *over.*

Then he shows up at my door today—Valentine's Day—with a bouquet of daisies. My favorite flowers. The card is simple and poignant: *My love always, Lloyd.*

I had nothing to give him in return. But I admit I made something of a show kissing Lloyd in front of Eva. Maybe that was mean of me. She retreated into the kitchen, examining the photos and magnets on my refrigerator door.

"I'd *love* to go to a circuit party with you all sometime," she's saying now, pointing back into the kitchen toward a picture of me and Zed, the leather guy I dated briefly last year. We're at the Folsom Street Fair in San Francisco, the only time I've ever worn the harness Javitz left me. Now I've loaned it to Henry for those clients who want him in leather. "Would you *take* me to a circuit party, Jeff?" Eva's asking. "They look like so much fun!"

I have to smile. Eva at a circuit party. Now *there's* an image.

"Don't encourage him," Lloyd tells her. "I've already told Jeff he does too much partying."

"Many times," I agree.

Lloyd nuzzles his face down into Mr. Tompkins's fur. Eva takes the opportunity to lean in close to me. "May I talk with you a minute, Jeff?" she whispers. "About something?"

I nod, a little wary. She takes my arm and leads me into the kitchen, away from Lloyd's ears. She looks up at me with those big, earnest eyes.

"I need some advice," she says.

"Advice? What kind of advice?"

She sighs. "Last week, Lloyd had a cold. I made him some broth and bought some sinus medicine, but nothing seemed to perk him up. *Tell* me. What did *you* do when he was sick? Is there some special food, some particular remedy he prefers?"

I just look at her.

"I feel rather silly asking," she continues. "Kind of like the new wife asking the ex."

She laughs. I don't.

"I was never a wife," I tell her.

Her eyes level with mine. "I just want to take seriously my responsibilities to him. After all, this is quite a commitment we've made to each other."

Has she no *clue?* Is she being catty or is she really so ingenuous?

"Look, Eva, I can tell you this much. When Lloyd's sick, he prefers to be *left alone.*"

She smiles. "Come, now, Jeff. I've heard how you and Javitz would sit up all night with him, changing the wet cloth on his head, tucking in the blankets around his legs."

"Oh, he likes *family* around," I say, fully aware of just how nasty that comes across. And I intend it to be nasty. I admit it. I just can't abide the phoniness anymore. She dislikes me as much as I dislike her. She knows that I see through her, and she's trying to win me over with her fakey warmth and talk of circuit parties. Yet she can't resist her own little digs about joint checking accounts and making commitments.

I move past her back into the living room. I don't know if she's upset, and at the moment I don't care. I just sit down beside Lloyd on the couch.

"He's missed me," Lloyd says, putting his face down near Mr. Tompkins's. Anyone else would lose half a cheek, but our baby just licks Lloyd's ear.

I smile. "Henry won't sit with his back to him."

"That's probably smart," Lloyd says. "You bad boy, you." He tickles Mr. Tompkins's belly. The cat purrs even louder. "How's he taken to your houseguest? What's his name again? *Andrew?*"

"Anthony," I correct him. "He . . . well, he's grudgingly gotten used to Anthony."

Truth is, Mr. Tompkins *loathes* Anthony. Anthony's offense was to usurp the throne: *the couch*. Every chance he gets, Mr. Tompkins makes a nest on top of Anthony's backpack, leaving it covered with cat hair. Yet Anthony never complains. Repeatedly he's tried to win the cat over, bringing home salmon-flavored treats and catnip toys. But while Mr. Tompkins is only too glad to wolf down the treats, he still tries to take a chunk out of Anthony's hand as he feeds him.

Eva's come out of the kitchen. I look over at her. "Don't you want to pet Mr. Tompkins?" I ask, unable to resist.

Her smile tightens. "Maybe later." She looks over at Lloyd. "Don't forget, we need to stop at Pottery Barn for new bath mats for our up-stairs bathroom."

Oh, she's *good*. I have to give her that. She's good.

"You know, Eva," Lloyd says, "you might want to check that place on Clarendon Street, the one I was *telling* you about." He looks at her as if he's trying to remind her of something. "Lots of nice things there for the house."

"Oh, yes." She smiles. "But I don't know Boston. I'll wait for you. I'm afraid I'd get lost."

But Lloyd's insistent. "Just walk up through Union Park, cross Tremont, hang a right, and a take a left on Clarendon. Easy as pie."

She flushes. "Oh, I just get *so* confused with directions. . . ."

I realize what he's doing. He's trying to tell her to get lost. He wants to spend some time alone with me. On Valentine's Day. My heart melts.

But just then, the door opens. It's Anthony. Coming home, after being out all night again on one of his weekly disappearances.

And he's carrying his own bouquet of flowers.

There are moments of such sublime awkwardness that they become almost magical. This is one of them. Here we are, Lloyd and I, trying to get rid of Eva, when in walks Anthony. And the flowers in his hand are wrapped in pink Valentine's paper with lots of hearts. Eva doesn't know who the fuck this guy is, while Lloyd knows fully well—and all I want to do is slip under the rug.

"Uh, hi," Anthony says, noticing the company.

"Anthony," I say quickly, "you remember Lloyd? New Year's Eve?"

"We never officially met," Lloyd says, extending his hand to Anthony.

I jump up off the couch and snatch the flowers from Anthony without acknowledging them. I set them down on the coffee table. "Oh, well, then, Lloyd, this is Anthony. Anthony, this is Lloyd."

The two shake hands. "I notice Mr. Tompkins is pretty content there," Anthony observes.

"Yeah. Well, he misses me." I notice just the slightest defensive tone in Lloyd's voice.

"And this is Eva," I say, finishing the introductions.

"Nice to meet you," Anthony says. His big mitt completely swallows her tiny hand.

"And it is a *delight* to meet you," she gushes in that same syrupy tone I know so well. "Jeff has spoken *so* warmly about you."

No, I haven't. I totally haven't. Lloyd asked me how it was, living with Anthony, and I said, "He's no bother." That's it. He's *no bother.* That's *warm?* This woman is too fucking *much.*

Anthony blushes a little, looking over at me. "I brought you something," he says.

I look down at the flowers on the coffee table. Mr. Tompkins has jumped off Lloyd's lap and is now munching on the sunflower heads that hang off the side. "Hey!" I scold, whisking up the bouquet and rushing it to the kitchen. "Thanks," I call back to Anthony.

I know he expected a kiss, but I just can't. Not in front of Lloyd. Actually, more to the point, not in front of *Eva.* I don't want to give her the impression that I've moved on, that I've found someone new, that Lloyd is all hers.

But haven't I? *No,* I tell myself as I fill a vase with water, *I guess I haven't.* I snip the ends off the sunflowers with a pair of scissors. Okay, so maybe I've tried to convince myself that I *have* moved on. And yes, I *do* care about Anthony, but seeing Lloyd again has only made me wonder if Henry is right: if those feelings for Anthony exist simply because Lloyd has seemed unavailable.

I set the flowers in the vase, placing them on top of the refrigerator so Mr. Tompkins can't get them. He's far too fat to jump that high.

Then I notice the card. It has fallen out and landed on the floor. I stoop down, pick it up and debate whether to open it. Lloyd's just a few yards away in the living room. My curiosity wins out. *To Jeff,* the card reads. *With thanks for taking me in. Happy V Day. Love, Anthony.* This time my heart melts for *him.*

Jeff O'Brien, you are one fucked-up fool.

I walk back out to the living room. I can tell, very little conversation has transpired in my absence. "Mr. Tompkins would eat the drapes if I didn't watch him," I crack, using the cat to relieve the tension. Everyone laughs.

"I know!" Eva announces, her eyes twinkling with an idea. "Maybe *Anthony* would show me where this place is on Clarendon Street."

"What place?" he asks.

"Fresh Eggs," Lloyd tells him. "She's afraid she'll get lost."

"I'd be glad to." Anthony smiles. "I've just learned my way around Boston myself."

"Oh, *would* you?" She beams. "How kind. And this way we'll have a chance to get to know each other a little better. I have a feeling we're going to be *very* good friends."

I look at Anthony. He's still wearing the same clothes from the night before. His hair is matted down. He's unshaven, grimy. *What's the matter?* I'm thinking. *Your trick not have a shower?*

But I don't really think that Anthony leaves here once a week to spend the night with some trick. In the beginning he had disappeared on Wednesdays, then Thursdays, and now it's Sunday that he takes off, only to return back, on cue, some time late Monday afternoon. He leaves early in the morning for work and then doesn't come back until the next day. It's gotten so that I don't even ask anymore and he doesn't even tell me. It just happens.

I watch him leave with Eva, my emotions roiling. I hate when I get this way. So hostile to Eva, so petty with Anthony. I took over at Lloyd. It's as if he can read my thoughts.

"Come sit by me?" It's a question, not a command. I oblige. I sit down next to Lloyd again with a long sigh, dropping my head onto my chest.

"It was nice that he brought you flowers," Lloyd says.

"Whatever." I squint up at him. "Has she tried to get into your pants yet?"

Lloyd seems to blanch a little, but ignores the question. "I wish you would come see the house. It's coming along really nice. We plan to be open by next month. I hope you'll at least come for the opening party."

Mr. Tompkins has wormed his way between Lloyd and me. He settles his front half over Lloyd's left thigh and his back over my right.

I sigh again. "Lloyd, I thought it was clear when I came down last time. I can't put myself in a place where I'm going to get hurt once more. I'm not going to get my hopes up only to find you can't make a commitment." I pause. "At least with me. You had no problem making a commitment with Eva."

"I miss you, Jeff," he says simply.

I make a sound of annoyance. "You *can't* just come knocking at my door like this." I look at him. "Especially not with *her* in tow."

"Why don't you like her, Jeff?"

I laugh. "It's not about liking or disliking. She's obviously threatened by me and tries to neutralize me any chance she gets."

Lloyd huffs. "Well, maybe *you're* feeling threatened, too. Otherwise you wouldn't react so strongly."

I look at him. *"Don't.* Don't start playing Dr. Freud with me. You know I hate that." He sighs, resting his head on the back of the couch. "Besides, what's to feel threatened about? You have your life; I have mine."

"I guess you do." Now it's Lloyd's turn to sound a little piqued. "Who'd have thought some guy you met on New Year's Eve would *still* be here?"

I shrug. "I'm surprised myself."

Lloyd scoffs. "I have never in my life known you to put up with someone in your space. It took you *two years* to get used to *me.* What's changed, Jeff? Why do you let him stay?"

I don't know the answer. Part of it may be that I'm not writing, so I don't feel the need for privacy the way I used to." Back in the days when I toiled over my computer banging out freelance articles in our second bedroom, I'd needed silence to hear the muse sing. Now it doesn't matter when Anthony turns on MTV first thing in the morning. I just flop down next to him on the couch and we watch that cute gay kid and his military boyfriend on *The Real World.*

"There's just something about Anthony," I say. "Something that intrigues me."

"Well, he's very attractive," Lloyd says, sighing, as if that were the reason.

"No. I mean, yes, he is, but that's not what intrigues me." I pause. "Maybe it's because I've gotten kind of hooked on finding out more about him. He's like an assignment, in a way. Who is he? What's his story? Where's he from?"

Lloyd looks at me dumbfounded. "You mean you *still* don't know?"

I shake my head. "No. Just a few clues here and there."

"Jeff, he could be an *ax-murderer,*" Lloyd says.

"Yeah, he could be. But I bet it's something more interesting than that." I lean in close to Lloyd. It feels good to be this near him, even with all the issues between us. "He's a mystery. Once a week he goes out and doesn't come back until the next day."

"Have you asked him about it?"

"At first. But I didn't want to seem like I was prying. He's paying rent now—just a token, really, but he buys his own food. So he doesn't have to report in to me." I run my hand through my hair. "Early on, all he'd say is that he'd gone to see a friend. Now he says nothing at all, and I don't pursue it. But as far as I know, he has no friends in Boston other than me and Henry and a few of the other guys. And he's not seeing them."

Lloyd makes a face. "Sure he's not sleeping with Brent? It would be just like Brent to want to keep that a secret."

"I thought of that, but I don't think so. Anthony can see through Brent. He's told me so."

Lloyd strokes the back of Mr. Tompkins's head. "So what else makes him mysterious?"

"He never talks about his past. No relationships. No jobs. No family. He's admitted to coming from a suburb of Chicago, and once he said his father was an asshole. Another time he said something about not doing well in high-school algebra. But that's it. That's about all I know."

I don't tell him about the laminated photograph of Robert Riley. I just can't. I still feel guilty about going into Anthony's wallet. I've been wanting to dig further, maybe try to find where the photograph came from, but something stops me. I just can't do it.

Lloyd looks at me with concern. "Do you think he's hiding something?"

I sigh. "Hiding, running away, covering up—I don't know. Something."

Lloyd takes my hand in his. "Jeff, if you're living with him, having any kind of relationship with him, you *should* know all you can about him."

"Oh?" I raise an eyebrow. "And are we following our own advice?"

He backs off a little. "That's different, Jeff."

"How so?" He's given me the perfect opening; I'm not going to let it pass. "Maybe I only knew Anthony a few hours before I let him move in, but how much longer had you known Eva? A few months? Come on, Lloyd. Isn't Eva as much a mystery to you as Anthony is to me?"

He shakes his head in that stubborn, obstinate, superior way of his, the one that used to drive me mad when we lived together. "Jeff, I know a *lot* about who she is," he insists. "*Too* much, sometimes, even." He pauses. "Though I'll admit that a friend of hers tried to tell me something, but I cut him off."

"Why would you do that?"

He looks at me as if the answer is obvious. "Because she's a *friend*. And I don't like talking about friends behind their backs."

I lean in closer to him. I can smell his aftershave. I've missed that smell. Part of me just wants to kiss him and forget all this. Suddenly, in my mind it's eight years ago, and Lloyd and I are vacationing on St. Croix, and we haven't a care in the world and man, he looks so hot in that bright-blue Speedo. We dive into the water, splashing each other. We make love on the beach. But I catch myself. I have to say what I'm thinking.

"Lloyd, I'll be blunt with you. I think Eva is far more likely to turn out to be an ax-murderer than Anthony is. I think she's unstable. I get the sense she could go a little loco on you if you don't live up the image she's got in her head."

"Oh, please, Jeff . . ."

"I mean it, Lloyd. It's *you* she wants. Not a guest house in Provincetown. You could be opening up a *laundromat* together and she'd be just as into it."

His face grows stem. "Jeff, I meant what I said. I appreciate your concern, but I'm not comfortable talking about her behind her back."

Oh, if this isn't so typical Lloyd. "So you think I ought to be running around doing background checks on Anthony, but it's not okay for you and me to discuss *Eva!*"

"Jeff, the two situations are very different."

"Come on, Lloyd! You're—"

The door opens. We turn to look up at Anthony and Eva coming back inside, their cheeks rosy. They're smiling and laughing together.

"The store was closed," Eva says, "but what a wonderful time we had throwing snowballs at each other!"

"She's so much *fun!*" Anthony exclaims to Lloyd, who just smiles tightly.

"I felt like a teenager again," Eva gushes, hugging Anthony around the waist.

I stand and walk into the kitchen. This is all just too far out. Why the fuck did Lloyd come here today, anyway? He messes up my head with those damn flowers and then pulls back yet again, all hands-off, when I dare to talk about Eva. God, I *hate* her.

But I hate even more feeling so petty.

I turn around. Anthony has come into the kitchen behind me.

"Jeff," he whispers, his face all red and shiny from the cold, "if you and Lloyd want to be alone, I can go stay somewhere else tonight."

"No, no." I look from him over at the flowers he brought me, sitting on the top of the refrigerator. "Lloyd's not staying. They're going back to Provincetown tonight."

Anthony smiles. "Well, I'm glad. I have to admit I feel a little jealous. I know that's stupid, but I do."

My heart melts. Damn, it sure has a habit of doing that.

"It's not stupid at all," I tell Anthony. "And hey. I really appreciated the flowers."

"Happy Valentine's Day," Anthony says. I smile.

When we get back to the living room, Lloyd is putting on his coat. "Do you want to have dinner with us?" he asks. "After we get back from Pottery Barn?"

Eva takes my hands in hers. They're icy. "Oh, I'd so *love* for you to join us," she says, looking up at me with those eyes, as if I hadn't been nasty to her earlier, as if she were really being sincere. "You and Anthony both."

I look from her over to Lloyd. There's no question I would like to spend Valentine's Day with him. No question I'd like to sit across from him at a restaurant with a bottle of wine. No question I'd like to be with him tonight, so many happy Valentine's memories living between us. But not with *her* along. Not with her going on and on about all they have to do and all the plans they're making. *They, they, they.*

"Thanks, but I promised Anthony we'd go out," I say at last. I feel awful, especially when Lloyd looks away in disappointment. But in exchange I see a small, grateful smile creep across Anthony's face.

"Are you *sure?*" Eva's asking, busy with her gloves. "Oh, well, some other time, then. You must come down and visit us soon, Jeff. I'll cook a marvelous dinner!"

Anthony extends his hand to her, but she moves in for a tight hug instead. "Thank you *so* much, Anthony. I so enjoyed spending time with you. You *must* come with Jeff when he comes down to the Cape."

Lloyd comes over to me. We embrace. "Happy Valentine's Day, Cat," he whispers.

My throat is too tight to reply.

After they're gone, I let out a long sigh.

"I think Eva is going to write to you," Anthony says as he heads into the shower.

I look after him, puzzled. "Write me? Why?"

"I don't know. She asked for your E-mail. I hope it's okay that I gave it to her."

Whatever she has to say, I'm not sure I want to read it. My heart feels all melted down to nothing. I press my face into Lloyd's daisies, inhaling their tangy fragrance. From the shower I can hear Anthony singing: *"I'm naked without you . . ."*

His voice seems to dislodge Mr. Tompkins from the couch. The cat jumps down, stretches, then walks over to the door from which Lloyd has so recently departed. Plopping down his enormous body, he completely obliterates the doormat. As always, he's determined to wait there until Lloyd has returned.

A Few Hours Later on Route 3, Forty Miles South of Boston

Lloyd

"Lloyd," she's saying, "I haven't given you my Valentine's gift yet."

I grimace. It's dark, and it's started to rain slightly, a slushy, snowy mix. The wipers are having trouble keeping the windshield clear. I'm certainly not in the mood to be opening up Valentine's trinkets while trying to keep my eyes on the road. Besides, I'm still in a bad mood from the visit with Jeff. Yet again I'd gone to see him, made the effort, trying to get us back on track. I even brought him daisies. But he remains so intractable, so stubborn about accepting my venture with Eva, irrationally jealous of her and making outrageous claims.

Sure, I have my own worries about Eva, but *unstable?* Just *who's* unstable here? Who's the one who took in some unknown stray who keeps his past a deep, dark secret? *That's* not exactly the most stable act, in my opinion. Once more, Jeff has gotten caught up with a trick, just as he did with that Eduardo kid a few years ago, completely blind to what it's doing to *us*.

Us. Maybe such a construct no longer exists. Is it *over*, then? The thought hits me like a physical force. Could all those months of reconnection really have been leading nowhere? Is Jeff really so—

"Lloyd?"

I turn. Eva's leaning in closer to me, holding something in her hand. She switches on the overhead light. It's a small package wrapped in a piece of silk.

"Eva, I can't really . . ." I gesture with my head to the road in front of us.

"Oh." She nods. "Of course. Here, let me unwrap it for you."

I sigh. "Eva, you shouldn't have done anything. I didn't get you a gift. I'm sorry."

Part of me had, of course, expected her to do something. Part of me knew she wouldn't just let Valentine's Day pass without offering some token of her affection. It's sweet, it really is—and I truly believe that gift-giving is about the giving. If she *wants* to give me something, then she should. But still I feet awkward being empty-handed. True, I paid for dinner, but that didn't come wrapped in silk.

"It's okay, Lloyd," she says softly, reassuring me. "I didn't expect anything."

She unfolds the silk wrapping to reveal a small wooden box. "Hang on," I say, aware that I'm not fully participating in the romantic mood she's trying to set up. But there's an eight-wheeler coming up fast on my ass, and I really don't want to get us killed. I switch on my signal and more over to the right lane. The road is getting slushier. The wipers squeak across the glass.

"What's in the box?" I ask, a little reluctantly, even a little petulantly.

She lifts the lid. I can't see right away. "What do you think?" she asks.

"What is it?"

She holds the box up in front of my face.

"Eva! *Please!* I'm trying to drive here!"

She withdraws the box quickly. "I'm sorry." She makes a little sob. "It's just that this *means* something to me. And you seem as if you don't even *want* it."

I sigh. "Let me see it again." She holds the box out in her hand. It's a ring. A ring with a green stone. "What—what is that?"

She smiles weakly. "It was Steven's. I bought it for him on our fifth anniversary. It's an emerald, Lloyd. To match your eyes."

I'm flabbergasted. "Eva," I say slowly, "I can't accept that."

"Of course you can!"

"No, I can't. It was—yours and Steven's. You should keep it!"

"Oh, darling," she says, leaning over toward me again. "I want to give it to you. For all you've given to me."

"First of all," I say, my eyes in the rearview mirror, "please don't call me 'darling.' Second of all, I can't accept it because it's just too much. Too intimate. Too much like we're lovers, and we're *not*, Eva. We are *friends*. We are *business* partners. We are not *lovers* and *that* is a lover's gift!"

There's silence, except for the steady squeaking of the windshield wipers. I reach up and switch off the overhead light.

"Eva?"

No response from the darkness.

"Eva?"

Suddenly she bursts out with an enormous sob. As if all at once she'd been stabbed with a spear up her gut. I jump, grabbing tight onto the wheel, trying to keep the car steady. I catch a quick glimpse of her as we pass under a streetlamp. Her face is contorted, her mouth open. It looks as if she's baying at the moon.

"Eva, please!"

"Stop this car!" she demands. "Stop—this—car!"

"Eva, I can't stop—"

"Pull into that rest stop there! Stop this car!"

"Eva, I'm not—"

"Stop this car!"

I swerve all at once, feeling the slushy road under me, praying to God we won't skid off the road. Slamming on my brakes after pulling into the rest stop, I turn, ready to tell her to stop being so crazy, that she almost caused us to have an accident . . .

. . . when she opens up her door and runs off into the night.

I sit in stunned silence. *What the fuck just happened here?*

I feel the cold and dampness from the open door. I sit staring at it for a few seconds. Finally I reach over and pull it closed.

I will not enable this behavior, I think. *I will not go running out there looking for her. That is what she wants me to do. I will sit here and wait for her to come back. It is cold and rainy and she will come back in eventually. Hell, I should just drive off and leave her. That would . . .*

Ahead of me several yards there's a car parked. I watch as the driver's-side door opens, momentarily lighting up the interior. A man steps out, pulling a baseball cap far down onto his head. He slams the door and the light goes off. I hear a beep sound. An automatic security device. I think I can discern the man walk into the woods on the side of the rest stop.

Where Eva has fled.

Holy Jesus, I think. *I can't leave her out there now, with some guy . . .*

I take a deep breath and open my car door. It's just above freezing, thank God, but it's still cold, especially with the rain-snow mix sliding down the back of my jacket. I step through the slushy mess up onto the grass. "Eva!" I shout. "Where the fuck are you?'

I can't believe this is happening. I take a few steps toward the woods and call her name again. Nothing. No sound. No sight of her.

I venture past the first thicket of trees. In front of me stands an aluminum chain-link fence. A section has been cut from it, enough space for a person to pass through. I suddenly realize why, and *who* has done it. Men stop here and go into the woods to blow each other. Javitz used to tell me all about places like this. Jeff's recounted a few escapades here himself. *Oh, Christ,* I think. *That's what that guy from the car was looking for. He saw someone run in here. Wait'll he finds out she's a woman!*

I push on ahead. "Eva!"

I hear her before I see her. A low, wracking sob. I make out a figure huddled beside a tree. I approach her. She doesn't even look at me. She just keeps crying softly to herself.

"Eva, come with me," I say gently, taking her by the shoulders. She doesn't protest, just allows herself to be led away passively. On our way out, I spot the man from the car lurking in the bushes. *God, even in the snow and the rain they come,* I think with disbelief. "Sorry, buddy," I say under my breath as we pass. "Nothing here for you."

Though right now I'd gladly hand Eva over to him.

Once we're back in the car, I look sternly at her, though she keeps her eyes averted.

"Eva, something like this can never happen again. Do you understand?"

She turns her big round eyes up at me. "I know you slept with Tyrone. Were you never going to tell me?"

I don't know how to respond right away. I open my mouth but say nothing.

She unlatches the glove compartment and withdraws a Kleenex, dabbing at her eyes. "Oh, Lloyd, forgive me for being so silly. My behavior was atrocious. *Of course* it will never happen again."

I still don't say anything, pulling back in my seat instead to watch her carefully.

"It's just that I felt you and I were friends. Good friends. When you didn't tell me about Tyrone, I felt as if you didn't trust me. I was worried about a pattern starting between us." She looks at me suddenly, as if *I'd* been the one to misbehave, as if *I* were the one who needed scolding. "A pattern of deception, Lloyd. I can't tolerate that. If we're to have an honest, healthy relationship, there can be no deception."

"No deception," I repeat back emotionlessly.

"There needs to be one-hundred-percent honesty." She takes a deep breath to calm herself. "I suppose it's been building inside me. That's why I reacted so outrageously just now. I am sorry, Lloyd. It was so unlike me."

I wonder.

"Of *course* we're not lovers." She gives a sudden laugh and looks over at me. "What gave you the idea we *were?* I certainly don't think of you in that way, Lloyd, and I'm sure *you* don't think of *me* that way, either!" She sighs dramatically. "You see, my emotions have just been on edge. I wanted to give you that ring not for any other reason than to express my gratitude to you for giving me this new lease on life. I'm not sure if you can understand just how important that's been for me."

"I know it's important, Eva."

She reaches over and pats my hand. "Do you know why it mattered so much? Today, of all days? Not only is it Valentine's Day, but it's"—her voice chokes up again, and the tears return, though a bit less noisy this time—"it's also Steven's and my anniversary. We were married on Valentine's Day. Today was always so special for us: all the little gifts he'd leave hidden around the house for me; all the little sweet things he'd do"—she covers her face in her hands—"oh, Lloyd, I miss him so!"

I hesitate for a moment, not wanting to do it, but I do anyway. I put my arm around her. I can't help it. I'm such a sucker. Too softhearted for my own good, Jeff often says. I'm taken in by every sad story anyone ever wants to tell.

But she *can't* be lying. Not about *this.* I know how much she loved Steven. Running out of the car is still unacceptable, but I guess I can understand her grief. There are times I still feel like running away, as far and as fast as my legs can take me, and it's been *four years* since Javitz died. My heart softens toward her and I tighten my arm over her shoulders.

"Please take the ring," she says in a broken voice. She's retrieved it from the floor. "You don't know how happy it would make me."

"Eva, I'm not Steven," I say as tenderly as I can. "You can't turn me into him."

Her hands grasp my face. "Oh, darling, Lloyd. Of *course* you're not. You're *you.* I don't want you to be Steven. I want you to be *you,* the wonderful man who's given me so much." Our faces are only a couple of inches apart. I can smell her breath, slightly stale. I can feel the rush of her blood still thudding through her body. "Please accept this gift from me."

I sigh in resignation. She removes her hands and finds the ring in her lap. She slips it onto my finger. "There," Eva says. "It fits you perfectly."

"Thank you" is all I can say, softly and without emotion. I turn and grip the steering wheel. The emerald flashes in the glare of a passing truck. I turn the ignition.

It's going to be a long drive back to Provincetown.

The First Week of March,
A Skyscraper Downtown

Henry

Once again I'm carrying a case full of goodies—the same things, in fact, I would've taken to Mardi Gras had I left with Jeff, Anthony, Shane, and Brent this morning as I'd originally planned, on a nine A.M. flight to New Orleans. It was to be a two-city circuit extravaganza, with a first stop at Mardi Gras, then on to the Winter Party in Miami. We couldn't choose between them, so we decided to do both. Except then I backed out altogether.

I was sorry to cancel. I'd had a great time last year, and I know Jeff is disappointed. He says I've been neglecting him lately, and maybe I have. But he's got *Anthony* to keep him company now, hasn't he? Why go and watch the two of them nuzzle on the dance floor for four and a half days? Anthony's time is soon to be up; Jeff is going to tire of him soon. I know the routine very well. Jeff's last few infatuations—Alexei and Zed and that kid from Missouri—had been all over him, barely allowing me a word in edgewise. Until, of course, they overstayed their welcomes and Jeff bid them *so long, farewell, auf Wiedershen, good-bye.* Of course, *then* Jeff was all too glad to have me back in his life.

So, no, I wasn't *that* upset about not going to New Orleans and Miami. This is one romance of Jeff O'Brien's where I'm not going to play voyeur. Besides, Kenneth promised me a much better time. With Kenneth, I'm never on the sidelines.

I take the elevator up to his penthouse. This is a repeat visit. Actually, it's my *third* time with Kenneth, probably the wealthiest of all my clients. And this is to be my first overnight job. A cool *grand*.

Even before I get to his door, I can hear the music. The low, steady, throbbing bass beat coming through the walls. I knock. It takes a few times before Kenneth hears me.

When the door opens, I can't believe what I'm seeing.

The penthouse has been transformed. It's dark, with all the furniture pushed up against the walls. A revolving disco ball has replaced the usual chandelier, and dry ice on the floor sends fog throughout the room. Donna Summer is playing in stereophonic sound. Her comeback club hit cover of Bocelli's *Con Te Partirs.* "I Will Go With You."

"Do not be afraid, afraid," Kenneth's singing along to the lyrics, holding out his hand to draw me inside.

I do my best to suppress a little gasp. Kenneth is shirtless, and he's shaved off all his gray chest hair, making his tits look even longer and floppier than usual. His skin shines bright pink, and above his tight black Lycra pants a tire tube of flesh bounces as he gyrates to the music.

Can you guess Kenneth's fetish? You got it. He has a thing for circuit boys. When he discovered I was one of them, it all came tumbling out. How once, years ago, he'd done the scene, but felt he couldn't keep up: graying, balding, putting on weight. But instead of railing against body fascism and the obsession on youth, Kenneth has turned it all into a fantasy. He picks up *In Newsweekly* and *Genre* just to drool over the photos of shirtless boys at the clubs. He subscribes to *Circuit Noize* and keeps track of every party on his calendar—when it's happening, where it's held, and how many boys are there—even though he no longer attends. From *International Male* and *California Muscle* he orders sexy little numbers like the Lycra pants he's wearing, putting them on as soon as they arrive and jacking off to his image in the mirror. He might not be a part of the scene, but he knows it very well.

"I fantasize about wearing spandex in a huddle of manflesh on a dance floor," he confided to me. "I fantasize about getting a tribal tattoo around my bicep. I fantasize about taking Ecstasy and Special K and getting really twisted listening to Cher sing 'Believe' over and over again."

He's not being ironic. That's the thing. You're probably laughing and shaking your head at him, but Kenneth is *sincere* about this. He's totally, completely serious. Believe me, he makes me want to crack up even more than the guy with the shoe fetish. Kenneth is Brent raised to the nth degree, Brent gone bald and fat and completely crazy, locked away in a penthouse at age fifty.

I don't mean to make light of it. Please don't take it that way. Kenneth is an affluent corporate exec, a pillar of the business community, and not an unattractive guy. The times just passed him by before he'd had his fill. Married until he was thirty-five, the father of two girls, Kenneth spent the last decade chasing young muscle boys, desperately trying to prove he could still keep up. Jeff and I have seen him around for years, at Buzz or Machine on Saturday nights, after hours at Rise, or at Tea Dance at the Boatslip in Provincetown. He would be there shaking his tush, swinging his love beads or whatever jewelry happened to be in fashion that year, licking boys' armpits in an Ecstasy haze. He was, in a word, *tragic*. I remember once Jeff pulled me aside and made me promise never, *ever* to let him get to that point.

But you know what? There's always been something about Kenneth that I admired. True, he cut a sad figure, a lost and lonely ghost dancing by himself with his eyes closed. *But good for him, too*, I always thought. *Good for him for not going "gentle into that good night."*

Turning the big five-oh, however, had finally put an end to Kenneth's ventures onto the dance floor. Circuit culture might not be dominated by twinks, but there is an age limit, especially if you've committed the gay cardinal sin and allowed yourself to (horrors!) *look your age!* Now Kenneth lives only with memories and fantasies, and the wistful knowledge that the party's still going on as gaily as ever—without him.

So what does he do? He turns his penthouse into his own private version of the Winter Party. His own—and mine.

"Come on, Hank, dance with me!" Kenneth exclaims. I smile. feeling a little silly, but I do my best.

Kenneth presses up against me. "Got to get rid of these clothes," he says, pulling my sweater up over my head and then attacking the buttons of my flannel shirt. In moments I'm shirtless, hard and dry against Kenneth, who's soft and wet.

"Dance for me," he says suddenly, backing away. "Dance like you would at a circuit party. Come on, baby. Show me."

I laugh. "It's a little hard without the drugs."

"Ah!" Kenneth dashes over to a side table. He comes back with a couple of small pills in his hand. "Let's bump!"

My heart breaks at the man's awkward eagerness. But if this scene is to be done right, a little X will help. Kenneth assures me he got the drug from a reputable source, that there's no PCP or anything hidden in the pill. I trust him and accept his gift, as much as Jeff's voice is scolding me in my head.

"And look," Kenneth says, gesturing toward the wall. There's a cooler filled with bottles of spring water. "Everything we need."

So we dance. Donna Summer segues into Madonna's "Beautiful Stranger" and then some older stuff from the late eighties and early nineties, when Kenneth had been making the rounds: C&C Music Factory, Real McCoy, CeCe Peniston, Rozalla, and, reaching way back, that old classic "So Many Men, So Little Time." The X gets me pumped and I do indeed start to dance as if I were with Jeff in New Orleans and not with some old fat guy in a Boston penthouse.

And you know what? It's *just as good*. Somehow, it's just as good. That's important to understand. *I have just as much fun.* I look over into Kenneth's eyes and see how happy he is. How ecstatic, really, and it's not just the drug doing it. It's the fantasy; it's the illusion. I've made it real for him. I've made him happy.

See, Kenneth is a good guy. He gives money to AIDS and gay causes. He doesn't speak ill of other people, and he's a good dad to his girls. How can anyone begrudge him his fantasy?

I pull off my pants and open my carrying case. "How do you like this?" I ask, holding up a gold Jocko squarecut. I actually wore this at the Morning Party on Fire Island a few years ago, back when there still *was* a Morning Party.

"Oh, Hank, put it on!" Kenneth urges.

So Hank does. And then we dance some more. We dance all night, in fact, and well into the dawn, just as we would have at any circuit party, our hands in each other's pants, our tongues in each other's mouths. If not for the sun gradually illuminating the Boston skyline outside Kenneth's window, we could be in New Orleans at Mardi Gras. As far as I'm concerned, we are.

The Next Day, the Real Mardi Gras

Jeff

You're probably expecting me to describe all sorts of revelries here. Scenes of utter decadence. Crazed, mind-altering experiences. Hunky boys pulling down their pants to expose cocks and asses in exchange for strings of sparkly beads. Walking knee-deep through beer cans on Bourbon Street. Squeezing into Oz to dance to the awesome sounds of Manny Lehman until the sun is coming up and then stumbling outside to have sex in the street.

I can do that. I can tell you how we all immediately get shirtless and tweaked and parade through the streets, Shane in cutoff Lucky jeans, and Anthony and I in matching white Sauvage squarecuts. A week in the tanning booths in Boston has given our pale Northern skin enough of a healthy glow to pass under the Southern sun. Mardi Gras is all it's supposed to be: loud, riotous, colorful, dissolute, profane, wicked, and utterly shameless.

But no. I'm not going to get into all that. Truth be told, my mind just isn't on the scene. My mind is somewhere else, and that's what I'm going to talk about now.

Anthony. He's become an obsession with me. Oh, not him, really. It's the mystery of who he is, what he's hiding, where he comes from, what he was doing all those years he claims to have been just drifting. As I watch him dancing, strings of beads swinging from around his neck, he's oblivious to all the lustful stares around him. But I see him not as some sexy boy toy but rather as the subject of an article, a profile, an investigation. It's as if he's an assignment from the *Boston Globe* or *New York Times.*

Ever since Lloyd's visit on Valentine's Day, when he'd pronounced it my obligation to discover whatever I could about Anthony (even if sanctimoniously declining the same for himself and Eva), I've become a man determined. Maybe because it rekindles my reporter's instincts, three years dormant. Maybe because it simply takes my mind off Lloyd. Whatever it is, I've resolved to uncover Anthony's past—whether he wants me to or not.

"You're missing Henry, aren't you, Jeff?"

"Huh?"

It's Shane, leaning in toward me, all knowing eyes and self-satisfied smile. We're standing on a side street. Someone's puking into the gutter only a few yards away. "You seem so distracted this weekend," Shane says, "and I know what it is."

He has no clue. Sure, I'm annoyed at how absorbed Henry's gotten with this escort shit. I never see him anymore. But it's not Henry I'm thinking about at the moment.

Shane has his own ideas, however. He thinks because *he's* preoccupied with Henry, *everybody* is. He has a little spiel he wants to deliver and nothing's going to stop him.

"You've gotten pretty used to Henry tailing you around, haven't you, Jeff?" He smiles nastily. "Now he's found something on his own, and I think you're having a hard time with that."

I look at him impatiently. "Why are you harassing me?"

He smiles. "'Cuz you're the type of guy who can *use* a little harassment. I think you get your own way far too often."

I smile back at him. "You don't like me, do you, Shane?"

"Aww," he says, "let's not have any hard feelings." He grins. "Let's be friends, okay? Shake?"

My look turns into bemusement. I shake his hand.

Zap!

"Yow!" I pull back my hand. There was a sting, a sharp prick of electricity. Shane's cracking up.

His latest gimmick: a hand-zapper.

"Who are you, *Harpo Marx?*" I try to wave him away.

He reaches across me to place his palm against Anthony's abs. "Whoa, baby!" Anthony laughs, the zapper tingling his stomach.

"Okay, enough!" I command. "Go back inside the bar and dance, you two."

"You coming, Jeff?" Anthony asks.

"In a while."

I stand off to the sidelines, watching him. The mystery's unraveling, slowly, bit by bit. Back home, under lock and key, in the top drawer of my desk, is a print-out of several dozen names, followed by a social security number and place and date of death. All of the names are Robert Riley.

I showed it to Henry. It was the last time I'd seen Henry, in fact, and the *first* time we'd gotten together in over a week. Shane's right about one thing: I had gotten used to Henry being a much more frequent presence in my life than he's been of late.

"You *could* return my calls once in a while," I said to him.

Henry smiled. "Sorry, Jeff. You know how it is."

"Actually, I *don't*, and hope I never do. Any more shoe fetishists?"

He laughed. "No, but I had a guy into clothespins."

I leveled a look at him. "I don't even *want* to know."

Henry took the paper from my hands. "So tell me about this list. What is it? What does it tell you?"

I ran a hand through my hair, happy to move off the topic of his escorting. "It's from the Social Security Death Index," I explained. "You can get it online." I'd already told him about the laminated newspaper photo in Anthony's wallet and dating it to approximately 1985 to 1988. "I figured if it was in the newspaper, it was probably either an obituary or a news story. So I printed out all the Robert Rileys who died in those years. As you can see, there are quite a few—too many to narrow down. Even several in Illinois, which is where Anthony said he came from."

"It's a fairly common name," Henry observed. "But maybe it wasn't an obituary. Riley doesn't have to be dead."

"Exactly," I continued, lifting the next sheet out of the folder. "But finding all the Robert Rileys living in the United States would have been useless. So this is a print-out of all of the Robert Rileys living in Illinois, or at least listed in the white pages. You can get that online, too. Still quite a hefty number, as you can see."

"But Anthony could have *moved*," Henry pointed out. "He didn't have to still be in Illinois. By the mid-eighties, he would have been—what? About fifteen or sixteen?"

I nodded again. "Yes. It really *is* the proverbial needle in the haystack. I just wish I could determine what newspaper the photo is from. If I could do that, I could check the index for Robert Riley, see why his photo had been in the paper. I seem to recognize the typeface, but it doesn't match any of the papers I know, like the *Globe* or the *Herald* or *Bay Windows* or the *New York Times*. I could also probably recognize the *Los Angeles Times* and the *Washington Post,* but it's not them, either. The clipping was very different in style."

Henry rubbed his chin. "Well, how about the *Chicago Tribune?* You probably don't know offhand what that looks like, and if Anthony was from a Chicago suburb—"

"Been there already. I went over to the library and checked the index to the *Tribune.* No Robert Riley for those years."

"So who do you think Robert Riley was? His father? A lover?"

I sighed. "I considered the father angle, but the photograph's too young. He looked to be in his thirties, which would have meant he'd had Anthony when he was a young teenager. Possible, but not likely. Of course, there's the possibility that, if it *were* an obituary, they could've used a younger photo, which would mean Riley *could've* been his father—but the photo seemed very contemporary, very eighties. The hair, the tie. Plus, you have to factor in what Anthony has said about his father. That he was an asshole. Which seems to discount his carrying his photo around in his wallet all these years."

"So a lover, then."

I made a face. "Maybe. Except he's also said he's never had a relationship. None."

"He could be lying."

I shrugged. "Could be. I just don't sense he is. I get the feeling whatever little bit he's told me is true. It's not lies I'm dealing with here—it's the absence of information. But one thing is clear. Whoever this Riley was, he *mattered* to Anthony, for him to keep his picture around all this time."

"A friend, then. An uncle. A—*teacher!*"

"Any of those could be possible." I let out a very long sigh. "He mentioned getting a two-year degree, but won't say where. Says it's not important. Nothing I'd know, or care to." I looked over at Henry. "So tell me. What does a guy do between high school graduation and age twenty-nine? He has to do *something.* The only thing I can say for sure that he did during that time is work on his body, because you're not *born* with a body like that. Abs like this take a lot of time and dedication. *Years.* So he had both the time, money, and—just as important—the *inclination* to pursue a fitness program."

Henry was watching me keenly. "You know, you're *glowing,* Jeff. You're *into* this."

I smiled. "Well, it *is* kind of like I'm back on the job, researching a piece."

"But *why* the interest?" Henry drew close. "What's the motivation? There's no promise of a byline here."

I considered the question. And standing here on the sidewalks of

New Orleans, I consider i ... ocession of masked revelers sway around me. ... ...ic answer. I just know I'm *hooked*. Yes, it's about Anti... ...ting to know just who this guy is who's sleeping on my couch—...ave grown very fond of over the past few weeks. But it's about *me, too*—about Jeff O'Brien, who in another life won awards for his reporting, who was respected and admired, who boasted he could find out any story, anywhere, anytime. It is, perhaps, an exercise to see if I still have what it takes. To discover if, somewhere under my malaise and grief and disappointment, I'm still the same good reporter I've always been.

But I'm not sure what the next step is. I've hit a brick wall. Unless I can determine what newspaper that clipping comes from, I might never narrow the list of Robert Rileys down to the right one. And never discover his connection to Anthony. Or anything about Anthony's past. God, I wish I could talk about this with somebody.

I realize that Shane's right about another thing: I *do* miss Henry like crazy. Even more right now than I miss Lloyd. This escort thing is out of control. I expected after a couple of tricks, he'd give it all up as a lark. But he's seeing two, three guys a week now. Shane might think it's all fine and dandy, but I fear getting a call that Henry's been arrested. Or beaten up. Or killed. I worry that Henry might get raped, that he'll seroconvert, that he'll turn jaded and cynical and hard.

Most of all, I just miss having Henry on the other end of the phone or sitting across from me at my apartment, listening to me ramble about whatever was happening in my life. Or *not* happening. But whenever I call Henry these days, I usually get his machine, or if I *do* manage to catch him at home, he's either heading out to turn some trick or just too beat to talk.

His absence from my life has put a lot of things in sharp relief. I realize how alone I really am. I'm aware that since Javitz's death I haven't permitted myself to get close to too many people. Lloyd's right when he says that I've distanced from our old friends. As much as I might value my extended gay family on the dance floor, there's no denying that I haven't let any of them in too deep.

But something changed with Henry. Somehow, I let him in, bit by bit. Henry isn't like Brent or most of the other guys. He really *listens* when I talk. He's *there* when I need him. He even knows stuff about me that I haven't told him. He just figures it out, and Henry's usually right, though I'm often reluctant to admit it.

Okay, Jeff, no more feeling sorry for yourself, I think. *You're at fucking Mardi Gras, and the boys here on the gay block are beautiful.*

I consider going back inside to join Shane and Anthony on the dance floor. I've picked up on the first strains of Amber's "Sexual" in the mix: all the boys are chanting, "Li-da-di, li-da-di, li-da-di, li-da-di." But—and this just shows where my head's at, because I don't think I've ever felt this way before—*I'm just not in the mood to dance.*

I watch as the boys swarm onto the floor to wiggle in with Shane and Anthony. Billy, Adam, Eliot, Oscar. I'd met them in Lauderdale a couple of years ago, and we're all sharing a suite of rooms here in New Orleans. Billy and Adam live in D.C. and served as our hosts for the Cherry Ball last year. Eliot's from San Diego, and Oscar's from Atlanta. Each one in turn looks over at me, gesturing for me to join them. I blow a kiss but I don't move.

"Jeff, come on, you love this song," Anthony says, suddenly behind me, grabbing my arm.

"Let me just finish my beer."

He looks at me with concern. "You okay?"

"I'm fine."

"You sure?" He places the palm of his hand on my chest.

I smirk. "If my heart's still beating, I am."

Anthony kisses me lightly. "It is." He smiles. "You want to take a walk?"

"What? And leave a good song?"

Anthony nods. "Come on."

I put down my beer and take his hand. We walk off down Bourbon Street. It's a crazy fever pitch of activity out here. We don't speak, just soak up the sights and sounds. A juggler in a gold lamé thong. A heavy woman singing opera from a balcony.

It doesn't take long for us to wander a few blocks, where it suddenly turns very hetero. Anthony and I walk hand in hand into a mob of drunken straight boys.

"Faggots," I hear someone call.

Anthony's grip tightens on my hand.

"Just keep walking," I tell him.

"Lookit the fags holdin' hands," some brute bellows. "Isn't that sweet?"

I can feel Anthony trembling. My anger is surging, but my survival skills pull rank. We round a corner, heading smack into a crowd of people. A policeman stands not far away.

"No matter where we go," I mutter. "It's not fucking safe anywhere."

"On the dance floor," Anthony says. "It's safe there."

I look up at him and smile. "Yeah. It's safe there."

We find a spot under a trellised porch covered with vines and sit against the building. We have a good view of the festivities in the street, but we're hidden somewhat. Protected. Anthony sits close to me, still holding my hand.

"You're not just missing, Henry, are you?" he asks finally. "It's also Lloyd, isn't it?"

I look over at him. "I've told you. Lloyd never goes to circuit parties."

"You just miss him in general. I can tell."

I shrug. A big black transsexual with exposed breasts throws a handful of beads at us. I stand and unzip my pants, flashing my dick, and she hoots. I turn back to Anthony. "Truth be told, I think it's over between Lloyd and me," I tell him as I sit back down.

"You've thought that before."

I sigh. I've only known Anthony a few months, but the kid's picked up quite a bit. "Yes, I suppose I have. And things got good again and we seemed to be giving it one more try. Our last best chance, in a way. But that tanked pretty fast." I let my voice and my thoughts trail off. "But why go there right now, huh? Why get all serious when we're in the midst of all this revelry?" I try playfully nuzzling Anthony's nose.

"Well, I want to go there because I want to *know*." Anthony's voice is serious and he keeps his gaze steady at me. "I want to know what your feelings are for him."

"I see." I ignore another string of beads that lands at my feet. "Well, okay. My feelings. I love Lloyd. You know that."

"Yes. I know that he's family. Even more than the way family is defined by straights."

I smile, remembering my words. "Why do I feel as if you want to a add a 'blah blah blah' to the end of that?"

Anthony leans in closer to me, his blue eyes plaintive. "You know how I feel about you, Jeff, don't you?"

I tousle his hair as I might a child's. "No. How do you feel about me?"

Anthony laughs. He leans back, then quickly sits forward again, as if he had the words on the tip of his tongue. But he stops, shaking his head. All at once he jumps up, and he begins to sing. Yes, *sing*. As if we were in some gay movie musical.

"*Don't . . . you . . . know . . . that when you touch . . . me . . . baby . . . that it's torture?*"

Amber. He's doing Amber. From the dance floor. I'm flabbergasted.

He spreads his arms out wide, singing off-key and totally getting the words wrong. A couple of passing revelers start mimicking him, serving as impromptu backup singers.

"I watch your mouth when you're speaking. Stu-u-u-udy your body when you walk out of the room. You don't know what you do tooooooo—this heart of mine!"

He falls down on his knees in front of me. The guys behind him applaud, but he's oblivious to them. He's looking up at me with the widest, most adorable eyes I think I've ever seen. I cup his cheeks in my hands.

"You crazy, sweet thing, you," I say.

"Is that all you feel about me?" he asks. "That I'm sweet?"

I smile affectionately. "The whole *point* of that song, sweetheart, is that it's all about *sex*. That's what she's singing about."

Anthony's face clouds over. "It's more than the sex for me, how I feel about you."

There goes my heart again, melting. "And it is for me, too, Anthony. It is for me, too."

He sighs and returns to his place sitting next to me. "But you're not like—you know—you're not in love with me or anything."

I run my hand through his cornsilk hair. "Look, Anthony. When you've been going round the rodeo as long as I have, you just don't use words or phrases like that very easily. There's *twelve years* pulsating between Lloyd and me. I can't just put a knife in that. You get what I'm saying?"

Anthony nods but says nothing.

"I *do* like you," I tell him. "I like you a lot. I don't know. Maybe all this is happening for a reason. I believe in fate, you know. Maybe it was fate meeting you the same night that Lloyd told me he was buying a house with somebody else."

"But you still love him."

I sigh. "Yeah. Yeah, I do. But maybe I have to face up to the fact that I was daydreaming when I thought we'd ever get back together. Maybe a few romantic times together last year just turned my head."

"So I'm what they call the rebound," Anthony says, turning his face to took at me. I touch his cheek.

"We can use other people's definitions of circumstances and relationships, or we can make up our own." I look at him just as intently as he looked at me earlier. "But I can tell you this much. If we're going to have *any* kind of relationship, we need honesty. I've just been honest with you. How about returning the favor?"

"What do you mean?"

"Okay, for starters, where do you go every week when you disappear? I've stopped asking about it, because I felt it wasn't any of my business. But since we're getting closer here—"

Anthony closes his eyes. "I can't tell you, Jeff. I'm sorry. But I can't tell you."

"Look. I found a bus schedule under the couch. Are you taking the bus somewhere? Is that why you're gone overnight?"

Anthony says nothing.

I sigh. "Anthony, I want to respect your privacy, but you can't talk about wanting a relationship with me on the one hand and then not tell me anything about yourself."

He opens his eyes to look at me defensively. "I've told you stuff."

"Oh, come *on*. I don't even know the name of the town you were born in."

"Lake Bluff."

"Okay. Well, how about your parents? You never talk about them."

"My father's dead."

"And your mother?"

"She's still alive."

I laugh. "Come on. This is what I *mean.*"

"What? I'm answering your questions!"

"One-word answers. And it's more than just facts and dates." I scowl over at him. "I just can't believe you spent your whole life before coming out as gay without having a *single* significant relationship."

"Why not?"

"Because—because—it just doesn't happen, that's why!"

"Maybe not for you, but it did for me."

"Come *on*, Anthony. You can't see why I have questions? You can't see why I wonder? You're so mysterious about your past and then you disappear once a week to someplace you can't tell me about! What *is* it? A wife and kid hidden away somewhere? A rich sugardaddy you have to visit? A maiden aunt? A monastery? *What?*"

"No, Jeff, it's not—"

"Then what is it?" My voice rises without my even being aware of it. "Tell me what it *is!*"

"I can't tell you, Jeff!" Anthony stands up abruptly. "Okay? *I just can't tell you!*"

He seems as if he might cry, as if he's on the verge of a major fit, but then he calms down. "I just can't tell you right now, Jeff," he says. *"Please* accept that."

I stand up beside him and put my arms around him. "Okay, buddy.

It's okay. I'm sorry if I got you worked up." I kiss his ear. "You can't tell me right now. Okay. I *do* accept that. Because it means someday you *will* be able to tell me, right?"

"I hope so," Anthony says quietly.

"Well, well, well!" A voice from behind suddenly startles both of us. We look around. Brent. With three other guys in flower-print sarongs. Even from this far away I can tell they're majorly fucked up.

"Oh, Jesus," I groan.

"Well, will you look at these two lovebirds humping on the streets," Brent says, elbowing one of the other boys. "Don't they make for a pretty postcard from New Orleans!"

"Brent, we're having a conversation," I say, completely vexed.

"A *conversation!* Do gay men actually *have* conversations at Mardi Gras?"

"Yes, gay *men* do," I snarl. *"Boys,* however, are apparently incapable of such behavior."

"Oh, *my!* Quick! Somebody get a pad and pencil! Jeff is getting *wry!"* His gaggle of sarong boys all laugh hysterically. "Somebody call the writers for *Will and Grace!"*

"I'm going to punch him," I whisper, more to myself than Anthony. "I'm actually going to *fucking punch him."*

"Hey, Brent," Anthony says. "You know the guys we're staying with? Eliot, the tall, dark, *really cute* guy with the amazing brown eyes? He thinks you're hot."

"No *way,"* Brent says.

"Total way," Anthony says. "They're in dancing with Shane right now."

Brent sparkles. "Okay. See you boys later." He turns to his entourage. "You can either come with me or stay here and have a *conversation."* They elect to follow him back to the bar.

I look up at Anthony with bemusement. "Eliot will have your head on a silver platter."

Anthony sits back down and laughs. "Got rid of him, though, didn't I?"

I sit down myself and kiss him. "You never cease surprising me, kiddo."

"Jeff, I love you."

I smile. "Oh, be careful where you go, my friend. Others before you have trod that very same path and later wished fervently that they'd taken a detour."

"I don't care. I've never felt this way before in my life. I love you."

I put my arm back around his shoulders. I know it's not love. It's infatuation; it's lust; it's gratitude; it's all those wonderful pheromones bouncing around inside both of us. Of *course* Anthony would think he's in love. He came out into the world of circuit parties and gym queens and easy, fast, furious sex. Hell, the very words he used to express his so-called love for me were taken from the lyrics of a throbbing circuit anthem. Of *course* he'd confuse all of that with love.

But love it isn't. That much I know for sure. You can only talk about love after being in a relationship, up and down, around and about, back and forth. You can only talk about love after surviving sickness and death and betrayal and anger and jealousy. You can only talk about love after you've untangled the emotional fabric of your own life. And neither of us seems to be in any position to do that right now.

Oh, maybe I'm being far too dogmatic. I *do* have that tendency. Javitz used to scold me for it. The world is never as black and white as I might presume. I can't play the hardened sophisticate all the time. I can't deny that the sheer youthful ingenuousness of Anthony's words has touched me. Is it really so long ago that I myself was so young?

I tighten my grip on his shoulder and pull him in closer. Together we stare out into the mind-numbing assault on our senses. A clown is fellating a naked man in a cowboy hat. A woman covered in gold metallic paint gyrates on the shoulders of a midget. The rhythmic disco beat pulses down the street from Oz.

"You're not in any trouble, are you?" I ask softly, close to Anthony's ear. "If you are, and you need help—"

"Thanks, Jeff," Anthony responds, leaning his head down on my shoulder. "That, I can assure you. I'm not in any trouble."

We sit that way for close to an hour. My mind is starting to wind down, my body beginning to wear out. Some of these boys can keep going for days, but more often than not lately, I've been retiring early. At my age, my dad was barely making it through the eleven o'clock news; usually he'd be snoozing in his chair during *Kojak*. And here I am pushing myself to stay awake until dawn. The chemicals can only work for so long.

I rest my head on Anthony's shoulder and I realize my investigations will have to come to an end. How can I continue going behind his back now?

We never go back to the dance floor. We don't find out until the next day that Eliot told Brent to go suck rope and later on Brent passed out. While he was being carried out of the bar, Shane pulled out his laser guns to create a light show as a distraction. That was kind of Shane, I think, to spare Brent any added humiliation. Though in my opinion he deserved every bit he got.

I'm not sorry we missed all that fun. We spend the rest of the night and the following day back in the apartment of our hosts, resting up for our next stop, the Winter Party in Miami. We make love, make breakfast, then make love again, making believe that for the time being, at least, nothing matters but each other. That there are no secrets, no other boyfriends, no questions left unanswered—no obstacles standing in the way for two guys to simply fall in love.

A Month Later, Nirvana

Lloyd

"It's really okay," Eva's insisting.

"Are you sure?"

"*Ooh*. It hurts! Rub it again, okay?"

I oblige, using my thumb and forefinger to gently massage Eva's ankle. She fell, trying to retrieve a vase from a shelf, just as all our guests were arriving. She shrieked in pain, and I feared she'd broken her ankle. And at our grand opening party, too. I asked the guests to wait just a moment and helped Eva into the kitchen.

"Here," I say, pressing the ice pack around her ankle again. "This will ease the swelling." She's looking down at me with such appreciation. She blinks back tears.

"Does it hurt that much?" I ask. "Maybe I should take you over to the clinic."

"No, no. I'll be okay." She smiles. "Thank you, Lloyd. It's been an awfully long time since anyone has taken care of me like this. Thank you."

"You sure it's okay?" I feel her ankle again, reassuring myself it isn't broken. "Just to be safe, I don't want you walking on it for a while. We'll sit you down on the couch and you can greet guests from there."

She touches my face. "Thank you for caring so much."

I blush. "I need to get back out there." She nods. "You just sit here for a few minutes more with that ice pack."

"Yes, Doctor."

We exchange smiles. I dust off my pants and head back into the parlor, where the guests are doing their best to make small talk, but not everyone knows each other. I resume the introductions. It's a mix of lives and lifestyles: the old friends from the Javitz days; Provincetown locals; and Jeff's party crowd. It seems everyone has come: Ty, Henry, Shane, Brent, Ernie, Melissa, Rose, Chanel, Wendy, Naomi—even my old flame Drake, looking particularly natty in a black turtleneck and leather pants. He keeps catching my eye as he moves through the rooms, popping cheese and crackers into his mouth, carrying his glass of white wine.

"It's just beautiful," says my old friend Melissa, her two-year-old daughter Rachel in her arms. The girl's head is down on her mother's shoulders, her arms and legs wrapped around her like a koala bear.

"I'm so glad you could come," I tell her.

"We wouldn't have missed it. I just know Javitz is beaming somewhere. To own a guest house in Provincetown! Who doesn't dream of *that!*"

I smile. Yes, it *does* seem like a dream. Last night our very first guests arrived. A gay man, alone, and a straight couple. All three are here at the reception, too, offering firsthand testimony to our hospitality. They've been treated to breakfast in bed and a four-course dinner. We can't guarantee such service all the time, but hey, they're our first guests. The gay man—his name is Ira—is across the room regaling the crowd with tales of sumptuous salmon almondine and a long lazy afternoon in the Jacuzzi. "It's like being at a *spa,*" I hear him gushing.

I'm glad they're pleased. Word of mouth is the best advertising. Still, I can't deny how tired I feel. In the past four days I've maybe had nine hours of sleep, total. Eva, as usual, has had even less, staying up until three in the morning washing windows and ironing cloth napkins, polishing brass, and setting up VCRs. I marvel at her energy. Things have rebounded between us. She wants this to work as much as I do. Maybe even more.

I'm relieved, of course, since after that episode on the highway, I had started to think maybe Eva really *was* as unstable as Jeff had charged. I'd insisted that she start seeing a therapist. "Therapy is a *good* thing, Eva, nothing to be ashamed of," I told her. "You need someone to process your grief with. Losing Steven isn't something that you can process all by yourself, or with me."

She agreed, and immediately I felt better. I gave her a list of names of local therapists that I admired, and she promised to choose from among them. She hesitated when she saw all of the names were women—"I've never been as comfortable with women as I have with men," she said—

but I urged her to work through her feelings. It could make for very good therapy, I argued.

Who she ultimately chose I still don't know: I haven't wanted to badger her or appear to be supervising her. We're partners, friends, equals. But whoever she's seeing seems to be doing a good job. For the past few weeks Eva's been like her old self: confident, wise, strong.

"They seem to be enjoying themselves," she says, coming up behind me.

"Hey," I reply, turning around. I wasn't even aware of her approach. "I don't want you walking on that."

She slips an arm around my waist. "I'll be fine," she says. "Your tender loving care did the trick. It's all I needed. Besides, I can't miss out on this. This is it, Lloyd. Our dream come true."

I smile, dropping my arm around her shoulders. "And to you goes most of the credit."

Even this afternoon's gala was largely orchestrated by her. Catered by a couple of top-notch local chefs, the spread is both delectable and elegant: caviar, gingered scallops, flame-roasted pears, chocolate-covered strawberries. Candles flicker everywhere. The wine flows freely.

Drake catches my eye again from across the room. I smile, and he raises his glass.

"What a handsome man," Eva says, observing. "Who is he?"

"His name is Drake. He's—an old friend."

"Very handsome. Classic, even."

"Mmm." I watch him. He's now talking with Henry and Shane and Brent. Yes, Drake is indeed classically handsome. Tall, square-jawed, silver-haired. The penultimate New England Wasp. When I first moved apart from Jeff, I saw a lot of Drake, who'd been very persistent in trying to win me over—determined, in fact, to get me to move in with him. But as much as I liked him, as much as I found him very attractive, something always held me back.

Something named Jeff.

I scan the crowd again. Still no sign of him. We haven't spoken much since Valentine's Day, but my anger toward him has subsided and I find myself, yet again, hoping against hope. Henry told me he *presumed* Jeff was coming, but admitted he hadn't talked to him in a few days. I'd sent Jeff an E-mail reminding him of the opening and asking him to come, but I never got a response. There's absolutely *no excuse* if he doesn't show. The weather's fine for either driving or flying—an early taste of spring, in fact: warm and sunny, with the sun spilling in from the windows, including the new one that completely opens up the kitchen. We couldn't have asked for a better kickoff for our venture.

Suddenly hands are covering my eyes. "Guess who?"

"Uhhh . . ."

The hands disappear. A face moves into view. It's Ty.

"How soon they forget," the attorney says, smirking. "Hey, you've got a packed house. Congratulations!"

"Thanks," I say, feeling ridiculously uncomfortable all at once, with Ty grinning at me, Eva at my side, Drake watching me from across the room, and Jeff expected any minute.

Ty reaches down to kiss Eva on the cheek. "And hello to you, too, darling," he says. "Keepin' the boys entertained?"

She smiles tightly. "Help yourself to a glass of wine, Tyrone. And there's plenty to eat."

He winks at me as he moves across the room.

Eva's hurt, I can tell, that Ty greeted me first, and far more enthusiastically than he did her. I place my arm around her shoulders again. "You doing okay?" I ask softly.

"I'm just tired."

"As well you should be. You've been working your butt off nonstop. I want you to take a few days' rest after these guests leave. Our next crew doesn't arrive until the weekend, but then it's nonstop for the rest of the season. So I want you to rest up. Okay?"

She smiles up at me and pats my hand on her shoulder. "Ay, ay, Captain."

"We should mingle," I say. "Come on. You haven't met Henry and Shane yet."

We cross the room, excusing ourselves past people who all repeat the same congratulations, the same good-lucks. I spy Drake off to one side, shaking Ty's hand. His eyes, however, never leave me for long. He's making me distinctly uncomfortable.

"Well, here comes our handsome host," Brent says as we approach.

I smile. "I'd like you all to meet my partner—er, I mean, my partner in Nirvana, my *business* partner—Eva Horner." Isn't it weird how a word like *partner,* which is really the only way to describe Eva, has taken on a romantic connotation within gay culture? I withdraw my arm as she steps forward a little bashfully. "Eva, this is Henry, Shane, and Brent."

"Bravo!" Shane crows, clapping his hands. "I had no idea what to expect of this place. So many guest houses are *tacky* affairs. But *this!* I am *so* impressed with the style and the obvious care you have put into it!"

"Oh, my, thank you so much, Shane," she says, clearly touched.

"It really *is* fabulous," Henry agrees.

I feel a hand on my back. Two hands, actually. I turn. Drake and Ty are both behind me.

"What charming friends you have here, Lloyd," Ty says, indicating Drake.

Drake's eyes are locked on mine. "Well, when one is as charming as Lloyd, his friends can only be the same."

So *smooooth*. They're both so goddamn smooth.

"How are you, Drake?" I ask.

He kisses my check. "You know the answer to that question, handsome," he says, winking.

I force my eyes not to roll. I introduce him to Eva.

Drake extends his hand and Eva takes it warmly. "I was just delighted to get an invitation in the mail," he tells her, but his eyes are still on me. "A wonderful excuse to see Lloyd again. It's been a while, hasn't it, Lloyd?"

"Yes," I say. "It's been a while."

"Where's Jeff, by the way?"

I feel myself flush. "He'll be here."

Drake just smiles and nods.

"Is it *true*," Shane's asking Eva in a mock-conspiratorial stage whisper, "that you do impressions of Mae West?"

She blushes, slapping my shoulder playfully. "*Oh*. Has Lloyd been telling tales out of school again?"

"I was just bragging about your talents."

"*Please!*" Shane actually gets down on his knees, looking like the jolly green giant on TV. "Will you do it for us?"

"Oh, I couldn't . . ."

"Just one little 'Come up and see me sometime'?" Shane begs.

"She hurt her ankle earlier," I explain.

"Now, don't be party poopers," Brent scolds.

Eva laughs. "Well, maybe after some of these other people have left."

"Okay," Shane says, standing. "Then it's a promise."

She laughs again. Gay men certainly do seem to take to her, and she certainly seems at home with them. They're all smiling at her, Henry commenting on her black velvet pantsuit and Shane admiring her ruby brooch. I step back a bit to watch them fuss over her, then notice that alone among them, Drake isn't paying attention. He's still looking at me.

"You must be very proud of this achievement," Drake says quietly, moving closer. "I had no idea you wanted to open a guest house."

I nod. "It just sort of came to me one day. I guess I've been looking for something to do for a while."

He keeps staring at me. It's really making me uneasy.

"It's been a long time," he says again, sipping his wine.

"Yes. Since Javitz's memorial service, I think."

"I saw you a few times afterwards." Drake smiles, flashing his steel blue eyes. "In my dreams."

I want to barf. What had I ever seen in this guy? He thinks he's so suave, so sophisticated. I look around to be rescued by someone. Anyone.

The timing couldn't be worse. There, in the doorway, is Jeff.

Jeff

"Oh, just great," I groan. "Just fucking great."

"What?" Anthony asks, coming up behind me.

"Oh, only somebody I didn't expect to see and really wished I never would again."

Lloyd has spotted me. I watch as he makes a beeline away from Drake toward me.

"Cat!" he calls. "You're here!"

We kiss quickly, perfunctorily, on the lips. "You remember Anthony?" I ask.

"Sure, sure, hi," Lloyd says, not even shaking his hand. He takes my arm. "I can't wait to show you all we've done."

"A good turnout," I say, looking around. "You invited a lot of people." A beat. "A few I didn't expect."

Lloyd stops in his tracks and looks over at me. "He's on my mailing list. I wasn't even aware he got an invitation."

"Yeah, whatever. Anthony, you want a glass of wine?"

Lloyd lets go of my arm. "All of our old friends are here."

"I see them," I say, pouring myself and Anthony some wine.

Oh, yes, I see them. It was only with major reservations that I came here at all today. The idea of walking into a roomful of people I haven't seen in quite some time is almost as unnerving as the prospect of having to deal with Eva again. No, it's not a day I've been looking forward to, despite how much I've been missing Lloyd. Part of me wanted to be spiteful and stay home: after all, he's apparently been too busy to respond to any of the E-mails I've sent him. E-mails in which I've tried to reconnect, tried to establish something—tried in my own feeble way not to let him go.

I hand the glass of wine to Anthony, who accepts it gratefully, as if he wanted something to do with his hands. I know Anthony feels awkward coming here, too; he was nervous the entire flight over on Cape Air, and it wasn't just the ride in the eight-seater plane that made him anxious. He knew there would be people here who would view him with some degree of suspicion, or even hostility: all my old friends, who've been rooting for a reconciliation between Lloyd and me. It's been a reminder to him that things aren't as free and clear as we've been pretending they are these last few weeks.

It's been easy to live with illusions. At the Black Party last week in New York, Anthony used the word "boyfriend" to describe me for the first time. "Is it so?" Eliot asked me. "Has our Jeff really been snared again?" I let it go for the time being. A heady conversation about relationships was the last thing I wanted to get into while watching a couple of porn stars rim each other on stage.

But ever since I suggested we come to Provincetown for Lloyd's opening, Anthony's been edgy, and now Lloyd's discourteous greeting has only made things worse. It's not like Lloyd to be so abrupt.

"Do you want a tour?" he's asking.

"Maybe in a bit," I say. "I don't want to keep you from your guests. You were in the middle of what looked like a deep conversation when I came in."

Anthony pulls away a little from us, pretending to admire a painting on the wall.

Lloyd moves in close to me and speaks in a lowered voice. "Knock it off, Jeff. I was just *talking* with him. I have been waiting *all day* for you to get here. Don't start with attitude."

I really don't want to be a jerk. I *did* come with the best intentions. "Okay," I say. "I'm sorry. No more about Drake."

"That cleared up," Lloyd says, lowering his voice even further, "why'd you bring *him?*"

"Anthony? What was I going to do? Leave him sitting alone in my living room?"

"You have before."

"But this was a party."

Lloyd rolls his eyes. "Whatever."

I shake my head. "You know, Lloyd, every time we've seen each other for the past three months, we get into something right off the bat." I feel genuinely sad all of a sudden. Was it just a few months ago that everything had seemed to be going so rosy?

Lloyd sighs. "I'm sorry, Jeff. You're right. We should just let it go."

We smile wanly at each other. Anthony approaches us again. "It's a really nice house, Lloyd," he says carefully.

Lloyd extends his hand. They shake. "Thanks, Anthony. I'll be glad to give you a tour. There's plenty of food, so help yourself, okay?"

"Thanks!" Anthony beams at the change in attitude.

Lloyd turns back to me. "I should mingle. But I'll be back in a bit, okay?"

I nod. I watch him move off. Oh, man, I wish I hadn't come. My eyes fix on Lloyd and Eva as they move through the crowd together, stopping to talk with people, basking in their goodwill and congratulations. At one point Eva even slips her arm through Lloyd's. It's like a goddamn wedding reception, that's what it is.

"Jeff O'Brien!"

I turn. It's my old friend Chanel. Once we were as thick as thieves, the first person either of us would call whenever anything good or bad happened in our lives. She helped us care for Javitz in his final illness, and next to Lloyd and me, she was probably the one who loved him best. We have a lot of history, Chanel and I.

But times have changed. Javitz is dead and Chanel is now a mom, and we don't call each other anymore. She's heading toward me, leading her three-year-old daughter Gertrude by the hand. They make the most multi-culti family you can imagine: Gertie was born in China, Chanel in the Philippines, and the other mommy, Wendy, is a white Anglo-Saxon Protestant. I smile as they approach.

"Gertie, scold Uncle Jeff for never coming to see you," Chanel says.

"Bad Unca Jeff."

I try to laugh. "I see we're teaching our children how to impose guilt at an early age."

Chanel eyes me stiffly. "We miss you, that's all."

We exchange brief kisses. "Chanel, Gertie, this is my friend Anthony."

She gives him only the briefest of acknowledgments, keeping her eyes on me. "Jeff, how *are* you?" she asks. *"Seriously.* I ask Lloyd about you all the time. I haven't heard from you in *months."*

"I'm sorry, Chanel. I've just been busy."

"Busy with what?"

I stammer a little. "Well, I've been traveling . . ."

She harrumphs. "You haven't been busy writing; I know that much."

I'm getting a little annoyed at her attitude. "You don't know that."

"No, I don't. You're right. And *why* don't I know? Because I never hear from you."

Anthony leans in a bit. "I'm going to get some more wine. Can I get anybody anything?"

I shake my head and Chanel ignores him. Anthony moves away as quickly as he can. I don't blame him.

"Chanel," I say, trying to smile, "you know I don't take well to being interrogated."

She smirks, nodding her head in Anthony's direction. "Is he one of your circuit-party boys? Is that where you met him? Are you doing *drugs,* Jeff? I've read the articles about the circuit scene. I know what goes on at those things. Raising all this money supposedly to fight AIDS while encouraging all sorts of unsafe sex and drug use."

I blink my eyes in disbelief. "Chanel, you don't know what you're talking about."

She scowls. "I'm sorry if I sound bitchy, but I *worry* about you."

"Well, I'd appreciate it if you'd stop. Being bitchy *and* worrying."

She sighs. Gertrude is standing at the edge of a table, popping grapes from a platter in her mouth. "That's enough, sweetheart," Chanel says, taking her hand. "They give you gas."

"So how are *you?*" I ask, trying to change the subject. "Gertie's gotten so big—"

"I'm *angry* with you, Jeff," Chanel says, spinning on me suddenly. She draws herself up straight. "I just can't stand here and make small talk with you."

"Well, okay." I try once again to smile, to get her to laugh. "Shall we *sit* and make small talk, then?"

She seems infuriated that I'm not giving her what she wants. And what is that? Repentance? Humility? Mea culpas? A quick and easy reconciliation with Lloyd so that everything could be just like it was between all of us—a lifetime ago?

She just glares at me. "Javitz would be so disappointed in you," she says finally, surely knowing that's the cruelest thing she could say to me. "He didn't leave you that money just so you could squander it all away." She hustles Gertrude off into the crowd.

I just stand there. It's as if she'd just slapped me across the face. I don't move, don't blink. Anthony returns and waves his hand in front of my face.

"You okay, Jeff?"

"No." I down the last of my wine. "I want to get out of here. I don't belong here."

"We can't leave. Henry's over there. Shane and Brent, too."

I'd actually been looking forward to getting the chance to throw some attitude Henry's way, laying the guilt on him for being so out of touch. But now, after Chanel's little scene, I don't have the heart for it. Instead, I greet Henry warmly, hugging him close, doing the same to Shane and—saints preserve us—even to Brent. I'm glad to see them. I relax a little in their presence, keeping as far from my old friends as I can.

"You know, Eva is *so* nice," Shane's saying. "We were talking and she told me her husband had been gay. She just opened right up and told me that."

"Yeah, she told me, too," Henry says. "She started sharing about how he had died of AIDS. She even started to cry a little. Jeff, you never told us all that."

I just shrug.

"Well, look what she gave me," Shane says. From his pocket, he pulls out a rhinestone-covered cock ring. I'm not kidding you. A *rhinestone-covered cock ring.* "She said it was Steven's! Can you *believe* it? I just met this lady and she gives me her husband's cock ring!"

They all laugh. Except me, who can manage only a tight little grin.

"I *really* want to get out of here," I whisper again to Anthony.

"Jeff, we've got to wait a little bit. We just got here."

Henry's leaning in to me, having overheard my words. "Eva is really nice, Jeff. You ought to give her more of a chance."

"Oh, she is *awesome,*" Shane adds. "I *love* huh!"

A tall black man in Prada has climbed up onto the coffee table and is trying to get everyone's attention. "People, please! I'd like to propose a toast."

Folks quiet down. "To Lloyd and Eva." The guy waves his glass of wine over the crowd like a priest wielding an incense burner at Mass. "To Nirvana." He lifts his glass.

Who the fuck *is* he? I don't even know Lloyd's friends anymore.

"To having the courage to follow your dreams and make them come true," the guy says, completing his toast.

"Hear, hear!" several people call out as everyone raises their glasses to Lloyd and Eva. They smile. They clink glasses. They kiss. Everyone applauds.

"Kind of like a wedding reception, huh, Jeff?"

It's Brent breathing in my ear.

Lloyd

The party is winding down. The sun's dropping lower in the sky and many of the guests have already departed. Ty has brought out Eva's wedding album, much to her giggles and halfhearted protestations. She sits on the couch beside Ira, our first night guest, who's by now pretty plastered. I watch him carefully, not wanting to have to clean up after him if he gets sick. Eva has her wedding album on her lap, and Ira's leaning in eagerly to see each photo. He's a middle-aged man with a receding hairline and barely any chin. He keeps gushing over how handsome Steven is. Eva's clearly delighted.

I begin to surreptitiously clear off plates from the tables, hoping the remaining guests might get the clue and hit the road. I'm tired, and I still haven't had any time alone with Jeff. Something went down between him and Chanel; I don't know exactly what, but Chanel and Wendy left in a hurry. Jeff hasn't moved much since he got here, standing off in the corner talking with Henry and Anthony, seeming to keep as far away as he can from old friends like Melissa, Rose, and Naomi.

"May I help you with these?"

I look over at a pair of hands stacking plates beside me. I move my eyes up and there's Drake.

"Oh. Thanks. You can just put them in the kitchen."

Drake winks at me. "I'd like to make a reservation for Memorial Day weekend," he says, adding a couple more plates to the stack and grabbing the stem of a wineglass with his forefinger.

"Actually," I tell him, "I think we're already booked."

"Ah. Good for you. Business is booming." He follows me into the kitchen and sets the plates on the counter. "Actually, I'd make a reservation for any night you have available. Just to get the chance to see you again."

He tries to kiss me. I pull back.

"I don't want to go there, Drake," I say. "I hope you understand."

He looks puzzled. "I'd heard that you and Jeff had reconciled, but then I'd also heard that it was off again. Still the same old dance, huh?"

I feel defensive. "Don't comment on something you know nothing about."

Drake holds up his hands. "Hey. I didn't mean to make you mad. I apologize."

"It's okay." I sigh. "Look, I appreciate your coming today."

He leans up against the sink and folds his arms against his chest. "So there's no chance, huh? No chance you'd have dinner with me?"

I hesitate, not sure how to respond. Jeff's always said Drake is the kind of guy who grew up always getting what he wanted—prep schools, trust funds, the right connections to get the best jobs—and he's right. It's one of the reasons nothing could ever have worked between Drake and me. His interest in me stems from the fact that I said *no*. I'm one of the few things in life Drake hasn't gotten when he wanted it.

"I'm really busy, Drake," I tell him. "Please understand."

He nods, but he looks perturbed. "Oh, I do." He smiles bitterly. "Better than you think."

He turns to walk out of the kitchen when he nearly collides with Ty. "Well," Ty says, looking from Drake to me. He seems a bit arch. "Hope I wasn't interrupting anything."

"I was just leaving," Drake insists.

Ty sweeps his eyes across him. "Then allow me to escort you out," he says flirtatiously, taking Drake's arm in an apparent attempt to get back at me. Drake grins. Ty walks with him out into the parlor.

I laugh to myself. How *do* I get myself in these situations?

When I follow them, I see Drake hand Ty his phone number. Their eyes hold several seconds longer than necessary as they shake hands good-bye. Drake doesn't even turn to look back at me before he heads out the door. I laugh again. So maybe his trip out here to Provincetown hasn't been entirely in vain.

In the parlor, Shane's sitting on the back of the couch, peering over Eva's shoulder at the wedding album. "You are so right, Ira," he's saying. "Steven was a major hunk and a half."

"He certainly was," Eva agrees fondly.

I look down at the album. Are they just being kind? Steven looks like a zoned-out hippy. Given that they got married in 1970, I figure Steven probably *was* a zoned-out hippy. He's got a big, bushy head of black hair, a beard, and for his wedding outfit he's wearing a green poncho with a gold star in the center of his chest. Eva's all in white lace, daisies woven through her long, free-flowing hair. Except for the fact that she keeps her hair tied up now and rarely exposes that much cleavage, she looks the same, her skin still as unlined as it was thirty years ago.

"Come on, Eva, enough people have left," Shane suddenly urges. "You *promised.*"

"Promised what?" Ira asks.

She closes the wedding album. "Oh, I don't know," she says.

"*Please?*" Shane begs.

"Please *what?*" Ira repeats.

"*Ladies and gentlemen,*" Ty suddenly intones, jumping up onto a chair. "May I present to you *Tira!* The lady of the sideshows—who can tame more than lions!"

All at once Eva springs from the couch and leaps up on top of the coffee table. I'm taken aback by how agile she is.

Apparently that twisted ankle healed *really* fast.

She moves this way and that, becoming Mae West immediately, one hand on hip, the other pushing at her hair. "*They call me Sister Honky Tonk,*" she sings. The hips start swinging. "*They call me Sister Honk Tonk . . .*"

I watch in wonder. This little unhappy lady has learned to find herself in moments like these. I think of how hard she's worked these past few weeks, how determined she is to make our venture a success. As I watch her swing her hips and sing to the cheers of the boys, I can't help but love her. I want to laugh and cry at the same time.

Henry, Brent, Anthony, and Jeff have gathered closer to watch. The other three laugh and cheer, but I notice how Jeff holds back, his arms crossed over his chest, only the smallest smile fixed on his face. I sigh. I'd hoped he might melt a little toward Eva, seeing her do Mae West.

"Ah, but you were wonderful tonight," Ty says, in character, feeding her lines.

"*Oooohhh.* I'm always wonderful at night."

Laughter from the crowd.

"Yes, but tonight you were especially good," Ty says.

"When I'm good, I'm very good, but when I'm bad, I'm better."

More laughter, hoots.

"If only I could trust you . . ."

She puts a hand behind her head. "Oh, you can. *Hundreds* have."

"You *go,* girl!" Shane shouts.

The whole room erupts into cheers. She giggles, covering her mouth and stepping down off the coffee table. They keep hooting and hollering for her. She dissolves into laughter, sitting back down and burying her face in Ira's chest. Shane lifts a shiny glass figurine of the Buddha from a side table and presents it to Eva like an Oscar. It's one of the many we've filled the house with, and for a second I recall the little wooden Buddha we found, and wonder where it is. It was our good-luck omen, a gift from the house on our first night here. What has happened to it?

But who has time to think? Everybody's on their feet, cheering. Henry places his pinkies in his mouth and whistles. I beam. My eyes catch Eva's and we exchange a look. It's good. Everything's going to be okay.

Jeff

I can't take it, all the cheering. I have to back away. I mean, am I really the only one who can see through her? See how pathetic her bids for attention really are? Why are all these gay men so eager to think she's so special?

"Come on," Henry's saying, noticing my reticence. "Go congratulate her."

"For what? Making a fool of herself?"

He scowls at me. "You are one mean queen, Jeff O'Brien. She didn't make a fool of herself. She was *funny*. Give her a *chance*, Jeff. She seems like a terrific lady."

I ignore him. I want to get out of here. I've made my appearance. I don't care for a tour. This isn't my house. It's Lloyd's and hers. Why do I care to see any more of it than I have?

Okay, you're right. I'm being totally snarky. And I'm smart enough to know that even in my snarkiness I'm not being entirely honest. Eva's little performance *was* funny, and these guys have every reason to think she's just grand. I'm jealous. Plain and simple. I'm admitting it. What more do you want me to do?

"Jeff," Henry says, melting a little and putting his arm around my shoulder. "Do you need to talk?"

"I'm fine, Henry."

He sighs. "Jeff, there was a time I would have spent a lot of energy trying to get you to talk. But I'm not doing that anymore. If you want to talk, I'm here, but I'm not going to beg you to do so."

I look at him. Doesn't he realize he's part of the problem? *He's* pulled away, too, and lately there have been times I've felt as if I were all alone on a goddamn deserted island. "Henry," I say, trying to hide some of the desperation I can feel building in my chest, "are you sure you won't reconsider going to Palm Springs for the White Party with us? It's a Jeffrey Sanker event, and you know Sanker's events are awesome."

"No, Jeff." Henry won't meet my eyes. "It conflicts with the Weekend of Hope. Don't you want to stay for Boston's own party?"

I frown. "And see the same old tired faces? Come *on*, Henry. You had a fabulous time last year."

"*You* had the fabulous time, Jeff. Remember? You met that hot guy from Germany. I had to sleep out by the Wyndham pool because you guys took the room."

"You *told* me you had a good time," I protest.

"No, Jeff. I'm not going to Palm Springs."

"I just miss you, buddy," I say, suddenly unable to hide how vulnerable I feel. Maybe it's the wine. Maybe it's all that cheering for Eva. Maybe it's being here in a house that Lloyd is sharing with someone else. "I just miss hanging out with you on the dance floor."

Henry looks over at me. I can see he's struggling with this, too.

I grip his hand. "Will you at least come to Wild and Wet in Montreal? *Please?*" Damn, I sound like I'm begging.

Henry sighs.

I give him a little smile. "I'm sure Shane's bringing an *awesome* water gun."

Henry laughs. "I'll bet it's an Uzi." He smiles back at me. "I'll think about it, Jeff."

Lloyd approaches us. "So what did you think of Eva's rendition of Mae West?"

Henry laughs. "She was awesome! Totally!"

I smile. "Your guests won't need to go to the Crown and Anchor for drag shows this summer. They can just stay right here."

"I still haven't given you a tour, Jeff," Lloyd says.

"Well, we've got to hurry. Our plane leaves in less than an hour."

Lloyd gestures for me to follow. I say all the appropriate things about the new paint jobs, the new art, the new curtains, the new carpeting. I make no specific comment about Lloyd's room, and Lloyd says nothing about me sitting at the desk, writing with a view of the bay. Neither of us acknowledges the big canopied bed or the photo of the two of us with Javitz from almost a decade ago, hanging prominently in the middle of the wall. All we exchange are pleasantries, as if I'm just one more visitor passing through.

And maybe I am. Ever since I've gotten here, I've felt distinctly unspecial. Just like anybody else, with no more claim to the place than

Brent—or *Drake*—and even less than Ira, who at least is a paying guest. Eva embraced me once, in her usual effusive style, but then kept her distance, doing her thing, hanging on to Lloyd's arm. And so long as Lloyd refuses to talk about it—about how that dynamic makes me feel—I can see no future in continuing anything with him. As we start back down the stairs, I tell myself it's really over this time. I don't even feel sad. Just numb. And restless. All I want to do is get on the plane with Anthony so we can go home and start packing for Palm Springs.

Lloyd looks at me. "When am I going to see you again?"

I sigh. "What for, Lloyd? Why are we pretending things are still happening between us?"

We stop in the middle of the stairs. Lloyd takes my hands. "I love you, Jeff."

I sigh. "It's not about that and you know it."

Eva's suddenly in front of us, trying to help Ira walk. "He needs to go upstairs and lie down," she says.

"I'll be okay," the drunken guest insists. "Just make everything stop spinning."

Lloyd and I take him from her, gripping him under the arms. We help him up the stairs and into his room and ease him down onto the bed. Eva places a cold damp cloth across his brow. "You just rest a while," she whispers.

We close Ira's door behind them. "Poor man," Eva says.

"An innkeeper provides many services, I guess," I observe.

Eva smiles. "From now on, no more free wine for the guests." We all laugh without much conviction. She looks up at me. "Are you leaving, Jeff?"

I nod.

"Well, don't be a stranger," she says, heading back down the stairs. I notice I don't get a hug good-bye. "Feel free to visit us anytime," she calls back over her shoulder. "You're always welcome here."

Lloyd looks at me. "Please, Jeff, don't go yet," he says. "I just want to say good night to some folks who are leaving. Please let's talk more before you go."

I promise nothing. I follow him down the stairs and watch him disappear into the parlor.

"Get our coats," I whisper to Anthony. "We've got to get a cab and get to the airport."

Henry sees us planning to escape and tries to stop us. "Wait, Jeff. I can give you guys a ride back to Boston. I drove down with Shane and Brent. We'll be leaving shortly."

"No, I want to go *now*," I tell him. I don't want to say good-bye to Lloyd. Not again. I can't bear it. Anthony hands me my leather jacket and I slip it on. He buttons up his pea coat.

"You can't just *leave*," Henry admonishes me.

"Watch us," I say as Anthony and I quietly slip out the door.

Lloyd

It's late. I sit alone on the couch, listening to the grandfather clock tick loudly from the other room. Both Eva and Ty went up to bed over an hour ago, with Ty giving me the eye as if to say, *My door will be unlocked.* But I'm not in any mood for that tonight. I sit and watch the fire go down, bit by bit, until all that remains are a few smoldering cinders.

Why are we pretending things are still happening between us?

I've tried, but no matter what I do, I can't get Jeff's words out of my mind. He left without even saying good-bye, and I feel certain he won't call, either. Is it really over, then? Is this it?

No—I just can't give up. Not yet. I can't believe our karma's been exhausted, our story fully told.

Memories dance through my head. A warm spring day, out on the back deck of our old apartment in the South End of Boston, grilling tofu dogs on our tiny barbecue, then eating them together, one of us at either end, nibbling toward the middle and ending with a kiss. How silly we were. How young and giddy and in love.

I love you, Jeff.

It's not about that and you know it.

Then what *is* it about? If we love each other, why is it all so hard?

I start to stand up, then notice Eva's wedding album on the coffee table.

Something makes me flip open the front cover and look down at the inscription.

Steven and Eva
April 15, 1970

I stare at it for several seconds before realizing what's wrong.

She said they were married on Valentine's Day. That's why she was so emotional that day she ran out of the car. . . .

Why would she lie about something like that?

I put out the fire and shut off the last of the lights. I grip the banister and make my way up the stairs. I need to sleep, put thoughts of Jeff out of my mind, at least for now. Morning will come early, and I'll have three guests waiting for Belgian waffles and poached eggs—though I doubt poor old Ira will want much to eat.

I should probably check on him. He may have gotten sick, or fallen out of bed. As I approach his door, I can hear sounds, low and guttural, that at first I take for retching. I steel myself and place my hand on the doorknob, ready to turn it and walk inside.

Something makes me hesitate. Should I do it, or just leave him alone? Ira's a grown man, after all. He'd probably prefer being sick in private. But it had been me who'd provided the wine. In some ways, it's my responsibility as a guest-house owner to check in on him. I'll just see if he needs anything. If not, I'll just let him be.

I open the door.

Ira isn't retching. He's fucking Eva.

Her head is hanging off the bed, her hair flowing down almost to the floor, her big breasts bouncing, her eyes closed as she moans in delirious ecstasy. Ira's pumping hard on top of her. His eyes lift briefly to lock with mine.

I quickly close the door.

"Holy shit," I whisper to myself. I stand there for several seconds, unable to fathom what I'd just seen. I can't move or think. Then all at once I hurry to my room, not wanting to hear either of them orgasm.

Needless to say, sleep is not a visitor this night.

The Third Weekend in May, Wild and Wet in Montreal

Henry

My torso is dripping wet and my jeans are drenched. Not from sweat, as you might expect out here on the dance floor, but from three dozen squirt guns, aimed at me by as many hot boys.

Shane did indeed bring an Uzi, a big assault weapon he positions between his legs from which he pumps tremendous volleys of water. "Oh! Oh! *Ohhhhhhhh!*" he cries, as if orgasming, suddenly shooting a wet cannonball across the dance floor. He douses more than one small guy completely from head to toe.

Water, water everywhere, and not a drop to drink. My mouth, as usual, has gone dry. "You want something to drink?" I shout over to Jeff and Anthony.

They don't respond—of course—too engrossed in singing to each other the words of Abigail's "Let the Joy Rise." Something about looking for one friendly face. I scowl. Screw 'em. Didn't I know this was how it was going to be?

I stagger over to the bar and order a bottle of water. "Why not just wring out your jeans?" the bartender asks me with a smirk.

I smile. I'm glad I didn't wear underwear. Wet boxers under wet jeans would have been unbearable. Some of the guys have stripped off their pants and are dancing in briefs and jockstraps. What the hell. The tag line to the party is "Get Naked."

I look back at the dance floor. Jeff and Anthony still have their pants on, but they've both slipped so low you can see the cracks of their asses. Why was it, on *Designing Women*, the plumber's ass crack was considered a disgusting joke, but when circuit boys let their cracks show, it's hot as hell? I laugh to myself. Maybe because the plumber hadn't looked like these boys, with their rounded pecs and sharply cut triceps and twenty-nine-inch waists. It's a misperception that circuit boys are body-builders: the few really bulky guys stand out, ungainly, from the sea of tiny-waisted, sculpted boys with abdominals for days, those sexy inter-nal oblique lines leading down into their jeans.

"The really big guys have HIV," Brent assured me once. "You can pick out the positives from the negatives just by looking around the room."

An ironic flip-flop, I supposed: it used to be you could tell the ones with HIV by their wasted appearances. Now they're the huge guys, bulked up by steroids, which are sometimes shared with their non-poz brothers.

"So how do you know so much, Brent?" I asked. "*Your* arms are get-ting pretty big there yourself."

I remember how he rolled his eyes.

"Trust me, Henry. There's not much I *don't* know."

Of course, we were all at the gym just before we got here, giving our-selves that last-minute Party Pump. I know I look good—*very* good, in fact, given the number of glances I've gotten since I arrived. I move my eyes back to Jeff and Anthony. *They* haven't been doing much looking in my direction, however. Their legs are locked, their arms entwined over their heads, their hair dripping down into their eyes.

So they're having a good time. Good for them.

Except the only fucking reason I *came* to Montreal this weekend was because Jeff had practically begged me to. He'd *missed* me, or so he said. See, I hadn't gone to the White Party in Palm Springs, and Jeff pouted for weeks. *I just miss hanging out with you on the dance floor, buddy,* he said. *Please come to Montreal. Pretty please?*

And I melted. Damn, I hate that Jeff can still have that effect on me. Here I am, having paid the outrageous entrance fees, put up my cash for the X, and then Jeff barely says two words to me the whole time. Even in Shane's car on the ride up, Jeff and Anthony smooched in the back seat most of the way. "Hey, it's like getting a free porn channel," Shane quipped, not complaining, simply adjusting the rearview mirror so he could keep an eye on the action.

Oh, what the fuck. I take a swig of water. Let Jeff and Anthony maul each other all weekend. I don't care. I know it's not going to last. Things like this never do for Jeff. They get all hot and heavy and then Jeff backs out when it gets too serious. I still have the letters from poor Alexei in

St. Petersburg, imploring me to intercede with Jeff on his behalf. And then there was that tragic kid from Missouri, who I'd driven to the airport and advised to forget he'd ever met Jeff O'Brien.

"He won't be calling you," I said. "It's over."

"He'll call," the kid insisted.

"He's not going to call."

The kid was crushed. Better to give him the hard truth than let him live with false hopes.

I wager it won't be long before Anthony is history, too, and Jeff and Lloyd are back in their never-ending game of cat and mouse. Or cat and dog. Whatever the fuck they call each other.

I try to stop watching them but I can't. Why am I making myself so miserable? All I know is that I wish I were back in Boston, with a client. Now, that's *sad*. Here I am, surrounded by hot, hunky guys, and I'm missing my old trolls. At least my old trolls seem so *happy* to be with me. These guys—Jeff included—just seem so preoccupied with themselves. Maybe the critics of circuit culture are right. Maybe it is just a self-absorbed, narcissistic, headfirst plunge into hedonism.

And maybe I'm just lonely. On the way up here, I actually allowed myself to dream about finding a boyfriend in Montreal. Now, wouldn't *that* be nice? Finally, a man to call my own. I can't even imagine what that would be like.

The X is making me horny, hornier than I've been in a long time. A different kind of horny than I feel when meeting clients, maybe because I'm on the hunt rather than on the payroll. It's been weeks since I've been out on my own like this. *Months,* even. I look around at the flesh around me. Every bit of it looks good enough to eat. Strange how I feel the need to "dehorn"—Brent's term for having sex after a long hiatus. I've been having sex two, three, or more times a week since February. But not this kind of sex. Not the kind of sex I'm hoping to find here.

I love Montreal. Here the men are far friendlier than in just about any city in the U.S., save Atlanta and New Orleans. Wild & Wet is held on Canada's Victoria Day Weekend, so the boys are definitely in the holiday spirit. Montreal has an undeniable old-world charm with its brick sidewalks and narrow streets. A year ago, as I was wandering down Rue Ste. Catherine, some guy smiled and we struck up a conversation. Just like that. It was one of the rare times I actually scored on a circuit weekend: Francois and I made mad, crazy love all night. We might have even become boyfriends if he hadn't been moving to Vancouver. I could deal with Montreal, but Vancouver was just a bit too much of a commute.

But I figure, if lightning struck once in Montreal, it could strike twice: the city rates high on Brent's PH factor. The odds of finding a potential husband here are better than just about anywhere else, I tell myself.

Is it so terrible to want a husband so bad? Someone to call my own? Jeff always has a couple backup husbands in reserve, while I never have one. Not *one*. Not one significant relationship in my whole, entire life. Unless you count Sean with the Cheeto breath. And I *don't* count Sean.

I sigh, leaning in on the bar with my elbows. I turn, suddenly making eye contact with a guy standing next to me. He smiles. He's definitely yummy. Dark. Maybe thirty-two, thirty-three. Goatee. Closely trimmed body hair.

"Awesome music," I say.

He nods, looking at me.

"Dance music doesn't get the respect it deserves in the States," I tell him. "In Europe, you hear it on the radio. In the States, it's considered too gay. What about in Canada?"

He doesn't respond. He just keeps looking at me. I feel like a dork. *Henry Weiner,* I scold myself, *you can pump up all you want and give yourself star-burst tattoos on your stomach, but you're still just the geek who once stood on the sidelines and couldn't imagine ever talking to these delicious boys. You still don't know how to do it.*

The guy continues studying my face. Maybe he just didn't understand me. That's it! Duh! We're in Montreal! He probably only speaks French.

Wrong again. "I know you," he says, in English, with that delicious Quebecois accent both Jeff and I find irresistible.

"Don't think so," I say, taking another sip of my water, trying to look casual. "I'd remember you."

He peers closer at me. "I *know* I have seen you."

I smile. "Ever come to Boston?"

Suddenly a light goes off in his eyes. "Boston! The Web site! You're Hank, no?"

I feel my face redden. So it's finally happened. The Internet is big, wide-open space, and my mug, albeit turned a little away from the camera, is plastered all over several Web sites for anyone to see: *HANK. STUDLY ESCORT, BOSTON-BASED. MUSCLE WORSHIP SPECIALTY. $200. OUT ONLY. TRAVEL BY ARRANGEMENT.*

"Uh, yeah, that's me," I admit.

"Cool," the guy says. "My name's Sylvain." He extends his hand.

I shake it. I feel myself putting my shoulders back, deepening my voice, shifting into my escort guise. "Good to meet ya, Sylvain," Hank says.

"You here on business?"

Business. He means, *Are you here with a client?* "No," I tell him. "I'm here with friends."

"Are they escorts, too?" asks Sylvain.

"No." All at once, I feel a little uncomfortable talking about my escort life with a stranger. With a stranger not looking to hire me, that is. At least, I don't think Sylvain wants to hire me. . . . We're just two guys meeting in a bar. Aren't we?

But Sylvain says nothing more. He just stands there, looking around the room. I'm about to ask him if he wants to dance when he turns back and says, "Well, good to meet you, Hank. Good *luck.*"

My mouth opens, but I manage only a nod in reply. Sylvain pushes into the crowd and disappears.

Good luck. Translation: *I don't have to pay to bring somebody home.*

I want to shout after him: *I wasn't going to charge you!* But I just settle back against the bar, a horrible sensation spreading through me.

No husband is going to want an escort for a mate. As soon as they find out what I do, they're not going to be interested.

Panic grips my chest.

So I won't tell them. And if I meet someone nice, someone who might turn into a boyfriend, it'll be easy to give up the escorting . . . Won't it?

I finish my water and place the empty bottle on the bar. I realize I'll meet no one here. I feel bitter, resentful for coming. Wasn't that the way it always happens at these things? So much sex on the dance floor and no one goes home with each other. Why is it that men line up to *pay* me for sex, and the guys at these parties won't even take it for *free?*

I look over again at Jeff and Anthony, sending curses. I feel guilty when Jeff looks over, catches my eyes, then lights up with a big smile and waves.

"Don't they make a lovely couple?"

I turn. It's Brent purring in my ear.

"Actually, they do," I say matter-of-factly, not even turning to look at him. "Both are very hot. All eyes are on them."

"Not mine," Brent snorts. I can tell from his eyes he's rolling. X, but *more,* too. There's always more with Brent. He has letters in his alphabet soup that I can't even *imagine* what they stand for. "But *your* eyes sure seem glued to them."

"Don't *start,* okay, Brent? Don't start in on how I'm secretly in love with Jeff, okay?"

Brent laughs. "There's nothing secret about it, sweetheart. Everybody knows. Except maybe him, and even *he's* probably got a pretty good clue. Jeff's thick, but not that thick."

I just sigh.

"Okay, I'm sorry." Brent orders himself an Absolut and tonic. "Want anything?"

"No. I'm as buzzed as I want to be."

Brent looks at me as if I've just expressed a concept he cannot begin to fathom. "I've yet to ever reach that state myself," he says, paying for his drink and then settling against the bar, shoulder to shoulder with me. "I've got a date with Tina later."

I smirk. "Of course you do. You're going steady, aren't you?"

"She's a wonderful girl," Brent says coyly.

I've never done crystal. Jeff told me long ago that crystal is the big, bad dog lurking on the dance floor, and he's insisted I never try it. "Keep away from Tina and Gina," he's said, predicting that one of these days Brent is going to OD right on the dance floor in front of us.

But I'm starting to think Jeff can be far too judgmental. There *is* such a thing as successful, casual drug use, isn't there? Sure, Brent can be annoying as all hell, but he seems to handle his drugs well. He gets twisted; he's passed out a few times at circuit events—but he gets to work on time every Monday. He's successful in his job, happy in his life. At least, he seems to be.

"Tell me something," he's saying, eyeing me. "Is it true you're whoring yourself?"

I laugh. "Well, finally, Brent, you're the last to learn a very juicy piece of gossip." I level my eyes with his. "Yes, it's true. I'm an escort. Big deal. I don't care who knows anymore. All that's different between me and everybody else here is that I actually *have* sex—and get paid two hundred bucks a pop for the effort."

Brent smiles. "I pass no judgment on you, Henry. Don't get all huffy. In fact, I think it's awesome. More power to you. I'd do the same thing if it wasn't for the thought of all those potbellied trolls who'd want to hire me."

I feel defensive of my clients. "They're not all trolls."

Brent flicks his wrist at me like an auntie. "The point is, Henry, when I saw your photo on a Web site a few weeks ago, I was just hurt that you never told me." He takes a sip of his drink. His blue eyes peer at me from over his glass. "I thought we were better friends than that."

"*Better friends?*" I make a face. "Brent, I've *never* confided anything to you. *Ever.*"

Brent frowns. "No, I guess you haven't." He sighs. "I wish you would, though. I tell you stuff all the time."

"You do not."

"I *do*. I tell you about who I trick with. Who I fall in love with. Which, granted, happens every other week, but still I tell you. I tell you *all* about every trip I ever take. I'm always telling you about the parties you miss, Henry. I'm always keeping you up to date." He positions himself a little aggressively in front of me. "Who's the one who's always inviting you out to Geoffrey's for breakfast or to Club Cafe for happy hour? Not Jeff O'Brien, Henry. *Me*. When I walk into a club, you're always the very first person I talk to. Can you say that about *him?*"

Our eyes hold each other. In his own way, Brent has a point.

"Henry Weiner, I consider you one of my best friends in the entire world."

Brent sounds a little emotional. Sure, it's the drugs and the alcohol, but in his own fucked-up way, Brent's being sincere. And trying—as best as he knows how—to tell me that he *cares*.

I smile. "Okay, Brent. I'll confide something to you."

"What?" he asks eagerly.

"If I found a husband tonight, I'd give it all up."

"The escorting?"

I nod. "Yeah. And this, too. All this traipsing around to party after party. I'd settle down, watch figure skating on TV on Saturday nights, get up early on Sunday to go get doughnuts and the paper. Maybe get a dog."

Brent shakes his head. "No, you only need the dog when you're single, Henry. My pug, Clara, not only keeps the bed warm but offers the perfect conversation-starter walking on Tremont Street. I *adore* Clara, but truth is, once you're married, you don't need a dog anymore."

I smile. "So how come *you* haven't found a husband, Brent?"

He looks away. "Husbands before the age of thirty-five never last. They just break your heart."

I try to find his gaze, but he keeps his eyes averted. Was there some pain in his words? Some hidden human experience to Brent Whitehead?

He turns back to me, cocky again. "I think thirty-five is the best age to settle down. I've got two years left to go. Then I'll consider settling down. Not too young that I'll be missing out on anything, but also not too old that I'm being forced into retirement." He grins. "I want to go out when I'm still on top. Like *The Mary Tyler Moore Show.*"

I laugh in return. "You know, under your nasty little exterior, Brent, you're not such a bad guy."

He beams. "You *see*, Henry? I can be a *much* better best friend than Jeff O'Brien."

"Did I hear my name?"

It's Jeff. He's pushing his way toward us, slipping his torso past others just as buff and wet and glistening as he is.

"Only to say that here you come again," Brent sniffs.

"Lookin' better than a body has a right to," Jeff sings in response. No one laughs. He makes an exasperated face. *"Get* it? Dolly Parton? *'Here you come again?'"*

"And here I go," Brent sings back. He winks at me. "Ta, Henry. I'll be in touch." He moves off back to the dance floor, cocking his squirt gun.

"What's up with *him?"* Jeff leans over the bar to order waters for the troops he's left behind on the dance floor. He makes a face as he hands over the cash. "Christ, I'll have to liquidate my 401k to pay for all this." He moves in close to me. "So how come you're not dancing?"

"Oh. You noticed."

Jeff frowns. "Are you mad at me for something?"

I sigh. "I'm not *mad* at you, Jeff. What would be the point?"

"Oh, God, you *are* mad at me."

"I'm not mad at you. Go *on*. Before Anthony trots off with someone else."

Jeff smirks. "Not likely." God, he can be such an arrogant fuck.

I shake my finger at him. I don't care if he calls me an old schoolmarm. "Don't hurt him, Jeff," I scold. "He's still too JV to understand you."

"Look, Anthony *may* be a little junior-varsity, but he's learning fast."

"Then how come he's not savvy enough to see that you and Lloyd are still just as entangled as ever?"

Jeff unscrews the cap of a bottled water and takes a slug. "I don't intend to hurt Anthony," he says seriously.

"You never *intend* to hurt *any* of them." I pause, looking away. "You just do."

"It's over with Lloyd. Henry, I realized it that day at the opening party. He's made his bed, and as far as I am concerned, he can now sleep with her and get it over with. He won't even *listen* when I try to offer my insights into her. So it's *over*. Anthony's totally into me, and I should just be grateful for that."

"But you don't even know the first thing about him."

Jeff begins ticking off points on the fingers of his left hand. "I know that he's kind. He's sincere. He's smart. He's compassionate." He takes another swig of water. "He's even dancing better, don't you think?"

"Haven't been paying attention," I lie. "Okay, so he may be kind and smart and all that, but he still disappears once a week. Who knows what's up with that?"

Jeff creases his brow, looking at me.

"Don't do that," I warn. "Wrinkles."

"What's going on with you?" Jeff asks. "Why are you trying to burst my balloon?"

"I'm sorry. But have you ever found out where he goes when he disappears?"

"I don't want to know," Jeff replies, but he doesn't convince me. "Not until Anthony wants to tell me himself. You've got to trust somebody if you're going to be in a relationship."

I try to smile. "It's *so* easy for you, Jeff. You know that? Let me tell you something. This guy hires me last week. He was just forty. Not all that much older than you."

Jeff scowls. "Your point is?"

"He was good-looking, smart, successful. But *lonely*, Jeff. So goddamn lonely. Do you know why he hired me? No worship scenes, no kinky stuff. Not even any sex. He hired me just so he could *hold* someone. That's all we did for the hour. Just laid there and held each other."

"Two hundred bucks for just lying there?" Jeff smiles. "Give him *my* number."

"You don't get it."

Jeff moves in close, nose to nose. "I *do*, Henry. I'm just trying to have fun. Why do you get all serious when we're supposed to be having a good time?"

I glare at him. "The guys who hire me are so much more in touch with what's *real* than any of these guys here."

Jeff frowns. "Come on, Henry. The guys who hire you are closeted, scared—"

"*Real*, Jeff. They're *real.*"

"The guy with the *shoes*, Henry. *He* was real?"

I pull away from him. "Look around you, Jeff. Look at these guys. Guys who don't want to grow up. I mean, come *on*, Jeff. Isn't it a bit odd that thirty-year-old men know the lyrics to *Britney Spears* songs?"

"*You* own every one of her CDs," Jeff reminds me, poking me in the chest with his finger. "And Christina Aguilera, and let's not forget Destiny's Child—"

"I'm including myself in this," I insist. "I'm just tired off the immaturity. The narcissism."

"Uh, hello? Who's made a career out of his own narcissism?"

"That's not what it's about anymore for me. It's changed. Jeff, what I want is something *real*. Some basic human interaction. Half of these guys here won't talk to you, won't say hello. It's all attitude."

"That's not so, Henry, and you know it. You're just feeling sorry for yourself."

"It *is* so. Everybody's so self-absorbed. 'Look at me, look at me.' Don't deny it, Jeff. You're caught in that same body image trap. You can't have sex with somebody unless you feel your body is in perfect shape. That's *fucked*, Jeff."

"I thought you felt the same way," he says.

"I'm thinking it's time I wake up. This scene is all about guys with too much time and too much money on their hands. Privileged white guys who can afford to jet-set around the continent—"

"Hold on just a fucking minute, Henry."

Okay, I know I'm tapping a nerve here. So much nasty stuff has been written about circuit boys and circuit culture that Jeff has long had an immediate, visceral, defensive reaction.

"These are *not* all white guys here," he snaps. "And yes, I wonder sometimes about priorities, too, about how I'm spending my money. And yes maybe our body image has gotten fucked up. Maybe we *can* be narcissistic posers at times. I'll look at that about myself, Henry." Jeff pauses. "But don't assume all these boys were born to privilege. *I* wasn't. *You* weren't, either."

I stand my ground. "But we're privileged *now*, Jeff. Even if we struggle, we find the cash for airfare, for hotel rooms, for drugs."

Jeff has no reply. I know I've stumped him with that one. Jeff's always been so sensitive to class stuff. Especially now, with the bank account Javitz left him. I keep going.

"And everybody pumped up with X or K or G or whatever they use. Ambulances routinely parked outside clubs. Is that craziness or what?"

"I say it's taking realistic precautions. Like passing out condoms." He's being stubborn.

"What goes up," I warn, "*must come down*, Jeff."

He looks at me with concern. "Is that what this is all about? You did some K, didn't you? You're going into a K-hole."

I just sigh impatiently. "Jeff, I'm going back to the hotel. I'm tired of coming to these things and not meeting anyone. At least when I escort I connect with someone. There's *contact*. There's *intimacy*."

Jeff puts his arms around me. "You just need to come out and *dance,* buddy."

"Yeah, for what? So that some guy can paw me and we can suck each other's tongues and then once the drugs wear off we'll each go home alone and realize our Prince Charmings were just fucked-up, nameless party boys?"

Jeff rests his forehead against mine. "You want to get all cerebral here, buddy?" he whispers. "You want to talk culture and theory here on the sidelines while they're mixing in Pepper MaShay out on the dance floor? Okay, Henry, let's *do* it, then. I'll go there with you. I'll admit to you that gay culture celebrates the ephemeral while always yearning for the eternal. But one does not necessarily nullify the other. Maybe it's just fleeting, and maybe a lot of it *does* have to do with the drugs, but you know as well as I do that what happens out there on the dance floor is just as *real* as anything you've experienced with your johns. Go ahead and lump all circuit boys into one big, fleshy mass just because you're feeling lonely. But you know it's not true. You can either stand here and feel sorry for yourself or go back to the room and jerk off to a Falcon video, or you can come back out to the dance floor with me and get back into the swim."

And then he kisses me. Mouth to mouth, lips to lips, even a little tongue—Jeff kisses me. He's never done that before. The X must be really having an effect on him. I blink back my surprise.

He pulls back, staring at me. "Well, what's it going to be?"

I have no idea. I have no idea why suddenly I'm so depressed. Maybe I *am* having a bad reaction to the X. It happens sometimes. Maybe Jeff's right: I *am* out of the swim, out of the loop, having spent too much time standing on beds while my clients adored me.

"Come on, buddy," Jeff whispers, encouraging me.

I smile. I allow him to lead me back to the dance floor. For a song or two, Jeff remains attentive, even grinding his crotch into my butt, holding me from behind—but eventually he pairs off with Anthony again. Whatever. Across the dance floor, I spy Brent lip-locked with some hunky Asian guy. I try to pretend I don't mind dancing alone, but I'm very glad when Shane sidles up alongside me, dousing me with a blast from his Uzi.

"Still the sexiest guy on the dance floor," Shane tells me.

I pull him close, running my hands up and down his wet, shapeless torso.

"Oh, I see where this is leading," Shane says.

"Oh, yeah?" I ask. "Where?"

"Right back to your hotel room."

I laugh.

Shane bears down on me. "What's the matter, Henry? Giving up so fast on all these hunky Montreal boys? Thinking it's going to be a dud of a night, so you might as well grab me? Just like in Philadelphia."

I look up at him. "Shane, it's not like that—"

"Yes, it is, sweetie. Come on. We don't lie to each other, remember?"

He's right. We'll have sex and it'll be good, but there's no getting around the fact that I'll be using Shane because I'm lonely.

I let him go.

"That's okay, stud muffin," Shane says, grinning. "I didn't mean that I didn't *want* to go home with you. I was just being honest. Anytime you're ready to go, I am, too."

I look at him. I feel as if I might start bawling right there on the dance floor. Shane just pulls me close, pressing my face into his chest. We slow-dance that way for a while. Then, hand in hand, we go back to the room.

A Few Days Later,
A Town Outside Hartford,
Connecticut

Jeff

"Unca Jeff! Unca Jeff!"

The top half of Little Jeffy's face suddenly appears over the library's computer terminal. His big brown eyes and bushy dark hair make him took like a Muppet. I can't help but laugh. "I thought you were going in for Storytime," I say to him.

"It didn't start yet." The five-year-old scurries around to the front of the computer. "Whatchadoin'?"

I help him up onto my lap. "I'm ordering some flowers to be sent to my friend. You remember Henry, don't you?"

Jeffy nods. "How come you're sendin' him flowers? Is he your sweetheart?"

I smile. "He's my *friend*, Jeffy."

"That's right," the boy says. "Unca *Lloyd* is your sweetheart. My mommy told me."

I sigh, saying nothing.

Jeffy presses his nose up against the computer screen. "So how come you're sendin' *Henry* some flowers if he's not your sweetheart?"

"Because the last time I saw him," I explain patiently, "he was feeling a little bit sad. Move out of the way, Jeffy, so I can see what I'm sending."

"Why was he sad?"

I tousle the kid's hair. "I don't really know, kiddo. He just was."

"Will the flowers make him happy?"

"I hope so," I tell him, clicking the SEND button after typing in my credit card. "I really hope so."

When we dropped him off at his apartment after getting back from Montreal, Henry still seemed so gloomy. I wished I could have *done* something, *said* something, fixed whatever it was that was bugging him. I know I don't show it often enough, but Henry's my best friend in the whole world, and I love him. More than I've loved any other friend since Javitz. And though I try to play Javitz to Henry's Jeff, I'm doing a pretty shitty job of it. Javitz would've done far better for me than I'm doing for Henry. Javitz always knew how to discern exactly what was going on for me when I was down. He would have zeroed in on the problem and teased it right out of my system. He'd have done a whole hell of a lot more than just send me flowers. But for the moment, it's all I can think to do.

Henry's been on my mind all day, even as I drove down to Connecticut for my regular outing with Jeffy. It's been fun, as always. I took Jeffy and his mom, my sister Ann Marie, for lunch at the Big Boy, then we headed over to the mall, where I bought Jeffy a new pair of sneakers and some glow-in-the-dark monster stickers. In the car, NSYNC blasted from the radio, and Jeffy just *loved* that I could sing all the words of "Bye Bye Bye" along with him. Ann Marie laughed. "As if any of my boyfriends could ever do *that*," she said.

See, Henry? Knowing teenybopper lyrics is good for *something*.

Now we're at the library for Storytime. They're on the final chapters of *Charlotte's Web*. I love this old library. It has the hush that all libraries have, an enveloping stillness I treasure. Some of my best articles have been researched in libraries like this all across the country, from small-town repositories to the grand, gargantuan Library of Congress in D.C. I know all of their secret hiding places, their little cubbyholes: the alcove at New York Public where you can sit for hours without anyone ever walking by; the quiet burrow in the basement of Boston Public where they keep the old city directories; a study room on a top floor of the UMass library, where students do a lot more than study.

This one's the most special, however, for this is the library of my hometown, where as a kid I spent many an hour hidden away in the stacks, reading about black holes in space or Perseus slicing the head off Medusa or the early film career of Barbara Stanwyck. My parents thought I was playing softball with the neighborhood boys, but I was really lost in a world of fantasies and dreams. Such a devious little fag boy I was, and with such eclectic tastes! I checked out books on Greek mythology, old-time radio, and the Charles Manson murders all at the same time. I once photocopied every single page of Agnes Strickland's five-volume *Lives of the Queens of England*. Like anybody who saw me couldn't figure *that* out.

Of course, back then, the library had no bank of computers, and the ugly drop ceiling that now obscures the magnificent marble dome had yet to be installed. But the brownstone walls remain, and the high stained-glass windows. As a boy, I came here for Storytime, too, and *Charlotte's Web* was my favorite tale. I remember staring up at the blue glass of the windows and imagining Charlotte up there, spinning her web. When Miss McGeowan got to the part where Charlotte dies, I bawled so hard my mother had to take me into the bathroom to calm me down. That book is still the saddest one I've ever read.

It's funny. Sitting here with Jeffy on my lap, my mind makes a sudden leap. I wonder all at once if Anthony has ever read *Charlotte's Web*. As much as Henry might be on my mind, Anthony's there, too. These past few weeks have been a blur of emotions, and, as I predicted might happen, Anthony's come to mean a whole lot more to me than just a leftover New Year's Eve trick. Am I falling in love with him? Sometimes it feels that way, when we sit together on the couch, him nestled between my legs, sharing take-out Chinese food and watching *Bewitched*. Sometimes it feels that way, when I introduce him to all the Gay 101 he missed—Bette Davis movies, Broadway soundtracks, John Waters, Barney Frank, Armistead Maupin, Harry Hay—and he beams with such gratitude. But how can I fall in love with anyone when my feelings for Lloyd are still all jumbled up inside me?

Still, there's no question that for the past few days, all sorts of silly questions have been popping into my mind about Anthony. Has he ever been to Disney World? Did he watch *The Electric Company* when he was a kid? Did he go to his prom? What kind of Christmas tree did his family have—real or artificial? All the little things you're supposed to know about someone you live with, someone you might want to stick around for a while. I know all of those things about Lloyd. But it feels as if I'll never know them about Anthony.

Little Jeffy is getting fidgety. "Unca Jeff, can I send my sweetheart some flowers?"

I laugh. "Your sweetheart? Who's your sweetheart? Your mom?"

"No. Michael."

I laugh even harder. "*Michael!* Who's Michael?"

"He's in my kindergarten class."

I can barely contain my mirth. "And have you told *Michael* he's your sweetheart?"

Jeffy nods, pressing the space bar on the computer keypad. "Yup. Hey, Unca Jeff, are you a top or a bottom?"

I almost drop the kid on the floor. "Where did you learn about *that,* mister?"

"On *Will and Grace,*" the boy replies.

My sister Ann Marie has appeared on the other side of the bank of computers. "Jeffy. Come on. They're starting Storytime."

I look at her, wide-eyed and grinning. "Do you know what this child just asked me?"

She makes a face. "I shudder to think."

"If I was a top or a bottom."

"Well," the boy persists, "which *are* you?"

"Jeffy," his mother says sternly, "Storytime."

The child climbs down off of my lap. He looks back at me. "Michael's a big old bottom," he tells me before running across the lobby to the children's section. I just took over at my sister and burst out laughing.

Ann Marie gives me an exasperated smile. "I let him watch the show because I think it's important for him to see gay people and straight people together."

"You're a good mom," I assure her. "Oh, and by the way, *speaking of Moms.* You won't tell her I came down, huh? She'll start in about the fact I didn't come see her."

"My lips are sealed," she promises. She sits down at the computer next to me. "Jeff, I've been wanting to talk with you. We haven't seen Lloyd in a while. Can I ask if there's a problem?"

I sigh. "Problem? No, there's no problem. Not if I just accept the way things are. He's consumed by his guest house." I pause, looking away. "It's his choice."

"Well, couldn't you spend more time there? You're not *working.*"

I frown. "Ann Marie, you don't understand the situation, and I really don't want to get into it, okay?"

"Okay. I'm *sorry* for asking." She can be just like me, quick-edged and dismissive. "It's just that I thought the two of you were getting back together. I love Lloyd. So does Jeffy."

I try to smile. "Well, what did you think of that guy Anthony? Remember, the blond guy who came with us a few weeks ago? He played GameBoy with—"

"I remember." Ann Marie looks at me plainly. "So is he the new one?"

"Well, he's living with me right now. . . ."

She nods. She doesn't seem happy. "What does he do? Where's he from?"

Perfectly appropriate questions, I acknowledge to myself, but questions for which I have no adequate answers. "Never mind," I say. "It's very much in the formative stages. I don't know where it's going."

"But you like him?"

I nod. "I do. I do like him."

She narrows her eyes at me. "Because Lloyd isn't available?

I make a face at her.

"Look, Jeff. I don't want to sound like Mom here, lecturing you. But I'd give anything for the kind of devotion I've seen between you and Lloyd. I look at you guys and say, 'Why can't I find that?' You guys have something special."

I look away. "Thanks, Ann Marie. But I really *don't* want to get into it."

She sighs. "Okay. Well, I promised the reader I'd help monitor the kids today. Some of them start acting up during Storytime. Let me cook dinner afterward before you head home."

I nod.

She smiles at me as she stands up. "You know how much it matters to Jeffy that you come down and spend the day with him like this. And to me, too." She kisses me on the cheek.

I watch her walk away. Since she left Jeffy's father, she's had no one. No significant other. Oh, she dates, but they never last for more than a few weeks. No wonder Ann Marie wants to believe it can work out between Lloyd and me. It's the same for Chanel, who's broken up with Wendy more times than I can count and who—I've heard through the grapevine—is considering taking Gertrude and leaving her again. It's the same for Henry, too, who's never had a relationship in his life. *Everyone* wants Jeff and Lloyd to work out.

Except maybe Jeff and Lloyd.

But you like him?

I do. I do like him.

Because Lloyd isn't available?

Is that it? Is that the reason I stick with Anthony, despite the mystery? Despite not knowing much more about him than I did on New Year's Eve?

That's when it hits me.

"Of course," I whisper to myself.

Suddenly I know what paper that clipping came from. The photo of Robert Riley.

The Hartford Courant. The paper I grew up with. My hometown Connecticut newspaper. That's how I recognized the typeface. I saw it every day for the first twenty years of my life.

I stand abruptly, walking quickly over to the reference desk. "Excuse me?" I ask.

The woman looks up at me. It's old Miss Crenshaw, the same woman who sat here twenty-five years ago. As a ten-year-old boy I'd stand in front of her requesting a copy of the atlas of the British Isles, circa 1600. She looks just as old now as she did then, her face a maze of leathery wrinkles, her small, round blue glasses perched at the end of her nose, her hair cut short and severe.

"Yes?" she asks.

"I wonder if you have an index to *The Hartford Courant.*"

"What year?" she asks efficiently.

"Uh, well, I guess I'd need 1985 to 1988."

She nods and reaches under her desk, rummaging around for a moment and then producing three thin, blue spiral-bound volumes. "Do you have a library card?" she asks.

"Um, well, I used to," I say.

"Name?" she asks, hands poised at her computer terminal.

"Jeffrey O'Brien, but it was a long time—" She ignores me, typing in my name.

"Here you are," she says. "Card expired in 1981. Care to renew?"

I smile. "Actually, I don't live here anymore. I just want to—"

"And I see you never paid a fine on *The Films of Greta Garbo.* My, my, with interest building all that time, that adds up to . . ."

She looks up at me from behind her blue glasses. I gulp.

Miss Crenshaw smiles. "Maybe I'll grant you amnesty. You don't think I remember you, do you, Jeffrey?"

My mouth opens in surprise.

"Oh, but I do. I remember you very well, sitting over there, reading all day, when you could've been outside playing with the other boys. I pegged you then as a special one. One who was going to go *far* in life." She winks at me.

I smile. "I was always harassing you for books from the special collections."

"That you were." She removes her glasses to look up at me. "And don't think I didn't notice when your byline started appearing in various places. I took some pride in that, thinking maybe those afternoons here in the library had helped get you to where you are."

I nod. "They *did,* Miss Crenshaw. They certainly did."

She beams. "I especially enjoyed that piece you did in *The Advocate* a while back on elderly lesbians. Thought it was right on target." She looks at me significantly, her old eyes twinkling. "I convinced the board to finally subscribe to *The Advocate* after that. Now anybody can read it over in Periodicals. *Anybody.*"

I feel my throat tighten a little. How awesome would *that* have been for my ten-year-old self?

"Here you go, Jeffrey," Miss Crenshaw is saying. "I hope this means you're researching another fine article. Or a *book*. I would *love* to catalog a book from Jeffrey O'Brien on these shelves someday before I retire."

I take the volumes from her. "Thank you, Miss Crenshaw. Maybe you will."

Yeah. Maybe she will at that.

"But do me a favor," she says. "Don't be one of those writers who gets all sensitive and prickly when someone calls you a *gay author*. Whenever I hear someone bitching about how the label limits them, or ghettoizes them, well, I just want to slap them upside the head."

I laugh out loud. I can't help it. Miss Crenshaw just gives me a look. "It's just such a culture-hating thing to say," she says. "Don't be like that, Jeffrey. Now go do your research." She turns back to her computer.

I'm smiling all the way over to the table, where I sit down and open the index in front of me. Very quickly I find what I'm looking for.

And then some.

Robert Riley is indeed listed in the index.

September 15, 1986: RILEY, ROBERT. Man found blundgeoned to death in yard. A-14: 3–5 (photo).

But there's more, too: a whole list of related articles about the investigation into the death and the arrest of suspects, continuing through December. I eagerly pull over the Index for 1987, and sure enough, the stories continue. Almost a year after the murder, sentencing was held for the two killers. Ortiz and Murphy were their names. They pled guilty; one got thirty-five years; the other turned state's evidence and got twenty.

My mouth is as dry as if I'd had three hits of X. I can hear my heart beating in my ears.

Robert Riley was murdered.

Even before I know for certain, I intuit a gay-bashing. I copy down the notations from the index and hurry over to the metal cabinet that contains the rolls of newspaper microfilm. I locate the correct reels and slide open the drawer. It makes a loud squeak, causing several people at nearby tables to lift their eyes from their books and glare over at me. Miss Crenshaw puts her finger to her mouth. I carefully extract the reels I need.

Into the microfilm reader I maneuver the film. It's been a couple of years since I've done any research, but I still remember how the thing works. I can't deny how pumped I am. It's always like this when I find myself hot on the lead of a good story. Except this isn't an assignment for *The Advocate* or *The Boston Globe*. This is about *Anthony*. Anthony's *life*.

I stop. I sit back in my chair. Can I really do this? I swore off it, not wanting to go behind Anthony's back. He said he'd tell me when he could. I promised myself not to snoop.

But I *have* to know. Lloyd's belief in fate has rubbed off on me: I was *meant* to realize the *Courant* connection. That's why I'm here at the library today. I was *meant* to find this information. All sorts of questions suddenly flood my mind. The bus schedule I'd found, making me consider that Anthony's overnight disappearances weren't in Boston. Did he come here, to Connecticut?

I can't stop now. I *have* to find out why he carries Riley's picture. I begin turning the crank on the microfilm reader as fast as I can, watching the edges of the film for the date. Finally, there it is. Monday, September 15.

I make a small gasp. There, staring out at me, is the same photo that Anthony keeps laminated in his wallet. Robert Riley, smiling and staring at me.

> A West Hartford attorney was found bludgeoned to death in his front yard early Sunday morning. Police are looking for two suspects a neighbor saw fleeing the scene several hours earlier.
>
> Robert Riley, 36, was pronounced dead at the scene after a call was made to state police by his newspaper carrier, who discovered the body facedown in the grass at 6:55 Sunday morning. Mr. Riley's head had been repeatedly struck with a blunt object, and his mouth and hands were bound with duct tape.
>
> A neighbor, Mrs. Franklin Toomey, told police she was awakened by the sounds of shouting around 2:00 A.M., and observed two persons running through Mr. Riley's yard. They drove off in what she described as a "white two-door vehicle."
>
> Police at this time have no suspects and are not speculating on a possible motive for Mr. Riley's death.

Mr. Riley was a well-regarded corporate attorney, working for such clients as Aetna and the Travelers. Friends are remembering him today as a committed, caring community member.

Riley was recently recognized with a community service award from Junior Achievement for volunteering his time teaching about the law to students at Lewis Fox Middle School in Hartford.

Riley was a bachelor who had "many friends and no enemies," according to his roommate, Anthony Sabe.

I sit back in my chair hard, as if I'd been pushed.

"Anthony," I whisper.

After that, I can't read straight. I keep trying to finish the article but can't seem to focus.

His roommate, Anthony Sabe.

But Anthony would have been only sixteen.

Roommate?

He cared about young people.

What does it mean?

I think of one other thing.

I'm the same age as Robert Riley when he was killed.

"Unca Jeff!"

I look up, startled. Jeffy's been crying. His little checks are red and blotchy.

"Unca Jeff," he sobs. "Charlotte *died!*"

"Yeah, I know, buddy," I say, trying to bring myself back to his reality. "You okay?"

"Yeah," he says, drying his eyes as I put my arms around him. "It was just a story." He's talking loud, but then remembers he's in a library. He cups his hands to his mouth and whispers: "And besides, she left lots of babies to keep Wilbur company."

I kiss the top of his head. "Yes, he'll always have them."

He grins, moving from sad to glad effortlessly, as only children can do. "Mommy said we'll meet you in the car," he chirps. "Okay?"

"Okay," I manage to reply. The boy runs outside, Miss Crenshaw cautioning him to take it slow. I turn back to the microfilm reader, in somewhat of a daze. I quickly find the next article, not stopping to read it, just hitting the PRINT button on the reader. I find each successive story listed in the index and print them all, right up through the sentencing of the killers. It costs me $3.20, ten cents a page. I hand the money over to Miss Crenshaw, who places it in a little box on her desk.

"Don't forget, now," she tells me. "I want to see a book from you one of these days."

I smile but say nothing. Outside the library, the sun is low in the sky. It's still warm, and the leaves have popped on all of the trees, tender and bright and green. I punch in Henry's number on my cell phone, desperate to share all this with someone, but of course all I get is a message that "Hank" is unavailable and to leave a message. I do, begging him to call me back *right away,* but of course, it'll be over twenty-four hours before Henry returns the call.

By then, I know so much more.

Memorial Day Weekend, Nirvana

Lloyd

It's an awesome start to our first summer season. A beautiful warm day, the sky an unbroken umbrella of blue. In the harbor, dozens of white sailboats dot the turquoise bay, and the street is thronged with tourists. Ty is one of our guests for the weekend, surprising us by filling the house with the most fragrant white lilies I've ever smelled. He also left a single red rose on my pillow. If not for all the complications in my life, I might welcome his persistent advances. But as it is, I simply said good night and shook his hand when it was time to go to bed last night.

Now it's Friday morning, and I'm sitting in our office, behind the front desk, going over the payroll account. We've hired three houseboys to help run the place. Believe me, we need them. Poaching eggs, flipping pancakes, washing linens, turning mattresses, changing sheets, and folding towels for four or five visitors each week was one thing. Doing it for ten to fifteen people *per day* is quite another.

We're booked to capacity for the whole holiday weekend, and despite our *NO VACANCY* sign out front, bedraggled tourists still wander in, asking if we've had any cancellations.

I hear the bell on the front door tinkle; another forlorn lot of bad planners, I presume. "Just a minute," I call.

"Take your time," comes the reply.

I know the voice. I try to place it, then shake my head in disbelief. I walk out front.

"Innkeeping becomes you, Lloyd. You took great."

Drake.

"Thanks," I say, a little wary. Two cloth suitcases sit at his feet.

"I was *thrilled* that you had a room available at the last minute," he says, leaning in over the counter. "My lucky day."

"Drake, I'm afraid to say your luck has run out. I don't have a reservation for you, and we are completely full."

He smiles. "Not according to your partner, you aren't."

I frown. "Eva? When did you talk to her?"

"A couple of days ago. At first, she told me you were booked, but then I reminded her how we'd met at the opening party, and she suddenly said there was a room." He smiles. "It's a beautiful day out there, Lloyd. Maybe I can persuade you to take a break and join me on my boat?" His eyes twinkle. "Did I mention I bought a boat?"

"No," I say. "You didn't mention that." I hold up my hand to him. "Wait a second, okay?" I pick up the phone and press Eva's extension. She answers cheerily. "Eva," I ask, keeping my voice level, "could you come down to the front desk, please?"

I hang up and look over at Drake. "I'm being up front with you here, Drake. I don't know why she said we had a room. We just *don't*. We've been booked solid for months, and there have been no cancellations."

He shrugs, seeming so fucking cocky in the belief that I'll be eventually proven wrong. Eva comes down the stairs. When she spots Drake, she beams, rushing over to embrace him tightly. "How *good* it is to see you again," she enthuses.

"And you, too, Eva," he says. "Now, maybe you can explain to our friend here that you really *did* find a room for me."

She lets him go and turns to look at me. "I did. Come into the office with me for a moment, Lloyd. I'll show you which one on the house diagram. Drake, we'll be right back."

He gives us a jaunty little salute.

Eva closes the door behind us. "Lloyd, I cleared out *my* room so he'd have a place to stay."

"*Your* room? Eva, that's crazy! You can't give up your room!"

She offers a brave little self-sacrificing smile. "It's okay. He's your friend. I'd like to do it for you."

I'm flabbergasted. "This is absurd. Where were you thinking *you'd* sleep?"

"In the attic."

"*The attic!* With the *houseboys?*"

"There's an extra cot," she says simply.

I grip her by the shoulders. "Listen to me. I don't *want* Drake here! Do you understand? He wants to see me romantically, and I'm just not interested."

"Oh." Her brow furrows. "I see."

I sigh. "You need to explain to him that you made a mistake."

She looks at me with some anxiety. "Oh, I can't do that, Lloyd. Everything's booked up all over town. He came down here expecting a room." She puts a hand on her forehead. "Oh, dear, I've made a mess of things, haven't I? It was just that when he said he was your friend, I figured you'd be *glad* to see him."

"Why didn't you tell me about it?"

She smiles wanly. "He thought we ought to surprise you."

I just shake my head.

Her smile changes a little. Suddenly she looks more sassy than distressed, as if she's just thought of a plan. "Well, you don't have to worry about him, Lloyd. I promise I will keep him away from you."

"Eva, we have a houseful of guests. You can't be patrolling Drake all weekend."

She grinned. "I'll get him to take me out on his boat. He told me all about it when we talked. That will keep him occupied for at least half a day." She looks off in the direction of the door. "He *is* awfully handsome, isn't he?"

I look at her sharply. "Oh, is *that* what you're thinking?" I lean down close into her face. "Do you want to sleep with *him,* too? Not all gay men are as easy marks as Ira, you know."

Okay. I suppose I need to take a breather here. Just talking about it gets me worked up. Because ever since that night I walked in on her and Ira, things just haven't been the same between Eva and me. All of my old fears about her state of mind have been revived. When I confronted her about Ira, she acted surprised that I knew, and immediately burst into tears. She claimed she'd just gone in to check on him and discovered him lonely and depressed, and they'd started talking, and before she knew it they were kissing, and well, one thing led to another. . . .

"But he's a gay man, for God's sake!"

"I know, I know," she said, tears dripping off her chin. "He said I was the first woman he'd slept with in fifteen years!"

"Are you planning on seeing him again?" I asked.

She was trembling. "No. Not if you think I shouldn't."

I sighed. "You can't be seducing guests, Eva."

She burst into a new torrent of tears. I found myself consoling her. "Did you at least use a condom?" I asked.

"No," she whimpered, and that set off a round of paranoia and a long discussion of safer sex. She hadn't had sex since Steven, she said. She should have known better.

"It will never happen again," she promised shamefacedly. "Even though I think Ira has feelings for me . . ."

Even though he's a gay man.

I needed to talk with someone, so I described the situation to a friend, a therapist practicing here on the Cape. Without naming any names, I asked her what diagnosis she might make in this case.

"From what you're telling me, I'd say this person is a little delusional," my friend told me. "There's definitely a personality disorder. She might even be borderline."

I shuddered. No, that much isn't possible. I'm a trained psychologist. I'd have recognized a borderline personality. There's *no way* I could have missed that.

No way? None at all? I force myself to remember what my own frame of mind had been like when I met Eva. I was depressed myself, drowning in my own confusion and grief. I was looking for a lifesaver, and it seemed that Eva tossed one in the water for me to grab on to. When you're *this close* to drowning, you don't take the time to inspect the thing to see if it has any holes.

What makes this even more troubling is the fact that I'm starting to think Eva *lies* to me. I don't think she's in therapy. She said she was, but I don't think she went *for even one session.* In the past couple of months, she's rarely been far from my side: if she's been seeing somebody regularly, I can't imagine *when.* She's never talked about her therapy, either, and for someone who discloses as easily and as often as she does, I tend to think that's significant. No, I don't think she's in therapy, and that troubles me a great deal.

But if she *is* personality disordered, then so much of what I've been observing makes sense. Every male guest—gay or straight, young or old—has been practically smothered with attention from Eva. Some love it, singing her praises and promising they'll return for more. Others seem puzzled by it, often finding themselves trapped for hours looking at her scrapbooks and listening to her stories. One night I came downstairs to find her on the couch with a very handsome guest in his forties, and she was crying. The man was consoling her about something. I just bit my lip and walked back upstairs.

It's as if she's this black hole of emotion, sucking into her void every male who happens to cross her path. I ponder my evolving diagnosis. Just suppose those bedtimes with Daddy weren't as innocent as she makes out. Sexual abuse would help to explain a good deal of her behavior. I'm beginning to feel Eva's dependence on me isn't just about her grief over Steven's death. It goes back much farther than that.

I don't know what to do, how much more I can take. Every time I turn around these days, there she is. Forget the solitary walks along the breakwater I once so treasured. Now a quiet half hour alone in my room is hard enough to achieve.

Can I talk to you just a minute, Lloyd?
I'm sorry to bother you, Lloyd.
I don't know how to fix the toaster, Lloyd.
Lloyd, can you take a look at this, please?
I am so frazzled, Lloyd. I need a shoulder to cry on. Please???

Her clever little machinations to coerce what she needs from me have only increased. Like that day of the opening, when she'd *supposedly* twisted her ankle. I wonder about that now. Then there was the fainting spell at the Unitarian Meeting House, where I carried her downstairs and tenderly placed a cold cloth on her head. A few nights later there was an episode of sleepwalking. I found her staring out from the front door in her nightgown and gently escorted her back to her room. "Thank you, Lloyd," she said as I tucked her in. "Thank you for taking care of me."

Another evening she sat on my bed, talking dreamily and playing with her hair, eventually falling asleep, apparently hoping I'd simply crawl in next to her. No, thanks. I'm not Ira. *This* gay man does not sleep with women. I took my pillow and headed down to the couch.

It's you she wants. Not a guest house in Provincetown. You could be opening up a laundromat together and she'd be just as into it.

"Lloyd?"

I blink. She's looking up at me with those big round eyes.

"Lloyd, what do you want to do about Drake? I'll do whatever you say."

I give in. She wins. She convinces me that we simply can't turn him away; he does indeed take her room. But I can't bear the thought of her sleeping up in the attic with three randy houseboys. I give her my bed, and instead, it's *me* who climbs the ladder up to the attic and takes the cot beside Ian, Justin, and José. Queer, isn't it? I trust *myself* with them more than I do her.

The next day I barricade myself in the office, not wanting to run into anyone. But forget that: there's always *somebody* knocking at the door.

Around noon I hear a voice. "Lloyd?"

I look up. It's Ty. I give him a small smile.

"I had dinner with your friend Drake last night," he says. "What a charmer."

I shrug. "If you say so."

Ty smirks. "I tried to show him some charm myself, but all he wanted to talk about was you." He stares down at me. "Not that I blame him."

I run a hand over my buzzed head. "Ty, I'm kind of swamped with work right now. . . ."

He moves around behind me and begins giving me a shoulder massage. "You're missing a fabulous day. Can I entice you into a walk?"

"Really, I can't—"

"Just to clear your head. Get out of this place for a while." He pauses. "Before Eva gets back from the grocery store."

I look up at him. He raises his eyebrows.

"Yeah," I say. "A walk might do me good."

We're on our way out the door when we run into Shane coming up the front steps. He's dressed in a pair of leopard-print Lycra shorts and a Bundeswehr tanktop. I like Shane. He's not filled with attitude the way so many of Jeff's circuit friends are.

"Hey," I greet him. "In town for the weekend?"

"Sure am," he says, snapping his fingers like a drag queen. "Kickin' off the season!"

"And in *style*," I say. He pirouettes for us. "We're going for a walk," I tell him. "Care to join us?"

Shane looks a little awkward. "Oh. I'd love to. But actually . . . I'm here to see *Eva*. We're having lunch."

I just nod. But of *course*. He didn't come to see *me*; he came to see *Eva*. I smolder as Ty and I walk down Commercial Street. I don't say anything, but I sense he understands *exactly* what's on my mind.

A drag queen dressed as Cher, complete with ass-revealing fishnet stockings, motors past us on her scooter. Straight tourists gasp and snap photographs as she passes. The town is alive with rainbow flags and the smell of cotton candy. A trio of lesbians in leather are listening to a woman play a gigantic harp in front of Town Hall. The summer has begun.

"You want to talk?" Ty asks finally.

I laugh. "I'm not sure what I'd say."

"Maybe that she's driving you a little crazy. Maybe that everywhere you turn, there she is."

I look at him. "Let's get a burrito."

We each order the Saucy Tofu at Big Daddy's, then head out to the picnic tables on the pier. Gulls alight immediately at our side, hoping for a handout.

I tell Ty a little of what's been going on, but still I try to be respectful.

I want to be appropriate. I want to respect boundaries. I want to be all the things Eva isn't. Ty is *her* friend first, after all.

"I guess the stress of the past few months has just made me cynical," I say. "I know viewing her every move with suspicion is unfair. Maybe I ought to give her the benefit of the doubt more often."

"Maybe you should," Ty responds noncommittally.

I wipe peanut sauce off my chin with a napkin. "Maybe she really *did* innocently fall asleep on my bed. She works hard. I have to give her credit. She's up at the crack of dawn, making fabulous breakfasts for the guests. She keeps a spotless house, and pays all the bills on time. Do you know we're already exceeding expectations and the summer has just started?"

"You've both worked very hard," Ty says.

I laugh. "Maybe I'm just cranky because I miss male companionship."

Ty makes a palms-up gesture with his hands. "I'm all yours, handsome."

I shake my head. "I don't think we should, Ty. She was very upset about the last time. I think it wounded her ego. She thought you were in love with her."

"Lloyd, I'm a *gay* man. She knows that and always has known that."

I sigh. "Well, it's not the only delusion she's had. But I need to respect that you're her friend first, before me."

"Actually, I was *Steven's* friend. To be honest, I've never fully trusted Eva enough to call her a friend."

Okay, so that nearly knocks me off my seat. I just sit there staring at him.

"I could tell you things," Ty is saying, throwing bread to the gulls, "that would make your hair stand on end."

I recoil. "No, Ty. I can't talk about her anymore. This just isn't right."

He shrugs. "You're a man of great principle, Lloyd. But this isn't just about you. You have a *business* to run. *Guests* you're responsible for. Guests who might not come back if Eva pushes too hard."

I look off at the bay. How peaceful it is out there. The way the boats rock lazily back and forth, the sparkle of the sunlight against the surface of the water. I can't deny wanting to talk about all this with Ty, but neither can I ignore my discomfort. In my work with patients, I've always respected confidentiality to a fault. Talking about someone to a third party without speaking to them first is wrong. Just *wrong*.

But Ty's right: I need to talk to *someone* or I'll go crazy myself.

"I just think that sometimes," I begin, weighing my words carefully, "Eva has a little trouble with boundaries."

"A little trouble?" Ty grins. "Dr. Griffith, you *are* discreet."

I grow impatient. "You were there the night of the opening, Ty. Didn't you see her with Ira?"

He sighs. "Oh, I saw her all right. *Heard* her, too. I imagine she *wanted* me to hear. After hearing *us* together several weeks earlier."

"You think she slept with him simply to get back at us?"

Ty shrugs. "That was only part of it. She has all sorts of motivations and needs. They're all tumbled together, bouncing off each other and working overtime—as you've learned."

I feel as if I might cry all of a sudden. "But she seemed so *strong* when I met her. I saw her in action, Ty! I *saw* her with Alex—"

"Who died a few weeks ago."

My jaw drops.

Ty nods. "Yes, he died. I called Eva to tell her." He pauses dramatically. "She never came for the funeral."

"Maybe . . . maybe it was just too hard for her. I mean, after Steven . . ."

"And maybe she didn't care. Maybe she had *stopped* caring. Because there was a new man in her life to care about."

I remember Eva telling me how she might have fallen in love with Alex. I had seen her devotion to him, seen the concern and the care on her face. And she never told me he died. She hasn't seemed in the least affected by it. The realization hits me: *she had written him off.* She never saw him again after she left New York. She probably never even thought of him.

Because there was a new man in her life to care about.

"It's all or nothing with Eva," Ty says. "That's what's so disturbing."

"Maybe," I say, still searching for a way out of this, "maybe in her grief, she's shut down parts of herself. Compartmentalized things . . . I mean, I *know* there's something good and strong and wise about Eva. The talks we've had, the things we've shared . . ."

Ty looks at me gently. "I remember when she started volunteering. I saw that side of her, too." He pauses, seeming to consider something. "Did you know that, as part of her volunteer efforts, Eva worked as a tutor for the New York school system?"

"No."

I feel a chilly hand settle on my shoulder.

"She did it for about six months. Then she was asked to leave."

I lean toward him. "Maybe I shouldn't—"

But he won't allow me to cut him off. "She had grown a bit, shall we say, too *attached* to one particular boy. A sixteen-year-old recovering addict. His mother put in a complaint."

"I'm sure Eva was just—"

He levels his eyes at me. "The mother found them in bed together."

I haven't had sex with anyone since Steven.

"Nothing ever came of it," Ty tells me. "She was just asked to leave."

I know I shouldn't have heard that. I have no right to learn of this incident without Eva's consent. It's in the past and I shouldn't hold it against her. Everybody makes mistakes. There are two sides to every story.

But it sure as hell fits the pattern.

"Do you want to talk more?" Ty asks.

"No," I say definitively. "That's more than enough."

He sighs. "I worry about you sometimes, Lloyd. She can be—"

"Please, Ty. No more."

"It's just that Steven—"

"No more!" I hold my hands up at him. "I'll talk with her myself. Anything else that I need to know, let her tell me on her own." I pause. "But you're right. I do need to talk to her."

That's the only way. The only way this venture of ours can succeed. The only way I can stay with this and not go crazy. If she gets into therapy, really works at things, then we can still make it work.

"Speaking of talking," Ty says, "have you had any communication with Jeff?"

I frown, puzzled at the change in topic. "No," I tell him. "Not in a while."

In fact, since Jeff hasn't answered any of my E-mails in weeks, I've stopped trying to contact him. He must be so busy with Anthony that he can't be bothered. I heard through the grapevine that he's down in Pensacola, Florida, for yet another party this weekend.

"Well, I think your funk may have other causes than Eva alone," Ty says sagely. "Maybe you'd rather we talk about *that.*"

He raises his eyebrows at me again, hoping I'll say more. But I don't. I just can't. Talking about Eva is upsetting enough; I can't start thinking about Jeff, too.

"Well," Ty says, giving up, "if you ever *do* want to talk more, please call me." He places his hand over mine. "Remember that, okay?"

Our conversation ends there, because suddenly—speak of the devil— Eva and Shane are behind us, laughing like two schoolgirls. He's taking her to Tea Dance, he explains, and Drake is meeting them later for dinner. Eva's wearing zebra-print spandex to complement Shane's leotard; her fleshy thighs are exposed for all to see. Needless to say, I decline their invitation to join them. I turn down Ty's offer for dinner, too. I just rent *All About Eve,* watching it alone in my room. I miss Javitz more than I've ever missed him before.

A Few Days Later,
Mike's Gym, Boston

Henry

There's no place to hide. Jeff has spotted me. I finish the last of my curls and set the barbell back on the rack.

"I returned your call," I say, a preemptive strike, even before Jeff has reached me.

He just smirks. "Yeah. A day later."

I try to smile. "The flowers were beautiful, Jeff. Thanks. I appreciated them."

"So you said in your message."

I raise my eyebrows. "Jeff, don't give me attitude. *I called you back.* The ball's been in your court, and I haven't heard back from you."

Jeff sits down on the bench. "I've been in a weird space."

I try not to react. No, my first reaction is not what you're thinking. I *don't* want to put my arms around him and cajole him into telling me what's wrong. That was the old Henry. The new Henry takes one look at Jeff's woebegone face and begins thinking up excuses to rush off. I'm *through* letting Jeff O'Brien drag me down. I'm *finished* being his wailing wall, his punching bag. I don't want to hear any more details about how much he misses Lloyd or how confused he is about Anthony. *Jeff and his men* is a topic that has ceased to hold any interest for me.

But I find I can't rush off. Maybe the flowers he sent have softened me up a little. I sit down beside him and look into his eyes. God, I hate to see that look there. Every now and again, Jeff gets that look, all lost and ragged-looking, with dark circles under his eyes. Usually it's when he's blue about Lloyd, or near the anniversary of their friend Javitz's death. It makes me weak to look at it. God, I hate feeling weak around Jeff.

"What's up?" I ask despite myself. "What's going on?"

He sighs, looking over at me. "I found out some stuff about Anthony."

"What did he tell you?"

He shakes his head. "I found out on my own."

Just then some muscle queen taps me on the shoulder, wanting the bench, so I suggest to Jeff we move over to the corner to talk. The gym is packed, as it usually is this time of evening, pulsing with the aroma of perspiration and lubricating oils. It's a smell I've come to find strangely comforting—strange because that very same odor had so oppressed me in high school. I smile at familiar faces as we walk across the gym, but Jeff barely seems to notice them. He just leans against the wall, folding his arms across his chest.

I lean in beside him. "What is it, Jeff? What did you find out?"

He looks me straight in the eyes. "The guy in the photo, remember? Robert Riley? He was *killed*. Murdered. A gay-bashing. And Anthony *lived* with him."

"No shit."

Jeff nods. "Anthony would have been fifteen or sixteen. I don't know why he was living with the guy. The newspaper accounts just called him a roommate."

"Code for lover?"

Jeff shrugs. "Maybe. But the guy was in his thirties. And Anthony just a kid."

"So? That's not so unheard of."

"But he wasn't even of legal age," Jeff says, clearly not satisfied with the scenario. "All I can figure is that the guy must have taken him in. Maybe Anthony got kicked out of his parents' house. Maybe he was having sex with the guy and maybe he wasn't. The point is, Robert Riley clearly *meant* something to him, if he still carries his picture around. And the guy was murdered in an antigay crime."

"Matthew Shepard," I say.

"What?"

"Remember how Anthony reacted to the PSA on Matthew Shepard. He was really affected by it. No wonder."

"Yeah." Jeff looks off into space. "No wonder."

I sigh. The news makes me feel gentler toward him, and toward Anthony. "It must have been really hard for him," I say, "being so young and the guy getting killed." I think of something. "But didn't

Anthony say he'd just come out some time last year? And that he'd never been in a relationship?"

"Yeah," Jeff says. "That's what he said."

"So he must have been lying."

Jeff sighs. "I guess."

I consider something. "Unless he didn't view himself as gay then. Maybe the guy wasn't a lover. And maybe his murder so traumatized Anthony that it really *did* take him all this time to come out."

It seems logical to me. I feel as if I've solved the mystery square on its head, but all Jeff does is put his hands in front of his face and sigh once again.

"So what's the matter?" I ask. "What's eating you up?"

He looks at me as if it were obvious. And maybe it is. Maybe I've just so detached myself from Jeff's life that I fail to see it.

"What's *eating me up*, Henry," he says, a little impatiently, "is that he's never talked to me about it. And I can't let him know what I know without revealing that I went behind his back. We went down to Pensacola for the Memorial Day party, and it was awful. I could barely look at him the whole time. I'm sure he sensed something was up."

My heart tugs, just a little. I hadn't even known Jeff had gone to Pensacola. Last year we'd gone together. I try not to dwell on it, to just stay in the moment. "So what did you do?" I ask. "Go back into the old Chicago newspapers?"

"Not quite." Jeff smiles slightly. "Here's the really ironic part. All this happened not twenty miles from where I grew up in Connecticut."

"*Connecticut?* How did Anthony get to Connecticut?"

Jeff shrugs again. "I don't know. But that's where Riley was murdered. Where Anthony was living with him."

"So you must remember this case, then, if it happened so close to you."

"No. I'd already left for college in Boston. But I asked my sister about it. She remembered it vaguely. It was the first big gay story to hit all the Connecticut papers. Apparently, it motivated activists in the state to form an antiviolence project and ultimately led to the legislature passing a hate crimes bill."

"So it was pretty big. They caught the killers, then?"

"Yep." Jeff's face clouds over. "The usual suspects. Straight high school kids who went out looking for fags to beat up. Shining stars of American malehood."

"Poor Anthony."

Jeff stretches. "Yeah. So I just have to figure how to process all of it."

He bends over, trying to touch his toes, but fails. "Oh, man. I've been out of the gym a whole frigging week. I need a workout something *bad.*"

I smile. "You look fine, Jeff. I thought you said you'd work on that body image of yours."

He smiles back at me. It's good to see him smile. "So, buddy," he says, "you want to grab something to eat with me after this?"

I sigh. "Oh, Jeff, I'm sorry. I have—plans."

He just smiles and holds up his hand in a "Say no more" gesture. He moves off toward the treadmill. Halfway there, he turns around and says, "Thanks for listening, buddy."

My heart breaks watching him walk away. I can't deny there's still a very large part of me that wants to sit with Jeff all night, consoling him, making him laugh, making him forget his troubles. But that isn't my job. It never should have been. I have another job now, and a new client. A new, *very wealthy* client on Comm Ave.

I turn and head into the locker room. I check the mirror to see if I'm sufficiently pumped. I flex quickly before anyone spots me. Yes, I look good.

I step into the shower and let the spray hit me full force. I need to invigorate myself, psych myself up for the job. It's been a while since I've taken on any new clients. I can handle the regulars; I know what they want; I've got it down to a routine. But new clients take a little more motivation. I have to admit that the edge is off my escorting. Whereas in the beginning it was hot, risky, exciting, empowering, now it's different. Some encounters still leave me as satisfied as ever, seeing the gratitude on the face of my client. But other times I just feel weary, and going back to my empty apartment I just flop on my bed and fall asleep in Hank's clothes. Sometimes I don't even bother to shower until the next morning. I know: how gross is *that?*

Maybe it's the spring, when young men's thoughts turn to love, or however that old saying goes. Maybe it's the fact that, without Jeff to occupy my every waking moment, I've come to realize just how alone I really am. I want a boyfriend. A husband. Is that so much?

I think maybe I should get a dog.

I step out of the shower and towel myself dry. At the sink, I cup some water in my hands and use it to swallow a little blue pill Shane secured for me. Viagra. "Don't take it if you're using poppers," he instructed. I was a little skittish about admitting I needed it—after all, Hank is such a *stud*—but lately a little lift has been helpful. Me and Bob Dole, something in common. Who knew?

I look at myself in the mirror. I try to see Hank standing there, but all I can glimpse is Henry Weiner. I'm up for a promotion at work: a little more responsibility for a whole lot more money. If I get the promotion, which seems a shoo-in, will I continue escorting? It's never just been about the money, I know, but the extra cash has been a good rationale for continuing. I sit down on the bench and pull on clean Calvin Klein boxer briefs, the precise brand and style my client asked for. I sigh and begin rolling on my socks.

"Hey, best friend!" The voice of Brent suddenly breaks the silence of the locker room. He drops his gym bag beside me. "You coming or going?"

"Going," I tell him.

"Oh. Too bad. Thought we could spot each other." Brent pulls off his shirt, revealing his awesome physique. I wonder again if Brent takes steroids. It wouldn't surprise me, and might even account for his mood swings and the sprinkling of acne across his shoulders.

"Here's a funny story, speaking of spotting," Brent's saying, chattering along as if he doesn't have a care in the world. And maybe he doesn't. "The other day I was at the bench press and I say to this guy, 'Hey, will you spot me?' And he says, 'Baby, I spotted you the moment you came through that door!'"

He erupts into his high-pitched laugh. I just smile a little wearily. I watch him step into his gym shorts. "So you going to Gay Disney?" he asks.

I shake my head. "Nope."

"Is Jeff?"

I stop as I'm tying my shoes. "Gee," I have to admit, "I don't know."

"Well, *I'm* not." Brent moves in closer to me on the bench. "Don't you want to know *why*, Henry?"

I smile. "Even if I didn't, you'd tell me anyway."

"Of course. Because we're *best friends*." He grins madly. "And I want you to be the *first* to know." He grabs me by the shoulders. "Henry, I've *met* someone! And this one is going to *last*, I can just tell!"

I manage a smile. "Good for you, Brent."

"I know you think I'm just being excitable, that you've seen me like this a hundred times. But this is *different*, Henry. *Very* different." Brent beams. "He's *totally* not into the scene. No drugs. Nothing!"

"Nothing?"

"Nothing more than a beer once in a while. A real guy. *Hates* the club scene. Wouldn't be caught *dead* at a circuit party."

I stand. "You seem to have *so* much in common."

Brent stands to face me. "That's just *it*, Henry. We *do.*" He draws closer. "Since you're my best friend now, I'll let you in on a little secret. I've been wanting to retire from the scene for a while now. You can't keep at it forever, you know. You'll end up looking like what's-his-name—you know, the one we always made fun of? Kenneth! How *tragic* is he?"

I cringe. If Brent only knew I see Kenneth once a week, dancing for him, making his dreams of relevance come true, even if for a night.

"And with *Jorge,*" Brent continues, "I've found a *companion.* Someone to come *home* to."

"I thought you didn't want to settle down until you were thirty-five."

"When did I say that?" He looks at me intently. "You know what my biggest fear is, Henry? Ending up an old queen, all alone. You know the type. Every gay movie they make these days has the middle-aged guy whose sole reason for being in the film is to console and counsel the younger set. He's usually fat and queeny and wears lots of rings. Oh, God, Henry. I do *not* want to become *that.*"

He secures his locker and checks himself in the mirror.

"Thankfully, now I won't *have* to!"

He grins like an idiot. "Have fun wherever you're going, best chum of mine! Will you be the maid of honor at my wedding?"

Thankfully, he's off into the gym before I can answer.

Outside, it's started to rain, a light, warm, spring drizzle that brings that ripe, earthy smell up from the park. I pop open my umbrella and make my way across Tremont and then up Dartmouth. I want to be happy for Brent and not take solace in the fact that I'm quite certain that this one will last no longer than any of the other "husbands" Brent has thought he'd corralled.

But what if he does last? What if Brent has indeed found lasting happiness with someone who will love him until the end?

Waiting for the WALK sign in Copley Square, I think about Jeff and Lloyd. For the first time, I think maybe I understand why they've invested so much time, energy, and passion in that frustrating, maddening, back-and-forth relationship of theirs. *Because they've tasted it,* I think. *They know what it can be like.*

And they know it's worth fighting for.

In one week, I'll be twenty-nine. The last year of my twenties, and no sign of a husband. Here I am, off to pose in my Calvin Kleins for some rich guy on Comm Ave, and I've never had a real boyfriend.

What the fuck is wrong with me?

It's raining harder now. I cross Boylston and then Newbury in a funk.

Maybe I should've called a cab. I pull in tighter under my umbrella. Crossing Marlborough Street, I almost get hit by a Volvo. I give the driver the finger.

Yeah, a dog isn't such a bad idea. At least I'll have someone waiting for me when I get home.

I ring the bell at the guy's building. "It's Hank," I call, and the buzzer lets me in. At least the guy's rich. Maybe he'll give me a good tip. It's a fashionable brownstone, with a majestic staircase and gilded banister. The guy is on the second floor. I knock.

My jaw drops. The guy who opens the door must weigh four hundred plus.

"Are you . . . Maurice?" I stammer.

The guy nods and motions me inside. I step around him, which is no easy task. The apartment is a mess, piled high with newspapers and magazines and a couple of empty pizza boxes. The furniture is tacky, and there are no curtains on the windows, only dirty Venetian blinds. But this is Comm Ave! The guy's supposed to be *rich!*

Maybe he is. But he's also a *slob.* It looks as if he hasn't washed his hair in weeks. There are stains on his shirt.

"Did you wear the Calvins?" he asks.

I nod.

"Let's see."

Good, I think. *Let's just get down to business so I can get out of here.*

The place has the unmistakable stench of boiled chicken. I feel a little nauseated. But Maurice doesn't seem to pay any attention to the body I've just revealed to him. He simply takes off his own clothes—a sight to see, let me tell you. He struggles out of his pants, grunting and sweating. By the time he removes his dirty shirt, he's breathing so heavily I think he might have a heart attack.

Pass no judgment, I tell myself. *He needs love. Like all the rest of them.* I've given affection to others who have been less than the physical ideal. I can do it again.

Yet I can't even see Maurice's genitals behind the enormous barrel of stretched, hairy gut. A distinct wave of body odor strikes me. I close my eyes. No amount of Viagra will help me now.

"Come here," Maurice orders, suddenly pulling me roughly to him, gripping my head with his hands and pushing it deep between his moist, sagging pectorals. I stiffen instinctively. "Don't resist me, man. Go for it. Suck my tits."

I swallow hard. "I . . . can't . . . breathe," I manage to say.

Maurice lets my head go but immediately replaces his hands on my shoulders, pushing me down to my knees. "Then suck my cock," he barks.

I open my eyes to see a small, flaccid, uncircumsized penis tucked in the shadow beneath the man's heavy stomach. I open my mouth and place my lips around it. *Give him love,* I repeat over and over in my head, like a mantra. I begin to run my tongue over the sweaty hood of his cock.

"That's it, suck it," Maurice moans.

But I can't get past the terrible cheesy smell down there between his legs. And the *taste*—gritty and bitter. I feel myself close to retching.

"Come on, suck it harder! I'm paying for this! *Suck!*"

Something foul passes from his penis into my mouth. I spit suddenly onto the floor.

"*Suck it!*" he commands, angry now.

I pull my face away from the revolting thing. "I can't," I say.

"What do you mean, you can't?"

"I just . . . can't. I can give you a hand job."

Maurice glowers down at me. "I don't want a hand job. You said you did oral."

"Yes, but . . ." I stand up. "Maybe if you showered . . ."

"It's what *I* want, not you," Maurice says, stabbing a finger into my chest. "*I'm* the one paying *you*, buddy."

I take a step backward. "You know what?" I say all at once. "I don't want your money." I begin pulling on my jeans. "I just want to go home."

Maurice takes a step closer to me threateningly. For the first time in all these months of escorting, I feel fear. My mouth goes dry.

"You're nothing but a little whore," Maurice says. "And you have no idea who I am, how important I am." He motions over his shoulder. "Get the fuck out of here."

"Gladly," I say.

I run out with my shirt and shoes in my hands. My socks are still crumpled up somewhere on the guy's floor. Maurice slams the door behind me, and I'm left in the hallway to pull on my sweatshirt and slip my bare feet into my shoes. An elderly woman coming out of an apartment across the way spots me, shakes her head in disgust, and hurries off. She's evidently become used to seeing a parade of trash in and out of that place.

Trash. I just thought of myself as *trash.*

I practically stumble outside onto the sidewalk, the torrential rain quickly making me realize I left more than my socks in Maurice's apartment. My umbrella's still in there, too. I walk back home in the driving rain. It's better that way, I think. With the rain coming down all over my face, and my hair plastered down in front of my eyes, no one can tell I've started to cry. All I want in that moment is to find Jeff and to have him hold me, to have him make me feel better—to make me feel as good about myself as he had that day he'd first invited me to dance with him. That's all I want. I want Jeff.

But Jeff has never looked at me that way, never seen me even for a moment's consideration as more than a sister. He's never loved me the way I've loved him.

"Well, fuck you, Jeff," I say into the rain. "Fuck you."

I've never come this close to admitting to myself the truth of what Brent and Shane and so many others have always insisted. Okay, so I'm in love with Jeff O'Brien. I can't deny it anymore. I'm in love with Jeff and I'm a fucking whore. *Trash* kicked out of apartments on Comm Ave. What the fuck has happened to me?

I get home a blubbering mess. The silence of my apartment overwhelms me.

I pick up the phone and punch in his number. He's home.

"Shane?" I croak into the phone. "Can you come over?"

And of course, he does. He makes me dinner and massages my shoulders, and I find the Viagra is still working. He goes down on me, and I do my best not to pretend it's Jeff. Afterward, we lie awake on my bed for a long time, looking up at my skylight as the rain hammers a steady beat against it. Shane reaches over and begins outlining the features of my face with his finger. First my eyebrows, then my eyes, then my ears, then my nose.

By the time he reaches my chin, I'm asleep. He apparently lets himself out then, or some time soon after, for when I wake up in the morning, he's gone.

I wonder why he didn't spend the night.

That Weekend, Walt Disney World

Jeff

They call it "The Happiest Place on Earth," and Anthony sure seems to agree. I can see it on his face and hear it in his voice: the way he laughs at the campy antics of the Incredible Tiki Birds; the way he throws his arms into the air as we come speeding around the corner on Big Thunder Railroad; the way he lets out a whoop as we plunge from the top of Splash Mountain; the way he befriends every gay man and woman who passes by us wearing the telltale red shirt.

"Hey!" he's yelling to a group of red-shirted fags ahead of us in line on the way to the Epcot monorail. "Where you guys from?"

"Baltimore," one of them, a tall blond muscle boy, calls back.

"Boston here!" Anthony shouts. "Happy Gay Disney Days!"

I smile, looking over at him. "Are you *sure* you didn't do any X?"

Anthony beams. "I'm totally straight, Jeff."

I smirk. "Now *that's* a misnomer if I ever heard one."

"*I love Disney World!*" he shouts, throwing his arms into the air.

He's such a kid in some ways. True, I've never been able to resist the Disney magic myself, especially during my first visit here with Lloyd and Javitz some years ago. I still have the photos somewhere: Javitz making faces with Goofy, Lloyd posing with a hunky Alladin, all of us perched atop the slide at Typhoon Lagoon. It's a trip I'll never forget, and as much as I enjoy watching Anthony's spirited reactions, there's a little cloud of melancholia following me around, as I keep remembering how Lloyd and I kissed all the way through the Haunted Mansion and how Javitz lost his baseball cap in the wind tunnels of Space Mountain.

But this is my first time being so overtly gay here at the Magic

Kingdom, and I can't deny the excitement at seeing so many red shirts throughout the park. It's the agreed-upon code to identify all us queers, as if that's even really necessary. We're *everywhere*. Only the most tolerant or clueless straights have stayed in the park today; the whole complex is practically transformed into a private gay playground. All of the gay Peter Pans and Snow Whites who, for the rest of the year, have to smile and wave innocently at toddlers and their moms, can now indulge in winks and quips with the hordes of horny gay tourists, if you get them out of earshot of the Mouse.

Earlier today I made eye contact with one such "cast member," an attractive young Filipino boy who snuck Anthony and me into the underground catacombs for lunch in the Disney commissary. There, Belle from "Beauty and the Beast" smoked cigarettes with a headless Donald Duck, who cruised Anthony up and down. After lunch, we all made plans to meet for the big party that night at Mannequins on Pleasure Island. I carefully stashed away their names and numbers in my wallet.

"I love this extended family you're always telling me about, Jeff," Anthony's saying as we take our seats on the monorail. "It feels like a giant family reunion, with cousins you never even met!"

From another car, a group of queens are singing "Someday My Prince Will Come." I look over at Anthony and nod. "That's a good analogy," I tell him.

He smiles broadly. "I could never have imagined such a thing a year ago. To have found all this—*man!* Jeff, you brought me in! I'd never have found my way if it hadn't been for you."

I wink at him. "I think you would have done fine, Anthony."

He shakes his head adamantly as the monorail begins to move. "No, Jeff. I *mean* it. I owe *all of this* to you. And I don't just mean you paying for my plane ticket here. I mean *all* of it. My whole life. My whole gay life."

I give him a small smile and turn to look down at the passing scenery. Behind us, Cinderella's Castle fades into the distance. We pass over the flat manmade greennness of Central Florida. It's hot, very hot, and I'm glad I opted against the red-shirt uniform. My loose white cotton prevents those icky perspiration stains most of the other boys are doing their best to hide, including Anthony. Besides, I've put on a pound or two—in the wrong places—and the shirt does a good job covering it up.

I don't doubt that Anthony is sincere in his gratitude. A year ago, I suppose, he was still a scared young man, unwilling to admit to his gayness, still traumatized by the murder that had taken place over a decade before. The killers of Robert Riley had claimed more than one victim that night. The fireplace log they'd used to beat Riley to death had proven almost as fatal to Anthony, even if it never touched him. Those two fuckers sent Anthony into a decade-long exile, causing him to miss out on what should have been the best years of his youth.

If only I could figure some way to get him to talk about it all, without having to admit I'd gone behind his back. I look over at Anthony now, chatting up a couple of gay boys with Southern accents, exchanging stories of Alien Encounter and Star Tours and the Tower of Terror.

"This is my first time to Epcot," Anthony's telling them. "Jeff's been there before, so he's going to show me I around."

I enjoy playing tour guide. I know that the best way to see Epcot is to work from the back to the front, so I take Anthony by the hand and lead him quickly under Spaceship Earth across the bridge to the World Pavilion. This way we'll be going against the usual flow of the crowd, and can enjoy the different countries at our leisure.

Ahead of us I spot a couple of folks looking up toward the sky. There's a small plane trailing a banner through the bright blueness. I strain to read it against the sun. *REPENT,* it says. *GIVE UP YOUR LIVES OF SIN AND COME TO JESUS.*

"No matter where you go," I grumble, "there's always somebody."

Anthony just stares up at the banner.

"Don't look at them," I say, taking his hand again as some in the crowd shake their fists up at the plane. "Don't give them even that. We have countries to explore."

I've been to the real England and the real France and the real Mexico, but Anthony has never been outside the United States (with the exception of our trip to Montreal), so he takes particular delight in seeing each national pavilion. In Norway we ride Maelstrom, then take a break to eat a couple of cream pies.

"You having fun, Jeff?" Anthony asks me.

"Sure."

"You seem kind of distant."

I shrug. "I don't mean to be. How am I distant?"

Anthony has cream filling on his upper lip but doesn't seem to realize it. "You just kind of are. Maybe it's just that you've been here before and aren't as excited as I am."

"Maybe."

He looks at me warily. "And maybe you're missing Lloyd."

I sigh. "Anthony, wipe your lip."

He obeys. "Do you, Jeff? Do you wish you were here with Lloyd instead of me?"

"Anthony, why do you always ask such things?"

"You know why." A little of the boyish enthusiasm seems to dim in his eyes. "Because I like you and want you to like me."

"I *do* like you," I insist. "You know that."

He smiles. "I like that you've started letting me sleep with you."

Now, that's a surprise to me as well. It happened quite unexpectedly. We were sitting on my bed, watching MTV, as we often did, and Anthony fell asleep. But this time I didn't wake him. I just pulled the covers up and slipped in beside him. The next night it happened again, Anthony falling asleep as we watched TV. Did he finagle it that way? Could he be as crafty as all that? I don't care, because in truth, I enjoy having him there. It's the first time I've ever enjoyed sleeping with anyone other than Lloyd.

"Anthony," I say, leaning across the table a little, suddenly inspired by all this happiness around us, "don't you think maybe it's time to tell me a little more? About yourself?"

He pulls back a little, taking another bite of his cream pie.

I press on. "You promised that someday you would. You'd explain where you go when you disappear. You'd tell me more about your family . . . and your *friends,* Anthony." I mean Riley. I want him to talk about Riley.

Anthony says nothing. He finishes the last of his cream pie, licking the filling from his fingers.

"No?" I ask. "There's *nothing* you can tell me?"

He looks at me pleadingly. "Why *here,* Jeff? We're at Disney World."

"Why not here? It's the Happiest Place on Earth, remember?"

Anthony says nothing.

I sigh. "Anthony, did you ever have a special friend? Someone who really mattered to you? Somebody you maybe looked up to? Maybe . . . *mentored* you?"

"Why are you asking me this?" he asks suspiciously.

"I'm just wondering, Anthony. I'm just wondering if maybe there's ever been anyone else, any other man, who you came to care about."

Anthony shakes his head firmly. "Jeff, there's been no one. You're the first man I've ever been in love with." He tries to smile. "Believe me."

"Okay, okay. That may be true." I scratch my head. "But maybe there was someone who meant a lot to you, maybe when you were younger . . ."

"*No!*" Anthony stands up suddenly. "Why are you going on like this?"

His reaction seems to rattle me, make me angry. "Because I want some *answers,* Anthony! You're living with me. You're sleeping in my bed. And still you disappear overnight once a week and still I don't know anything about you. I *deserve* answers! And if you don't tell me, then—well—I may just have to find them out on my own!"

Anthony just stares at me. He still has some cream filling on his face. His lips draw tight and his brow creases.

"Anthony?" I ask.

Suddenly he turns and shoots off across the pavilion. He runs as fast as he can into the passing crowd. He darts around a lesbian couple pushing a baby stroller and then disappears. I call after him, running a few feet, but quickly realize it's ludicrous to pursue him. He's gotten too much of a head start and the crowd is too large.

I sigh, shaking my head in disbelief. All I can do is go back to the room and hope he shows up there. I didn't mean to push him over the edge like that, but you know what? Instead of guilt, I feel anger. What the *fuck* is he hiding? Why can't he just *tell* me about his past? He claims to love me, but he sure doesn't seem to trust me.

Back at the room, I flop down on the bed and start missing Lloyd like crazy. I begin thinking again about my last trip here, with Lloyd and Javitz, and how much fun we had. What am I doing here with some mystery kid who goes running off like a scared antelope?

And why hasn't Lloyd responded to my E-mails? Is he really *that* busy running the guest house? I fall asleep hating my life.

I awake at ten minutes to eleven. The room is dark. I flick on the light and realize Anthony hasn't come back. I grow a little worried, then tell myself to stop. Anthony's a big boy; surely he just stayed in the park and fell into another group of gay boys. In fact, he'll most certainly be at Pleasure Island, where we all planned to rendezvous. I hurriedly shower and change my clothes.

But he's not at Mannequins, either. I stand on the revolving dance floor so I can scope out the entire crowd, and I don't spot him. None of the guys we'd met have seen him either.

Then screw him, I think. *If he thinks he can just run off on me and—*

"Hello, Jeff."

I turn. It's the last person I expect to see. Or want to.

"Drake," I say, without much emotion.

"Having a good time?" he asks, with that little edge to his voice, as ever.

I look past him. "I'm just . . . waiting for someone."

He feigns incredulity. "The famous Jeff O'Brien hasn't been stood up, has he?"

I sneer. "If thinking that makes you feel good, then go for it, Drake."

I've never cared very much for this guy. It's not just that Lloyd dated him briefly when we first moved apart. It's the fact that he's an affluent, arrogant upper-middle-class snob, and what he's doing at Disney World, I can't imagine. I know he still carries a torch for Lloyd; that much was obvious that day at the guest house opening party.

Yet I have to admit that Drake looks awfully hot standing there, his silver hair offsetting his tanned face, his black tank top revealing surprisingly muscular shoulders and arms. A few years ago I'd never have looked twice at a guy his age. But I've become far more eclectic in my tastes. I can understand what Lloyd saw in Drake, at least physically. Suddenly the image of this man and Lloyd in bed together makes me horny, although I find myself embarrassed to admit it, even to myself.

"Jeff," Drake is saying, "I was joking. I certainly didn't mean to offend."

"None taken," I say.

"Good." He smiles. "The friends I came with are a little too drunk for my taste. You, however, seem pretty sober, Jeff."

I nod. "I'm not much in a partying mood tonight."

"Who'd you come with? That good-looking blond boy I met at the party?"

I sigh. "Yeah. Guess he's not going to show."

"Funny, isn't it?" Drake muses. "You and me, running into each other, alone."

"Yeah. Especially when you could be in Provincetown, staying at Lloyd's."

He snorts. "I tried that. Memorial Day weekend. Lloyd's a busy boy. I saw him at check-in and check-out. That was it."

I laugh bitterly. "That's more than *I've* seen of him."

We stand there silently for a few minutes, watching the dance floor revolve.

"I never noticed how pretty your eyes are, Jeff," Drake finally says.

I give him a quizzical little smile. "I never noticed you were a flirt."

He laughs. "I've *always* thought you were attractive, Jeff." He puts his hands on my shoulders. "And what have you thought about me?"

I look squarely at him. "Drake, what I have thought about you is not far from what you have thought about me. We have never liked each other. We have been civil only because of Lloyd."

His eyes dance. "I suppose you're right."

He leans in and kisses me. Without even thinking about it, I kiss him back. No X, no drugs, just an unexpected passion. It turns into quite the kiss, with lots of tongue and hands on butts, and when it finally ends, Drake puts his arm around me and begins leading me out of the club.

Part of me is hesitant—after all, my body isn't feeling exactly perfect—but then I remember my promise to Henry to give that up, and so I continue walking.

I stop just as we walk out into the humid, starry night. "Just so that we're being honest with each other," I say looking over at Drake, "I'm fully aware that the only reason you want to sleep with me is because of Lloyd."

Drake smiles. "Just as *I'm* fully aware that the only reason you're sleeping with me is *also* because of Lloyd."

I can't help but laugh. "Fine, then," I say as we start walking again. "Just so we're being honest."

The sex, I can't deny, is awesome.

Fourth of July Weekend, Nirvana

Lloyd

The phone rings early, but I am, of course, already up, scrambling eggs and squeezing fresh orange juice. And I know before I answer it that it'll be Jeff. I just *know*. Remember? I told you this right at the start, and it's still true. That's just the way it is between us. Even if it's been months since we talked last.

"Hey," Jeff says.

"Hey," I say in return.

There's a momentary silence between us. I look up to notice Eva at the toaster, running through several slices of bread for the guests. She seems to pause, listening. Somehow I sense that she knows I'm talking to Jeff. I take the phone out onto the back porch.

"Cat," I say. "How *are* you?"

"I'm in town," he tells me. "It was a last-minute decision. I'm staying in North Truro, actually. Figured you guys would be all booked up this weekend."

We are. It's our craziest weekend thus far, the traditional kickoff to Provincetown's two-month high season. I knew this was going to be a killer. Eva had been up even earlier than I was, getting the four pots of flavored coffees perking, and arranging into vases our daily delivery of fresh flowers. Sunflowers and peonies today. The past couple of weeks have been rainy and chilly, dampening everyone's spirits, but the weather report promised different for this weekend, and so far the day is cooperating. Already, at nine A.M. all our windows are open, and fresh, salty sea air fills the house.

"I was hoping, maybe . . ." Jeff's voice trails off. "I was hoping maybe we could see each other."

I hear the screen door slam shut. I turn. Eva has come outside and is looking at me, raising her eyebrows and gesturing, as if she wants to ask me something.

"Maybe we can meet somewhere," Jeff's saying.

I know just the place. "The breakwater," I suggest.

I can tell Jeff's smiling on the other end of the phone. How many countless hours did we spend on the breakwater, ruminating about life and love with Javitz? It's also the place where, nearly four years ago, we sprinkled Javitz's ashes, watching them swirl into the outgoing tide and finally disappear, merging into the sea.

"Perfect," Jeff says. "What do you say, maybe four o'clock?"

"Four it is."

His voice sounds buoyant. "Okay. Great! See you then, Lloyd."

"Bye, Jeff."

Could he really be as happy as I am about reconnecting? If so, then why has he ignored all my E-mails? Why has he never *called*?

I click off the phone and turn around. Eva is practically in my face. "We have a house full of guests," she says immediately.

"And your point is?"

She assumes a defiant posture, standing up straight and lifting her bosom. "I *won't* be left alone to handle them all by myself."

"We have three employees, Eva," I say impatiently. "And I'll be gone a couple hours at the most, in the late afternoon, when no one's around."

She looks as if she might suddenly cry. "Lloyd, it's just that—well, *Jeff*. I know your long history with him, and I'd hate to see you—well, you know, get hurt again."

I imagine for the past few months she's allowed herself to think that Jeff was finally gone for good. And why not? *I'd* even come to think it. But never entirely. Deep down, I always believed we'd reconnect somehow.

"I don't think it's a good idea to see him," she says. "We're so busy, and you might get upset. . . ."

I refuse to get into anything with her. I just walk past her into the house.

Eva follows.

"Lloyd," she says, and her voice has taken on that all-too-familiar shaky, teary cadence, *"please* don't see him today. My nerves are *shot*. I'm *so* overworked and rundown. If something were to *happen* . . ."

I spin on her. "Are you saying I can never leave the house? That I'm trapped here just because you're afraid you can't handle a crisis on your own?"

She recoils from my words. "Please don't yell at me," she says in a tiny voice.

"I'm not yelling," I say, sighing, closing my eyes, leaning against the refrigerator.

So it's come to this: sniping and shouting. The rift between us has only grown in recent weeks. I've become increasingly distant, finding that when I'm with her, all I do is analyze her every word, her every action. It's not fair to her and it's also driving me crazy, so I just retreat to my room as early as possible, plug in my earphones, and get lost in my music. Sarah McLaughlin. Alanis Morrisette. Jewel. A couple of times Eva has told me she's knocked on my door but I haven't heard her. Which is exactly how I intended it.

Oh, this is *not* what I imagined Nirvana would be. This isn't why I got involved in this venture, followed this path. Believe me, I've *tried* talking it out with her. I asked her point-blank if she was in therapy, and she became evasive, finally admitting she hadn't found someone she "clicked" with. I tried getting her to level with me, to admit to her insecurities, to face them and deal with them. I tried to get her to disclose the incident Ty had told me about, to explore what had motivated her, how her loneliness and grief can sometimes cause her to do unwise things. But nothing. She just started to cry.

A week ago, I sat her down and asked if she was happy. She insisted she was. I told her I felt she needed to make some friends on her own, that she couldn't rely only on me as support, or simply co-opt my friends. I explained gently that I needed more space from her, that given how stressed we both were from running the guest house, I really, *really* needed some quiet time, all to myself. She assured me that she completely understood.

Yet the very next day she developed a terrible headache, weeping and trembling, and begged me to sit next to her on her bed and hold her hand. "I don't know what's wrong with me," she lamented. "I feel so *depressed.*" She fell asleep with me holding her hand. I felt as if she'd conned me, yet again, into giving her what she wanted.

After episodes like these, I distance myself from her. She'll attempt to reel me back in with little gifts: candles and incense and hazelnut chocolate and even a pair of boots I admired at one of the leather shops in town. But the more she tries to buy back my favor, the more I resist being bought. And so it continues.

The topper came just yesterday, when, retreating to the sanctuary of my room, I detected the unmistakable fragrance of Eva's perfume. Lilacs. *She'd been in my room.* The aroma lingered strongest among the sheets of my unmade bed. I actually felt *violated.*

I went right out to Land's End hardware and bought a new doorknob lock, the kind I could secure with a key from the outside whenever I left the room.

I know this is no way to run a business together. Yet confronting her seems to do no good.

Unless she's in therapy, working on these issues, I don't know how we can continue. I told that to her. She promised she'd find someone. But it's a promise she made once before and failed to keep.

I can't help but wonder just what it was that Ty had twice tried to tell me. *I can tell you things that would make your hair stand on end.* What insights into Eva's character, into her past, have I refused to hear?

So here it is Fourth of July, and I'm at my wit's end. I pass the rest of the day doing my best to avoid her and concentrate instead on seeing Jeff again. The return of the sun assures that all of our guests are quickly out of the house. Once the beds are made and the laundry complete, I let the houseboys go for the afternoon and take an hour myself to lie in the sun on the deck. Eva, thankfully, is nowhere in sight.

In my room, I decide to nap before seeing Jeff. I want to be fresh and energized for him. Flopping down onto my bed, I think about Jeff and Javitz and me, how long ago those days seem now. I've been feeling so alone these past few months, despite the steady crush of guests and Eva's ubiquitous presence. I'm consumed suddenly with the desire to *see* Javitz physically, to *hear* him once again. I reach down and fumble under my bed through my videos. I have quite the porno collection—necessary for getting through the bleak isolation of a Provincetown winter—but I'm not looking for Tom Chase or Cole Tucker. I'm looking for David Mark Javitz. And I can tell simply by touch which video is him.

I pop it into the VCR at the foot of my bed. It's a video we made one summer seven or eight years ago, Jeff and Javitz and I, with a videocam borrowed from Javitz's friend Ernie. Just a goof, really, just playing around. There are about sixteen minutes of banter, the three of us on the deck of a rented summer house off Commercial Street. It was a glorious sunny day, much like today. I settle back against my pillows and hit PLAY on the remote control.

After the blue lead, the video crackles into life. "Is it on?" Jeff's asking.

"I think so," Javitz replies. He's behind the camera. "Though I can't claim videography to be one of my many talents." He laughs unseen, that raw, throaty, smoke-chewed laugh of his I miss so much.

The camera trembles as it focuses on Jeff, sitting on the deck, squinting into the sun. How young he looks. No lines on his face. Then it pans over to me. I wave. I cringe watching myself, as I always do. Why do people always wave at the camera in home movies?

I haven't watched this in a long time. After Javitz first died, I watched it often, desperate to keep his image in my memory. I didn't want to forget. I wanted to remember every little detail of him, keep them burned into my brain: how he moved, how he sat in a chair, how he held his cigarette.

In the video, Jeff is standing up, insisting Javitz give him the camera. "You're going too fast," he scolds, in the way only Jeff can scold. There's a blip of darkness, then suddenly a close-up of Javitz fills the screen. What a star entrance. It always takes my breath away.

"Is this my best angle?" he's asking as Jeff pulls back to take in a full-length shot. Javitz poses like a pinup girl in a little black Speedo, showcasing his long, thin body. He puts a hand on his hip and sashays across the deck, shaking his shoulder-length curly black hair. It makes me think momentarily of Eva as Mae West. But Javitz isn't imitating anybody. He was way too much of an original to do imitations.

"No," I'm saying, moving into the frame. *"Here's* his best angle!"

I grab Javitz around the waist and bend him forward, so that his ass sticks up straight. Jeff zooms in until everything is out of focus. All you can hear is Javitz's laugh. "Haw haw haw haw!"

Darkness again. We set the camera on a tripod, and now there's a long shot of the three of us, grinning ridiculously, our arms around each other's shoulders. It's not just Jeff who looks young, it's all of us. How old was I then? Twenty-six? Twenty-seven? Such babies. So full of life. Even Javitz. Thin, but not with the wasting that came later. His face is round and full. Jeff isn't nearly as muscled as he is now. And all that *hair* on my head!

Another little blip of darkness, and then there's Jeff's voice back behind the camera. "Okay," he's saying. "Just wanted to get it for posterity. Javitz was about to say something profound."

Javitz arches an eyebrow at him and exhales smoke over his shoulder. I can smell it.

"Go, ahead," Jeff's saying, unseen, the camera framing Javitz and me at the table, the sparkling blue bay behind us. "Keep talking. Forget I'm here. I'm just playing a little cinema verité."

"You don't even know what that *is*," Javitz growls, arching an eyebrow.

"Do, too. I'm a film buff, remember?"

Javitz rolls his eyes. "Bette Davis never made any cinema verité."

"Cat," I'm saying, "turn it off. We're having a conversation."

"No! Javitz, finish what you were saying."

"What I was saying, *Lloyd*," he says, turning away from the camera as Jeff zooms in for a close-up of his profile, "is that when the three of us are together, when we're sitting around the wood stove at your place, or up here on the deck in Provincetown, and we're talking, talking about the world and what it means and how we could make it better—when we're like that, and you settle back into my arms and Jeff comes out with hot chocolates for all of us, when we get so tired we begin to fall asleep on each other's shoulders—in those moments I have the greatest passion of my life."

I can feel his breath. I can see the little red lines in the whiteness of his eyes.

That's when the video stops. I think Jeff felt it was a little too intrusive and turned the thing off. But how glad I am now that he captured that moment. How often I have watched it, over and over. I have it memorized, every scene, every word. How happy we had been then. All of us.

Jeff's seen the video only once, right after Javitz's death. He was overcome. He couldn't even make it through the last scene, walking out of the room in tears. Ever since then, he's refused every time I've suggested watching it again. He just can't bring himself to see it.

I hit STOP. The video has the opposite effect on me. It soothes me, comforts me. It lulls me into a place of memory, a time when I was happy. I feel very drowsy suddenly, slipping down among my pillows, falling asleep, dreaming of Javitz and Jeff and me, playing Frisbee on the beach . . .

"Go get it," Javitz is urging me.

I turn around. The Frisbee has landed in the water and is floating out to sea.

"Go get it," Javitz tells me again.

I look out at the waves. Jeff is out there, trying to get the Frisbee.

"*Go*," Javitz insists.

But I hesitate. I put my foot into the surf. The water is cold.

All at once I sit up. My dream fades from my consciousness even as I try to hold on to it. I blink my eyes. I look over at the clock. My little nap has lasted for an hour and a half! It's now ten minutes past three. I hop out of bed. I have just enough time to shower and ride my bike over to meet Jeff.

I begin to whistle as I wash. For the first time in weeks, I feel happy. I'm very glad I've gotten a little sun, too. *Jeff can't fail to appreciate that glow,* I think to myself as I give myself one final check in the mirror.

I put my hand on the doorknob, cocky as a jaybird.

It won't turn.

I try again. It won't budge.

"What the fuck . . . ?"

It's *locked.*

From the *outside.*

But that's crazy. The only way to lock the door from the outside is with the key I bought.

And the key is on my key ring.

And my key ring is . . .

Downstairs on the kitchen counter.

I bang on the door. "Hey!" I bang harder. "Eva! Eva! Are you out there?"

I look at the clock. It's twelve minutes to four.

Meanwhile, at Herring Cove Beach

Henry

"So it's over."

I rub the lotion into Brent's back. It sure is a nice back, I admit to myself. Hard, rippled, defined. Even with the sprinkling of acne, it's a back I enjoy touching, especially given the kinds of bodies I *have* been touching for the past several months. It almost doesn't matter whether Brent uses roids or not to build it. It just feels *awesome* to run my hands across it.

"I'm sorry, Brent," I tell him. "Really I am."

Just as I'd predicted, his relationship with Jorge didn't last. Brent's "perfect" union didn't even endure as long as some of his "imperfect" ones. He's been lamenting it ever since I picked him up to drive down here to Ptown.

His back lifts in a long sigh. "It's just that I thought Jorge was the *one*. He seemed so *perfect.*" He turns his head to look up at me. "I even didn't mind not going out to Avalon on Sunday night. Can you imagine? *Me!* I actually *liked* staying home and watching *Who Wants to Be a Millionaire?* Do you know it was the first time I'd ever seen it?"

I just smile, keeping my hand moving on his back.

Brent puts his head back down. "But it was too good to last, I guess. Do you know what he said, Henry? He said he just didn't have *those feelings* for me. What the fuck does that mean? What are *those feelings?*" He covers his head with his hands. "Guess I *am* going to end up that tired old queen I was so afraid of becoming, all by myself."

"No, you won't, Brent."

"I will. You know, it's not very PC to say this, but at least all those guys who died young from AIDS will never have to face growing old and irrelevant. You tell me which is worse."

"Brent, you're being ridiculous." I knead his shoulders. "It may be an old cliche, but there *are* other fish in the sea." Not that I believe it much myself, but what else do you say in such a moment?

Brent isn't listening to me. "Yet again," he cries, "I strike out."

I stretch out beside him on the blanket. *"He's* the one who struck out, Brent. Not you."

Brent turns to look at me. "Hey, thanks, best friend. What a nice thing to say."

I just laugh.

The late-afternoon sun is still strong and full, and it feels wonderful on my skin. Damn the sunblock; another hour won't hurt. Herring Cove is packed, although by now, one by one, people are leaving, giving themselves plenty of time to freshen up before Tea Dance. Brent and I have decided to forego the tea dances today, saving our energy for tonight. It's a long weekend, after all. Why not take advantage of the sun? The summer has been so rainy so far.

Facing out onto the bay instead of the ocean, Herring Cove isn't nearly as impressive a beach as Race Point, but it's *ours.* Everyone knows it's the gay beach. Over near the parking lot, you might spot a few families, but as soon as you walk in just a few yards, you notice a distinct absence of men among the hundreds of women, and then, a little farther down, not a gal among the hundreds of guys. At the very farthest point, you notice something even more obvious: a mix of men and women without bathing suits. The nude beach isn't officially sanctioned, so you have to keep watch for rangers, but I'm not interested in taking off my Speedo anyway. I like a tan line, and so do most of my clients.

Not that I've done any escorting since that disaster on Comm Ave. E-mail from my Web site has gone unopened, and I turned off my cell phone. I just can't bear it right now. I feel as if my whole life has been turned inside out. At work I've sat through *six different interviews* hoping for this goddamn promotion. It was supposed to be a shoo-in, but instead I'm left ragged. Then, when I went home last week for my birthday, my mother, in an attempt at being supportive, asked if I was dating anyone. "You should feel free to bring anyone home with you, Henry," she said. It only made me feel worse—because I *have* no one to bring home.

The crowning indignity, however, is the fact that Jeff forgot my birthday. Sure, I know he's caught up with all the Anthony drama, but isn't that always the way? *Jeff gets wrapped up in his own life and only calls me when he needs something.* Yes, he sent me flowers a few weeks ago, a lovely gesture. But it's not enough. Not anymore. I've settled for too little too late far too often.

I sit up, resting my arms on my bended knees. In front of me, each lap of the waves brings the sea farther up the beach. The water is a murky blue-green with considerable foam, leaving thousands of sparkly little stones along the sand in its wake. I let out a long, relaxing breath and scope out the beach. So many men. Big men and little men, hairy men and smooth, young and old, beautiful and plain. How many of them are having conversations just like mine and Brent's? Lamenting their singlehood and misfortune in love? Other than Cher and Madonna, it sure seems to be the favorite topic of gay men.

At the next blanket, a quartet of middle-aged queens are drinking mimosas. They seem to be lamenting something, but I can't make it out. On their portable CD player the Backstreet Boys are playing too loudly for me to hear anything else. I notice that Brent is quietly singing along: *"And that makes me larger than life . . ."*

I smirk, correcting his lyrics: "Makes *you* larger, not me."

"That's what I said."

I laugh. "Forget it."

Brent sits up on an elbow. "So, Henry, if we're going to be best friends, we've gotta know something about each other."

I squint down at him. "What's that?"

He looks at me with all seriousness. "NSYNC or the Backstreet Boys?"

I roll my eyes. "Well, I guess I'd have to say Backstreet, just because of Kevin Richardson. How hot is he?"

Brent makes a face. "You mean you have *no* opinion in the great NSYNC debate over who's cuter, Justin or JC?"

I shake my head. "No. I admit I haven't pondered the ramifications of such a profound conundrum."

"Well, for *my* money," Brent says, reaching for the sunblock, "I'll take ninety-eight degrees any day." He squirts the lotion over his chest. "They're *all cute,* except for scary Justin. And have you noticed how often they put those boys in tank tops? Nothing like those wispy other bands. These guys are *built.* They could be gay boys."

I smile. "Aren't they?"

Brent sighs. "No. Not yet, anyway. I say, give all these boy bands a few years. Look at what happened to the New Kids on the Block. Don't a couple of them live in the South End now, hanging out at the Eagle late at night for last call?"

"That's the rumor."

Brent lies back down. "I'm sure even Ricky Martin someday will settle down with a nice guy, and the world will simply shrug and say, 'Big deal.'"

"We can only hope."

"By the way, Henry," Brent announces, keeping his eyes closed against the sun. "I've got some really good party favors for this weekend. I just want to get blotto. We can forget *all* our troubles and really have fun."

Forget all our troubles. I smile to myself. I need to keep a balance here. They're killing each other again in the streets of Jerusalem; it's pretty audacious of me to think of *my* life as being troubled.

But *still.* I've heard from the grapevine that Jeff is in town. I should've suspected he'd be here. He doesn't come to Provincetown all that often anymore, but this is Fourth of July, Ptown's only real circuit party weekend. He wouldn't miss this. I wonder where he's staying, if he's going to try to see Lloyd.

I know he'll think me a jerk for hanging out with Brent. But it's been fun. I can't deny that. It all started at Gay Pride, where I ran into Brent at the Block Party. He was calling me "best friend" and everything and we started hanging out. We did a little K and we danced our asses off. He did a bump of crystal, too, though I declined. "What are you afraid of, Henry? Tina is a good girl. She won't hurt you."

But Jeff's words still made me anxious: "*I could have had a bad problem, Henry. I caught myself just in time. You stay away from crystal. It's not worth the risk.*"

I don't know what to think. I know lots of guys who've been able to manage a casual use of crystal meth, but I also know some spectacular fuckups. But Jeff's rigid admonition to keep away from the stuff suddenly feels controlling to me. Like he always knows better, and I can't find out anything on my own. I have to admit I've been enjoying hanging out with Brent. As dippy and druggy as he is, at least it's just been him and me. Not the way it is with Jeff. There's no Lloyd, no Anthony to obsess over. Just the two of us having fun.

"Hey, Brent," I say all at once. "I'll race you to the water."

Brent makes a sound of disbelief. "Go in the *water?* You crazy? I just slogged all this lotion all over me."

I leer at him. "But think of how good your square cut will look all wet and clinging as you walk back up to the blanket."

His eyes dance. "Last one in pays the cover at the A House!" He leaps up and makes a mad dash across the sand.

I hoot out loud and follow him in.

Meanwhile, Only a Few Yards Away, at the Breakwater

Jeff

I look at my watch. It's 4:40. Could Lloyd be standing me up?

I'm dangling my feet in the water at the spot where we scattered Javitz's ashes. Remembering that day isn't something I do very often. I watch the little ripples my toes make in the water, and recall the way his ashes swirled around and around, a beautiful sparkling spiral, before they headed out with the tide. Touching the water gives me a surprising sense of comfort: it makes me feel connected to Javitz. His *atoms* are here. Simply breathing in the air brings Javitz inside me. I understand finally why this place has been so healing, so *sacred*, for Lloyd.

"I'm sorry, Javitz," I whisper, probably for the five-thousandth time in four years.

Why didn't I come down that night, the night he died?

There was a hurricane, a voice inside me tries to rationalize. *You would have been a fool to risk it.*

Yeah, that and the fact some hunky Russian flight attendant was in my bed.

I think back to the morning we scattered the ashes. It was warm, warm like the mornings of our happiest memories, mornings when Javitz and Lloyd and I would get up early and walk through town, solving the world's problems if not our own. The smell of fresh-baked Portuguese bread would be wafting through the air, braiding with the fragrances of fudge and a briny low tide. We'd stop for coffee and look out at the bay, laughing about something, anything, everything.

We'd end up at Tips or Cafe Heaven for breakfast, where Javitz—the Jew—would always make an outsized point of ordering sausage and bacon, to the exaggerated horror of Lloyd, the vegetarian. Oh, yes, I smile to myself: those were the mornings I prefer to remember.

But sitting here on the breakwater, I force myself to recall another morning, the morning we carried the urn containing Javitz's ashes all the way down Commercial Street, past the shops and the cafés and all the pretty tourist boys, past the houses we had rented all those summers, past the dick dock and the Coast Guard station and all the way out here, one last walk for the three of us. That day there were no tears. We'd shed them all at the memorial service, and by now our eyes were dry. In fact, I've hardly cried at all since. It's easier not to cry.

Okay, so maybe it's time. Maybe I ought to finally tell you what Javitz meant to me. Maybe you'll understand all this better if tell you that I met Javitz when I was just twenty-two, a wide-eyed, eager young grad student. Javitz was the wry, caustic college professor more than a decade older than me. He was a big-time gay activist, too, who quickly embroiled me in a world of civil disobedience, direct actions, and ACT UP rallies. It was the Eighties; it was the way gay men lived back then. We were lovers for a time, Javitz and I. His HIV seemed merely a fact of existence, the thing that inspired us to fight, but somehow it wasn't *real.* Though we might discourse endlessly on its ramifications, not once—at least not in the early days—did I ever imagine him actually *dying.*

But he did. He died and I wasn't there.

I look at my watch. Where the fuck is Lloyd?

See, what I've never been able to let go of is the idea that I failed Javitz. Let him down. Oh, sure, I helped take care of him when he got sick, sitting up all night outside his room on the really bad nights, in case he tried to get up and walk. He had no balance and no strength, and the dementia kept him from understanding those two salient facts. I did my part wiping his ass, feeding him cold chunks of watermelon, holding an unlit cigarette to his mouth so he could think he was smoking. The saddest thing was to watch him, out of ingrained habit, lift two empty, tremulous fingers to his mouth. As much as I'd cursed those damn cancer sticks when he was well, I'd have given anything to smell their tar and nicotine again.

But despite all I did, in the end I failed him—when he had *never once failed me.* He had *always* been there, whenever I needed him, for almost the entirety of my adult life. And now I find myself playing Javitz to Henry and Anthony, pretending to be the man with the answers, the wise old sage. But I'm a *fraud,* and I'm certain Javitz knows it. He's watching me. He's keeping track.

Javitz would be so disappointed in you.

Chanel's right. I knew it even before she articulated it. *Javitz is disappointed in me.* I wasn't there at the end as I'd promised him I'd be, and now all of the lessons he taught me are proving pointless. Because I can't pass them on. I bounce from party to party dispensing bad advice to boys whose lives are as fucked up as mine. Henry avoids me, and Anthony is impossible to reach. And look at the mess I've made of my relationship with Lloyd. To top it all off, I've stopped writing.

Javitz is disappointed in me.

The sun is lower in the sky. It's now almost five o'clock. I lift my eyes toward shore. What could be *keeping* him?

I spot someone approaching. No, two people, actually. I peer at them as they get closer, realizing it's not Lloyd. It's two twenty-something gay men in khaki shorts and Abercrombie T-shirts. I catch just a snippet of their conversation as they pass.

". . . tired drag queens."

"Yeah, I'm so over them."

"I hate gay culture. It's so . . ."

They pass out of earshot. I can only imagine the adjectives he was about to use. I want to yell after them, *"So what are you doing here in Ptown? Why not vacation in Biloxi, Mississippi? Or Laramie, Wyoming?"*

I shake my head. No matter where you go, there's always somebody ready to jump on us. Sometimes it's even our own kind. Javitz's words are in my head. "They've bought the line. They've actually bought the line that gay is bad."

I let out a long sigh. Where the fuck is Lloyd?

So you're no doubt wondering what prompted me to break down and call him, especially after he hasn't answered my E-mails in so long. It's simple. *I miss him.* I miss him something fierce.

Especially these past few weeks, ever since Anthony and I returned from Disney World. You see, Anthony's become a body without a name, a face without a history. I've pulled away from any kind of intimacy with him, stung by his lack of trust. Yet he seems almost oblivious to my distancing; perhaps he's just glad I've stopped asking questions. At our hotel in Orlando that next morning, he'd shown up with bags under his eyes and baby-fine stubble on his cheeks. I'd just returned from Drake's, but neither of us asked what the other had done all night. He just came into the room, hung his face like a sad puppy, and we moved on from there.

But it can't go on like this—not with such a vast cavern of deceit gaping between us. Anthony wants us to be lovers. A month ago, when he started to share my bed, I maybe considered the same thing. I was melting, and his soft, innocent eyes had been so easy to fall into. Yet how can I look at him that way if he won't share the most basic facts of his existence?

Just what to do about it, however, remains the dilemma. For now, I just feel too inert to make any kind of a move. Except call Lloyd. *That* I found the strength to do.

"Jeff!"

I turn. It's Lloyd—*finally*—bounding over the rocks of the breakwater. I look at my watch. It's ten minutes past five.

"Thank God you waited!" Lloyd exclaims, out of breath, face flushed, grabbing me by the shoulders and kissing me spontaneously.

"I was just sitting here thinking about Javitz," I say. "Guess I got lost in thought."

Lloyd sits down next to me. "Javitz kept you here until I arrived. I know he did."

I look at him suspiciously. "Why were you so late?"

He scowls. "I was locked in my room."

"*What?*"

He shakes his head. "Jeff, the door was locked form the *outside*. I'd just bought a door lock with a key, so that I could seal off my room when I wasn't in there." He removes his sneakers and slips his feet into the water beside mine. "The only way it could be locked was for *someone to use the key.*"

"So who locked you in?"

He shivers slightly. "There was only one other person in the house. *Eva.*"

"Eva? You think Eva locked you in your room? On *purpose?*"

He sighs. "All the guests were out. I had to bang and holler for over half an hour. I couldn't go out a window because the drop is too steep. I didn't have the phone in my room, so I couldn't call for help. Finally, I spotted one of the guests coming back up the walk, and I shouted for him to get my keys on the kitchen counter. He was the one who let me out."

My jaw is nearly down on my chest. "But . . . *Eva?* Why would she lock you in your room?"

He looks at me. "Because I was coming here to see you," he says significantly.

I blink at the directness of his statement. *Lloyd . . .* talking this way about Eva? To *me?*

"Did you confront her?" I ask hesitantly.

Lloyd hangs his head. "Yes. She pled total innocence."

"But you don't believe her."

Lloyd turns to face me plaintively. "Oh, Jeff."

"Dog, this is serious."

He sighs deeply. "She insists she was sound asleep the whole time in her room. But a lock like that couldn't just lock by itself, could it?"

"Not likely."

"It made me think of the last time I was heading out to meet you. Last winter, when you first came down to see the house. Eva tried to stall me then with her tears. I think maybe she hoped you'd give up and not wait for me. Head back to Boston without ever seeing the place."

I consider it. "If I'd done that, things might have ended between us even sooner." I run my hand through my hair. "And you think now she was hoping to prevent us getting together again?"

Lloyd just lets out a long sigh. He doesn't have to answer. We look into each other's eyes.

"This is serious," I say again.

"I know," he says. "I've kept hoping against hope that it would get better, telling myself that she was simply having some kind adjustment disorder based on her grief." He looks so sad, so lost. "But I have to finally admit that it's a far more serious diagnosis than that."

I put my arm around him.

"I've missed you," he tells me, taking my hand.

"I've missed you, too." I try to smile. "So why haven't you responded to any of my E-mails?"

His eyes open wide. "*Your* E-mails? You haven't responded to *mine!*"

"I *have*. But the last one I got from *you* was well over a month ago."

He looks at me queerly. "I stopped writing because I wasn't getting any answers."

I grip his hand. "Lloyd. Does Eva know your password?"

He seems to not to want to admit it, but finally he nods. "Yeah. I gave it to her a long time ago. She needed to go online and she didn't have an account yet." He moves his eyes back to mine. "She was deleting your E-mails."

I just hold his gaze.

"I *trusted* her, Jeff."

I touch his cheek. "You don't want to talk behind her back, right?"

"I think I have to," he says plainly, looking at me again. "I *need* to,

Jeff. It's gotten very difficult. If I don't give her what she needs, she twists her ankle or has a fainting spell. If I talk to her about it, she gets all weepy or runs out of the car away from me into the woods."

I squeeze his hand.

He looks at me sheepishly. "Aren't you going to say 'I told you so'?"

I laugh. "If I did, you could say the same thing to me."

Lloyd studies me. "What do you mean?"

"Anthony."

"What about him?"

I smile wryly. "Oh, well, he's been known to run away, too, when I push a little too hard."

Lloyd looks at me with concern. "What has he told you about his past?"

"That's just it. Nothing."

"*Jeff,*" he says, "you don't mean to tell me you *still* don't know where he disappears to? Or *anything* about his background?"

I sigh. "I know some, but not nearly enough, and what I know I found out on my own." I fill him in briefly about Robert Riley. "Anthony was only a teenager then. I think the murder did a real number on him. Yet when I've tried to talk about it, he goes ballistic." I shrug. "Now I feel trapped by this mysterious stranger in my house."

Lloyd pulls me close. "Oh, Cat. How did we ever get ourselves in such situations?"

We watch the sunset, holding each other. Each without speaking it, we're both remembering Javitz's oft-repeated line about Provincetown being the only place on the East Coast where the sun sets over the ocean. It feels like a hundred years ago that Javitz was with us, and no time at all.

I feel brave. "Tell me about how he died again, Lloyd," I whisper.

He looks at me. "You sure, Cat?"

I nod. He told me the story once, on the morning I arrived only to find Javitz's body cold, but never again after that. I couldn't bear to hear it. I couldn't bear to remember that I wasn't there.

But now I want him to tell me. I want to hear how the winds beat against the house, threatening to break it down, as if God Himself was as pissed as we were that such a man had to die. As if the only way Javitz could be torn from this life was through forces mightier than Him, and there were damn few of those, believe me. I want to hear how Lloyd described for him the power of the wind, and how he told Javitz he could become one with that wind and be free.

I cry as he repeats it all to me. I sit there in Lloyd's arms and sob, the tears running down my face and dripping off my chin.

Finally, after four years, I'm grieving Javitz.

"I told him that I loved him," Lloyd's saying, "and he mouthed the words back to me. He died saying those words, Jeff. He died saying, 'I love you.' I saw the life disappear, like a candle going out behind his eyes."

"And then the wind," I say. "The wind again."

He nods. "Suddenly there came such a wind outside, so fierce that I thought the roof would be ripped off above us. Tables and chairs fell over. A vase in the living room flew from the mantel and shattered against the floor. I thought the house was collapsing inwards, but it was only Javitz, finally released from this world."

My eyes are wide, remembering. "And then when I got there," I say, "you and I went out onto the deck and shouted, 'Javitz doesn't have AIDS anymore! Javitz doesn't have AIDS anymore!' until our voices were hoarse." I look at Lloyd. "Do you remember that? Do you remember?"

He's crying now, too. "I remember, Jeff. I thought *you* had forgotten."

I shake my head. "I've never forgotten." I wipe my eyes. "It was just so hard, never having the chance to say good-bye. . . ."

"None of us did, really, Jeff. The dementia came on so fast. He was here one day and then lost to us the next. That's what was so cruel."

The tears come back, harder now. "But you at least got to tell him that you loved him. He heard you say that. He answered back that he loved you, too." It's too much for me to articulate. "I didn't—even—"

He pulls me close. "Don't be feeling guilty, Jeff. We both thought you'd have time to get here. And the storm . . ."

I can barely speak. "I should've come when you first called."

"Look, Jeff." He straightens me up. "Things happen for a reason. I believe that."

I scoff. "What reason could there have been to keep me from Javitz as he died?"

"I'm not sure, Jeff. But I know that you and I maybe needed to go our separate ways after his death. We each had our own paths to follow."

I look at him with confusion.

"What I mean is, Jeff, you and I needed to find out who we were, apart from each other, and apart from Javitz. The three of us had been enmeshed so long. I've been thinking about this. When we reconnected last fall, it was because we *wanted* to. We saw the new people we each had become, and we *liked* each other. We were stronger, wiser. Our paths had diverged only to cross once more."

"So what happened to change that?" I ask. "Why have we been apart these last few months, so angry and embittered at each other?"

Lloyd laughs. "That part I haven't figured out yet."

I laugh in return. "So what now? What do we do now? Our predicaments are so different and yet so uncannily similar, too."

Lloyd looks at me. "Tell me the truth. You *do* care about Anthony, don't you?"

I let my eyes wander off toward the water. "I care about him," I admit.

"And well you should." He squeezes my hand. "You couldn't boot him out of your life any more than I could boot Eva out of mine. We've woven them both pretty tightly into the fabric of our lives, and we owe it to them to handle this right."

I nod. "Do you think it's still possible to work this out with her, get through all the bullshit, and run the guest house?"

"Who knows? I'm going to have the heart-to-heart talk with Ty that he's been wanting to have for months, and then I'm going to talk with Eva. It's the only way." He looks at me deliberately. "And I think you should also get as much information as you can about Anthony. Then sit him down and tell him what you know. I believe they'll both respond well if we do it with compassion and respect."

I hold his hand to my lips. "But what about us?"

He gives me a small smile. "We can't know about us until we work through the rest of what's going on in our lives."

"But maybe . . ." I hesitate, looking at him. "Maybe we can do it together."

He sighs, reaching his hand down to break the surface of the water. "Do you remember how Javitz's ashes swirled in the tide?" he asks. "What a beautiful design they made?"

"I remember."

We put our heads together.

"Well," I ask again. "Can we find a way to work through this together?"

He looks at me with a sudden brightness. "Come with me to New York," he says. "I'm going to call Ty and visit him once things settle down after the Fourth. Come with me. Maybe I'll even go out dancing with you at the Roxy."

"All right," I agree, emboldened by the idea. "So long as you come with me to Connecticut first. I have a few inquiries I want to make there myself about Anthony."

"It's a plan," he says. We both smile at each other, smiles that bubble up into sudden, giddy laughter. How good it feels to be with him again. How right.

We sit there until the sun disappears behind the moors.

The Next Night,
The Crown & Anchor

Henry

It looks like poppers, but the label on the bottle in Brent's hands reads *BLUE NITRO*.

"Brent," I say, my shoulders suddenly stiffening. "That's GHB."

He scrunches up his face. "Don't freak, Henry. Just consider it liquid Ecstasy."

I'm still rolling from the regular X, several bumps of which Brent and I have taken over the past twenty-four hours. I've never sustained such a party high for so long: Jeff always put the brakes on me much earlier than this. And there's been none of the usual sustenance that Jeff always brings to circuit parties: the fruits and the water, the protein bars and carrot sticks.

Yet being free of Jeff this weekend has meant I could do a lot of things I normally could not: prime among them (I'm still hoping) is *meet somebody*. As in *potential husband*. Brent's convinced me that my cusp-of-thirty singlehood can be blamed, at least in part, on how preoccupied I've been with Jeff, and the fact that strangers always assume we're a couple. Without Jeff in tow, maybe I can finally connect, finally meet Mr. Right. Hell, the way I'm feeling, I'll even settle for Mr. Right Now.

So I kept my distance from Jeff last night at the A House, a fact he noticed but did not comment upon. He was too consumed (as usual) in his own dramas: awkwardly dividing his time between Lloyd, standing at the bar, and Anthony, shirtless on the dance floor with the extended family of Billy and Oscar and Eliot. Of course, Shane tried to engage me, but I'm getting weary of Shane's antics, too: last night he went around sticking "Hello Kitty" stickers on boys' nipples. I mean, how long can anyone put up with this stuff?

Okay, so maybe I'm being bitchy, but it's how I felt. I just stuck as close as I could to Brent. We were really wasted, and I think Brent passed out at some point during the night. Mostly alcohol on top of the X, though he may have done some crystal. I made out with a dozen hotties on the dance floor and then headed to an after-hours party on Bradford Street, where I made out some more. But when I woke up today, around four in the afternoon, I was still alone. Tonight, I vowed, I wouldn't get so twisted.

Except now Brent's raising the ante.

"Look, I know you're scared of crystal," he says "so I didn't bring that. I figured this would be better for you. Henry, now don't make a face. G is not addictive. It's actually *good* for you."

The night is warm, and we stand facing each other by the club's pool, as all around us the crowd of shirtless hunks swells. There are so many hot guys here this weekend, and I'm determined to meet one of them before the night is over. That's why I'm reluctant to go where Brent wants to take me. "I don't know," I say.

Brent rolls his eyes. "Don't be such a pet. I just need to get really twisted and forget all about Jorge. And you need to forget about Jeff. Don't deny it, best buddy. I know he's on your mind."

I just sigh.

"G is perfectly safe if you know how much to take." He unscrews the cap on the bottle. "You don't have to do as much I do. Just start with half a capful and see how you feel." He grins. "It's really a wonder drug. Not only does it give you the most fucking awesome buzz you've ever had in your whole life, but it helps you develop lean muscle mass." He laughs, patting his abs through his tight ribbed tank top as if presenting evidence.

Still I hesitate.

Brent leans in close. "You know how X releases your inhibitions and lets you approach anyone without any fear?" He rubs my cock through my jeans. "This is even better. You will be so *smooth*, man."

I sigh. Why do I need a drug to be smooth? Haven't my clients thought I was pretty smooth all on my own? Haven't I been the cocksure man of their dreams?

Okay, here's where it gets really weird. You ready? Let's just say fate has its own timing, and nothing you can do will change that. While Lloyd may be the expert on fate and psychic phenomena, I can tell you this much: too often have I thought of someone and then had them show up for it to be merely a coincidence. Like right now: I'm thinking about my clients, and who do I see across the courtyard but Kenneth. You remember Kenneth, the guy who created a disco in his downtown apartment and paid me a grand to dance all night to Donna Summer. Kenneth is here at the Crown, shirtless, with his chest shaved and sunburned. He's buzzed his head. He spots me and waves.

"*Eeew,*" Brent says, looking as if he's just sucked a lemon. "I hope that old troll doesn't come over here. He's so *pathetic.*"

I look at Kenneth but don't wave back. I'm not proud of the fact. He looks so lost standing there, so beside the point. My heart breaks for him. Even though he paid his cover and stands here among us, he still looks as if his nose is pressed up against the glass. He waves again, but I avert my eyes, pretend I don't see him. I feel like such a shit.

"So what do you say?" Brent's demanding. "You going to try Miss Gina, or am I going dancing with her by myself?"

The weirdness only continues. I'm still watching Kenneth, and I see that as he turns away from me, he's looking at someone else. I follow his line of vision and observe he's gazing longingly at a couple of guys who've just come in. Two hunky, perfect, shirtless guys. I realize all at once they're Jeff and Anthony.

And then, of course, my eyes meet Jeff's.

"Okay, fine," I say, and quickly down the capful of liquid Brent is offering me.

He's looking around to make sure we aren't being watched. I hand him back the cap and shudder.

"What's the matter, best friend?" Brent smirks. "Scared of a little salt water?"

"No. I'm just afraid of getting caught."

Brent's eyes spot Jeff now, too. "Well, well. Look who's just sauntered in and is heading our way." He quickly takes a much more substantial dose of the liquid, then stuffs the empty bottle into the pocket of his baggy jeans.

"Just be cool, Henry," he instructs.

I feel nothing. I see Jeff and Anthony approach. We all make small talk, but for the life of me, I'm having trouble following exactly what we're saying. Whether it's the drug or just anxiety, I'm not sure. I just know that when we go our separate ways into the dance area, that fucking hypocrite Jeff O'Brien still hasn't said "Happy birthday" to me.

Jeff

Henry's acting weird, but he often acts weird, and lately he's been even weirder. It hurts that we're estranged, and confuses me, but I feel powerless to do anything about it. Let him hang out with that asshole Brent Whitehead if he wants. I have too much else on my mind right at the moment to think about it for long.

"God, the place is *packed*," Anthony observes as we push our way onto the dance floor. "Hey, look! There's Rudy! And Eliot and Oscar! And Michael from L.A.! *Hey, guys!*"

Anthony rushes forward to embrace the extended family. I hang back to scan the crowd for Lloyd. I don't spot him. He told me he'd consider coming out tonight, although two nights in a row is hardly his style. Maybe it's just as well if he doesn't come, I think. Last night was certainly awkward, trying to juggle my time between him and Anthony.

"Jeff! Over here, Jeff!" Anthony is calling, frantically motioning me over. I do the round of kisses and hugs and quickly fall into the rhythm of the dance. The boys are already rolling, licking and pawing Anthony. I haven't had my first bump yet, and I'm not sure I want to. Not if there's a chance Lloyd might show up.

"What's up, Jeff?" Eliot asks. "You seem distant." He puts his arms around me, kisses me on the lips.

"I'm just—looking for someone."

"Who, baby?"

"It doesn't matter. He's probably not coming."

"You going to Hotlanta? We're talking about getting a block of rooms."

"I don't know. I haven't decided."

"Anthony said he wants to go."

"Well, let him. We don't have to do everything together."

Eliot scrunches up his face at me. "You are being quite the pet, sister. You need to talk about anything?"

I look into his eyes. Eliot is a good guy. This time he brought us all little stick-on plastic gemstones, and he's been spelling out friends' names with them on their backs. But he knows nothing about me. Not really. How could I talk to him?

I give him a kiss and tell him I need some air. I let them dance. Why spoil their time? I slip out onto the back deck, and what do you know? I run smack into Lloyd.

"I had a feeling you were somewhere nearby," I tell him.

Lloyd smirks. "It's just that way between us, isn't it?"

We kiss gently, taking each other's hand and walking over by the pool.

"You know," I say, hesitant to broach the subject, "but I should probably tell you something."

He looks at me oddly. "What's that?"

I brace myself. "I tricked with Drake in Florida."

Lloyd stops walking and looks over at me. I knew he might be angry, but I had to tell him. Drake might say something, and well, we're trying to make a go of at least being honest with each other.

"Well?" I ask.

Suddenly he cracks up. Bends over and holds his knees laughing.

I feel suitably chastised for considering it such a momentous revelation. I laugh too. "You know, we each spent the entire time talking about you."

He can barely contain his mirth. "Glad to know I wasn't forgotten."

Suddenly we're distracted by a commotion behind us. Applause. Some hooting and hollering. I can make out a flash of feathers and flowers above the heads of the crowd. A small smile creeps across Lloyd's face. "Must be the Hat Sisters making their arrival."

I assume he's right: every summer the crowd can count on Boston's most famous drag queens making an appearance.

But then I narrow my eyes and look closer. "That's not the Hat Sisters," I say.

Lloyd looks, too. "No, it's not. It's . . ."

Shane—in an outrageous flower bonnet and skintight leopard-print dress, big balloon bazooms bouncing in front of him. There's another drag queen behind him, much shorter, in a velvet dress and feathered hat, with the most amazing hourglass figure.

No, not a drag queen . . .

"Eva!" I gasp.

"What the *fuck*?" Lloyd can barely speak.

She spots us and blows a kiss.

"I can't believe it," Lloyd says, shaking his head. A crowd has gathered around them, making ribald comments and snapping photographs.

I make a wry face. "Gay boys just love her, don't they?"

Lloyd's jaw is still open.

"They think she's a man under all that padding," I tell him.

"Yes. Precisely." He sighs. "Just what she wants them to think."

Eva waltzes onto the dance floor, surrounded by her entourage.

Henry

It seems to me that the music is louder than I've ever heard it before. It's awesome. Just awesome! It's like the volume has been turned all the way up on the TV set of life. *The TV set of life!* That's *so* funny! I crack up laughing to myself.

Brent's laughing, too. Man, I'm having such a kick-ass time with him this weekend. Better than any time I've ever had with Jeff. I feel suddenly wild and free, giddy and high. Brent's ordering us vodkas and tonic and I'm so happy I kiss the back of his neck.

"To love," I say, accepting the drink and holding it aloft as a toast. "To finding the love of our lives!"

Brent seems to go serious all of a sudden. He leans in close to me. "What would you say, Henry, if I told you I'd *already* found the love of my life?"

I can't keep from laughing. "I'd say you were fucked," I tell him, cracking up. "How many boyfriends have you had, Brent? Each one you called the love of your life."

I realize I'm shouting, partly because the music is so loud, partly because I just feel like I need to shout. If I talk too quietly, I can't tell what I'm saying.

Brent's looking at me strangely. "You didn't know Theo, did you, Henry?"

"Who's Theo?"

"Theo was my lover." Brent leans back against the bar, smiling grandly now. I think he's slurring his words a little, but I might be wrong. It's hard to tell. "He was my great love. The kind of love you want to find, Henry. And I've already had it. So there."

"No way, Brent. You said you had never found true love." I'm still shouting, but Brent seems not to notice. I try to lower my voice but find I can't. "That's what you said."

"I never said that, Henry. I had true love with Theo."

"So what happened to him?" I yell, laughing again, finding all of this ridiculously amusing.

"He died." Brent looks at me with eyes that suddenly frighten me. He shouts now, too. "He died seven years ago, Henry! He died of AIDS!"

I just laugh stupidly.

"No one that I meet lives up to Theo," Brent yells into my face. "No one!"

"So why didn't you ever tell anyone about him?"

He sneers, as if it's a stupid question. "Because nobody talks about it anymore." I realize he's no longer shouting. I watch as he turns back to order another drink. A voice way down deep inside tells me that I should stop him, that he's had enough—that we've both had enough— but I don't. Maybe if he gets drunker we'll start laughing again. I don't want to talk about this. I want so much just to laugh.

The DJ is mixing in "Glorious" by Andreas Johnson. What an awesome song. Brent's back, and to my great relief, he's smiling. He throws his arms into the air, spilling his drink.

"Gloooooorrrious!" we sing out, dissolving into laughter. We stumble onto the dance floor.

"Henry! Brent!"

I turn. It's *Eva,* dressed as Mae West. And *Shane.* In *drag!*

"You guys look *fabulous!*" I scream, leaping onto each of them in turn, kissing both on the mouth.

"You are fucked up," Shane says, waving his finger at me.

It's quite possibly the funniest thing Shane has ever done. The way his finger moves back and forth. Like he's a cartoon character on a television screen. That's what it feels like: like I'm *watching* this whole scene, not living it. It's just so funny. I can't stop laughing at his little finger moving back and forth. I leap up at Shane again and hug him close.

Brent pulls off his tank top and immediately begins tearing at mine. I turn from Shane and suddenly find myself liplocked with Brent. I run my hands up Brent's sides and into his pits and over his biceps. I'm hard instantly.

"Gay men sure know how to have a good time!" Eva calls out, clapping her hands.

I let Brent go. I look over at Eva. How happy she looks. What a fucking awesome lady she is. Jeff's so fucking unfair to her. I pull her close and kiss her.

She responds eagerly, tongue first.

Lloyd

"You want to go back in and dance a while?" Jeff asks.

I touch his face. God, it feels so good to be with him again. "Yeah, okay," I say. "So long as we steer clear of Mae West and Sheena, the leopard queen."

Jeff laughs. We walk back inside holding hands. I wonder how Jeff will feel if Anthony sees us. He sure doesn't seem to be worrying about it.

But it isn't Anthony we run into. It's Henry, liplocked with Eva. I pull away automatically, but Henry's on us in a second. "Come on!" he shouts. "Dance with us!"

"He's *manic*," I observe.

"He is *majorly* fucked up," Jeff says.

I peer over at him. "Ecstasy?"

Jeff shakes his head slowly. "That doesn't look like X to me."

Eva's approached us. I marvel at her cavalier ability to pretend there's nothing wrong between us. This is a woman who has been methodically trashing Jeff's E-mails to me for weeks. This is a woman who deliberately locked me in my room. This goes far beyond any adjustment disorder, any grief reaction. This woman is certifiably personality disordered. I just need to find out how *far*.

I watch as she embraces Jeff. "How *good* it is to see you, Jeff," she coos. "It's been so *long.*"

"Yes, it has, Eva," Jeff says, trying to smile. "You certainly look festive."

She giggles coquettishly as Shane suddenly wraps his arms around her and lifts her up two feet from the floor.

Glorrrrrrrious. . .

Jeff leans into me as we watch them twirl off onto the dance floor. "You know, despite all she's done, it's hard to begrudge her." He actually seems to be melting toward her. "She looks so happy."

I laugh in disbelief. "Jeff, if she's as unbalanced as I think she might be—"

Suddenly Brent is upon us, poking his face between us. "Take your shirts off!" he's shouting. "Take your shirt off!"

"Keep your pants *on*," Jeff cracks, clearly annoyed. "All in good time."

"Take your shirt off!" Brent continues shouting, accosting any reveler who dares to keep his torso covered. Shane makes a big production of peeling down his leopard-print top. "Take your shirts off!" Brent is still shouting. He now looks at at Eva. "Take your shirt off!" Her eyes open wide.

"Oh . . . my . . . God," I manage to say, bracing myself.

I watch her. The boys on the dance floor are now cheering for her. "Whoop, whoop, whoop, whoop!"

"She'll never do it," I whisper to Jeff. "She's very self-conscious of her breasts."

But she seems spurred on by the chanting, by the sudden wave of adoration swirling around her, this sea of gay men surging in, cheering her on. All at once she throws back her head in utter rapture, seemingly lost in the sound of their voices. "Go, go, go, go!" the boys shout, as if they were at a football game. I grip Jeff's arm as Eva begins unbuttoning her blouse.

"She's going to do it," Jeff says. "She's actually . . . going . . . to do it. . . ."

Making her glorrrrrrious!

Suddenly her velvet dress pops open, and two enormous breasts bounce forward for the whole world to see. A huge roar erupts. It's as if Cher herself had just appeared on the dance floor.

"I can't bear to look," I say, putting my head down on Jeff's shoulder.

Everyone else, however, can't take their eyes off them. It's like gaping at a car accident on the side of the highway. Eva keeps her eyes closed and her head back, smiling ludicrously, surrounded by a sea of adoring gay men, her gargantuan breasts with their pancake-sized nipples jostling in time to the music.

It is, I know, her dream come true.

Henry

"Yeahhhhhh!" I shout as Eva removes her blouse. I run up to her, hugging her close, lifting her up as Shane had, spinning her around.

"I've never had so much fun!" she calls down to me.

I settle her back on the floor awkwardly and almost topple into her. She braces me, her breasts bouncing, holding me up. My legs seem to want to give out. I laugh and kiss her again. Full tongue.

"Henry," she says in my ear, "do you ever escort for *women?*"

I can't answer. My tongue feels stuck, trapped against the roof of my mouth.

The music is slowing down. I can't hear what Eva is saying to me anymore. Man, I've been jumping around this place like a fucking *nut*.

Suddenly I'm so *tired,* as if lifting Eva has used up the last of my strength. I try to dance, but now I can hardly hear the music at all.

Maybe I can just rest somewhere . . . oh, yeah, just take a little nap. Me and Brent. I look for him but can't find him. I can't see much of anything.

"Brent?" I call. "Brent?"

Jeff

"Oh, Christ," I say to Lloyd. "Look at Brent." He's staggering, holding on to the wall for support. Just like in New Orleans. And so many other times.

"He's going to be sick," Lloyd says, turning away in disgust. "Tell me what appeal these club drugs have, Jeff. Just tell me one good thing about them."

"Lloyd, let's not start. We're having much too good a time."

And we are, despite Brent and Henry and Eva. But then someone else arrives. . . .

Anthony.

"Jeff." He pushes his way over to us when he spots us. "Hello, Lloyd."

"Hey, Anthony," Lloyd replies.

Anthony doesn't look at him. He keeps his eyes glued on me. "You guys having *fun?*" he asks. There's an edge to his voice. An ironic edge. Is Anthony learning . . . *sarcasm?*

"Yeah," I say, smiling awkwardly, "we're—"

Anthony cuts me off. "Eliot and Oscar want to know if we're having dinner with them."

We. Notice how he just used the presumptive "we." Just as Eva always does.

Okay, so it's a quandary. Since yesterday Lloyd and I have been reconnecting so well. Part of me just can't bear to ditch him now. But we also agreed we owed something to these two people we'd drawn into our lives. I can't just turn my back on Anthony.

I'm saved from choosing between them, however, at least for the moment, by the arrival of the fourth member of our little quartet. Eva hurries up to us, frantically trying to button her blouse.

She's clearly overwrought. "I hope you don't think I was being too outrageous, Lloyd," she's saying.

I can see his exasperation. "Eva, you need to stop looking to me for approval. You can do what you want."

"Well, Jeff?" Anthony's asking, looming in at me, clearly getting impatient. "You coming to dinner with us or *not?*"

"Oh, Lloyd," Eva says, the joy on her face suddenly replaced with despair. "Please don't be cross with me anymore! I can't take it!"

Anthony draws himself up tall and moves in close to me. "Jeff, just tell me *yes or no!*"

"*Oh, my God!*"

It's Shane.

He's screaming.

We all spin around.

"*Somebody help!*" Shane's hands fly up, knocking the wig off his head. "Please! *Help him!*"

Brent is on the floor, his body spasming, his arms thrashing wildly.

Henry

It's like I'm watching it all on TV, but kind of in a half-awake state, not really caring. I see Jeff and Lloyd and Anthony all suddenly pounce upon Brent, but I can't hear what they're saying, or really understand why they're jumping on him. It all just seems so irrelevant, really. All I want to do is go stretch out on the beach and look up at the stars.

Jeff

We manage to get Brent out onto Commercial Street. The spasms have stopped, but he's passed out. Anthony and Lloyd are supporting him under his shoulders.

"It's G," I say.

"We've got to call an ambulance," Eva says.

"Yes!" I shout. "Go back in the bar and call 911!"

She does as she's told, picking up her long Mae West skirts and running inside. I turn my attention back to the cause of the commotion. "You stupid idiot!" I yell at Brent. *"You stupid fucking idiot!"*

"Jeff, take it easy," Lloyd scolds me.

We ease him down so he can sit against a telephone pole. The crowd on the street is staring at us. "Huddle around him," Lloyd instructs. "Don't let people see him."

Anthony kneels down beside Brent. He taps his cheek. "Brent," he says, distraught. "You gotta talk to us. *Please,* you gotta talk to us."

"He can't hear you, Anthony," I tell him.

Shane's looming over us, a crazy-looking man in a leopard-print dress. "Of course he can't hear you!" He looks at me frantically. "I saw him drinking. He's been drinking all weekend. Not to mention everything else he's been doing. You mix G with alcohol . . ."

All at once Anthony looks up, tears running down his cheeks. "Is he going to *die,* Jeff? *Please* don't let him die!"

"Henry," I mutter suddenly, looking around, the realization hitting me that Brent wasn't partying alone. *"Where's Henry?"*

Just then Brent suddenly retches, vomiting a thick orange ooze all over Anthony's bare chest and arms. Lloyd tries to support him, but he just keeps vomiting.

"Good," Shane's saying. "The vomiting is a good sign."

I dash back into the bar. Eva meets me in the doorway and tells me an ambulance is on its way. The managers have clearly figured out what's going on and are both concerned and really pissed off. "Keep your drugs out of here," one guy says to me.

"Believe me, I'm with you on that," I tell him. I spot Henry leaning inside against the wall. "I've just got to go in to bring him out."

Lloyd

"Oh, God." I'm holding Brent. He's stopped vomiting, but now I don't think he's breathing, either. That's what happens in GHB overdoses. The breathing slows down and sometimes stops. I slap his face. "Brent! Brent!"

I utter a silent prayer as I put my head close to his mouth. I count one breath, then nothing. Eight, nine seconds pass. Finally, another.

"What's wrong?" Anthony is sobbing hysterically. Brent's puke drips off him in globs, but he seems oblivious to it. "Is he *dying*, Lloyd? *Please don't let him die!*"

I know enough about comas from my days at the hospital to recognize that Brent is slipping into one. If he were in an ER right now, the doctors would be beating on his sternum.

"He's not going to die," some guy is telling Anthony. "He just needs to sleep it off."

I stare up at the fool and look around. *"Where's the fucking ambulance?"* I shout.

Jeff

Inside the bar, Henry's barely responding to me—just smiling absurdly.

"Henry!" I shout at him. *"Henry!* Tell me what you and Brent did! Did you do G?"

Henry nods. I notice he's languidly chewing gum.

"Give that to me before you fucking choke," I bark, reaching into Henry's mouth and extracting the gum. "You can lose your gag reflex."

"Hey," he protests mildly. "My gum . . ."

"Just shut up, Henry."

He suddenly frowns. "You forgot my birthday, you asshole," he says, alert all of a sudden and snarly as hell.

I just glare at him. "Then consider this my way of making it up to you, buddy." I put my arm around him and help him walk out onto the street.

"What's the big deal?" he's asking. "So I did a little G."

"Apparently, Brent did more than a little," I tell him.

It takes a few seconds for my words to penetrate Henry's skull. Suddenly he stops walking. "Brent?" he asks. "Where is Brent?"

"Out in the street, waiting for an ambulance," I tell him.

Henry breaks free of me and starts to run but loses his balance. He nearly falls. I come up behind him and steady him.

In the distance, we can now hear the ambulance beeping at pedestrians to get out of its way as it attempts to pass down Commercial Street.

"Hang on, Brent," Lloyd is urging.

Henry stands over Brent in a state of confusion. All at once he drops to his knees and grabs Brent's shoulders.

"Brent!" he screams. "You've got to be all right! You've got to be all right!"

I put my arms around him. "Come on, Henry," I say gently. "Let's go."

"Best friend!" Henry's shouting, resisting my attempts to move him. "You've got to be all right! *Best friend!*"

Lloyd

The paramedics are great. They've handled GHB calls before. Seems they're becoming routine in Provincetown during the summer. Brent is taken to Cape Cod Hospital in Hyannis, with Shane following in his car.

Henry says nothing as we take him back to Nirvana, where he pukes and falls asleep. We put him to sleep in my bed and take turns looking in on him.

Downstairs, as a soft breeze tickles the curtains at the open windows, we can hear the booms of homemade fireworks over the bay. Occasionally we spy streaks of pink and blue shooting up over the trees, but none of us seems to be paying much attention.

Anthony, freshly showered, sits on the couch with his face in his hands. Eva makes us all a pot of ginger tea.

With all the commotion, I forget momentarily how angry I am with her, how concerned I am about her state of mind. Jeff seems to have forgotten, too, so consumed is he with anger toward Brent.

"He's such an idiot," he snarls, pacing the room. "He ruins it for everyone else!"

He sits down hard on the couch.

"Jeff," I urge, "take it easy."

But he's on a roll. "There's no *way* he couldn't have known about the dangers of GHB. How could he possibly do so much? And then drink on top of it! He knew about that guy who died at the Morning Party a couple years ago. We all did. It was all over the fucking gay press!" He slams his fist down on the coffee table, rattling the glass statue of the Buddha. "There's no excuse for this. How stupid could he *be?*"

I just shake my head, wondering again for just a moment whatever happened to that little wooden Buddha, the one we had found when we all still had so much hope. "It's just a tragedy," I tell Jeff. "That's all."

His face remains white with rage. "He took advantage of Henry. There's no way Henry would've tried G if Brent hadn't been pushing him." He looks away, furious. "Henry could have *died.*"

I understand Jeff's anger. Henry's his best friend. He loves Henry. And they've been having issues, torn up by conflicts I don't really understand. I don't need to. I just know that Jeff would've had to live with a whole new layer of guilt had Henry died while they were estranged.

But if I can pinpoint the root of Jeff's outrage, *Anthony's* reaction is harder to figure. He looks up at us, his eyes puffy from crying. He's clearly been tremendously affected by this. I never knew he and Brent were so close. Maybe it's less about Brent and more about reliving traumatic memories of that guy Riley's death. Is he thinking about Riley's body lying there facedown on his front lawn as Jeff had described it to me?

Whatever he's thinking, Anthony's looking at all of us for some kind of reassurance. "Will Shane stay with him at the hospital all night?" he asks. "I mean, so he can call us and let us know when Brent wakes up?"

Jeff snaps, *"If* he wakes up."

"Oh, please, Jeff, don't," Eva says, looking over at Anthony with concern.

"He *can't* die!" Anthony cries out. "He *can't!*"

"Why *can't* he?" Jeff shouts, getting up off the couch and storming away.

"No one can know at this point," Eva says tenderly, walking over to Anthony and taking one of his hands in hers. "Maybe you ought to try and get some sleep, dear. We'll wake you the moment we hear anything."

His face just crumbles then, and silent tears fall from his eyes.

Eva moves around to sit on the arm of the couch beside him. She puts her arm around his shoulder. "Would you like some tea, Anthony?"

"Okay," he mumbles like a little boy. My heart breaks for him.

"I'm going to go check on Henry," Jeff says, seemingly oblivious to Anthony's anguish.

"I'll go with you," I respond.

I look back once as we're climbing the stairs. Anthony has put his head down on Eva's shoulder, and she's stroking his hair.

Jeff

Henry's snoring. "He's gonna have one hell of a hangover," Lloyd says.

I nod. "As well he should." I'm glaring down at him, arms folded across my chest.

Lloyd looks at me. "You've got a lot of anger about this, Jeff."

"It's just stupid. It didn't need to happen."

"Jeff, do you think maybe, just maybe you've been a little cavalier about the drug use on the scene? About your own?"

My head hurts. I can't think, can't get into a philosophical discussion about all this. "Maybe. I don't know. Maybe I don't want to believe so many of my tribe are addicts."

I can tell Lloyd's pleased I used his word. He thinks of us as the despised gay tribe, and our spiritual journey is about healing the wounds inflicted on us from eons of hatred and persecution. I don't know what I believe. Except that it's Henry's own stupidity as much as any spiritual wounds that's put him in the spot he's in.

"Addicts come in many shapes, sizes, and dispositions," Lloyd says. "And I do think drug use has acquired a certain cachet among some segments of the gay community. It's cool to use drugs, not cool if you don't. Even Ecstasy has shown some brain damage in tests."

I just cover my face with my hands.

"Jeff, I've treated so many gay men with substance abuse issues. They believe it makes up for their shortcomings—deficiencies they've been brainwashed into believing they have. They think they need drugs to make themselves better lovers, more honest communicators, more valuable human beings."

I look up at him. "It's a complex issue." That's as much as I'll admit for now. My mind is shutting down.

"Maybe you'll write about those complexities," Lloyd suggests coyly.

I smile back wearily. "Maybe I will." I fall into an easy embrace with Lloyd. I still can't get over how good it feels to be close to him again. "Hey," I say softly, thinking of something. "Where are you going to sleep, with Henry hogging your bed? You've got a full house of guests."

Lloyd gestures to the floor. "Here. I've got a sleeping bag. Somebody should keep watch on Henry, anyway."

I look over at my sleeping buddy. "Well, I'll stay here with you. I want to be here in case he wakes up and starts freaking out."

Lloyd unrolls the sleeping bag and tugs at the zipper. "You sure you don't want to stay down on the couch with Anthony? He seemed pretty upset."

I shake my head. "I'll leave him with Eva. They might be good for each other."

Lloyd laughs. "Yeah. The woman who tells too much about herself and the guy who tells nothing at all." He winks at me. "Maybe they'll cancel each other out."

I smile. "It'll be nice to sleep with you again," I say softly, the anger that had been choking me suddenly dissipating, as if a release valve had just been turned on.

Lloyd meets my gaze. "Yeah. We can fall asleep in the breathing position like old times."

It's our term for spooning. Once, when we were young lovers, the breathing position conjured magic. In each other's arms the enchantment would begin: the bed would rise like a space ship, and we'd ride it toward dawn. We dubbed it our Incredible Magic Flying Bed, and in the mornings, sometimes we could remember glimpses of our adventure: passing over rooftops and church steeples, like Wendy and Peter Pan, gliding over mountains and valleys—the whole world, really. *Many* worlds, in fact. Lloyd usually remembered more of it than I did. "I saw a long, long river last night," he'd say, "leading to the ocean"—and something about his description would sound familiar to me if I thought about it hard enough.

And this is how we would wake: my lips on the back of his neck, his legs snared between mine. There would be a passionate blink of recognition in the first flutter of our eyelids, a wash of faith, of surety. This was our first moment of consciousness every morning for six years—an awareness of the other, how each had become an inextricable part of ourselves.

I want that again more than anything tonight. We slip easily into the breathing position, as if it's been no time at all. I snake my arms, around him and pull him close.

We fall asleep in each other's arms, listening to Henry snore.

A Week Later, Avon, Connecticut

Jeff

We're parked in my car on a quiet street in a tiny suburb of Hartford, shaded by tall oak trees. In the branches above us, the birds are having a gay old time for themselves, singing back and forth. We spot a fox sneaking out of the woods, all sleek and snouty and golden. In its mouth dangles a dead skunk.

Just then my cell phone rings.

It's Henry. I listen to what he has to tell me.

"Okay," I say. "Keep me posted."

I hit END and look over at Lloyd.

"What is it?" he asks.

"Henry says Brent's family wants to pull the plug on all the machines."

Lloyd runs a hand over his buzzed head. "Poor Brent," is all he says.

"Yeah," I echo. "Poor Brent."

I look out the car window at the big white house across the street. Why are we waiting? Why are we hesitating before we walk up that driveway and ring the bell?

Lloyd lets out a long sigh. "So much tragedy on such a lovely day."

In his lap sit printouts of the newspaper accounts of the Riley murder. And across the street is Robert Riley's childhood home, where his mother still lives.

The two images have become superimposed over each other in my mind: Riley facedown in the grass; Brent in a hospital bed, hooked up to machines.

"Henry hasn't given up hope," I say. "He's been going every day to the hospital to sit by Brent's bedside. He's been talking to him, joking with him, determined to bring him back. He reports seeing eyelid flutterings, vague movements of his lips. But no one else has seen such things—not even Brent's parents."

"Poor Brent," Lloyd says again.

"Poor Henry," I add.

I look again over at the house. It's a huge, white Colonial, with large picture windows and a typical New England stone wall separating it from the street. A wide wraparound driveway cuts through the very green front lawn. Sitting near the walk is one of those statues of a black guy with a lantern. I shake my head in disgust. Hasn't anyone ever told them how *racist* those things are? Maybe they *have* been told. Maybe they don't care.

"You know, my natural instinct," I admit, "would be to sympathize with Murphy and Ortiz, not Riley. He was Mr. Upper Middle Class. These kids came from working-class families, drove around in beat-up old cars. Riley had the world given to him."

"And then taken away," Lloyd reminds me.

I let out a long sigh. "Yeah. That's when my sympathy always shifts backs to him." I think of Riley again, his head beaten down into the bloody grass.

"It's nasty stuff," Lloyd says, looking down at the papers on his lap. He read them on the ride here in preparation of going into that house. They disturbed him, as they disturbed me.

"These kids—these killers," he says. "They actually called themselves 'The Reformers'?"

I nod. "Well, Frankie Ortiz did, anyway. He seems to have been the ringleader. Brian Murphy, the other killer, turned state's evidence and squealed, told the whole story of their after-school activities."

I close my eyes. I think of how distraught Anthony had been when I left, still in a state over Brent. I've softened toward him, realizing he's reliving this trauma. The death of Riley. Where had Anthony been the night Riley was killed? Was he inside, asleep? Did he stumble out onto the lawn to find his friend—his lover?—facedown in the grass?

I made sure that before I left I held Anthony in my arms.

"It's going to be okay," I told him, not sure what I was promising.

"Tell me Brent is going to live."

"I can't tell you that."

"I love you, Jeff," he said, so frightened, so young. "Do you love me?"

How could I answer that? Of course I loved him—though the love he wanted from me wasn't something I could ever really give to him. I just kissed his forehead. "I'll be back in a few days," I told him. "Call me on my cell phone if you need anything."

I slam my fist now against the steering wheel, causing Lloyd to look over at me with surprise. "A fucking bunch of testosterone-crazed brats from South Catholic High School," I spit. "They'd go looking for queers behind the old Chez Est bar in Hartford. Tease them, taunt them, then beat them up and rob them. And, at least once, kill one of them."

"They were kids struggling with their own sexual demons," Lloyd says.

"Maybe. And maybe they just figured fags were an easy mark." I look over at him.

"Remember, this was the mid-eighties. We're not talking Boston or New York here, either. This was the height of Reaganism in Hartford, Connecticut, a very provincial city where not a lot of homos were out and proud and standing up for their rights." I gesture to the papers on Lloyd's lap. "You read the reports. You saw how many robberies and bashings these kids were charged with. It all came out after Riley's murder. Who knows how many more went unreported?"

Lloyd shakes his head. "The Reformers," he says again. "They saw themselves as *reforming* homosexuals."

"Yeah." I look over at the big white house in front of us. "All those little boys thinking they were so tough . . ."

"Murphy doesn't seem so tough to me," Lloyd observes. "The accounts say he was blubbering like a baby all through his court appearances. When they were denied youthful offender status and it was clear they'd stand trial as adults, Murphy broke real fast, giving prosecutors all they needed to know."

"Yeah. Ortiz was then pressured into pleading guilty. So there was never any trial, just the sentencing."

"And both are still in jail?"

"Yep." I look back up at the big white house. "Murphy gets out in a few years, but Ortiz will be in there until he's a middle-aged man."

We fall silent. Neither of us relishes the idea of getting out of the car and walking up that driveway. But I have to do it. It's the first step in finding out the mystery of Anthony's past.

"You ready?" I ask.

Lloyd nods. We get out of the car. Mrs. Riley hadn't responded to my letter, but I called this morning, anyway. The woman who answered the phone informed me that "Madam" would be receiving "visitors" after two this afternoon. What does *that* mean? I'm not sure, but it's a way in, and I'm not going back to Boston until I've at least tried to talk to her.

I ring the bell, a deep chime reverberating inside. We glance over at each other anxiously.

The door is opened by a dark-haired, dark-eyed woman in a white uniform.

"Hello," I say. "I'm Jeff O'Brien. I called this morning."

She nods. "Yes. You're here to see Mrs. Riley."

"Yes. This is my colleague, Lloyd Griffith."

She motions for us to come inside. The first thing that strikes me about the foyer is how spotless it is. Gleaming. A high-gloss parquetry floor, sparkling chandelier, gold-gilt frames around two giant-sized mirrors that hang on opposite walls.

"Come this way," the woman is saying. "Mrs. Riley sees visitors in the sunroom."

We follow. We pass through a hallway, our footsteps echoing in the quiet house. A large framed photograph on a side table jumps out at me. It's the same as the one in the newspaper. Robert Riley, he of the big smile and eighties hair.

We stop before French doors that lead into a glass four-seasons room. It's a greenhouse of sorts, filled with lush plants and tropical flowers, as well as wicker furniture and a large television screen. Our guide turns to look at us. "My name is Gloria Santacroce," she says. "Have you ever met Mrs. Riley before?"

"No." I look at her plaintively. "I tried to explain on the phone. I'm a journalist. I wrote her a letter." I swallow hard, certain that my Adam's apple bobs in my throat as I lie my way through this. "I'm writing about her son. Robert."

Actually, it's not a lie: I *am* a journalist, even if I haven't written so much as a sentence in a couple of years. And I *am* thinking about writing about all of this—someday, if Anthony gives me permission. For the first time in a very long while, I truly feel inspired to write.

Gloria Santacroce smiles. "Yes. I remember your letter now. I'm sorry I never got back to you." She seems to consider what she should say next. "I think I hesitated because, well, I wasn't sure how much Madam would be able to tell you. You see, she has Alzheimer's disease."

"Oh," I say, my heart sinking, looking over at Lloyd. He makes a sympathetic face.

Gloria sighs. "There are days she's very alert. Today is a good day. When I tell her in the morning that it's Tuesday, she always perks up, because this is the day she leaves open for visitors. She very much enjoys having visitors." She smiles sadly. "But not too many come by to see her anymore. It's hard for people. I understand that. And Robbie was her only family."

"I don't want to upset her, talking about him," I say.

"Oh, she loves talking about Robbie." She pauses. "Just be gentle with her."

She opens the door and we step inside. The room is at least five degrees warmer than the hallway, with the sun full upon the glass. The day is bright and warm, and through the open windows I can hear the lively chatter of birds. The deep fragrance of honeysuckle suffuses everything.

"Mrs. Riley," Gloria announces, "you have visitors."

"Oh!" The old woman attempts to turn in her chair but finds it difficult. I step quickly around to the front so she can see me. She's dressed in a yellow sundress and slippers. "Hello!" she calls out, reaching with both hands for mine.

"Hello, Mrs. Riley," I say, taking her cold hands.

Gloria leans down close to her. "They're writers, ma'am."

"Oh? Writers?" Mrs. Riley is studying us with rheumy blue eyes. Her face is not nearly as wrinkled as I imagined it might be. Her skin looks soft, even youthful. Her hair is still full and very white. Her lips bear a trace of lipstick, and she wears a pair of clip-on pearl earrings. She sits looking out into her backyard, a thicket of honeysuckle and blueberry bushes. A stone path leads down to a birdbath and small lily pond.

"Yes, ma'am, my name is Jeffrey O'Brien and this is Lloyd Griffith."

Lloyd steps forward to take one of her hands.

"You're writers?" she asks.

"Yes, ma'am." I sit down in one of the chairs opposite her. Lloyd takes the other. "I'm writing an article about your son."

Her old eyes light up and she smiles. "Robbie? Is he here?"

I exchange a glance with Gloria Santacroce.

"Mrs. Riley," Gloria tells her, "you know that Robbie passed away."

The old woman sits back in her chair, seemingly annoyed by her caretaker's reminder.

"Yes, yes, go on with you," she says, waving her hand. Gloria withdraws a little, sitting in a chair a few yards away. "Did you know Robbie?" Mrs. Riley asks me.

"No, ma'am. I didn't. I was hoping maybe you could tell me a little bit about him."

"He put in that path there," she says, pointing out ahead of her. "He did . . . what do they call it?"

"Landscaping," Gloria reminds her.

"Yes." She smiles widely. "He was a landscaper."

"I thought he was an attorney," Lloyd says.

Mrs. Riley leans forward, a little agitated. "Yes, yes, of course. He was an attorney. He worked for the Aetna, you know. A lot of them. In Hartford."

I smile. "Yes. But he liked to do landscaping on the side?"

"Yes, oh, yes. Oh, he was so good at it, too. He put in that path. He had all the designers come out and they arranged the whole thing. He picked out the flowers and even—you see that pond? He put that in, too."

"It's lovely," Lloyd observes.

"Did you know Robbie?" she asks him.

He shakes his head. "No, ma'am. I didn't."

"Robbie was a landscaper," she says. "Do you see that path?"

This is going to be difficult.

"Robbie was a landscaper," she's continuing, talking more to herself than to us, as if trying to memorize the words, "and he worked for the Aetna." She shakes a finger at me as if she's just told me something very important. "He put in that path over there." Her eyes cloud over. "Oh, I miss him; I miss him so."

My heart breaks for her. "Yes, ma'am. I'm sure you do."

She looks at me, crystal clear all of a sudden. "They killed him, you know."

"Yes. I know."

Her blue eyes seem to focus on me, then look out over the garden again. "I have no one left. My husband died when Robbie was ten. Robbie was my only child."

I feel as if I might cry. I can see the tears reflected in Lloyd's eyes. "I'm so sorry, ma'am," I manage to say.

She smiles, revealing unnervingly even false teeth. "Are you an attorney, too?"

"No. I'm a journalist. I want to write about your son."

"About Robbie? Did you know him?"

I tell her no.

"Did you?" she asks Lloyd.

"I wish I had," he answers.

"Ma'am," I interrupt, figuring I might as well get to the point of why I'm here, "I'm wondering if you knew his friend, Anthony Sabe."

"Robbie liked to do landscaping," she says, oblivious to my question. "He did that path there. Behind you."

I look again. "It's very nice."

"Anthony helped him," she says. My ears perk up and I exchange looks with Lloyd. "They had all the designers in here. He put in that pond, too. We have real fish in there. Japanese koi."

She looks over at Gloria, seeming pleased at herself that she'd remembered the name.

I lean forward in my chair. "Did you say Anthony helped him, ma'am? Did Anthony do landscaping, too?"

The old woman's shoulders seem to slouch. "He was a nice boy, Anthony," she says quietly.

"I've met him, Mrs. Riley. I know Anthony Sabe."

She smiles. "You know Anthony? Oh, where is he? Is he in Hartford?"

"No, ma'am. He lives in Boston now."

She seems to consider something. "Okay. Then you tell him something from me. Will you do that?"

"Yes, ma'am."

"Tell him I'm sorry. Will you tell him that for me?"

I pause. "Sorry, ma'am?" I ask. "Sorry for what?"

She touches her face. Her voice seems far away. "What is your name again?" she asks.

"Jeff. Jeffrey O'Brien."

"O'Brien," she says, listening to the name as she says it. "Oh, a good Irish name. My maiden name was Fitzgibbons and I married a Riley. Good, solid Irish names." She's smiling, but the expression gradually fades. "It was a Murphy that killed him, though. An Irishman. That made it worse, even. You know?"

"Yes, ma'am."

"Did you know Robbie?" she asks again.

I smile wanly. "No, ma'am, I didn't."

"I miss him so," she says softly.

I look over at Lloyd. There's a tear falling from his right eye.

Mrs. Riley lets out a long sigh and sits back in her chair, as if suddenly very weary.

Gloria Santacroce walks up behind her chair. "I think she just gets frustrated." She smiles sadly. "I think the thoughts are there but sometimes they just get jumbled up in her head."

"I won't trouble her anymore," I say, standing up. I extend my hand to the old woman.

"Thank you, Mrs. Riley. I appreciate your taking the time to see me."

She doesn't take my hand. Nor does she respond to Lloyd's attempt to say good-bye. She just sits there staring straight ahead into the garden her son designed for her.

And Anthony helped to build.

Gloria Santacroce closes the door to the sunroom behind us. "I'm sorry she couldn't be more of a help to you," she says. "Who is the article for?"

"I'm not sure yet. Maybe *The Boston Globe*. Maybe something here in Connecticut." I look at her, a last glimmer of hope rising in my chest. "Maybe you remember something about him?"

She shakes her head. "I wasn't with Mrs. Riley then. I never knew Robbie. I feel as if I do now, though, because of all the pictures." She gestures around. There sure are enough of them: Robbie as a Little Leaguer, Robbie receiving First Communion, Robbie winning some award, Robbie as the corporate hotshot posing with Lowell Weicker. "She's always talking about Robbie. It's as if he's still with us."

"I suppose he is, then," Lloyd says.

She smiles. "I know the state prosecutor's office contacted us last year about something to do with the case. But of course, Mrs. Riley wasn't able to talk to him."

I sigh. "I wish I knew what she meant by asking me to tell Anthony Sabe she was sorry."

Gloria Santacroce sighs. "I presume he was the roommate." She looks back sadly through the glass at the old woman in her chair. "Robbie's lover."

"I . . . uh . . . yes, he was his roommate. But he was only a teenager then . . ."

Gloria shrugs. "All I know is that she felt guilty for a long time. She didn't let Robbie's lover come to the funeral. She wasn't comfortable back then with her son's homosexuality. I'm not sure how they dealt with it. I guess like many families, they just didn't talk about it. Oh, the lover may have come with Robbie to work on the garden, but she wasn't comfortable enough to let him share her grief."

"I see . . ."

Gloria isn't finished, however. "But I think that the nature of Robbie's death forced her to finally accept him for what he was." She gestures with her hand. "Come here. Look at this."

She leads us a little way down the hall and flicks on the light. There, hanging on the wall, is a plaque. Both Lloyd and I step closer to read it.

TO MILDRED "MILLIE" RILEY
WITH OUR GRATITUDE AND LOVE FOR YOUR
YEARS OF DEDICATION
THE HARTFORD COUNTY CHAPTER OF
PARENTS AND FRIENDS OF LESBIANS AND GAYS
JUNE 1, 1997

"Clearly, her attitude changed," Gloria says, smiling broadly. "And I think she must have carried around with her a lot of regret for how she'd treated her son's lover."

I look at Lloyd, then back at the plaque.

For your years of dedication.

"If you do know him," Gloria asks, "will you make sure you give him her message? Will you tell him that she's sorry?" I turn my gaze to look once more through the glass doors of the sunroom at the old woman sitting there, alone and confused.

"Yes," I promise Gloria Santacroce. "I'll tell him."

The Next Day,
84th Street at Eighth Avenue,
New York

Lloyd

So immersed have I become in solving Jeff's mystery that I've practically forgotten my own. But as we step out of the cab, suddenly assaulted by the honking, bleating sounds of Manhattan, it's Eva who's once again front row and center in my mind.

No, I haven't yet confronted her about what I suspect. The missing E-mails, the manipulations, locking me in my room. What, do you think I'm *crazy*? Do you think I'd *willingly* precipitate another episode? What would she do *this* time—jump off the pier? Set fire to the house? If she's indeed personality-disordered, I have to approach this correctly. And to do that, I need to talk with Ty first. I need advice. I need facts.

"Of *course*, Lloyd," Ty said on the phone when I called last night. "Come by my office. What do you want to talk about?"

"I think you have a pretty good idea," I told him.

"Ah." I heard him take in a long breath. "Yes, I think I do."

It's raining slightly as Jeff and I start walking up the block. I check the address Ty gave me again. It's just a few more doors down.

Jeff looks over at me. "As much as I'm glad Ty's talking with you," he says, "I wonder if he's heard of a little thing called 'attorney-client privilege'?"

I've thought of that, too. I'm not the only one who should have confidentiality concerns. But Ty assured me it wasn't a problem.

"Ty was *Steven's* lawyer," I explain to Jeff, repeating how Ty explained it to me. "Most of the work he's done with Eva has been in relation to Steven's estate. Anything else he's done has been pro bono, as a favor." I sigh, suspecting some lawyers might still see some conflict of interest. "At least, that's how he's justifying talking to me."

Jeff shrugs. "He must feel it's important, whatever it is that he wants to share with you." He smirks. "Either that, or *he's* in love with you, too."

I smile.

I pop open the umbrella. The gray, dreary sky overhead and the unusually low temperatures we've been enduring are enough to make late July feel like early April. This has not been an easy trip: the trauma over Brent, the meeting with the old lady, this snooping into Eva's past. I've had a knot in my stomach for two whole days, and a dull headache that repeated doses of Tylenol have failed to touch.

But you know what? No matter how unnerved I am, no matter how unsettled, all of it pales beside the joy of being with Jeff. So many months we've been apart, and now here we are, shoulder to shoulder, like Holmes and Watson, Batman and Robin, Scarecrow and Mrs. King—and it feels good. *Very* good. Last night we slept together at Jeff's sister's house, and we played with little Jeffy and rented a movie (*Now Voyager*) and made a pan of brownies and it was awesome. As if no time had passed for us at all.

And while I still feel some guilt about inquiring into Eva's life without her full knowledge and consent, somehow the synchronicity with Jeff—who's found himself in a similar position with a similar "third person"—only seems to convince me that I'm doing the right thing.

"Here we are," I say, looking up at the side of the building.

Ty's office is on the eleventh floor of an old brownstone, and we have to take one of those old-fashioned cage elevators to reach it. His is the first door after we step out of the elevator. On the frosted glass is printed in gold: *TYRONE POWER, ATTORNEY AT LAW.*

"His name is *Tyrone Power?*" Jeff asks.

"Yeah," I say, looking at him strangely. "Why is your jaw on the floor?"

He laughs. "*Lloyd.* You lived with me for six years. *Me,* the film-buff freak. We watched *The Razor's Edge* and *Nightmare Alley* together. I think we even watched the original *Zorro.*"

I still don't get it.

"Tyrone Power!" Jeff exclaims. "Javitz used to cream all over him. Gorgeous, drop-dead, old-time Hollywood movie star. And a closet queen, to boot."

"Oh, *right,*" I say. "*Tyrone Power.*"

Jeff's dumbstruck. "The name never registered?"

I smile shamefacedly. "I knew I'd heard it before somewhere."

"What's *become* of you?" Jeff laments dramatically.

I kiss him briefly. "See what happens when we lose touch?"

We step through the door. A red-haired woman with long pepper-shaped earrings looks up at us from her desk.

"Hello," I say. "I'm Lloyd Griffith and I have an appointment with Tyrone Power."

I hear Jeff chuckle under his breath.

"Just a moment," the receptionist says. "Let me check. . . ."

The door to Ty's inner office suddenly opens and he comes bounding out, his arms outstretched. "Lloyd!" he says. "I thought I heard your voice!"

Then he notices Jeff. He stops in his tracks, his grin fading a little, some of his enthusiasm tapered down.

"You remember Jeff?" I ask. "From the opening party?"

Jeff extends his hand. "Actually, we didn't get a chance to officially meet."

I watch Ty's expression as he shakes Jeff's hand. It strikes me that maybe he was hoping for a little—something—during my visit. "Nice to meet you, Jeff," he says cordially, if far less effusively than he'd greeted me. He gestures toward his office and turns to the receptionist.

"Dayna, hold all my calls."

"Yes, sir."

Jeff pulls close to me as we walk into the room. "You slept with him, didn't you?" he whispers.

"Shh."

"Okay. I get it. He *is* in love with you. Surprise, surprise." He chuckles under his breath. "You slept with *Tyrone Power.*"

Ty's office is small but well appointed: soft tan leather chairs, an imposing desk, an oil portrait of himself on the wall. "Brandy?" he offers, holding up a decanter.

We decline. He settles himself behind his desk, folding his hands together. An amethyst ring on his finger catches the overhead light. We make some small talk for a couple of minutes, about how rainy it's been this summer. Then I sit forward in my chair.

"Ty, I came down to talk to you about Eva."

"Yes," he says. "I presumed you had." He looks pointedly at Jeff.

"It's okay," I assure him. "Jeff's just here to support me."

Jeff nods. "I understand everything you say is confidential."

Ty leans back in his chair and brings his fingertips together. "Well, I suppose this visit is evidence enough that things have reached a breaking point."

I sigh. "You were right, Ty. There are things I need to understand, things I probably should have known about before getting invested in this business with her." I pause, not sure how to proceed, or even what I hope to get from this meeting with him. "I need some advice. I'm worried about the long-term stability of the business."

Ty looks at me seriously. "What happened, Lloyd?"

I hesitate. I look over at Jeff, who nods for me to continue. "She locked me in my room. For several hours. She claimed she didn't, but—"

"Dear God." Ty leans forward across his desk. "What if there'd been a fire? Or you were sick?"

I run a hand over the top of my head. "Precisely. It was the last straw." I look at him imploringly. "Tell me what you know, Ty. I need to hear it."

He stands, pouring himself some brandy. "Sure you don't want any?" he asks again.

"On second thought, why not?" Jeff says, smiling a little.

I shrug and accept some myself.

"Look, Lloyd," Ty says, sitting down now on the edge of his desk, "let me tell you what I know about her relationship with Steven. It wasn't—well, it wasn't what she presents it to be."

I sip the brandy. Apricot. It tastes warm and good. "What do you mean?" I ask.

He looks at me directly. "Steven and I were lovers."

I exchange looks again with Jeff.

"I met him when I was just coming out," Ty continues. "At the famous St. Marks Baths. It was 1983. I was just out of law school, and Steven seemed the most sophisticated man in the world to me. He took me *everywhere*: the opera, the ballet, *A Chorus Line*. Not for six months did he admit he was married. But he insisted that he was in love with *me*." Ty pauses. "He was planning on divorcing her, he said."

I sit forward in my chair. "He *was?* But Eva has said, many times, that even though he was gay, Steven remained in love with *her*...."

Ty takes a sip of brandy. "Maybe she's convinced herself that that's the case. But I was there, Lloyd. I saw how they interacted. Steven never gave her any reason to think that. At times he was openly hostile toward her." He smiles. "Remember, she thought *I* was in love with her, too, didn't she?"

"Yes." I struggle to adjust my image of Eva's marriage. "So why didn't he divorce her, then?"

Ty lifts his eyebrows as he looks at me, as if the answer were plain. "She threatened to kill herself."

I swallow hard.

"So they came up with an arrangement," Ty continues. "He had his life, and she, at least in theory, had hers." He reaches behind him on his desk and turns a framed photograph around to face us. "I look at us every day. Not a day goes by when I don't remember."

Both Jeff and I move in closer to peer at the photo. Ty is sitting on a couch with a man I recognize as Steven. They're holding hands. Two other men stand behind the couch, their arms around each other.

"From that picture, I'm the only one still alive." Ty picks it up to gaze for a moment at the faces there, then replaces it so they can continue staring out at us. Four happy-faced men, obviously gay, vintage Reagan-era: handlebar mustaches, Izod shirts, upturned collars.

"The other two are Pedro and Scott," Ty tells us. "We were all lovers, off and on, sometimes at the same time. It's hard to describe exactly what we all were to each other." He hesitates. "No definitions seem to do us justice."

"I think we understand," I say softly, looking over at Jeff.

Jeff smiles, lifting his brandy in a little salute to Ty. "You were a family," he says plainly.

"That we were." Ty's voice is even and his eyes are dry, but the emotion is palpable just the same. "We were indeed a family, Jeff. For a time, I lived with Steven. We had our room; Eva had hers. I'd come and go every day. Sometimes we included Eva in on the dinners we cooked. Oh, they were fabulous. Five-course meals with Pedro and Scott and some of the other guys. Sometimes we even took her out with us to the movies or to a club. How she loved going out with us to gay bars, the way gay men always made a fuss over her."

Jeff and I exchange a look.

"But as time went on, that happened less and less. Steven had spent many years married to her, and he could take only so much. He had to set limits. But she knew how to manipulate him. Sometimes she'd pretend to sprain her ankle so that we'd stay in with her, or make believe she was sleepwalking."

My head spins. I set my brandy down on Ty's desk and look up at him. "It's all just such a different picture than she described. She's told me how Steven would leave little gifts for her, hidden around the house."

Ty laughs. "She's got that reversed. She'd leave little trinkets for *him!* And it drove him crazy!" He shakes his head, pacing across the room suddenly. *"She* drove him crazy, Lloyd. She was always *there,* hovering in the background, even though they'd agreed to live separate lives. He would tell her she needed to find her own set of friends, but she never would. She'd just sit in the kitchen all alone as a bunch of us were in the living room watching *All About Eve* or whatever." He smiles sadly. "Sometimes I'd feel bad and invite her in to join us, even though Steven would give me the evil eye."

"Poor lady," Jeff says, but I can definitely relate to Steven's reaction. Definitely.

Ty settles back down at his desk. "That's when she started doing the Mae West thing. My heart just broke for her, and I encouraged her in it. For a while all the guys thought it was a hoot, and how she loved their applause. But after a while, Steven just couldn't take it anymore. She was always trying to find a way into our group, a way to stay in his life. She just wouldn't accept the fact that Steven had moved on, that their marriage was over."

"So why *didn't* Steven move out, make a clean break?" I asked. "Was he really so trapped by her threats?"

Ty smiles wanly. "He and I spoke often of buying a place in Westchester with Pedro and Scott, getting out of the city. Away from Eva. But she held *on.* Divorcing her would have been hell. Even if she didn't kill herself, she never would have let him go easily."

I look over at Jeff. No, I didn't imagine Eva let anything—*anyone*— go easily. Suddenly a wave of fear strikes me and makes me feel slightly nauseated.

"Then all of it became moot, anyway, because our little family started dying off. First Scott got sick. Steven had him move in with us, and I admit that Eva was a very attentive nurse. She could be counted on to get meds on time, to change linens regularly, to clean out bedpans. She felt needed, I guess, and she rose to the occasion. I can't take that away from her. We were all grateful." He laughs. "I remember her once saying that she fell in love with Scott while taking care of him. So typically Eva."

"Yes," I say. "She told me once she'd even loved Steven's lovers."

"When Pedro got sick, she did the same," Ty continues. "And then, finally, of course, for Steven."

His eyes wander to some place far away. I think he might cry, but he goes on.

"I can remember so well, toward the end, when Steven couldn't get out of bed, he'd sometimes grab me by the shirt and beg me to keep her away from him. 'She's crying and weeping all over me!' he'd say. 'She's telling me I'm the only man she's ever loved!' You have to understand how hard it was for him. Because she was still his wife and she would have had the law on her side had we ever tried to kick her out. So Steven's gay family—what was left of us—was forced to endure Eva's often overbearing presence through his last illness. And you can be damn sure she demanded to play the grieving widow at his memorial service. As well as for many years later."

He looks directly at me.

"That is, until she met *you*, Lloyd."

I drop my face into my hands. It's all such a different a picture than the one she'd painted for me. And yet it fits. It fits perfectly. I'm dealing with a seriously ill woman here.

"Eva is the most lonely lady I've ever met," Ty says, "and I don't really know why. She has a lot to give. There's just something inside her that seems incapable of being on her own."

"I think it goes back long before Steven," I say. "Her father . . ."

Ty shudders. "Oh, yes. We all heard how Daddy slept with his little girl, how the nanny thought it improper but Eva thought it was lovely. But Daddy was gone most of the time. Maybe that's why she latched on to Steven and wouldn't let go. She would do *anything* to be included, *anything* to believe she was still part of his life."

"And then he died," I say.

Ty nods, folding his hands in front of him on his desk. "When Steven was gone, she was adrift. She tried latching on to me. That's when I think she started deluding herself that I was in love with her. After me came Alex. But *you*, Lloyd—*you* wanted to buy a house with her. That's why it was so easy to just forget Alex. You were willing to make the kind of commitment no man had ever made to her before."

"You make it sound like a *marriage*," I say, aware that I sound defensive. "It was a *business* proposition."

"Sure. That's precisely what it was. That's how you and I and Jeff and everyone else saw it. But not Eva." He smiles. "Do you know how often she refers to you as her 'other half'? Before I met you, she would often hint to me that you and she were more than just business partners, more than just friends. Then, when I saw the situation for myself, I realized it was simply the same old pattern of Eva believing what she wanted to believe."

"Oh, boy," Jeff mumbles.

I just hang my head.

Ty tries to smile. "Lloyd, I think on some level she honestly believes everything she's told you is true. That she and Steven had this great love affair. Even the truth of his gayness she won't allow to disturb that image."

I finish my brandy. "And now she wants me to take Steven's place in her life. The clothes she's given me, the ring . . ." I think of something. "Ty, did Valentine's Day ever mean anything to the two of them?"

He looks at me strangely, almost defensively. "Why?"

"She said it did. She once claimed it was their anniversary, but I saw from their wedding album they weren't married on that day."

He stands, cursing under his breath. "Valentine's Day was Steven's and *my* anniversary! Damn her for appropriating even that."

I share his anger. I look over at Jeff. But his eyes aren't angry. They're . . . *moist?* He actually wipes away a tear. Why is he all of a sudden going sentimental about Eva—when he's lost no opportunity to denounce her from the heavens for *months?*

I think Ty wants us to hang out longer, but I need some air, even if a light mist is still falling. I explain to Ty that we have to get back to Connecticut so that I can make an early return trip the next morning to Provincetown. I'd told Eva I'd be gone just a couple of days, and it is, after all, high season.

"Well, maybe we can have dinner soon," he says, keeping eye contact longer than necessary. "Come back to the city or I'll come up there." He looks from me over to Jeff, and seems to accept that something has changed. "Actually, maybe we can make it a double date. I've had dinner a couple times with your friend Drake. He's very persistent."

"Persistent he is," I agree. I see Jeff smirk and look away.

"It was good to meet you at last, Jeff," Ty says, extending his hand.

Jeff shakes it. "Well, I'm still in awe of meeting Tyrone Power."

Ty grins. "Next time I'll introduce you to Linda Darnell. She's an attorney down the hall."

We all laugh. Ty and I exchange a look. It's a look of both good-bye and gratitude. He's a good man.

Outside, Jeff and I don't speak for a long time as we walk down Eighth Avenue. I'm replaying what Ty told us over and over in my head. Finally I look over at Jeff.

"You were right," I say. "It *could* have been a fucking laundromat. She used me to fill a void in her life without ever really caring about this guest house in the way she pretended to be. She pretended to share my dream of finding a new life just because it was the only offer she had!"

Jeff stops walking and looks at me. "Lloyd, I can understand you feeling that way. But I can't get over how *sad* I feel for her. I can't dislike her anymore, despite everything she's done to keep us apart. All I can feel is so sad for how lonely she is. How *lost*."

"Pitiful," I say, almost spitting the word. "That's what she is." I feel betrayed, *used*—and it's with great effort that I try to remember that she's ill, that it's about pathology and not malice.

Jeff lifts my chin with his forefinger to look me in the eyes. "Don't you think compassion might be a more useful emotion than pity?"

I look at him. He's right. I just feel such a shattering disappointment. I stand there on the street, my clothes getting wet, and I feel like such a fool. Why hadn't I seen it before? How did I allow this to sneak up on me? Some great psychologist I am. "I bought a house with a borderline personality!" I shout, the full weight hitting me.

Jeff smirks. "Like the Madonna song?" He sings a couple of bars.

I laugh. Thank God Jeff's here with me. He's keeping me sane. "Look, I don't know for sure that it's an appropriate diagnosis for her," I say. "Borderline is pretty serious, and some psychologists don't even use the term. It's been very misunderstood. But she seems to have some of the traits of a borderline. She needs to be in therapy to determine her problem."

"So you think she can get better?"

"Borderlines are very difficult to treat. Not impossible, but it takes a long, long time." I feel tremendously sad. "And I don't know if I can last that long."

"Maybe I can talk to her," Jeff says. "Maybe I can tell her that I've been in therapy in the past. That it's nothing to be afraid of. Nothing to be ashamed of. Maybe I can encourage her to seek some help."

I have to admit that Jeff's about-face, his surprising counsel for compassion, impresses me. This is the guy who only a few weeks ago hadn't been able to tolerate Eva's presence in the same room. Now, instead of using the occasion to rail against her, he actually finds it in his heart to feel sorry for her. Now he's actually considering *talking* with her, advising her.

True, I wish Jeff had gone into therapy himself to process his grief over Javitz's death. When I suggested it, he'd been as rigid as Eva was evasive about the subject. The sessions he refers to are, in fact, from long ago, while we were still together, and they lasted only a few weeks. Still, his compassion for Eva shows that he's made some breakthroughs on his own, and it heartens me to see it.

Maybe, in fact, the vulnerability he'd shown on the breakwater the other day, when he'd finally grieved for Javitz, hadn't been a one-time thing. Maybe the cold, hard, distant Jeff is disappearing. Maybe my soft old Cat was coming back to me. Certainly his sudden compassion reminds me of the Jeff I fell in love with all those years ago, the one who cried seeing dead animals in the road. Underneath his hardened, cynical circuit-boy exterior, maybe he's still as soft as marshmallow fluff on Wonder bread.

We hail a cab. It's starting to rain harder. I don't want to think about Eva anymore. I suddenly lean across the seat and—cabbie be damned—kiss Jeff full on the mouth. He reacts with surprise but quickly begins kissing me back.

"I just want you to know how wonderful it's been being with you these past few days," I tell him.

He smiles. "Well, it's likewise, Dog. It means a lot to have you with me, supporting me through this stuff with Anthony."

I kiss him again. I notice an eyebrow lift in the rearview mirror. Hey, I'm sure New York cabdrivers have seen a lot more than this.

Suddenly I'm struck with an idea. "Jeff," I ask, "where did you say you and Anthony spent the night New Year's Eve?"

He looks at me oddly. *"What?"*

"I'm shifting gears here. I have to or I'll go nuts thinking about Eva." I pull back to focus on his eyes. "Anthony was staying in Chelsea with some guy, right?"

"Yeah," Jeff says, still puzzled.

"Do you remember *where* in Chelsea?"

"Nineteenth Street and . . . Seventh Avenue, I think." He makes a face. "But Lloyd, what does this have—"

"Trust me." I tell the driver to scratch Grand Central and take us to the corner of Nineteenth and Seventh instead.

"But *why?*" Jeff asks.

"For *clues,*" I insist. "Maybe the guy Anthony was staying with is home. Maybe Anthony talked to him, told him something."

A grin slowly stretches across Jeff's face. "You'd make a good reporter yourself, Dr. Griffith."

I wink at him.

Of course, Jeff has a hard time remembering exactly which house it was. It had been dark, and late, and he'd been a little tweaked. But he finally settles on one address.

"Yeah," he says, pointing up at the building, "I remember that little moon carved over the door." He's certain the apartment they slept in had been on the second floor, in the front, facing the street. Given that it's only a little after three o'clock, we suspect that the guy is probably still at work. But we ring the buzzer anyway, noting the name of the tenant: **R. PHILLIPS.**

As we expected, no one answers. But as we turn to head back down the brownstone steps, a guy comes walking up past us, a little out of breath. Back from a jog. He's cute, with a receding hairline and a nice set of rounded pecs bouncing beneath his wet T-shirt, clinging to him from the rain. Obviously a Chelsea fag.

"Are you Mr. Phillips?" I ask, completely on a whim.

Now, I believe the universe helps you out when you're doing the right thing. It sets up little chances like this, so-called coincidences that later you can't believe really happened. If this is the guy we're looking for, *and* he just so happens to be returning home just as we are on his steps—when we might otherwise have missed him by a slender moment or two—well, then, wouldn't that just confirm that we—*both* of us—are justified in our quest into the lives of both Anthony and Eva? Wouldn't that just be our vindication from the powers that be?

The guy in the T-shirt looks at me strangely. I repeat my question. "Are you R. Phillips, from the front apartment, second floor of this building?"

"No," he says, scrunching up his face. "I'm just here visiting my girlfriend."

Okay, so whatever. Jeff and I look at each other and crack up, linking our arms around each other's waists as we hail another cab.

The First Week of August, Nirvana

Henry

"Come on, Clara," I call. "Come on, girl!"

Brent loved this little dog. Clara made his singlehood bearable, he said. I couldn't bear to think of Clara in the kennel, so I went down and picked her up a couple of days ago. There was no one else to take her.

"That's a good girl! Come on!"

Clara's a pug. You know pugs: so ugly they're cute. Little round jellyrolls, perpetually in motion, with apoplectic eyes over faces defined by twists and folds. I adored her from the moment the lady at the kennel placed her in my arms. I was wearing one of Brent's shirts. I hoped his scent might comfort her.

It seems only fitting that my first trip with Clara should be to Provincetown. I needed to get out of Boston. The city felt too confining, too dreary, too much of a fuss over nothing. And I wanted to be in Ptown. You know. Because of Brent.

I toss the squeaky rubber bone across the grass. Clara runs after it, yapping wildly, fetching it in her mouth and bringing it back to me. I wrest it from her teeth and throw it again. She makes another manic dash across the lawn. When she comes shooting back at me, a furry little cannonball, I roll onto the ground, my arms and legs in the air, and let her climb on top of me. She loves it when I do that. She drops the bone onto my chest and licks me all over my face.

"That's my girl," I laugh. "That's my baby girl!"

A couple of the other guests at Nirvana are passing through the yard. They stop to comment on how cute Clara is. I grin and accept their praise on her behalf. Brent was right. Having a dog *does* make you popular. *Everyone* stops to chat.

Lloyd has been great, refusing to charge me for my room, even though I insisted that wasn't necessary. Except maybe it is. Remember that promotion I was up for? Well, I didn't get it. They gave it to some woman who had less seniority than me but apparently better connections. All those years slaving dutifully away in my cubicle suddenly feel wasted. So money remains tight. And it's been some months now since Hank has contributed anything to the household income.

The sun is dropping lower in the sky. Out on the street I watch as a gaggle of boys heads toward Tea Dance, chatting animatedly like boys do on the streets of Provincetown, all hands and eyes. I recognize them as Boston boys. The same old tired faces. One waves over at me. I manage a smile.

I'm not planning on joining them. Instead of the bars and the beach, I've spent my time walking with Clara through Beech Forest and sitting out on the stones in the East End, as far from the crowds as I can get. It's a different Provincetown, one far removed from the throbbing beat of the Crown and Anchor and the "see-me, see-you" crowds at Spiritus. It's a Provincetown I didn't know was available during the height of summer, but Lloyd has revealed it to me.

"There's so much here that so many never see," he explained. I followed him out on my bike to the other side of Route 6, where we hiked up into the dunes, the place where the artists lived in their shacks and where the vast horizon of sand looks like the Sahara Desert. It was the first time I'd ever really spent any time alone with Lloyd, and I found his slower, easier, more spiritual energy so different from Jeff. So refreshing. It's been just what I needed, just what I'd been looking for on this trip.

Lloyd has come out onto the porch now and is watching Clara and me wrestle on the lawn.

"You two want to take a walk on the beach?" he calls over to us.

"Sure!" I stand, clapping my hands as Clara trots alongside me. "Come on, Clara! Come on, girl!"

I spot Eva coming out of the house behind Lloyd. "Did I hear you boys say you're heading to the beach? I'm finished with the work here, so maybe I'll—"

I watch as Lloyd shoots her a look. It's a look that surprises me in its intensity. "We've talked about this, Eva," Lloyd says. His voice seems hard, definitive.

Her face crumbles. "Right," she says, trying to smile. "I'll watch the house."

Lloyd is already down the steps and crossing Commercial Street. I can't help but keep my eyes on Eva. It looks as if she might cry. Then suddenly her expression changes: it's almost scary, like Madame Jekyll and Sister Hyde. Something twists, and she looks furious. She seems not to know I'm watching her. She turns and goes back inside the house.

Something has definitely gone down between Eva and Lloyd. I don't know what it is, but it must have been something *fierce*.

"Lloyd!" I call. "Wait up!"

Clara and I follow him onto the beach. The little dog keeps running up to the edge of the waves, backing off when they come in too close.

I catch up with Lloyd. "You seem to be keeping Eva at arm's length," I observe.

He sighs. "Yes. I suppose I seemed a little harsh back there."

"Actually, yeah."

"It's not easy," he says. "I keep wanting to melt, to give in. But I have to be firm, Henry. Otherwise everything will collapse."

"Wow," I say. "That sounds pretty dramatic." I try to smile. "Letting her walk with us along the beach wouldn't have been a problem."

He shoots me a look almost as ferocious as the one he gave her. "You think not? Then she would have wanted to cook us dinner. Then we'd have all sat around and she would gotten you talking about Brent. Then she would have told you about Steven. Then she'd be in bed with you. Give her an inch and she takes a mile."

I make a face. "Lloyd, you're exaggerating a little."

He relaxes. "Maybe. But trust me, Henry. I've learned some stuff. . . . Believe me, this is the only way for now. It's called *tough love*. Eva has some problems she has to deal with. I've told her the only way I can see us continuing with this business is for her to be in therapy. I've asked her to start making some friends of her own. She can't always be tagging along with me."

I shrug. "She's always been very sweet to me."

"There comes a time when the mother bird has to kick the babies out of the nest." He smiles. "I'm coming across hard, I know, but it's the only way. I can't go on enabling her. She needs to prove she can do the work."

"Well, I trust your judgment, Lloyd," I tell him. "I figure you know best."

You see, I've come to view Lloyd as a wise man. No matter what we've talked about, he's been able to offer ideas and counsel I never would have thought of on my own. If he believes "tough love" is needed for Eva, who am I to question him?

We're quiet for a while, watching Clara play chicken with the tide. She seems fascinated by its possibilities, but terrified of actually finding them out.

"Jeff's been trying to reach you," Lloyd says all at once, just as Clara gets her paws wet and yelps out loud, running back to me as fast as her little legs can take her.

I pick her up. "Yes," I say. "I got his messages."

"I know he wanted to connect with you when he heard about Brent."

I sigh. "Yeah. I'll call him when I get back to Boston."

Lloyd levels his eyes at me. "Henry, I don't really understand the problem between you and Jeff, but I know he really cares about you. He really wants to know that you're doing okay with this."

I laugh, a little too harshly. "Doing okay? What's that supposed to mean?"

Lloyd picks up a stone and tosses it into the waves. Clara wants to leap out of my arms to go after it, but I hold her tight.

"We've talked about everything in the last twenty-four hours except the reason you came down here," Lloyd says, turning to look at me. "Do you want to talk about Brent?"

"I . . . I don't know what I'd say."

He looks over at me with the kindest, softest eyes I think I've ever seen. "Was anyone with you when you got the news that Brent died?"

There are those words again: *Brent died.* I've heard them over and over, of course, for several days. I've even said them, giving the news to friends and acquaintances throughout the South End. But still they seem so strange, foreign, ridiculously unreal. Brent. Silly, spirited, ubiquitous Brent. He turns up everywhere, annoying the shit out of everyone. How can he be dead?

I set Clara down. She runs around in circles a couple of times before deciding to check out the waves again. "I called Shane," I tell Lloyd, "and he came over."

Lloyd smiles. "Good old Shane."

"Yeah," I agree. "Good old Shane."

He came right over after I called, bearing Chinese food and two bottles of wine: one red, one white. He forced me to eat the sweet-and-sour pork (if Mother only knew), and then we consumed both bottles of wine. Even though we didn't talk much, just ate and drank, it felt good to have him there. Just somebody else in my apartment who was living, breathing. Of course he spent the night. We didn't have sex, but he held me, and feeling Shane's warm body next to mine all night was comforting.

"Too bad Brent's parents didn't allow a memorial service," Lloyd says. "It might have offered closure."

"Yeah." Brent's body was whisked out of Boston and taken back to Providence for whatever burial ceremony the Whiteheads had in mind. All trace of him was simply gone from our lives.

"You could still organize something," Lloyd suggests. "Arrange a memorial service on your own. Get Brent's friends together . . ."

"He had no friends," I say. "No one really knew Brent. Or liked him very much."

I watch Clara bark at a flock of seagulls. How much life in that little body. How much spirit.

"I guess I never realized you and Brent were all that close," Lloyd says.

"We weren't. That's what's so weird about all this. For most of the time I knew him, Brent bugged the shit out of me. He was flighty, self-centered, and could be nasty as shit. But . . ."

Lloyd looks at me. "But . . . ?"

"He was my friend," I say simply.

Lloyd just nods.

I hesitate a minute, then speak again. "Brent had HIV," I tell Lloyd. He's stunned.

I look off at the bay. "His mother told me. Apparently, she hadn't known, either. She was angry. She found me in his apartment, clearing out his porno collection. I was doing it for her, really, so she wouldn't have to see it. But she was pissed. Accused me of giving it to him."

"Oh, God, Henry." Lloyd takes my hand. "Did Brent know *him-self?*"

I feel the tears burn behind my eyes. "I have no idea. Whether he was on the cocktails or not, he never told me."

"Jesus," Lloyd says.

I think of Brent's body, so full, so pumped, that trace of acne across his back. I don't want to cry. Not again. I fight back the tears.

"I can only think that all his partying was an escape of some sort. He did tell me he had a lover who died of AIDS. Right before he died, he told me that." I look over at Lloyd. "Do you know Brent once said that dying of AIDS was preferable than ending up an old, lonely queen? He didn't want to turn into some irrelevant old-timer whose only role was as background chorus to a group of kids. He wanted to go out while he was still on top." I shake my fist up at the sky. "Well, you got your wish, you asshole!"

Lloyd slips his arm around my shoulder.

"I don't want people to remember Brent just as some drugged-out party boy." I laugh ruefully. "Even though that's what he was. But he wanted what we all want. To find somebody. To fall in love." I look at Lloyd and finally start blubbering.

Lloyd just pulls me closer to him.

"Before I came down here," I say, wiping my nose with the back of my hand, "I went for an HIV test."

Lloyd lifts my chin. God, his eyes are beautiful. "Have you been putting yourself at risk?" he asks.

I laugh. "Lloyd, I've been a goddamn *escort*. And not once did I ever think about AIDS."

Lloyd doesn't know what to say.

"Oh, sure. I thought of it in the abstract. I told clients I only practiced safe sex. If I guy asked me to bareback, I refused. So, no, I wasn't really at risk. But it struck me, finding out about Brent, how I never really gave that much thought to AIDS—how *nobody* seems to, really. How so many in the circuit scene don't ever talk about it. Everybody pretends that it's over, that it doesn't exist."

"And yet, as Brent proves, it's still there." Lloyd looks off at the waves. "How many guys out on the dance floor have HIV and either don't know or don't tell?"

"I get my results when I go back to Boston." I look at Lloyd and I'm sure the terror on my face is obvious. "I've never been tested before in my life."

Lloyd sighs. "What a difference a few years make. There was a time when everyone I knew was tested two, three, or more times."

I look down at Clara, who's sniffing around the dried shell of a dead crab. "I don't know anybody with AIDS," I tell Lloyd. "I've never lost anyone."

Lloyd looks suddenly as if he might cry, too. I know he's thinking about Javitz. He takes my hands and eases me down beside him on an old log. He kicks off his sandals and pushes his toes into the hot sand.

"I've never known anyone who died of *anything* before," I manage to say, the tears coming again, dripping down off my face. I feel ridiculous.

"It's so strange to me," Lloyd says, his voice low and thoughtful, "how there's a whole new crop of gay men today who can say the same thing." He reaches over, wiping the tears from my face tenderly with the back of his hand. "I guess the few years between us are enough to make that true. Jeff and I know so many people who have died. Our lives are littered with the corpses of dead people. They've become part of the landscape for us. They're part of the way we see the world."

I face him imploringly. "How do you go on when somebody you know is no longer here? Somebody who was so alive and now they're just gone? You can't finish the conversations you were having. You can't do anything."

He shakes his head. "There's no answer to that, Henry. You just go on."

"I guess I just never *got* death before. How *final* it is. I mean, of *course*, I knew that. But to *feel* it . . ." I shudder. "The only other person I ever knew who died was my grandfather, and I was eleven. We weren't all that close, but I remember thinking he was just away, that he'd come back. I think in some ways I convinced myself he wasn't really dead. But I'm not eleven anymore. I can't think like that now." My voice chokes up. "I used to dread seeing Brent's name appear on my caller ID. Now I'd give anything for it to show up again."

Lloyd is looking out at the waves. "One way to go on, Henry, is to see death as not being final, as not being the end."

I frown. "Lloyd, I know you believe that, but I'm just not sure about it. We Jews are kind of vague on the idea of an afterlife, you know. I *want* to believe that life goes on, but I just don't know. . . ."

"Javitz once said that it's the embrace of ambiguity that finally sets us free." He smiles over at me. "Accepting that we can never know anything for certain. That it's not about knowing, but *feeling.*"

I like that. That much I can accept, take in. We sit there watching the waves inch inexorably closer as the tide rises. Clara's getting braver, allowing her front paws to get wet. Overhead, the great dome of bright-blue sky is broken only occasionally by the flight of a gull.

"It's so peaceful here," I say. "I wish Brent had known about this part of Ptown."

"Maybe he does. Maybe that's why you and Clara came down."

I smile over at him. "How did you get to be so smart? Was it Javitz who taught you?"

"Javitz taught me a lot," Lloyd says.

"You had an amazing friendship. I envy you."

"That we did."

"What was that like? You know, Jeff has never talked to me much about Javitz."

"Never?"

I shake my head. "Not in any detail. He'll just go quiet when his name comes up, and I can see him thinking, but he won't talk about him."

Lloyd sighs. "It's been hard for Jeff. It's been hard for all of us who loved him, who took care of him at the end. You see, Javitz had always taken care of us, and then, when he got sick, it was us taking care of *him*. Feeding him. Cleaning him. Just sitting there and being with him."

"You were with him when he died."

Lloyd nods. "The greatest gift of my life."

"It's so awesome. That you did all that."

Lloyd smiles. "It wasn't just me. I have this image in my mind of Jeff sitting there, combing Javitz's hair, singing to him. 'Good morning, heartache.' Billie Holliday. It was Javitz's favorite." Lloyd laughs. "And believe me, while Jeff has many talents, singing is *not* one of them."

It's a very different image than I've ever had of Jeff. Sitting there, combing somebody's hair, singing to them . . .

"Why has Jeff never talked about Javitz to me?" I ask Lloyd.

He pauses. "Jeff carries some guilt. He wasn't there the night Javitz died." He looks at me gently, then reaches over and touches my face. "*You're* part of the guilt he feels, too, Henry. You see, Javitz taught us the meaning of friendship. What you *do* for friends. *Real* friends. How to be there—really *be there* for each other. And I think Jeff feels he's failed you, Henry."

I just look at him.

"Your distance hurts him," Lloyd tells me.

I'm torn, as ever, when it comes to Jeff. I want to melt, to feel compassion. But my back stiffens, my defenses go up. Yes, yes *indeed,* Jeff has failed me. All the times I was there for him, but our friendship remained a one-way street. I can't imagine *that* was the kind of friendship Javitz had taught him about.

"If it *means* anything," Lloyd says, "*I'd* like to be friends with you. I like you, Henry. I'm very glad we've had this chance to connect with each other."

"If it *means* anything?" I repeat, smiling broadly over at him. "Lloyd, it means the world!" I hug him.

He takes my face in his hands. "Henry, I believe Brent's in a better place. But that doesn't make the tragedy of his death any less. Particularly not for those of us left behind, who still have lives to live, heartaches to heal. If you ever need to talk, please know that I'm here."

I look at him. Sitting there, profiled against the blue sky, Lloyd seems a revelation to me. How have I never managed to realize what a deep person he is? Or, for that matter, how very, very *handsome?*

"I was such a fool," I say, all at once, not even aware of the words until I hear them myself.

Lloyd's brows pull together. "What do you mean?"

"I've been doing everything but facing up to what was really bothering me."

Lloyd smiles, as if he's been waiting for that little insight. "And what was that, Henry?" he asks, looking into my eyes. "What was really bothering you?"

I laugh a little. "Now that you ask, of course, I'm not quite sure."

He runs a hand through my hair. It feels awesome to have him touch me. My whole body tingles. "Why did you start escorting?" he asks.

I shrug. "Because it gave me one hell of a frigging ego boost."

"A boost you apparently *needed.*"

"Yeah, I guess I did. And it was fun for a while. Even *hot.* But . . . then it started to change."

"How so?" Lloyd asks.

"Well, in retrospect, I think the reason I really got into the escorting wasn't so much the boost to my ego. That faded out pretty fast. What made it so—so fulfilling—was meeting these guys. Feeling a part of their lives. Connected to them, in a way. Making them happy. Seeing their secret dreams and fantasies come true. I felt like I was really giving them something."

"You were." Lloyd smiles. "Yourself."

"Yeah." I laugh, struck by the simplicity of it all. "I guess I was."

"That kind of thrill is far more lasting than any ego boost," Lloyd explains. "So what happened to change that? Why did you stop escorting?"

I shake my head. "Because . . . well, I had some bad experiences. People who hired me not for *me,* but for the *act.* Not for the fantasy, not for any kind of connection, but for the *mechanics* of sex. Blow jobs. Hand jobs. You know. 'Fuck me in this position hard.'" I whistle over to Clara, who's running off too far down the beach. She comes racing back to me. It makes me happy to watch her. "I guess escorting just started to make me feel so *empty.*"

Lloyd nods. "Maybe because your clients had taught you something. Something about what you wanted *yourself,* in our *own* life. Your wanted your own fantasy fulfilled."

I grin over at him. "You must have made one very excellent psychologist."

He laughs. "I think most people can understand what this is all about, Henry. You said it yourself. It's about connection."

"Connection," I echo.

"Javitz used to say that life is only about connection," Lloyd says. "It's about people loving each other, learning from each other, helping each other. That's all." He laughs. "There was a time when I truly thought what I wanted most in this life was to become a contemplative monk living in some ashram. But I know now I couldn't live without the connection to other people. It's what keeps me going."

"Yeah," I agree. "I think that's the problem for me right now. I feel disconnected. Especially from sex. I feel *so* disconnected from sex."

"I can understand." Lloyd suddenly smiles, as if an idea occurs to him. "You know what you would enjoy, Henry? Have you ever heard of a sacred-sex workshop? There are all sorts of these things, held all over the country, where gay men get in touch with the sacred erotic. Do you know what I'm talking about?"

I do. Brent used to make sport of such workshops, claiming they were just a bunch of horny, desperate guys who got together and called sex "sacred" because it was the only way they could actually *get* any. *Which,* I'm suddenly certain, is a crock of shit.

"I've heard of them," I tell Lloyd. "And yes, I think a sacred-sex workshop might be exactly what I need."

He smiles. "There's actually a workshop being held here in Province-town on Halloween weekend. I know the organizer. I can probably get us both in. Do you want to go?"

"Yes!" I say passionately. "Yes, I do!"

"Well, you're sure an easy one to convince," Lloyd says, laughing, just as Clara comes bounding up on both of us, knocking us over backward into the sand.

The Next Evening, Nirvana

Lloyd

It's hard saying good-bye. I can see why Jeff loves Henry: he's thoughtful, introspective, kind. I watch him walk down the front steps, turning twice to wave good-bye.

Please, God, I pray. *Don't let him test positive.*

I close my eyes. It's an old prayer, one uttered too many times in my life, about too many, and not one always granted. I watch Henry unlock the door to his Jeep, lifting the dog crate that contains Clara and settling it gently onto the passenger seat.

Let him be okay, God. Please.

It's funny, my praying. I don't believe in the old God, the one you pray to for things to happen—or not—or to ask favors. I believe in a God, a higher power, a collective soul of consciousness, for whom there are reasons for everything. If Henry tests positive, then there is some greater purpose it can serve, some unknown path to enlightenment. Even Javitz came to see his HIV as an ironic gift, as a means by which he could transform. But still, in this moment, the God I'm praying to is indeed my old Lutheran god, the one my father taught me about in his Sunday sermons, a God of not only compassion but *retribution*. A God who was both merciful and angry, for whom divine intervention remained possible. It's to that God I find myself praying now, imploring Him to please, please not let Henry test positive.

I shut the front door after he's driven off. I can still smell him on my clothes. I'd kissed him as he got ready to leave: just reached over and kissed him, full on the mouth, after he'd said something that particularly touched me. It was about finding himself, his deepest truth, holding a frightened little man in a motel room one afternoon. He didn't use those words, but that's what he meant. His words moved me, and I'd just reached over as we sat there on the couch, and kissed him. He seemed surprised at first, but kissed me back. Afterward we laughed. It had been a lovely, spontaneous kiss.

I'm filled with him right now: his scent, his words, the memory of our talks. If I close my eyes I can see him clearly. Henry is a revelation. I've always liked him but never really knew him. It's odd, really, this feeling of connection: our worldviews, our experiences, are so different. Henry's like so many young gay men today who've never lost anyone, who often don't even *know* anyone who is HIV-positive. How different from just a decade ago. Who his age could have said the same thing then? Jeff and I have lost so many, even beyond Javitz: old friends like Paul and Roger and of course Tommy, our friend from our ACT UP days. Tommy's death had been especially hard, coming so soon after Javitz's. There had been issues between Jeff and Tommy, but at Tommy's memorial service Jeff had cried even harder than he had for Javitz.

"I guess," Henry had said just before he left, "I understand why it's so difficult for Jeff to talk about it. It's like coming through a war."

"A war where the truce is merely a mirage, a ploy of the enemy." I knew I sounded like Javitz, but there it was, right on the front page of *Bay Windows*: YOUNG GAY MEN SPREADING HIV IN ALARMING NUMBERS. Not having known the initial devastation, lulled into complacency by the new drugs, people Henry's age and younger are repeating all of our old mistakes. Because everyone looks so healthy, no one is forced into talking about the truth of AIDS. The fear is gone. Maybe reintroducing a little fear wouldn't be such a bad thing.

"Be careful," I pleaded with Henry. "Please be careful."

He smiled at me. "Lloyd," he asked, seeming to think of something, "would you be interested in coming with me to the Russian River next week?"

I looked at him strangely.

He laughed. "I know it's last-minute, but I've been totally dreading going. See, Shane bought us tickets a long time ago and I promised—but if you came, we could balance out some of the mindless party stuff with talks like these."

I was dumbfounded. "Henry, are you asking *me* to go to a *circuit party?*"

"This one's different. I promise. It's outside. The Russian River is beautiful—"

"I know. I love Guerneville. I love all of Northern California. Maybe we could spend a few days in San Francisco—"

Henry's face lit up. "So you'll come?"

"If I can still get a ticket." A trip would definitely do me good. I haven't had a vacation since we opened Nirvana. And a week away from Eva would give us both some time off from each other.

I climb the stairs to my room planning to call a travel agent. Maybe I'll even take Henry up to the Harbin hot springs. Suddenly I'm excited about something for the first time in weeks. I'm glad the last of our guests have left, and none are due in for a few days. I need to stop thinking, to just turn off my brain for a while.

But I can't. I can't stop thinking about Henry. *Worrying* about him, actually. The world Jeff introduced him to can't offer him the insight or solace he seeks. It's a place of denial, a place where the wounded run for refuge. Oh, who can blame them for dancing their asses off? But it's just running away from the inevitable. Brent didn't die from the virus that lurked in his bloodstream, but from his refusal to face it, to integrate it, to take power over it—and *from* it.

I let out a long sigh and open the door to my room. I switch on the light.

Eva's standing there, glaring at me.

"What . . . ?" I sputter. "What are you doing in here?"

I'd left the door unlocked only for the few minutes that it took to walk Henry downstairs and see him off. And here she is, standing in the center of my room, holding something in her hands.

She blushes. "I'm sorry, Lloyd. I was leaving you a gift."

"A gift?"

She holds out a framed photograph. The two of us standing in the snow outside Nirvana. The day of our closing. "Happy sixth-month anniversary," she says.

My heart is still thudding in my ears from the start she gave me. "You could have given it to me downstairs. I don't like anyone in my room."

I notice her visibly stiffen. "You had *Henry* in here all day," she says.

"That's my business."

Her face twists in desperation. "It's mine, too! I live here! This is our home!" She starts to cry. "You've been pushing me away because you're seeing Henry now. Isn't that right?"

I feel my cheeks flush in anger. "I'm not seeing Henry."

"Oh, Lloyd! Why have you turned on me?"

I sigh, dropping my hands to my side. "I haven't turned on you, Eva.

I've simply told you I think you need to be in therapy to work on your own issues. It's the only way I can see us moving forward together. And I think it would be much healthier if we each had our own sets of friends, our own lives."

"That's not how this was supposed to be!"

"Oh? And how did you *think* it was supposed to be, Eva?"

"I thought . . . I thought . . . we would be *together,*" she says in a little voice.

I feel exasperated. "Is that why you locked me in my room, Eva? To keep me with you, and away from Jeff?"

"I *didn't,* Lloyd. I *swear.*"

I lower my face close to hers. "Then how about all those E-mails, Eva? All those E-mails Jeff sent me that I never got?"

She looks up at me with sudden terror in her eyes. I know I need to be careful here, that confrontation might not be the best approach. But it's time—long past time, in fact—that she be held accountable for these things. Maybe it's the shock she needs that will finally get her to look at her behavior.

"Did you think I wouldn't find out, Eva?" I ask, trying to keep my voice calm and level. "Until I began using my laptop, I read all my E-mail on the main computer downstairs, the one you log on to every morning before I get up. It must have kept you busy, constantly checking for and deleting all of Jeff's E-mails."

"Stop!" she shouts, putting her hands to her ears, dropping the photo to the floor. The glass shatters. She makes a sound, shaking her hands in tiny fists.

"No," I tell her forcefully. "No more scenes!" I rest my hands on her shoulders. "I know that deep down inside you there's a decent, strong woman, and that's who I'm talking to right now. I can overlook a lot, but not dishonesty. Admit to me what you did and we'll find a way to work this out."

"No!" she cries, breaking free from my grip.

"Eva, you've got to stop trying to turn me into Steven. Steven was a gay man, just like me—with a life of his *own* just like me! You can't make me into what you hoped Steven would be!"

"Stop talking about him!"

"Why? Because you're afraid I'll tell you what I know? That your anniversary wasn't on Valentine's Day—that Valentine's Day was Steven's and Ty's anniversary? That Steven and Ty were lovers, and that he would have left you if he hadn't gotten sick?"

She slaps me across the face. I take a step backward in shock.

Her face is white. Her look is one I've never seen before. A mixture of rage, hatred, fear, and desperation. It terrifies me.

"I'd like the ring back, please," she says in a low, hard voice. "You've never cared enough to wear it."

I study her. It's as if she'd just drunk a potion and turned into something else. No more tears. Now her face is contorted, her mouth full of fangs. I just stand there looking at her.

"My ring!" she shouts.

I open my drawer and retrieve it, handing it to her. She takes it and looks down at it in her hand.

"This should go to someone who cares," she says, pushing it down into her pocket savagely.

"Eva, if you don't think I've *cared,* then you're wrong—"

She cuts me off. "Oh, you think you know me so *well,*" she growls in a voice alien to my ears. Low and full of contempt. "You think you know so *much.*"

I watch her. She moves toward me, her hands held out like claws at her side.

"Well, you don't know *anything,*" she spits. Her eyes grow large as they glare up at me. "Anything!"

"Eva," I say, trying to calm her.

She screeches suddenly like a banshee. She's in my face, her hands just inches from my skin, her nails ready to scratch my eyes out. Then she pulls back, shaking her head, the tears flying.

"You think you know me, but you don't, not at all," she sobs. "Oh, but you'll *learn,* Lloyd. You'll find out what I'm *really* like."

She rushes from my room, slamming the door behind her. I quickly lock it, thankful that the key is in my pocket.

Was that a threat? For the first time, I feel fear in this house. Fear of *her,* of what she might do. Of what she might be capable of doing. I'm bigger, stronger, but there was such rage in her face. She had hit me, and came close to doing so again. What had she meant, that I'll find out what she's *really* like?

I've got to get a grip here. It's my fear, my utter disappointment, the shattering of all my dreams. I stoop down to pick up the shards of glass from the photograph. I feel trapped here in my room. A feeling of despair washes over me, and I start to cry, looking down at our smiling faces. How much hope we'd had then. How had we gotten to this place?

I cry harder. For a man who believes in a purpose for everything in life, in this moment I can't see anything that makes sense.

One Month Later,
The Folsom Street Fair, San Francisco

Jeff

San Francisco. Is there any gay man on the planet who, on his first visit to the City by the Bay, hasn't fallen in love with the place?

Anthony sure does. He's standing here on top of Twin Peaks, his arms outstretched, the wind in his hair, looking down at the city, turning all at once in a circle, marveling at the panoramic vista of sea and sky and rolling land. "So *open*," he says, his voice choking up. He's actually getting emotional over it. "So *free*. Nothing in the way. You can see forever up here!"

We've come to San Francisco for the Folsom Street Fair, and I'm giving Anthony a tour of the city. From Twin Peaks we head down to South of Market, where the fair stretches from Seventh to Twelfth Street. We're hardly what you'd consider leather guys, but the Fair is a wide-open, inclusive event, three hundred thousand strong. Everyone is leather for a day—kind of like St. Patrick's Day, when everyone becomes an honorary Irishman for twenty-four hours. Just as I did last year, I proudly strapped on the leather harness Javitz bought for me so long ago. It does make my pecs look pretty good.

Anthony attracts the lion's share of attention, however, wearing a pair of my leather pants and no shirt. Strangers come up to him to run their hands down his torso, marveling at his abs. He's in his glory. It's still summer here, eighty degrees without a pinch of humidity; back home the weather has already turned chilly. San Francisco seems a Shangri-la to Anthony, a gay paradise of love and sex.

And isn't it? We started our tour in the Castro, where Anthony was struck by the history of the place, just as I had been over a decade earlier, when Javitz first showed it to me. This was ground zero for queer-dom, and Anthony drank up my tales of gay history with a voracious thirst.

"This was where Harvey Milk had his camera shop," I told him. He looked through the glass, then back at me. "Tell me again who he was."

So I filled him in, recounting Milk's legendary out-of-the-closet ca-reer in the seventies, and how the riots after his assassination proved once and for all what kind of collective power angry queers could wield.

"One more gay man killed by the forces of reaction," I mused, look-ing up Castro Street toward Market, thinking of the generations of gay men who had crossed at that intersection, so many now gone.

Anthony was looking over at me, the sun highlighting his hair. "What happened to Harvey Milk's killer, Jeff?" he asked softly.

"They let him out," I spit. "He served only a few years. Finally he killed himself."

"Is that what he *should* have done?" Anthony asked me. "Was that only right—that he took his own life?"

I remember thinking it was an odd question. "Yes," I said. "I sup-pose given that justice hadn't been served by the courts, it was the only way the whole tragedy could ever come to a close."

Anthony just nodded. What was he thinking? Why didn't he talk? *Why,* after all this time?

Despite my playing tour guide for him, things haven't really been all that rosy between us. Not for over a month, really, not since my meeting with Mrs. Riley. I mean, here I am, knowing about his past but unable to talk to him about it. I've wanted so much to convey Mrs. Riley's mes-sage to him, but after Brent's death it seemed impossible. Anthony be-came a high-strung bundle of nerves, easily rattled, quick to dissolve into tears. Raising anything I'd learned risked setting him off. I've come to realize just how emotionally fragile he is.

"Do you want to talk, Anthony?" I've asked several times, trying to get him to open up. "About the *real* reason Brent's death has so upset you? Do you finally want to talk about your past?"

"No!" he's cried. In his eyes I've seen—what? Terror? Shame? Madness? Maybe all of them, but mostly it's desperation. I let the mat-ter drop.

So the distance has only grown, and Anthony surely feels it. He's gone back to sleeping on the couch, a move I made no attempt to change. I've begun writing, the first tentative pages of a story, the first attempt I've made in almost two years. I spend my days at my computer, while Anthony watches television alone. He knows things have changed between us. On the flight out here, he looked over at me with those puppy-dog eyes of his and said, "Jeff, I have a feeling when we go back to Boston, you're going to want me to get my own place."

I agreed it might be best.

I just can't keep up the pretense with him anymore. You *have* to understand what I mean. How can I go on being intimate with someone who doesn't trust me enough to share the most basic facts of his life— *and* who continues to disappear one night a week without explanation?

And there's something else, too. Lloyd's been coming to Boston fairly regularly. Things between Lloyd and Eva have deteriorated pretty rapidly over the last month. He jumps at any chance to get out of Provincetown and come up to Boston—and not just to see *me*, as it turns out. He and Henry, wonder of wonders, have become quite the buds. Lloyd even went with Henry and Shane to the Russian River a few weeks ago. *Lloyd,* at a circuit party, dancing all shirtless and sweaty with several hundred other guys. I admit I felt a little piqued, given how Lloyd would never, ever consider doing that with me. "It was awesome," he told me. "I felt such a bond, such a connection with the guys there."

"What have I been trying to *tell* you?" I asked, exasperated. "The circuit isn't just about mindless drug abuse."

Still, I tried not to act all pissy about it. That would totally backfire. Lloyd would get aggravated, and I'd give Henry the satisfaction of thinking I'm actually *jealous* of their friendship. Isn't *that* a crazy thought? So I just said I was really glad Lloyd had had a good time and that maybe he'd cut me a little slack in the future about the whole circuit scene.

Besides, it wasn't like I could've gone with them or anything, not with Anthony on my hands. He's really been a mess these past few weeks since Brent died, and he's always worse right after one of Lloyd's visits. Twice Anthony came in to find Lloyd and me hunkered down on the couch watching old movies, Mr. Tompkins snoring between us. He just headed into the bathroom and stayed there until the movie was over and Lloyd left for Provincetown.

In many ways, I think both Anthony and I view San Francisco as a good-bye trip. Sad, maybe, but inevitable. At least we've managed a few smiles together over the past few hours. Anthony's thunderstruck by the fair: all the leather, the whipping demonstrations, the boys in studded collars being led around on leashes by their masters. Anthony's eyes bug at the sight of a rubber-clad woman dripping wax on the upturned nipples of a bound girl-slave. His head keeps whipping around to watch the hundreds of butts, some tight and hard, others flabby and hairy, protruding from black leather chaps.

"You'd never see anything like this in Boston," he gasps.

"Sodom by the Sea," I tell him.

The trip was planned months before, back when we all envisioned it to be a happy excursion. But the flight out here had been miserable. Not only had Anthony pouted the whole way, but Henry was still distant: cordial but aloof, as he's been for months. I'm not even sure if we're friends anymore. He and Shane have plans to stay elsewhere, while Anthony and I are crashing with Zed, the guy I dated briefly last year. That, of course, has made Anthony even more insecure, fearful that I'll end up sleeping with Zed again. All in all, a wretched flight, made worse by turbulence from Cincinnati to the Rockies.

But once we landed in the fabled Golden City, our spirits rose. I even permitted myself to take Anthony on the tour. It's a glorious day, the Golden Gate sparkling in the sun. I remember my own first visit to the city, as a bright-eyed twink on the arm of Javitz. How I loved the place; never, not even in New York, had I seen so many queers. Even then there were still a few Castro clones walking around, in their tight jeans, flannel shirts and handlebar mustaches, though most would be extinct, due to AIDS and the fashion revolt against them, within a few years.

I loved just as much the topography of the place. Turn a corner and suddenly you're at the top of a hill, looking down a long, long lane that rises and falls to the water below. Behind you, mountains scrape the sky, and it's rare that anything obstructs your view. Anthony, too, was in awe of this as he stood atop Twin Peaks, tears in his eyes, like a Jew on Mount Sinai, or a Muslim finally arrived in Mecca.

Yet Anthony's emotion, like so much about him, remains curious. His wonder is perhaps understandable to anyone from the East, where towns are tucked into valleys, not spread over hills, and where buildings reach so high and cluster so tightly together that even a view into the next block is often impossible. But why the tears? Why did Anthony weep at such a vast expanse of freedom, at seeing the wideness of the world, the limitless opportunity in front of him?

A snippet of conversation comes back to me:

"I can't stand being inside for too long. Especially in places as small as that apartment."

"A little claustrophobic, eh?"

"Yeah. Actually, a lot claustrophobic."

"Look, Jeff," he's saying now, pulling on my hand. "This guy's eating fire."

In front of us, a burly man in leather overalls is swallowing flames from a stick as if they were cotton candy.

"Anthony," I tell him, suddenly conscious of the time, "you can stay and watch, but I need to hustle if I want to catch Varla Jean." Varla Jean Merman, Provincetown's own drag queen for the new millennium, is performing in a few minutes on the stage at Seventh Street. "We can meet up later."

"No," he says, running after me to catch up. "I'll come with you." So like a child . . .

That's what Randy Phillips had said about him. You know who I'm talking about, don't you? Randy Phillips. *R. Phillips,* from the apartment in Chelsea. The guy Anthony had been with in New York before he met me.

"He was always afraid of getting lost," Randy explained. "He stuck to me like glue—until New Year's Eve, that is, when he met *you.*"

There was bitterness in his voice. I guess I can understand it. In his view, I took Anthony from him. Stole him away from his very house.

Yes, my investigations have continued. Lloyd's idea was a good one, and as soon as we returned from New York, I found the phone number for R. Phillips online. I called and left a message, explaining I was a friend of Anthony Sabe's; not surprisingly, he didn't call me back. But I was persistent, finally catching him at home on a Sunday morning. He wasn't too happy to hear from me, especially when he realized who I was.

But he didn't hang up on me. He seemed curious to know what had become of the golden boy he'd met in Miami, who'd so briefly brightened up his winter.

"Have you found out much about him?" he asked me.

"No. Actually, I was hoping maybe you might tell me a few things. You see, I'm worried about him."

"He know you're calling?"

"No," I had to admit.

"You're out of line, dude, going behind his back like this," Randy said.

I acknowledged I probably was. "But I wouldn't be calling you if I felt there were any other options. You see, I've come to care for him a great deal, and his state of mind has become very fragile of late. A friend of ours died, and he's been really upset. I was simply hoping you might have some insight."

"What do you want to know?"

"Well, to start, maybe how you met."

He laughed. "At the White Party in Miami. Where else do gay men meet these days?"

That much fit with Anthony's story. He told me he had come back to New York with this guy after meeting him in Miami.

"So tell me," Randy said, clearly no longer concerned about crossing any lines. "Does he still disappear once a week overnight?"

When I told him that yes, Anthony was still pulling his weekly disappearing act, Randy Phillips recounted a pattern of behavior that I recognized immediately. No talking about the past, a mysterious silence whenever the subject was pressed too hard.

"You ought to tell him to be careful with that ID I got for him. He's lucky I'm an old softie and didn't turn him in."

"What ID?"

Randy laughed. "He had nothing when I met him. He was just a total bum, getting by on his looks. If he was going to fly back to New York with me, I had to get him an ID. Good thing I have connections in Florida. With all the illegal aliens there, they're experts at whipping up fake IDs. We had one for Anthony in a day."

His New York nondriver identification card. It was *fake*. I said nothing, just let Randy Phillips keep talking. I could tell as I listened that, despite the fact that they'd been together only a couple of months, Randy had fallen hard for Anthony. And in his questioning of Anthony's past, he'd been much more aggressive than I've been.

"I asked too many questions," Randy said. "Made too many ultimatums. Guess that's what drove him away."

"Did he ever mention anybody in Connecticut? Any connection there at all?"

"Connecticut? No. Right before me, he'd been in Albany with some guy, some loser who drove him all the way down to the White Party only to have me snatch Anthony away from him at the end. Where he was before that, I haven't a clue."

Albany. Yes, Anthony had mentioned Albany to me, too.

"Take my advice, dude," Randy Phillips said. "Push too hard, and he'll bolt out of your life the way he bolted out of mine. The guy from Albany probably asked too many questions as well. Starting to see a pattern? We're just links in a chain of sugar daddies, my friend. I'd advise you not to get too attached."

I look over at Anthony now. He's watching Varla Jean suck down her trademark tube of Cheez Whiz while yodeling like Mama Cass. "Dream a little dream of . . . *cheeeeese!*"

Anthony laughs uproariously.

Is that all I am to him? A sugar daddy who pays his way to all these far-flung revelries, who buys him clothes and gives him a roof over his head?

As fate would have it, that thought is immediately followed by the appearance of a tall, bearded older man in full leather, who grabs Anthony's ass from behind as if to claim it for his own. Anthony looks up at him and smiles. Part of me wants to punch the guy out. And part of me really doesn't care if he takes Anthony back to his dungeon and hog-ties him.

That's when I spot Henry and Shane in the crowd.

Man, do I ever miss Henry right about now. I want his advice and counsel, his take on how I should handle the situation. I haven't always given Henry as much credit as I should have; his advice usually turns out to be very solid. I miss our talks. What I know about Henry's life these days comes primarily from Lloyd. Life sure has its interesting twists and turns.

"Hey, buddy," I say, coming up behind him.

He turns and offers me a faint smile. "Hey, Jeff."

I notice Shane look down at me and quickly turn away. I can feel his contempt. Why he doesn't like me, I can't fathom. I put my arm around Henry's shoulder. "Can we go for a walk?"

He sighs, allowing me to move him away from the crowd. He's shirtless but wears no leather. He seems not to want to call attention to himself, as if he just doesn't have the heart to get into the spirit of the celebration. I know he's been greatly affected by Brent's death, too: like Anthony, he seemed to grieve far beyond the bounds of their friendship. Lloyd says it's a personal grief, that Henry's mourning the loss of something within himself. I don't understand what it is that Henry's going through, and he hasn't allowed me near enough to find out.

I look at him plaintively. "I miss you, buddy," I say, finding his eyes.

He looks away.

"I was going to call you a couple weeks ago and surprise you with tickets to Southern Decadence in New Orleans."

He still doesn't look at me. "I already had tickets," he says. "I went with Shane."

"So I heard. That's why I didn't call." I try to smile. "So how was it? We had a blast last year."

"It was okay."

"Just *okay?* God, Henry, last year we were *wild* at Southern Decadence. Remember that guy? What was his name? Gregory? The one with the feathered headdress and big dick . . ."

Henry finally meets my eyes. He seems annoyed. "Why should I remember him, Jeff? He had the hots for *you.*"

"No, it was you." I'm sure of it. Or maybe it was Henry who had the hots for him. . . .

"It was you, Jeff." He's looking away from me again.

I sigh. "Henry, I was really hoping maybe we could hang out a little on this trip. Are you going to Universe tonight?"

"No." He looks at me. "I mean, I'm not sure. Maybe."

I squint my eyes at him. "You mean, you don't want to make plans to go with *me.*"

"Jeff . . ."

I take him gently by the shoulders. "What's *happened* to us, Henry? I thought we were *sisters.*"

He just stands there, unable to respond.

"You're my *best friend,* Henry. And right now I could really *use* a best friend. There's all sorts of stuff going on for me—"

"Jeff, I can't help you." Henry's eyes widen and he puts his hands up, knocking my own from his shoulders. "You just have to understand. I can't get sucked into your life. Not anymore!"

"Henry, I'm not asking you to get sucked in—"

"But I *do,* Jeff." He closes his eyes, calming himself, then opens them again. "I *do* get sucked in. Time and time again. Do you ever stop to think about what might be going on for *me?*"

"Of course I do."

"You say I'm your best friend. But you have *no idea* what's going on in my life." He looks at me hard. "Do you know I went for an HIV test?"

No, I sure don't. I can feel cold terror rise up inside me like bile. "Henry," I ask, my mouth suddenly going dry, "are you okay?"

"Yes." He seems almost reluctant to tell me. "It came back negative. I thought maybe Lloyd had told you. But I should have known he has far too much integrity and discretion to do that."

I'm touching his arms, shoulders. "Buddy, were you worried? I mean, did something happen? What made you go in . . .?"

He looks away. "Jeff, I don't want to go into it. The point is, you simply have no clue about my life."

I'm feeling exasperated. "That's not *my* fault, Henry. If you'd let me back in . . ."

"No!" He seems barely able to control his pique. "Look, for almost four years now, Jeff, you have been my whole world. My whole fucking world! And I'm *grateful* to you. Don't think I'm not. You helped me find parts of myself I probably never would have found on my own. But it came with a price, Jeff. You require an awful lot as a friend. Complete devotion, and I can't give that anymore. That's not what friendship is." He pauses, looking at me significantly. "And I think you know what friendship is supposed to be."

"Look, Henry, I *tried* to be there for you after Brent's death. How many times did I call you? You wouldn't let me even *try* to support you!"

"Because I knew it would somehow just get turned around back to you." He draws back and looks squarely at me. "All you could do for the whole time Brent was in the hospital was go on about what an asshole he was, what a jerk. Why would I turn to *you* when he died? Jeff, I don't think you really know how to be there for anyone except yourself."

"That's not fair, Henry."

"You *failed me,* Jeff." He spits the words, almost as if he knows how they'll sting. "Oh, sure, you taught me about drugs. Which ones you can safely party with, which ones should be avoided. But you didn't mention one drug in particular. And that's *you,* Jeff. *You're* my addiction. And I can't allow myself to remain addicted to you."

He stalks off into the crowd. I start to follow him when I feel a hand on my shoulder. It's Shane.

"Let him go," he says.

"We can work this out!" I demand. "He's wrong! I *care* about him!"

"If that's so," Shane replies, "then let him go."

I look up at him. He's wearing a rubber tank top, a silver-studded codpiece, and a pair of chaps that reveal his long, flat ass covered with blond hair.

"What does he mean," I ask, "he's addicted to me?"

"For such a bright boy, you can be horribly obtuse, Jeff O'Brien." Shane folds his arms across his chest. "He's always been there for you. Night and day. Whenever you wanted, wherever you wanted to go, he was sure to follow. He watched you trick, he watched you fall in love, he watched you wrestle with your conflicted feelings for Anthony and for Lloyd—and meanwhile, you never saw him as anything more than a sister."

"Sisters are important," I say, defending myself.

"Yes. And ever so easy to take for granted."

My eyes try without success to find Henry in the crowd.

"Admit it, Jeff," Shane's saying. "You knew he had feelings for you that went well beyond sisterhood."

I can't stand there and deny it. "Yes. But I always thought—well, I hoped—that whatever I was giving back, it would be enough."

"Well, it wasn't." Shane smiles, almost as if he takes some satisfaction in all this. "If you care about him as you claim, don't pursue him anymore. Just let him be."

I turn my eyes to look up at him. "And why should do I that, Shane? So you can have him all to yourself?"

He lifts his chin to spite me. "I can give Henry the kind of love and attention you never could."

"Maybe." I harden my gaze. "But aren't you just playing Henry to his Jeff? Think about it, Shane. When are *you* going to have your own little epiphany with him—the way he's just had with me?"

I see the look on his face. I see the smugness evaporate in an instant, the eyebrows relax their arch. I leave him standing there with his mouth open.

I search the crowd for Anthony. He's just where I left him. The leatherman is gone. He smiles when he sees me.

Maybe it's because I'm still riled up about Henry. Maybe it's because I'm tired of games, of deceits, of half-truths. Maybe because Henry had the balls to speak his truth to me, I can't go on another moment without being honest with Anthony.

"Come on," I say, taking his hand. "Let's go for a walk."

He follows obediently, like the little puppy I often think of him as. But he's an adult, a grown man, and seeing him as a child hasn't been fair to either of us. That the game has gone on this long is remarkable.

I lead him out of the crowd. Across the street there's a small patch of grass at the corner of the block; a few hippie types are sitting cross-legged, passing around a joint. We settle ourselves a few yards away. The tangy scent of marijuana wafts over to us. Anthony stretches out on the grass and looks up at the sky.

"Do you remember when we were in New Orleans, Jeff?" he asks. "When we sat there on the corner of the street and you put your arms around me? I always think back to that moment, how happy I felt."

Yes, I remember. How could I ever forget? It was the night he sang that silly love song to me. We had gone back to the place where we were staying, and cooked dinner, made love, pretended things were different, imagined that we were free to fall in love.

"We need to talk, Anthony," I say, fighting off the memory. "You know that, don't you?"

He just closes his eyes against the sun.

"We can't keep avoiding the truth," I say. "Things have changed between us."

He opens his eyes and turns his head to look at me. "Nothing's changed for me," he says calmly. "I still feel the same way about you."

"Not enough to trust me yet, though."

He sighs. "Maybe it's not about trust."

"Then what is it, Anthony?"

He just closes his eyes again. "I suppose I need to accept the fact that you and Lloyd are getting back together."

"Anthony, how could you have ever expected to have a relationship with me if you weren't being honest with me?"

"Stop saying I wasn't honest with you!" He's passionate about this, even though he keeps his eyes closed. "I have never lied to you!"

I look down at him, his face turned up to the sun, his long lashes remaining defiant against his cheeks.

"Anthony, I have a message for you." I pause, considering the impact of what I'm about to do. I take a deep breath. "Mrs. Riley says she's sorry."

There's no discernable emotion on his face at first. A little quiver of his forehead, perhaps, but that's all. His eyes remain closed.

"Did you hear me? Mrs. Riley told me to tell you that she was sorry."

He opens his eyes slowly. "Mrs. . . . Ri . . ."

The words fade on his tongue even as he says them. If there was some crazy flicker of a thought that maybe Mrs. Riley was somebody here in this crowd, somebody who maybe had elbowed him aside or stepped on his toe, somebody innocuous like that, it vanishes as soon as he begins to speak her name. Anthony knows who Mrs. Riley is. I can see that as his face begins to blanch, all the golden color seeming to drain out of his cheeks and down into his neck. His eyes lock on to mine.

"Mrs. Riley," I repeat. "I've been to see her. She told me to tell you that she was sorry. Do you know what she meant by that?"

Behind us the hippies are laughing and lighting another joint. A man has joined them, carrying a leather drag queen on his shoulders, causing a bemused commotion. The drag queen is tossing condoms out to the crowd. They throw some our way. A couple of condoms land on Anthony's chest.

"Say something, Anthony," I say.

He just keeps staring up at me.

"Let's go back to Zed's," I suggest, taking his hands, feeling suddenly protective of him once more, wanting to take care of him. "No one's there. We can talk."

"How . . . ?" He's trying to speak, but the words aren't coming for him. "How . . . ?"

"Anthony, I'm sorry." I sit up on my knees and grip his hands tightly. "I looked into your wallet. I saw his picture." My mouth has gone dry as I try to speak his name. All I can think of are the horrible details, the grisly death of the man found facedown in his front yard. "Robert Riley."

Anthony makes a sound down deep in his throat.

I lean in over him. "I know he was killed," I say in a rush. "I know you were living with him. I can only imagine how that's affected you."

He's growling low, like some wounded animal.

"I went to see his mother, Anthony." I feel as if I'm blathering. "And she wanted you to know that she was sorry. She's sorry, Anthony—"

"No!" He sits up all at once, causing me to pull back. His eyes suddenly burn with an intensity I've never seen there before. I'm actually frightened he might hit me. "Don't tell me that!" he shouts. "Don't you *dare* tell me that!"

"Why, Anthony? She wanted you to know—"

"*Stop it!*"

The hippies are looking over at us. Anthony leaps to his feet, with me quick behind him. I try to get him to calm down, but he pushes me away. He's gone wild, like an unbroken bronco at a rodeo. He gnashes his teeth and runs his hands through his hair. He flinches and twists as if he's having an epileptic fit.

"Is he okay?" some woman calls over to us in a marijuana daze.

"You lied to me, Jeff!" Anthony screams. He's ferocious. "You talk about trust! You said you would trust *me* until I was ready to talk!"

"Anthony, I'm sorry, but I had to know—I care about you—"

"Bullshit! You don't care about me! You were breaking up with me!"

"Anthony, please—"

"Fuck you, Jeff! *Fuck you!*"

I should have predicted it. In fact, I did predict it. He's done it before; why not again? Anthony pulls out of my grip and runs off back into the crowd, just as he had at Disney World.

All these people running off on me. I stand there alone, feeling like a fool.

"He okay?" the woman asks again.

I let out a long sigh. "Your guess is as good as mine," I tell her, crossing the street back to the fair.

So *let* him run off. Let him stew in whatever it is he needs to stew in.

330 William J. Mann

At least it's out in the open now. After all these months, maybe we can *finally* get to the bottom of it. Maybe after he's run off his anger, he'll come back and and we can actually talk. I can try to help him deal with all of the shit he's been carrying around for years.

Jeff, I don't think you really know how to be there for anyone except yourself.

"Shit," I say to myself.

I determine no one's going to ruin my trip to San Francisco: not Anthony, not Henry, not Shane. I head back to the fair and put on a glad face, flirting with hot muscle leathermen and applauding the acts on the stages. But it's all a masquerade, and by nightfall I can't keep it up, constantly looking over my shoulder for Anthony. I walk back to Zed's only to discover Anthony has been there and reclaimed his backpack, leaving no note as to when he'll be back. I stay in, skipping Universe to watch TV, my ears ever on the alert for the sound of Anthony's return. I fall asleep with the television on.

When Sunday morning rolls around and there's still no sight of Anthony, I take the Super Shuttle to the airport, expecting to see him at the gate. I have his ticket, and I stand waiting for him until the flight begins to board. With each passing second I grow more anxious. Where is he? Did something happen? Is he all right? I feel terribly responsible for him, and a horrible sick feeling eats at my gut. I consider not getting on the plane, thinking I should head back to the city and search for Anthony. But where? How?

I'm unaware that Henry and Shane have been watching me as they stand in line waiting to board the plane. Finally, Henry gets out of line and comes over to me.

"Jeff," he says tonelessly, "you should probably accept the fact that he's not coming."

"But he's all alone," I protest. "I just can't leave him. . . ."

"He's made his decision," Henry says.

I just look at him. Henry says nothing further, just sighs and then heads back to rejoin Shane in line.

Crazy thoughts go through my head. *He committed suicide. He was raped and butchered. He got drunk and is sleeping off a hangover. He forgot what time the plane was leaving. I should report him as a missing person to the police.*

And then another thought, maybe equally as crazy, but I can't judge, not now: *He's met another sugar daddy, another sap, who won't ask so many questions.*

I hand Anthony's ticket to the clerk at the desk. "If he shows up in the last couple of minutes," I plead, "will you make sure he gets this?"

She gives me a sympathetic look. But as the plane fills up, the seat beside me remains empty. The flight attendants are checking to see if seat belts are fastened. I insist I need to leave mine unhitched, that someone will soon be slipping into the seat next to me. Then the captain comes on to ask us to prepare for takeoff, and finally I buckle my belt, giving in to the inevitability.

He's made his decision.

I watch the flight attendants secure the door. As the plane speeds down the runway, lifting into the air, I feel the miles quickly rack up between Anthony and me. Ten, twenty, fifty, one hundred, growing into the thousands.

Our story's over. And its ending totally *sucks*.

Poor lost kid. For a time, I really cared about him, really wanted to help him.

Jeff, I don't think you really know how to be there for anyone except yourself.

Looking out into the brightness above the clouds, where all that exists is peace and serenity, I think about friendships. How my friends have come to take the place of my family. Except for my sister and my nephew, my blood family has become almost irrelevant to me. I haven't seen or spoken to my brother in years. With my father, I was never able to be honest about my life; he died without ever really knowing me. My mother remains an edgy, cautious, infrequent presence in my life: our approach to each other seems to be, "You go your way and I'll go mine."

But that's not what family should be. Family's about *being there* for each other—being involved, caring about what happens, sharing the highs and the lows, the joys and the heartaches.

I had replaced my biological family with one that *worked*, one that had sustained me—for a while, anyway. But that family is gone now, *obliterated*—and flying home, staring off into the clouds, I allow myself for the first time to feel absolutely and totally alone. Javitz is dead. Henry can't bear to be around me. The "extended family," the far-flung second cousins of the dance floor, suddenly seem like a bunch of clueless hunks to me, knowing only my image—my doppelganger—not my soul. And from all of my old friends, the ones who knew the old Jeff—the person I was before Javitz died, the person I've tried so hard to forget—I've distanced to the point where I can't even call them friends anymore.

There's only Lloyd. As always, it comes back to Lloyd.

But even Lloyd and I still aren't sure what we are to each other, if we even have a future together.

Have I done this? Have I created this fate? Have I truly been so selfish? Insensitive to Henry? Disloyal to Anthony by going behind his back? And why did his absence hurt so much? And—most disturbing of all—what did that say about my feelings for Lloyd?

What have I accomplished by being so guarded? What have I done except create what I always feared the most: a life without family, without support, without anyone there in the middle of the night?

When did it start? I wasn't always this way. Javitz's death, I suppose, and Lloyd's departure. After that, it felt safer to erect the walls, to keep my distance, to play Jeff the Stud, Jeff the Heartless, Jeff the Invincible. Henry was right: the whole thing about not sleeping with anyone unless my body is in top shape is just one more manifestation of my withdrawal from the world. My body as armor against my soul.

But the spears got through anyway. My invulnerability was a sham. And what good did the whole goddamn ruse do for me, except drive away anyone and everyone who might have made a difference?

I have no answers to any of my questions, and there's no one to help me figure them out. In the old days, of course, Javitz could have untangled my emotions in one brilliant session, out on our deck drinking red wine and watching the sun go down. But I'm no Javitz. That much has become abundantly clear. Henry spoke the words plainly, articulating what I've always feared: *I failed him.* On my own, without Javitz, I'm a big old useless *fraud.* And it's not just Henry and Anthony and even Lloyd I've failed: it's Javitz himself.

I pretend to sleep the rest of the way home. When we land in Boston, I nod good-bye to Henry at the baggage claim. Whether he tries to say anything to me or not, I don't know. I just sling my bag over my shoulder and push out into the chilly night, alone.

Halloween, Nirvana

Lloyd

Prepare yourself. This is it.

She's got a knife.

"Please," I beg. "Put it down."

I open my eyes to find her standing over me with a long, sharp kitchen knife in her hand. The moonlight glints off its blade, its sheen reflecting in her wide, wild eyes. Behind her, grinning hideously, sits a Halloween jack-o'-lantern, its flickering candle making horrible shadows dance along the wall.

"I told you that you'd *learn*," Eva whispers. "Told you you'd find out what I'm *really* like."

Her face is distorted, full of hate. I clutch at my blanket, push back into the pillows.

"Eva, don't! Please!"

She raises the knife over her head, prepared to strike. I scream. I hear the whoosh of the knife through the air. The last thing I feel is the blade pierce my flesh. There is pain. I scream again.

Then I wake up.

"Holy Jesus," I gasp, sitting bolt upright. The cushions of the couch are damp. My heart pounds in my ears.

From across the room the jack-o'-lantern still grins, its light still flickering against the wall.

The house is dark. I have no idea what time it is.

"Holy Jesus," I say again.

I swing my feet off the couch and try to steady my nerves. It's not the first time that I've had such a dream. Ever since Eva stormed out of my room, turning into Madame Hyde right before my eyes, I've had these recurring dreams. Each time she has a knife, and each time she gets a little closer. This was the first time the knife actually made contact, I realize, making me terrified of what the next dream might bring.

I stand, straining my eyes to make out the clock on the wall. It's after eight o'clock. I was just taking a quick nap after dinner, after all the guests had left for the evening. It's Halloween.

But why is the house so *dark?*

I look outside. There's no light anywhere. I realize Provincetown is in the midst of one of its frequent and unexplained power outages. I shiver. Why does the East End of town have to be so *dark?*

That's when I hear the sound upstairs. Like a single footstep. Is someone in the house? I thought I was alone. Everyone had gone out. I listen closely, but nothing.

Maybe I'm just jumpy because this afternoon Henry and I watched Jamie Lee Curtis scream her lungs out in the movie *Halloween.* We then carved an enormous pumpkin and set a candle inside, just like the one in the film. I look over at it now, the only light in the room. I shudder.

I light a few candles throughout the parlor and feel myself relax in their comforting glow.

Sitting beside the jack-o'-lantern is a more reassuring object: a vase of Montauk daisies, a gift from Henry. I smile looking at them. It's been another couple of awesome days with him. The sacred-sex worshop had gone very well; I think he gained a great deal from it. But he gained even more, perhaps, by what happened afterward. As did I . . .

I jump. That *noise* again. It sounds as if someone's walking down the upstairs hallway. But Eva's away for a couple of days—a nice relief—staying with a new friend she's made in town. All our guests are out. The last two left for dinner over an hour ago.

I shiver a little, embarrassed by my nerves. I light another few candles and determine to buy a generator before the winter. I should just stop being so jumpy and get ready to go out. I promised Henry I'd meet him and Shane in town to watch the parade of costumes on Commercial Street. I'll just take a quick shower and—

Squeeeeeak.

A floorboard. That's *definitely* a floorboard.

"Is someone upstairs?" I call up the stairwell.

No answer.

Dear God, why am I so *jittery?*

And why am I convinced it sounds like *Eva* walking back and forth?

"I'm spending a couple days with Candi," she'd said last Wednesday, coming down the stairs with a suitcase.

It was fine by me. Tensions between us had gotten almost unbearable. She'd begun spending afternoons away from Nirvana. On her days off, she only returned here to sleep. I had seen her in town walking with Candi Carlson, a twentyish lesbian who runs a local sex shop. They made an odd pair, that was sure, and it struck me that, for the first time, Eva was associating with another woman. She'd never been much at ease with other women before, preferring the company of men. What the exact nature of their relationship is, I don't want to know. I'm just glad Eva is no longer constantly underfoot.

In my head, I've been trying to figure a way out of this mess with her. It's clear she isn't willing to work on her issues in therapy. No matter what her diagnosis might be, if she isn't committed to seeking help, I can't go on with her in this venture. We can't run a business by avoiding each other. So what do I do? Do I offer to buy her share of the house? Do I bring in a mediator? There has to be a solution: I refuse to feel trapped.

Creeeeeeeeeeeeeak.

My blood goes cold. That's a door opening. That's *definitely* a door opening.

"Is someone there?" I call again, but once more, no answer.

My dream comes back to haunt me. *I told you that you'd learn. Told you you'd find out what I'm really like.*

I brace myself, taking hold of the banister and walking up the stairs. In my free hand I carry a candle. Its tiny flickering flame reveals nothing but shadows in the upstairs corridor. But all at once there's a rustle of fabric. I pause, noting that the door to Eva's room is slightly ajar.

She's inside the room, I think to myself with absurd horror.

You'll learn, Lloyd.

My palms begin to sweat, and I feel chills run down my spine like an electric current.

"Eva?" I call.

Borderlines can have psychotic episodes. They can commit irrational acts if they feel provoked, threatened . . .

I move closer to her room. There is unquestionably someone inside. I push the door open slowly and lift my candle. A dim light invades the darkness. I hear something: low and tinny.

Music.

It's Madonna. *Hey, Mr. DJ . . .*

Then I see her: a form, a figure dressed all in black, slinking in and out among the shadows. Something reflects in the moonlight. Something shiny. My mouth goes dry.

But the figure is too tall, too thin to be Eva. "Who's there?" I shout.

"Huh?" A woman's voice. "Oh, my God, you scared the shit out of me."

"Who *are* you?" I demand.

The woman pulls close into the light of my candle. I gasp a little. She's wearing a black eye-mask and has black whiskers painted on her cheeks. Her body's encased in a form-fitting black bodysuit. On her head is a Walkman. That's what the moonlight reflected. She rests the headphones around her neck to talk to me.

"It's Candi," she says. "Candi Carlson. I'm looking for Eva's shoes."

"Her *shoes?*"

"Yeah, for her costume. We're getting ready to go to the A House."

"It's pitch black in here," I say.

Candi leans in close to me and smiles slyly. "Don't you know cat-women can see in the dark?"

She disappears back into the shadows. "How did you get in here?" I ask. "I've been downstairs all night."

"Eva gave me the key to the back door." That's all she says. No "I hope that's okay" or "I didn't mean to intrude" or "I'm sorry if I frightened you."

I stiffen. "Well, when you leave, please make sure the door's locked. I don't let guests come through the back door."

She doesn't answer. She must have replaced her headphones.

"Here they are!" she exclaims. She's back in my light suddenly, holding a pair of white patent-leather pumps for me to see. "Miss West's shoes!"

I turn to leave.

"So what's the deal?" she calls after me. "You a stick-in-the-mud, pal? Aren't you going out to party on this, our gay national holiday?"

"I'm going out," I say, a little defensively.

Candi puts her face close to mine again. "Glad to hear it. Would hate to think of you all alone in this dark, gloomy house." She laughs.

I don't reply.

She smiles. She's young, no more than twenty-five. Pretty, with dark eyes and a pierced nose. A scattering of freckles dots her cheeks. But there's something hard in her eyes, staring at me through the slots in her mask.

"Let me give you a little advice, pal," she says, drawing as close as she can. Our noses almost touch. She lifts a finger to my face, and in the candlelight I discern Steven's emerald ring on her hand.

This should go to someone who cares.

"Advice?" I ask.

"Yeah. You accuse Eva of any more bullshit and you'll have *me* to deal with. Got it, bucko?"

"Excuse me?"

"Don't let the name fool ya," she says. "I'm not always so sweet."

She moves out of my candlelight and slinks back off into the darkness. I'm flabbergasted, *outraged.* How *dare* she? I hear her pad down the back stairs. Oh, great. Just *great!* Now I've got the *Cat-woman* after me! What's Eva *told* her?

I take a fast shower and dress quickly, deciding to forego any costume. The lights come back on and I breathe a sigh of relief, hopping on my bike to meet Henry downtown. I spot him sitting on the sidewalk, as unadorned as I am, in front of the post office.

"Lloyd!" he calls. "You're just in time. Look!"

Among the revelers making their way down Commercial Street is Shane, dressed as Glinda the Good Witch. On his shoulder-length red wig he wears a tall Plexiglas crown. He sashays back and forth in a big pink hoopskirt sparkling with sequins, waving a wand topped with a glowing yellow star. "Are you a good witch or a bad witch?" he asks the crowd in Glinda's unmistakable twitter. Tourists snap pictures. Shane drinks up the attention.

"He sure knows how to work a crowd," I observe.

"That he does."

I sit down beside Henry on the curb, shoulder to shoulder. Witches and dragons and George W. Bushes, each scarier than the last, pass us each in turn. Next comes a local drag queen known as Miss Izzy, done up in a Glinda costume nearly identical to Shane's.

"Oh, Shane is going to be so *pissed,*" Henry says. "He doesn't like being upstaged."

The night is chilly. At one point Henry, being gloveless, slips both his hands down into the deep pocket of my wool coat, resting his head on my shoulder. He smells good. I lightly kiss his hair.

I wonder briefly how Jeff would feel if he knew Henry and I had made love. The workshop had been intense. We'd spent the entire day in a state of constant arousal, trading back and forth with our partners, giving and receiving, touching, caressing, kissing, licking each other. Orgasm was discouraged; a couple of guys hadn't been able to hold back, and I heard their unmistakable shuddering moans from across the room. But Henry and I had managed to keep from coming—until we got back to Nirvana, that is, and we went straight up to my room to bring each other to climax.

I've been to such workshops before. I knew what to expect. But Henry was blown away. I mean, absolutely *staggered*. After he orgasmed, he collapsed in my arms, sobbing his heart out. It was to be expected after your first time. Our workshop leaders had emphasized that the sexual touch we were employing went beyond the mere physical, reaching through the skin, the nerves, and the brain to the heart and the soul—to the very essence of our beings. With guided imagery they'd led us to places deep within ourselves, taking us to places we had forgotten, to memories stored deep within the fibers of our cells. The erotic journey was not so much about our external erogenous zones as it was about our internal selves: who we were, who we had been in previous lives, and who we were yet to be.

"For me," Henry said, lying in my arms, breathing contentedly, "it was about feeling connected again. I have never felt so connected to *anyone* before in my life." He reached over and kissed me passionately on the lips. "Sex is so much more than what I'd always thought it to be."

He snuggled in next to me. That's the way we'd slept all night.

Sitting here beside him now, I think again of Jeff. Anthony's departure had affected him deeply, much more profoundly than I imagined it would. He was in a state of funk when I saw him last, just sitting there on his couch, and I left Boston considering the possibility that Anthony had meant much more to him than I'd allowed myself to believe. Jeff's reaction gave me pause: if he still grieved Anthony so much, what did that say about us? And what about my own feelings for Henry?

"Lloyd," Henry says, nudging me. "Look who's coming now."

My eyes move down the parade. Here she comes: Mae West, cooing and posing and shaking her padded hourglass figure for the delight of the crowd. Candi's there, too, and I can see her more clearly now, in her black Lycra and fishnet stockings, purring like Eartha Kitt, cracking her whip at the crowd. There are other young dykes surrounding Eva, too: one dressed all in silver lamé, another in leather. They form a moving ring around her. Miss West's bodyguards.

"She's *awesome*," Henry says, sitting up at attention. "Lloyd, you have to give Eva credit. She did what you asked. She found a niche for herself, her own group of friends."

She doesn't even look over at me as she passes by. To Henry she blows a kiss, but to me she gives no glance, not even an awareness that she knows I'm here.

Henry turns to me. "Shane says Eva's having an affair with some woman named Candi, who works at the sex shop. Shane talks to Eva a lot, and he says they're hot and heavy."

I scoff. "I'm sure it's not sexual. Eva's not gay."

"Which one is Candi?"

"The one in the fishnets."

Henry looks at her and raises his eyebrows. "Very hot."

"Yeah," I say. "I guess she is."

"Shane says Eva's been hanging out at Vixen, the lesbian bar, that she's discovering her true queer self after all these years."

It seems ludicrous to me. "Well, she *did* chop off all her hair," I say. "You can't tell because of that Mae West wig, but underneath it's short and spiky."

"A lesbian rite of passage, I guess."

"She's no lesbian," I grumble.

Henry shrugs. "Lloyd, if she's eating pussy, she's a lesbian."

"That doesn't mean a thing. She'll do anything, *be* anything, just so as to not be alone. It's really very sad."

I look at her now, basking in the crowd's adulation, her dyke cohorts surrounding her. She sure doesn't *seem* sad. She seems defiant, smug.

I'm the one who's left with an overwhelming sadness. I think of the photograph of the two of us, smashed on my floor. I remember the talks we once had, late into the night, how *present* she had been, how *involved* she'd been in my grief. Had it all been a ruse? Had I merely been a preferred substitute for Alex, who had been standing in for Steven, who himself had simply been a replacement for the father whose love she craved?

Still, no matter what, none of that can take away how she helped me. How she showed up when I needed someone most. How she was there to listen, to suggest, to advise, to comfort. I miss that person. Miss her terribly, especially with Jeff once again in a deep funk.

I know what you're probably thinking. Be careful what you wish for. I'd wanted Eva to find a life of her own, and she did, disappearing for entire evenings sometimes, whole chunks of the day. Yet if I sound like sour grapes, consider this salient little fact: because of her absences—because of the time she spends discovering this new "life of her own"—I'm frequently left to do the majority of the work at the guest house. Once, she would rise early to arrange the fresh flowers, to make up a tray of muffins, to set the coffee perking. Now I'm lucky if she manages to saunter in during the afternoon to help with the laundry. Peak season having passed, we've let our houseboys go, and we've resumed doing the work ourselves. Except it's been mostly me doing the work.

"Is that a gun in your pocket or are you just happy to see me?" she's asking some muscle stud in the crowd. The gay boys cheer her, and she saunters away, one hand on her hip, the other pushing at her wig.

Then, behind her, I note someone dressed as Darth Vader. All black cape and heavy breathing, no sign of a face. I imagine it's another of her lesbian friends, because Eva keeps turning around to make sure Darth is behind her. At one point she even takes its hand.

"That's one big dyke," I say.

All at once Darth Vader turns to look at me. The creature stops its march down the street and locks its vision onto me sitting there on the curb. For the second time tonight, I feel my blood suddenly run cold.

Henry notices it. "Ooh. She thinks you're Luke Skywalker."

Eva's urging Darth Vader on, tugging at its hand. Reluctantly the creature obeys.

"That was *creepy*," I say.

"Whoever it was," Henry says, "it seemed awfully interested in *you*."

It sure did. Was this another lesbian avenger I'd have to watch out for, another one Eva had turned against me?

Henry leans into me. "You're not into going dancing tonight, are you, Lloyd? I know how much you don't like crowded clubs."

"That's okay," I tell him. "It's Halloween. Let's go in and see who wins the prizes."

Crowded isn't the word for it. It's hotter in the A House than it is on the beach in the middle of August. How some of these folks keep their costumes on, I can't fathom. Shane and Miss Izzy command the dance floor, taking up more than their share of space, each with their gargantuan Glinda hoopskirts. They make faces at each other, sticking their tongues out and rolling their eyes. At one point they have a hissy fit, like two cats on a fence, and it takes four guys in gold mesh to separate them.

Shane, in a sulk, beckons to Henry to join him on the dance floor. But Henry declines, preferring to stay at my side, leaning against the bar. I see the disappointment on Shane's powdered face, the way he turns away to hide how he's feeling.

"Go on and dance," I tell Henry. "I'm fine here."

"Naw," he demurs. "I'd rather stay with you."

I notice something in his eyes that makes me just the slightest bit un-comfortable. Sure, our time together has been incredible, the intimacy between us empowering and rewarding. But just what is happening be-tween us? I recall how Henry backed out of going with Shane to the Black and Blue Party in Montreal, which, I gather, is one of the premier events on the circuit. He'd asked if I wanted to go, but I said no; Sundance had been fun, but I really couldn't get any more time off. So Henry declined Shane as well, choosing to come down here to Provincetown instead, where we bought pumpkins and decorated Nirvana for Halloween.

"Maybe you can come to my mother's house with me for Hanuk-kah," Henry says now, leaning into me. "I really wished I'd had some-one to bring home on Rosh Hashanah. My mother keeps telling me that if I ever meet anyone, she'd like for me to bring him home."

Oh, God. As if all our dramas aren't complicated enough, now Henry wants to bring me home to meet his mother. I just smile, making no commitment.

I decide to leave once Miss Izzy is announced the winner of the Best Costume contest. I figure Henry will want to stay and console Shane, but he comes with me, agreeing that it's too hot in the bar to enjoy him-self. I doubt he really believes that. Had a club ever been too hot for him and Jeff? Wouldn't they have merely peeled off their shirts and slipped into the crowd, reveling in the sweat and the huddled masses, groping and being groped?

We walk out onto the street where an orange autumn moon rides high in the black sky. The sounds of the music from the bar fade off as we head out to the bay, the moon reflecting off the water. There are a few revelers out here, some still in costume. Their drunken laughter tumbles across the sand.

"Henry," I say, "do you understand the problem between Eva and me?"

"I think so."

"What are they?"

He looks at me, unsure why he's being tested. "Well, she just got too caught up in your life at the expense of her own."

"And?"

He looks puzzled. "Well, I guess she had too many expectations of you. Wanted you to be something to her that you couldn't."

I nod. "Does that sound familiar to you at all?"

He makes an odd face, then looks off in the direction of the revelers down near the shore.

"That's Eva," he says.

I smile. "Yes. That *is* Eva. But maybe, Henry, maybe can you see yourself, too?"

He looks at me. "Lloyd, I meant, *that's Eva*. Over *there.*" He nods toward the group of giddy partiers across the sand.

I turn quickly. He's right. It *is* Eva. In the moonlight, I can see her removing her big blond wig. She accepts a plastic cup from Candi, who holds a bottle of wine. Oh, *great*. Now they're drinking in public. That's all we need. The co-owner of Nirvana arrested for public intoxication and getting her name printed in *The Provincetown Banner*.

But then something else catches my attention. I think Henry notices at the same time.

Darth Vader is with them, too.

Except without the mask.

Even at this distance, even with just the moonlight to illuminate the face, I can make out who it is.

"Holy shit," Henry says.

"Is that who I think it is?" I ask incredulously.

He shakes his head in wonder. "None other."

"But *how?*" I ask.

And—perhaps more important—why?

Meanwhile, in Boston

Jeff

I can't believe how much I miss him.

Good God, Jeff, you're fucked up, I scold myself. *You are so fucked up.*

I've been talking to myself like that for weeks. Every time I come back into this apartment, I start missing him again, and I have to yell at myself.

It's good that he's gone! It was a dead-end relationship! You were going to end it anyway!

I sigh and switch on the light. Mr. Tompkins makes a mad dash for his dish, and I shake some food into it. I've just gotten back from Connecticut, where I took Jeffy trick-or-treating around my mother's neighborhood. He went as Batman. Every time someone opened their door, instead of "trick or treat" he'd say "I'm Batman" in a surprisingly good imitation of Michael Keaton. His performance usually earned him an extra Milky Way or roll of Smarties.

My voice-mail light is blinking. As usual, my heart races. Maybe he's called. Maybe it's him. Picking up my phone, I press my code for messages.

But it's just Lloyd. "Jeff," he says. "If you don't get in too late, give me a call."

I hang up, angry with myself. *Just Lloyd.* How fucked up was that? A couple of months ago I was pining for Lloyd. Now we're in regular contact and I'm missing some mystery man who ran out of my life.

A mystery man whose smile used to melt my heart.

Who once sang me a silly love song on the street.

I look over at the clock. Is 11:30 too late to call Lloyd back? I know he usually goes to sleep early, since he gets up at the crack of dawn to make muffins for the guests. But it's Halloween, after all, and Henry's in Provincetown with him. He and Henry do *everything* together these days. How *nice* for them. Maybe Henry got Lloyd to go out to the A House, and now they're dancing shirtless together, maybe even on X.

I hope they're having a *fabulous* time.

All I really want to do is go to bed. I'm beat. I'm late getting back because Mom had insisted I stay for supper, Jeffy seconding her with an energetic refrain of "Please, Unca Jeff!" So I gave in. Mom whipped us up some tuna fish heavy with mayonnaise, Campbell's baked beans, and instant butter-flavored mashed potatoes. We sat around the same kitchen table where, as a kid, I'd consumed many similar nutritiously suspect meals. Still, it tasted yummy.

But her comfort food offered no palliative for what ailed me. If anything, my time around Mom's kitchen table left me even more depressed, for it pointed up the absence of any real family in my life. As much as I loved Jeffy and Ann Marie, what was missing were people with whom I could be *real*. People with whom I could be *myself*. People who knew my history, my culture, my life—and *understood* it. Driving back to Boston, I cried, for maybe the tenth time that week, thinking about Javitz. Odd, isn't it? I've been crying more about him in the last few months than I did for the entire first three and a half years after his death.

Lloyd says I'd been repressing my grief. Holding it back. Pretending it wasn't there. I'll tell you one thing: it sure as hell is a lot easier *not* to cry than to actually do it. Crying takes guts. I'd always heard you felt better after allowing yourself a good, long cry. Well, that's *bullshit*. Each time I cry I feel worse. The memories, the pain, the guilt. The tears bring the emotions to the surface, where they get all wedged up in the bottleneck between my chest and my throat.

Sometimes I feel as if I'm having a heart attack. Or at least heartburn. Driving back to Boston, I had to pull over on the Mass Pike and buy some Maalox.

But I don't want you feeling sorry for me. Please don't go there. I'm very aware that it's not a pretty picture that I'm painting, and if you've figured anything out about me by now, it's that I have a decided preference for pretty pictures when it comes to myself. Yet there's not much I can do to beautify the situation. Ever since coming back from San Francisco, I've been a mess. My friendship with Henry is over. I'd fucked up with Anthony. And my feelings about Lloyd are all jumbled in my head all over again. You'd think on some level I'd be glad that Anthony's gone. That sure, I'd feel some compassion for him, and hope that he's okay, but by bolting out of my life, he'd made things so much simpler, allowing me to concentrate on rebuilding my relationship with Lloyd. After all, that's what I'd really been wanting all along, wasn't it?

Wasn't it?

I think of Lloyd and Henry together at the Russian River. I picture them chest to chest on the dance floor in Provincetown. Is this simply one more episode that demonstrates Lloyd's long-standing phobia of commitment? Had he, just as we were reconnecting yet again, suddenly made a jump to Henry, just as he'd once jumped to Drake, and then to Eva? And if so, how ironic is that? Lloyd's presence was certainly as much of an impetus for Anthony's beeline out of my life as any revelation I'd made about Mrs. Riley.

And, if I'm being honest with myself, how much of Lloyd's jump to Henry was influenced by my own lingering attachment to Anthony, a reality Lloyd could not have failed to observe?

I walk into the kitchen and flip on the light. On my refrigerator is the little card Anthony had given me months ago. I'd found it in my drawer on my first day back here after getting home from San Francisco. *To Jeff,* the card read. *With thanks for taking me in. Happy V Day. Love, Anthony.*

I close my eyes. I can see him on the sidewalk of New Orleans, singing me that ridiculous song. I can see him at Disney World, his eyes all aglow, shouting "Happy Gay Disney Days!" to every faggot he saw. I can see him asleep next to me in my bed, the sheet rising rhythmically over his chest as he breathed, his full lips slightly parted, a speck of sleep stuck in his lashes. . . .

"Oh, God," I say, and the grief is physical again. I find the Maalox, gave it a shake, and swallow a generous gulp right from the bottle.

I walk into my office and sit down at my desk. My face is reflected in my dark computer screen.

We're just links in a chain of sugar daddies, my friend. I'd advise you not to get too attached.

Did I really mean no more to Anthony than Randy Phillips? Than that nameless guy from Albany? Than whoever he's surely taken up with by now?

"It can't be," I say aloud. Anthony *loved* me. He said so, many times. He wasn't pretending. There was never anything insincere about Anthony. *Never.*

I open the file on my desk. From my pocket I withdraw a piece of paper that I plan to add to it. Something I discovered today in Connecticut, at the end of a frustrating day. Yes, I've kept up the search. Something's compelled me to do so. Anthony might be gone, but my obsession to find the truth is not. So I took advantage of being in Connecticut for the day, making my first stop at probate court. But Robert Riley's will had proved of no help; he'd left everything to his mother, not naming Anthony as any beneficiary.

So next I called the state's gay advocacy organization, hoping somebody there could tell me something about the Riley case. But the young kid who answered the phone said he had been five in 1986; he knew nothing. He did give me the name of a veteran gay activist, and I'd left a message on her machine. But she'd never called back.

It was at the State Department of Public Health that I finally found something, and looking at it again now, I'm still not sure how it fits. Anthony had said his father was dead. I'd already written to Lake Bluff, Illinois, which he'd claimed as his hometown, and found no death of any man there with the last name of Sabe from 1969 to the present. I paid quite generously for that search, too. Of course, his father's last name didn't have to be Sabe, but it was all I had to go on.

Combing through the Connecticut indexes myself saved me some cash, but almost cost me too much time. The office was getting ready to close for the day when the entry finally jumped out at me: *SABE, ANTHONY, died 1-5-95.* I quickly paid for a copy of the record without really looking at it. I didn't want to be late meeting Jeffy for trick-or-treating.

It wasn't until later, as Mom was whipping up her instant potatoes, that I had time to look at the document fully. And what I saw made me exclaim out loud.

"What is it?" Ann Marie asked.

I couldn't answer right away. "Just something . . . I'm working on for a story."

"I'm glad you're writing again, Jeff," she said.

I looked again at the words written in the space for cause of death. *Pneumocystis, as a result of HIV infection.*

If this was Anthony's father, he had died of AIDS.

My eyes glanced up to the top of the document. *Anthony Sabe.* PLACE OF BIRTH: *Lebanon.* Hadn't Anthony said he thought the name was of Middle Eastern extraction?

But was it his father? The age worked: the guy was born in 1946, but he was also listed as "Never Married." Was *this* Anthony Sabe gay, too?

My Anthony had nothing good to say about his father. Was it because he was gay? How did all of this *fit*?

A thought strikes me as I sit here. What if it's *this* Anthony Sabe who lived with Robert Riley, and not *my* Anthony? Allowing for that possibility suddenly makes all the other pieces of the puzzle fit more logically. It explains better the relationship between the "roommates," given that they were roughly the same age. It would explain Mrs. Riley's apparent memory of the Anthony who lived with her son.

But if it was his *father* who lived with Robert Riley, why did *Anthony* carry around Riley's picture? There must have been *some* connection between the two. Had Anthony known his father was gay, and known Riley, too?

And why was Anthony so fair if his father was from Lebanon? Perhaps his mother had been of northern European stock, or maybe he'd been adopted, or maybe . . .

I'm moving too fast here. A good reporter acts on hunches, but mere speculation can't be used without absolute proof. I have no evidence that the guy in this death certificate has any connection whatsoever with my Anthony. What I need is a newspaper obituary. Hopefully, it will list this guy's survivors. Maybe it'd lead me to Anthony's mother. . . .

"What am I doing?"

I sit back in my chair.

"Jeff O"Brien," I say out loud, "you have become a man possessed."

I stand up, walking back out into the living room. Mr. Tompkins has reclaimed his spot on the couch since Anthony left, pleased as punch that the intruder has left our midst. I sit down beside him and stroke him behind his ears the way he loves. He starts to purr.

Why am I still pursuing this mystery? What would I say to Anthony's mother if I *did* find her? What did it *matter*? I'm being crazy. Anthony's *gone*. Out of my life. Finding out who he was and what his story had been is really moot now.

But there's no denying that the story has seized hold of my heart and mind. Is that what I really miss—the *story*? Not the man? Already I've banged out twenty or so pages, recounting our meeting, our friendship, and the mounting mystery of his life. I have no idea if or where I'll ever sell it; it's merely a way to return to my craft, a way through the terrifying blankness of my creative soul. I am indeed writing again, for the first time in a long, long while. Maybe there's some connection to my tears. Maybe bottling up my grief also bottled up everything else.

I pace back into my office, just as the clock chimes midnight. I open the file on my desk and withdraw a stapled set of papers, taking them with me as I settle into my rocking chair.

They're the newspaper articles on Riley's murder and its aftermath, arranged chronologically. I've gone over them so many times, trying to find something. Trying to understand . . .

Most fascinating to me is the account Brian Murphy gave of the night of the murder. He confessed to police, a sworn statement that eventually got him a lighter sentence than Frankie Ortiz. In his confession, Brian comes across as more of a follower than a leader, part of the reason he'll be up for a parole in a few more years.

I read Murphy's account for probably the twentieth time. The quarterback of the football team at South Catholic High School, Brian was a popular kid, with girlfriends galore. They were all "good kids"—all of the "Reformers"—their goodness attested to in glowing reports from their principal, their parish priests, their coaches, and their teachers. Sure, Brian Murphy's father had served time in prison for gambling and extortion, and Ortiz's older brother had a long history of drug arrests, but these kids, their supporters insisted, were *good* boys. Solid *achievers*. All they had been doing was working off a little aggression, having a little *fun*. Some priest was actually quoted as saying, "Boys will be boys, after all."

"Yes," I murmur, reading through the papers. "That they will be."

"A couple Saturdays ago," Murphy told police in his written confession, "I was with Frankie Ortiz who picked me up driving his mother's '87 Chevy Nova. We drove directly to a market on Lawrence Street where we bought two forty-ounce bottles of Colt 45. We then drove to the parking garage next to the Civic Center and drank all the beer. We went to Club 21 where Frankie got into a fight with another kid, Peter something, and got Peter thrown out. We stayed there until 12:30 A.M."

It wasn't so different from any Saturday night for any high school kid anywhere. After the juice bar closed, the boys headed over to a fast-food joint and ate barbecued spare ribs. But the fight at Club 21 had left a little too much testosterone racing around in their systems. They decided to drive down by the Chez Est. "We knew it was a fag bar," Brian Murphy told police. "We thought we could roll on some fags."

They'd been there before. They'd harassed and beaten at least a dozen gay men over a period of several months, making off with cash and wristwatches and other trinkets. But this night, Frankie and Brian apparently had designs to take their "reforming" one step further.

"We drove around the block behind the bar twice. All of a sudden a guy starts following us in his car, which I recognized as a new BMW. When we would slow down, he would pass us and stare at us. He also blinked his lights at us a few times. While we drove we were deciding if we wanted to roll on him or not, meaning beat him up. We finally got the guy to pull up next to us and we got into a conversation. He said we could follow him to his house in West Hartford."

So they did. These two working-class boys from blue-collar Hartford were invited to the home of a wealthy attorney in the posh suburbs. I can't deny part of me always feels a small flicker of sympathy for Ortiz and Murphy at this point. I'd grown up in a world far more like theirs than Robert Riley's. Riley came from old money; I'd seen the estate where he'd grown up. At the time of his death, he was living in a large duplex condominium and drove a Beemer. The boys were impressed with what they saw at his place, and they coveted his toys: an expensive stereo and sound system, a VCR (back in the days before they were readily available), top-quality ski equipment.

But class sympathy can't entirely diminish for me the picture of Robert Riley's mother, sitting all alone, talking to her dead son.

I read on. *"Once, when he left the room,"* Murphy wrote, *"we were hesitant about ripping the guy off because we thought he was kind of cool. But since we were already there, we decided to go ahead with it."*

I run my hand through my hair. This is the part that always makes me anxious, no matter how many times I read it.

"He asked us if we wanted something to drink and he said he had milk or Diet Coke and we both said Diet Coke. We sat back down on the couch, all three of us, with Frankie in the middle. The guy starts rubbing Frankie's back. All of a sudden he said Frankie's license plate numbers, 782 FFK, and he looked at us and smiled. Frankie asked him if he was a cop and he said no. He asked if we were. Then he asks if Frankie wanted to go upstairs with him. Frankie agreed and they left. I read a Far Side *comic book while I was alone in the living room."*

My hands go a little moist holding the papers. What was going through Brian Murphy's mind as he sat there by himself reading *The Far Side?* I mean, come *on.* Frankie agreed to go upstairs with Riley after getting a back rub. What took place upstairs—and what did Murphy *think* was taking place?

> *"After about ten minutes they came back down, Frankie first, his face red and watery eyes. This means he's really mad. Frankie drank the rest of his Diet Coke then asked for a glass of water. When the guy left for the water, Frankie went to the fireplace and picked up a log. The guy walked in and told him to put the log down. But Frankie swung at him and missed. The guy ran for the door but Frankie hit him on the back of the head and he fell down. He got back up and opened the door to run outside but Frankie hit him again and he fell down the front steps. He got up again and started to run across the lawn but I ran after him and tackled him to the ground. The guy said, 'I'll give you anything you want, just leave me alone.' I punched him in the head and told him to shut up. Frankie went to his car and came back out with the duct tape. He told me to tape his mouth and I did. I got blood on my jean jacket as I was doing it. Frankie went back in the house and came out with the CD player and the VCR and the skis. He put them in the car and then he came back over to the guy. Frankie picked up the log and hit him one more time in the head. The guy shook and made a noise."*

Mrs. Riley's words in my head: "Do you know Robbie? Robbie's a good boy."

> *"We drove away. While we were driving we talked about if the guy was dead or not. We decided to turn around and make sure because he knew our license number. Frankie got out with the log and hit him three or four times and then dropped the log next to him."*

They went back to make sure he was dead. It was that little detail that did them in with the judge.

Suddenly the phone rings. I yell out, startled.

"Hello!" I bark, not even bothering to check the caller ID.

"Jeff?"

It's Lloyd.

"Are you okay, Cat? I was just starting to fall asleep and I was concerned about you all of a sudden."

Yeah, you know by now: it's just that way with Lloyd and me, despite everything.

"Yes," I tell him. "I'm okay."

"Well, when you didn't call back, I got a little worried." He laughs. "Guess you were out at some Halloween party, huh?"

"Only at my mother's." I explain how I stayed to have dinner after seeing Jeffy. "So why did you call?"

"Well . . ." He seems reluctant to tell me. "It's just that I know how concerned you've been, wondering if he's okay . . ."

"Who?" I ask, but somehow, I already know.

"Anthony."

I swallow. My throat has gone dry. "You've heard something about him?"

Lloyd pauses. "Jeff, I've *seen* him. He's *here*. In Provincetown."

I hear a low growl. Down at my feet, Mr. Tompkins is staring up at me with ferocious yellow eyes.

A Few Days Later

Henry

"That's it, Kenneth," I tell him. *"Feeeeel* the power within yourself."

He's stretched out on his bed and I'm giving him the massage of his life. Now, I don't claim to be a trained masseur, but whatever I'm doing, I seem to be doing it right. He's *so* into it. His eyes roll back into his head and he can't frame his words. I tell him not to try, just to surrender to the feelings and go with the flow. So okay, those are Lloyd's words, but I like them.

I've just finished Kenneth's hands and now I've moved on to his feet, kneading his soles and the balls under his big toes. Every fiber of his body seems to respond: his arms jerk involuntarily, his thighs begin flexing, and his dick stands up as straight as the John Hancock building.

Notice anything different here? Yes, I'm back to escorting, but with a twist. I posted my name and picture online again, with one key substitution. I replaced "Muscle Worship" with "Ecstatic Massage." Instead of me being on the receiving end of adoration, it's my client who's getting the attention.

If I thought there was a demand for my previous services, I was completely unprepared for the response to my new advertisement. I quickly discovered people are yearning far more to *be* touched than to touch. As the leaders at my workshop in Provincetown had pointed out, we have become a society detached from one another. There is a *craving* for intimacy, for physical connection. It's a yearning I've felt, too, and giving ecstatic massage is far more empowering than standing there as some aloof deity being adored by men on their knees.

It's been an empowering journey back. Online to restart my Web page, I'd chanced across an Internet review site for escorts. On a whim I'd clicked under Boston and found, to my great surprise, several entries for "Hank."

"What a beautiful man," Vernon had posted. "Both inside and out. Kind, compassionate, indulgent. He fulfilled my fantasy with charm and with no judgment whatsoever." Wrote another man, an anonymous poster: "Too often escorts are thinking only about the money that will be exchanged later on. But Hank was giving as much of himself as I was giving to him." Which one might he have been?

From Kenneth had come this simple review: "Thank you, my friend. There is not a category high enough to rate you adequately."

I was staggered—humbled—by the gratitude of these men. Hank had indeed done good work.

But Henry can do even better. I wrap my lubed hand around Kenneth's cock and begin to slowly move it up and down.

I can't wait to see Lloyd this weekend, to tell him all about this new success. Part of what has made my new adventures in the skin trade so energizing and empowering is my relationship with Lloyd. We're so much more suited for each other than Jeff and I ever were. My God, who *knew?* All that time I'd been traipsing around with Jeff, trying to keep up, trying to fit in, trying to be somebody I wasn't. With Lloyd, I feel at home. I feel complete.

"Henry, you have so much to offer," Lloyd said a few days ago as we parked our bikes and walked out into the dunes. "You're good-looking; you've got compassion; you're bright. You'll find your soul mate. Don't worry. Trust that the universe will bring him around when you're ready to meet him."

He turned and smiled at me then, his green eyes reflecting the sunlight. There's something about the light on the Cape in autumn. Lloyd pointed it out to me; I'd never have noticed if he hadn't. It's got a glow to it, gold and green, as if the angle of the sun reflects off the water in a whole new way. In truth, I'm seeing the entire world with new eyes, and it's all thanks to Lloyd Griffith.

I understand why he wants to take it slow. Why he brings up Jeff, tries to get me to talk about him. When I reached over once to take his hand, as we were perched on top of a dune with a view of the ocean, he looked at me and said, "We've got to be honest with each other, Henry." I knew what he meant. This is all so new, for both of us. I know he and Jeff have been back and forth together for a long time. I know he cares for Jeff. And despite all my issues with him, I do, too. I don't want to hurt Jeff. We have to be honest with each other about the obstacles in our way.

"I want to make love with you," I whispered in his ear.

Lloyd looked over at me and smiled. "Let's just watch the waves, Henry. That's making love, too."

And he was right. Sitting there, holding his hand, watching a fishing boat way off in the distance gradually make its way back toward the harbor, it was almost as if we were making love with all the passion we had on that first day. I closed my eyes and remembered the taste of Lloyd's lips, the smell of his skin, the sensations I felt as his tongue made circles around my nipples.

"Oh, yes, that's the way," Kenneth moans, managing to find his voice.

"Like this?" I ask, a little saucily, already knowing the answer.

I run my hand up and around his erect dick like a corkscrew, kissing the head as I reach the top. Kenneth can just barely croak out a grateful "*Yes.*"

I can't believe how much I'm enjoying giving him pleasure. This whole session hasn't been about me at all. I told him simply to lie back, that I was going to take him places he'd never been before. I'd been carrying around a little guilt ever since not acknowledging him that night in Provincetown. That last night with Brent. In many ways it seemed the last night of my old life. I'm thrilled to have the chance to make it up to Kenneth now.

I've been busy with clients ever since Halloween, and loving every minute of it. Shane's called twice trying to get together, but I just don't have the time. It's like the early days when I first started escorting. Once more, I'm loving my work. Lloyd explained to me about sacred-sex workers, men and women who've taken the art of prostitution to a spiritual level, where it's not so much about genital manipulation as it is reaching the heart and the mind and the soul. I want to take more workshops, attend conferences and seminars on the connection between the erotic and the spiritual, and Lloyd's promised to get me the information.

Maybe, he suggested with a sly little smile, a smile that touched the very essence of my being, this was my karma. Maybe that's what all my journeying has been leading toward all along. "Henry Weiner," he said. "Sacred-Sex Worker."

I like how that sounds. I don't care if Jeff would laugh his ass off hearing it. Jeff doesn't understand. Jeff has never understood.

"Oh, oh, oh, yes," Kenneth stutters as my massage of his cock grows in intensity.

"You are *loved*, Kenneth," I tell him. "You are special. You are beautiful. You are part of the whole cosmos of connected beings. Your essence is sacred. You are one with all things."

"Yesssss!" he exclaims, ejaculating a thick, milky geyser that quickly covers my hands.

I smile.

I love my work.

Meanwhile, in Provincetown

Jeff

"**W**here is he?"

Eva looks surprised that I'm so direct. She's standing behind the front desk with a woman, a dark-haired dyke half her age wearing a neon blue halter top and leather pants. I've seen her around town for years. Lloyd says they're dating, that Eva's posing as a lesbian these days.

"Hello to you, too, Jeff," Eva says, giving me one of her phony smiles. "Are you looking for Lloyd?"

"I know where Lloyd is. I'm looking for Anthony."

She remains unflappable. Her girlfriend looks over at her with concern, but Eva remains calm. "Anthony doesn't want to see you," she says pleasantly, going back to shuffling whatever papers she'd been shuffling when I came in.

I lean in over the desk. "Don't play games with me, Eva. I need to talk with him."

"Hey, buddy, you back up," the halter-top woman says, quickly getting into my face, poking her finger at my chest.

"Candi, I can handle this," Eva assures her.

The woman harrumphs, giving me the evil eye. "I'm going out," she snarls. "I'll be back in a bit."

"Okay," Eva chirps after her. Candi glowers at me and slams the door as she leaves.

Eva lifts her little round Munchkin eyes to meet mine. "I'll repeat myself, Jeff. Maybe you misunderstood what I said. But it's simple. Anthony doesn't want to see you."

I'm not going to be put off that easily. "How did he get here? Why is he with you?"

I can see the impatience betraying itself on her face. She sets her papers down and again makes eye contact with me. "I'm not sure it's any of your business, Jeff." She's still trying to sound pleasant, but it's strained.

"Look, Eva, I *care* about him. He lived with me for *ten months*. I know he's going through a lot—"

"He's doing fine," she assures me, smiling again.

"What is this? Your fucking mission in life? To steal away every man who matters to me?"

"So," she says, "that's what you think."

I close my eyes, trying to regroup. A strategy of confrontation hasn't worked. Well, there's more than one way of dealing with Eva Horner. Maybe I ought to try taking a page out of her own book. . . .

"Oh, Eva," I say, gripping the counter as if I need support to keep from falling. "It's just that I—I'm so torn up about it all. I'm so—I feel so *unfinished*. I just need some closure. I just need to *understand.*"

I raise my eyes to hers, trying to will them to glow with moisture. I'm not really lying. I *am* torn up about it. I *do* need closure. I'm just giving it the full dramatic effect the way she always has.

"Haven't you ever felt that?" I plead. "The need to understand? To feel . . . *heard?*"

It's working. I can see her soften. Her shoulders relax their posture a bit, her mouth curling sympathetically.

"Jeff, I just *can't* tell you where he is. He really needs some time to be alone. To *think.*"

"But . . . I don't understand." I'm not acting anymore. I really do feel confused and upset. "How did he get here? How did you get involved?"

She sighs. "He called me. Simple as that."

"From San Francisco?"

She nods.

"And you . . . paid for him to fly back here?"

She nods again.

"Why?"

Eva looks at me as if it's plain. "Because he was in pain. Because he had nowhere else to go."

"But why call you?"

She smiles sadly. "We'd had some good talks, especially when he stayed here after Brent's overdose." Her face hardens again. "Don't you

358   William J. Mann

remember how upset he was? Oh, maybe you don't. You were too consumed with your own anger to offer him much support."

Okay, so she has a point there. Maybe I'm being crazy, bursting in
here like this, demanding to know where Anthony is. Lloyd wanted no
part of it. We had dinner earlier, and he remained defiantly noncommi-
tal in his support of my desire to see Anthony.

"What are your feelings for him, Jeff?" he asked me. "What's coming
up for you in all this? And what does it mean for us?"

I couldn't answer him. Truth is, I don't know. I just know I have to
see Anthony again. I have too many questions, too many unresolved
feelings.

But I'm ready to give up. There's not much more I can do. I can't exactly reach across the counter and grip Eva by the throat and demand
she spill the beans, the way Humphrey Bogart might do to Peter Lorre
or something. I just let out a long sigh.

Then I hear the door behind me.

"You want to see Anthony?"

It's Candi. She stands there glaring at me, her hands folded across her
small bosom. I look at her without replying.

"I just talked with him," she says. "He said he'll see you."

"Candi," Eva says. "Is he sure?"

The other woman nods. "Come on," she says to me, pushing back
out the door.

I follow her down Commercial Street. We don't speak a word for the
first five minutes.

The fog is rolling in, heavy and damp. From Long Point I can hear
the foghorn warning ships not to come too close.

"Thanks for talking to him for me," I finally say.

Candi turns to look at me. "I didn't do anything for you. In fact, I
advised Anthony to tell you to fuck off. Like he should ever trust you
again, with you going behind his back and all."

I don't reply.

"Okay," she says, seeming to reconsider her quick judgment. "So
maybe I don't know the whole story. But I *do* know that you and your
boyfriend Lloyd think you're both pretty perfect, and that you owe no
responsibility to the people you draw into your lives."

"Okay, hold on right there. You're right, you *don't* know the whole
story. And you don't know me from Adam. We've only just met."

"I know your *type,* pal. And I know how Lloyd lords over Eva,
thinking their whole dysfunctional relationship has been only *her* fault.

He can't see how *he* contributed, how it takes two to tango." She smolders. "I suspect it's been the same for you and Anthony."

Abruptly Candi makes a turn down an alleyway between two art galleries. Stretching out on a pier onto the beach is a row of wind-beaten cottages. In only one does any light burn. Candi raps on the door .

"I've brought him," she announces.

The door opens. Anthony stands behind the screen, looking out at me.

"Thanks," he says, pushing open the screen door so I can enter.

"You want me to wait here?" Candi asks. "In case he gives you any trouble?"

"No, that'll be okay," he says. She grunts and moves back toward the street. I step inside.

It's a single room, no bigger than a cell, really, probably twelve by eight. Room enough only for a bed and a chair, though there's a nice view of the beach and the water.

Anthony seems to notice my surprise at his squalor. "Eva's looking into getting me a better place," he says. "It's all she could get at such short notice."

I stuff my hands down into my pockets. "She's paying your rent?"

He nods. "Just until I get a job."

My eyebrows raise themselves. "You want to *live* in Provincetown?"

He smiles awkwardly. "Just until . . . well, just for a while."

We're quiet. I look at him. How beautiful he is. He looks a little haggard, and his beard stubble seems heavier, more mature, than I remembered. But his eyes still have that same glow.

"I've missed you," I tell him.

He looks away. "No, you haven't."

I feel at a loss to express myself. "Would I have come down here to find you if I hadn't?"

He shrugs, still not looking at me. "You came to see Lloyd."

I walk up behind him and place my hands on his shoulders. "I came to see you."

He turns to face me. He's crying.

"Why did you come back?" I ask him. "Why not stay in San Francisco?"

"I could've," he says, wiping his eyes with the back of his hand. "I met a guy who offered me a place to stay."

I'm sure he had. And probably within hours of running away from me. The next sugar daddy to give him a roof over his head, three meals a day . . .

"But I didn't want to," Anthony's saying. "I wanted to come home."

"Home?"

He nods. "For the first time in my life, I felt like I had a home here. In Boston. In Provincetown. With all my friends here."

I sit down on his bed. The mattress is horribly thin and soft.

"Come back to Boston with me," I say, surprising myself. I hadn't planned on suggesting such a thing. But seeing him again—seeing him here—I want him back.

He just smiles. "You don't really want that."

"I do," I tell him. "We can leave right now."

"Why? So you can ask me more questions? Try to find out what you still want to know?"

I'm silent. Could I promise not to ask any more questions?

"And what about Lloyd?" Anthony is shaking his head. "No, Jeff, you don't really want me to go back to Boston with you."

I look at him. "It's just that I haven't been able to stop thinking about you since you left."

"About me? Or my so-called secret past?"

"You, Anthony."

He stands over me. "Jeff, you have no idea how important those ten months with you were to me. I never really had a home or a family before. You gave that to me."

I look up at him hard. "You don't run out on family when they ask questions, Anthony. You don't keep secrets from family."

He sits down beside me. "You're also supposed to *trust* family. Not go behind their backs."

I have no answer for that.

"Jeff, I *want* to tell you everything, but I can't. I'm just not ready yet."

"Have you told Eva?"

He shakes his head. "No. And she's never asked." He looks at me pointedly. "She doesn't seem to require that in exchange for friendship."

I look away.

"She's been *so* awesome to me, Jeff. Paying my way back here from San Francisco, finding me a place to live, introducing me to all of her friends . . ."

So he *has* found another sugar daddy. Except it's a *mommy*. "Anthony, just a word of caution," I tell him. "Eva doesn't give anything freely. She expects a payback."

"No, Jeff. She's said I needn't ever repay her."

I laugh bitterly. "Oh, she doesn't care about money. She's got plenty of that. She expects your constant presence, your undying devotion. She's made Lloyd's life miserable. You know that. And if you don't fulfill her needs, she turns on you, like she has Lloyd. She's letting their whole business go down the tubes so she can play at being a lesbian."

Anthony makes a face. "She *is* a lesbian. She just finally realized it and came out of the closet."

I scoff. "She's as much of a lesbian as *I* am, Anthony. Eva is a black hole of emotion. She'll do and say anything to feel intimacy in her life. These Provincetown dykes start paying her a little attention and suddenly she becomes one of them, just to fill up the aching void in her life."

Anthony stands and crosses over to his little sink, wedged into the corner of the room. He turns on me. I can see he's angry.

"You just don't get it, Jeff," he says. "And you know why? Because you're Mr. Queer Activist. Mr. Professional Gay. You came out of the *womb* gay! Well, not everybody knows and accepts it that easily."

"Anthony, look—"

"No, you listen to *me* for a change, Jeff. You had Javitz to teach you. He took you down to all those big marches and demonstrations in New York and Washington. You went all over the country learning how to be gay. Well, not all of us had that, Jeff. Just because you've been gay all your life doesn't mean that everybody has had your same experience. You told me how you just stopped doing crystal. Just like that. You didn't need detox, you didn't need any help. You're a strong person, Jeff, and good for you. But not everybody is you. Not everybody is as lucky as you!"

"I understand that, Anthony, but—"

"You know what, Jeff? You *don't* have all the answers. I used to think you did. But you don't." He folds his arms across his chest. His eyes narrow as they stare at me, and a small smile shapes his lips. "You have it all wrong, you know," he says quietly. "About me and Mrs. Riley. You think you're so clever, Jeff. But you have it *all wrong*."

I look at him intently. "Then tell me where I've made a mistake."

He shakes his head. "You're the reporter, Jeff. You're the one who said you'd find out on your own. I'm sure your investigations of me haven't stopped. Why don't you just keep on going? You find out, then come back to me. I'll tell you if you're right."

I laugh a little. "Are you challenging me, Anthony? Daring me to find out the truth?"

"Yes," he says. "That's exactly what I'm doing."

I stand up. "Then you're on."

We shake hands.

"But I want you to know something," I tell him. "You may think I'm doing this because I'm some big fucking arrogant know-it-all who has to have all the answers. But that's not why I'm taking your challenge."

He narrows his eyes. "Then why is it, Jeff?"

"Because I haven't been able to stop thinking about the guy who dropped into my life last New Year's Eve, who taught me how to love again, who without even knowing it broke me out of my shell of grief and avoidance, who, despite all the odds, took the chance on loving me." I reach over and touch his face. "I *do* love you, Anthony. No matter what, that will remain true."

There's no reaction on his part. No embrace, no kiss, no further words. I just slip back out into the fog.

The Next Day, the Breakwater

Lloyd

In November the air changes. There's a snap, a bite, a tweak of your face that turns your cheeks red and hard even as the sun still shines overhead. How Javitz loved the air that moved in over the Cape during the late fall, with its chilly premonition of winter. It conjured up the promise of wool scarves and empty streets, of hot mugs of strong coffee sipped around a fire, the two of us discoursing on the state of our world.

Jeff and I settle onto a rock, looking down at the last spot where Javitz's atoms had all been in one place, where his ashes had spiraled around in his final journey out to sea. It was such a warm day when we'd scattered his ashes, and how the seagulls had chattered, as if unable to contain their sorrow, telling the world the news that Javitz was gone. Today the stones of the breakwater are cold, and the gulls overhead are silent. The day is bright, the wind tricky. One minute, the air is still; the next, I'm chasing my baseball cap over the rocks.

"Soon it will be too cold to sit here," Jeff muses.

"Oh, I'll come out here even in the dead of winter," I tell him. "Last year, I watched a blizzard roll in off the bay from this very spot. It was quite the scene."

Jeff smiles, flicking his eyes over at me. "I remember the last time we sat here, you and I."

I smile. I do, too.

How could I forget? It was the infamous day that Eva had locked me in my room. Her last-ditch attempt to prevent what was happening.

Jeff's looking at me. "That day, the last time we sat here, we made a pact to find out about these people we'd let into our lives. We thought we were embarking on the quest to resolve all our dilemmas, to find answers. But all it did was make the questions even more complicated."

It's true. If that day we had hoped we were finding our way back together, the sheer complexity of the other relationships in our lives has made that goal seem as far away as ever. I've seen first-hand Jeff's reaction to Anthony's departure. Quite simply, he was devastated, and that told me a lot. I can't pretend that it doesn't hurt. I saw last night how filled Jeff had been with a desire to see Anthony again, so determined he was to put right whatever had gone wrong between them. I can't help but wonder if he's ever had the same passion for making it right with *me*.

But I'm hardly a model on how to rebuild relationships. Indeed, my own passion has been reserved for Eva. I spent weeks being angry with her, feeling resentful of her, and now I'm wallowing in a strange kind of grief, a feeling of abandonment. That takes up enormous energy—energy I could have been channeling toward Jeff. Instead, while Jeff was out confronting Anthony, I was sitting on my floor, reading through Eva's old notes and E-mails, the ones she'd sent me in those first few glorious weeks of our friendship, where our talks reminded me of what I missed most with Javitz.

No matter what her diagnosis, no matter what her motivations may have been, she had come to occupy a special part in my life, and that's what I miss. That's what I grieve. How Eva had understood my words. How she seemed to share my dreams. How she listened, really *listened* to me. To an outside observer, I would have looked like a spurned lover going through a box of old love letters. And maybe that's not so far off the mark.

Then, of course, in the midst of all that drama, I allowed myself to seek solace in the arms of Henry. Jeff's best friend. Or at least, his former best friend. I know Jeff still cares about him, and he misses Henry something fierce.

He's looking at me as if he knows I want to tell him something. I sigh. Why is it always so *complicated* between us? Why can't it ever just be *easy*?

"Jeff," I begin, "do you remember when Henry came down on Halloween for that workshop?"

"Oh, God, Lloyd, don't tell me you slept with him."

I just close my eyes.

Jeff groans, covering his face with his hands. "What were you trying to do? Balance things out since I slept with Drake?"

"Jeff, it wasn't like that."

He sighs, looking over at me. "How did it happen, then? You got carried away at the workshop?"

"No. It was a conscious choice." I can't lie to Jeff. "We came back to the guest house and it felt natural to make love." I try to smile. "He's really a very sweet guy. He's going through a lot."

Jeff looks off across the waves. "I can't pretend I haven't felt a little jealous about your connection. I haven't quite figured out exactly the *nature* of my jealousy, however. Whether it was because you were with him or that he was with you."

"Nothing's ever simple with us, is it, Cat?"

Jeff laughs. "Maybe you were good for Henry. Maybe you're exactly what he needed."

"I *do* think I've helped him. He's really gotten into exploring some spiritual issues. Maybe . . ." My voice rises in a hope I don't quite believe. "Maybe it will help him work out his issues with you."

Jeff's looking at me sternly. "Lloyd. Be honest with me. Henry's fallen in love with you, hasn't he?"

I sigh. "I think so." I run my hands over my head.

"And what do you feel for him?"

"I care for him a lot. I love him. But not in the way he . . ." I can't finish the sentence for some reason. "I'm not in love with him."

Jeff just nods.

"I tried to get him to see that he has this pattern of attaching to people, of remaking himself in their image."

Jeff laughs wryly. "Oh, that's Henry, all right."

"I'm not sure he got what I was saying."

Jeff shakes his head in exasperation. "And you know *why* he didn't get it? Because for all of your talk of rising *above* the ego, Lloyd, you forget that first one must *have* an ego to rise above." He laughs sardonically. "Henry. Eva. Anthony. We're surrounded by them."

"Henry's trying," I insist.

Jeff just shrugs. "God, I miss Javitz," he says.

This is the place we always find ourselves when things get complicated: with our backs up against the wall, unsure of how to move, wishing Javitz were here to tell us what to do. Suddenly it feels so old, so tired, and I want nothing more than to get away from that wall.

"You know what, Jeff?" I ask suddenly. "As much as we miss Javitz, we've got to stop thinking we can't do it without him. We've got to start trying to figure things out on our own."

He sighs. "As if we could. We aren't any further along than we were four months ago in understanding where we—*you and I*—are going."

I look at him. "Maybe we'll only know when we look back. That's the only time anything ever seems to make sense." I take his hand. "I think you need to figure out how you really feel about Anthony before you and I can proceed any further."

He seems to take that in, but then looks back at me. "And what about you, Lloyd? What do you need to figure out?"

Just then, as if on cue, we hear her. The heaving, gasping attempts to catch her breath, and the hiccuping little sobs that keep interrupting her struggle. We look up. Standing above us is Eva, her face blotchy with tears.

"Oh, Lloyd," she says, "I thought I'd find you here."

"What is it?" I ask, looking up at her with alarm.

"She's broken up with me," Eva sobs.

"What?"

Eva struggles to find her words but can't speak. Both Jeff and I watch her, the way her face makes odd twists and contortions, the unconscious movements of her hands in the air. Neither of us budges from our place on the rock. Neither of us says a word. She just stands over us, crying like a frustrated infant in its crib. Finally, in a pique, she throws whatever it is she's got clenched in her hand. Just before it splashes down into the indigo water, I can see it's Steven's ring. Lost for good.

Understand that I do *not* want to stand and take her into my arms. That's the absolute *last* thing I want to do. This is old and familiar: her scheme of trying to win attention from me. And now, after weeks of distance—after weeks of smug passive-aggressive hostility, after all she's done—does she really expect me to jump to my feet and wrap her to my bosom?

Yet neither can I just continue to sit here. Her tears, growing louder and more desperate, would put the most hardened soul on edge. I look over at Jeff. He seems clearly embarrassed by this display on her part. With a long sigh, I stand, every muscle in my legs resisting me. I walk over to her and place my hands on her shoulders.

"Eva," I say, my voice even. "Please try to calm down."

She wheezes, gasping for breath.

Jeff's behind me. "I'll see you back at the house," he whispers. I nod.

As he's passing, he places his hand on Eva's arm. Just that. A tiny little gesture that makes me respect him. Makes me remember why I love him. I watch as he moves off toward shore, his hands pushed down deep into his pockets.

"Eva," I urge her again, "try to get a grip."

Her red, swollen eyes find mine. "She won't see me anymore until I'm in therapy."

I don't say anything. She knows how I feel about that.

"She said she didn't think I was really a lesbian. Just because I didn't want to do—*that.*"

"That?"

"Oh, Lloyd!" she sobs. "I love her! I really love her! How can I go on without her?"

"Eva, you need to try to get a hold of yourself."

"I thought you'd understand," she stammers.

I try to smile, careful about setting her off. "How can I understand, Eva, when you've given me the cold shoulder for weeks?"

She looks up at me with the saddest eyes you can possibly imagine, and despite myself, my heart breaks for her. Whether pity or compassion, I can't tell.

"I only gave you the cold shoulder," she sniffles, "because you gave it to me."

"Eva, you're a bright woman." I try to sound as gentle as I can. "You were a lost soul when I met you. You latched on to me and defined yourself in relation to me. Everything you did, everything you *thought,* was somehow determined by your connection to me."

She makes a little sob. "I loved you," she whimpers.

Standing here, I realize something for the first time. It wasn't about Steven. It was about *me,* all along. *I don't want you to be Steven. I want you to be you—the wonderful man who's given me so much.*

And yet, not about me, either. Not really. I look down at her splotchy face. "At first, I thought it was far simpler than it really was," I say to her, the words coming from my lips as quickly as the revelations enter my mind. "I thought you were just trying to re-create Steven in me. Giving me his clothes. That ring. But that wasn't quite it, was it, Eva? Steven's almost irrelevant, isn't he?"

She looks away. She's stopped crying.

"Tell me the truth finally, Eva. Did you ever really grieve Steven, or was it something else? Were your tears really for yourself, for how lonely you were?"

She puts her hands in her hair. "Oh, Lloyd," she rasps.

I feel as if I might start crying too. "It wasn't so much Steven you wanted to create, but anyone—anyone who might fill up that loneliness in the center of your soul. What is it that causes that loneliness, Eva? Where does it come from?"

She says nothing, but her tears have stopped. Might she possibly, at long last, admit the truth?

When she remains silent, I let out a long sigh. "Your heart wasn't so much in what we tried to do together, but in simply having someone to do it—anything—with."

"Is that so bad?" she asks in a small, unfamilar voice.

"Eva, we can't go on like this anymore," I tell her plainly.

Her eyes flicker up at me in sudden alarm. "Are you saying—you want to *sell* the guest house?"

"We need to look at all our options," I tell her.

"Oh, Lloyd, *don't leave me!*" Her face twists. "I'll—I'll kill myself if you do!"

Suddenly I know how Steven must have felt. But I will not be trapped the way he was. Never.

"No, you won't, Eva."

"I swear I will!"

"Eva, please don't talk this way. Find that woman I first met. Find her down deep inside yourself, the woman who was strong and wise. That's who you are. That's who you really—"

"I'll kill myself, Lloyd!" She's wide-eyed and frantic. "I'll kill myself!"

"Let's go back to Nirvana," I say.

"I swear I will! With you gone, with Candi gone, I'll kill myself! I have no reason to live!"

I feel exhausted. "How about for *yourself,* Eva? How about living for *yourself?*"

"I'll kill myself, Lloyd!"

"You'll do what you have to do," I tell her.

She just stands there, defying me to walk away from her. There's nothing more that can be accomplished here, so I do. I turn and make my way back across the breakwater. It's not until I get to the end that I turn back around. She's nowhere in sight. My first thought is that she's thrown herself into the water. But I'd have heard a splash.

Wouldn't I?

The Last Weekend of November, Miami, the White Party

Henry

"Who are you calling now?" Shane asks, all annoyed.

I punch the quick-dial digits into my cell phone. *"Lloyd,"* I tell him. Shane rolls his eyes. *"Again?"*

I give him a face. "He's *worried* about something, Shane. I want to *be there* for him."

But I get his voice mail. "Hey, it's me," I say. "I'm just checking in. Just wanted to let you know that I'm thinking about you. Hope everything's okay. Call me if anything happens. I don't care what time it is. If you need me, call."

Shane and I are out on the beach, heading back into the party. I'm wearing baggy jeans and no shirt; Shane, some white Lycra wrestling singlet he'd bought from International Male. He's done a couple of bumps of X but I'm completely straight, wanting to be clearheaded if Lloyd needs me.

I don't even really want to be here at all, despite the fact that I had a good time last year. But a year ago I was a far different person than I am now. All I really want to be doing is sitting with Lloyd in the living room of Nirvana, sharing a bottle of wine and talking about our souls' journeys.

Okay. So I'm coming across rather pompous and a bit too earnest. I don't mean to be. But in truth, Shane's just aggravating me no end, pawing me and kissing me and constantly dragging me out to the dance floor. The only reason I'm here at all is because he coerced me, having bought the passes and secured the airfare ages ago. "If you don't come, I'm out a *lot* of money," he bitched when I suggested that maybe I'd stay home. "The White Party is the *Crown Jewel* of the circuit. Passes aren't easily obtained."

"So you can make a profit scalping them."

"Henry, come *on*. Please? It's been so long since we've been out dancing. I *miss* you."

My heart melted. "Okay, buddy," I promised him. But ever since we arrived, he's been so manic, chattering away nonstop at every single party we attended: "This is what we'll do tonight," and "Here's our agenda for tomorrow," and "Look over there, it's Oscar and Eliot and—hey, boys! Yoo-hoo! Over here!"

"Shane," I scolded. "No talking on the dance floor."

I have to admit, however, the Miami White Party deserves its fabulous reputation. Sunday's big bash, pulsing to the sweeping trance and vocal anthems courtesy of the amazing David Knapp, was held amid lush Victorian gardens with a spectacular view of Biscayne Bay. No other circuit party can match this one for sheer beauty. And the men certainly complement their surroundings, as much wonders of nature themselves as the flowers and the sea.

I look around at all of them as Shane and I slide back onto the dance floor. How many of them are like Brent? I wonder. How many of those fabulous shells mask what's really going on inside their bodies? How many even *know* they're carrying the virus? And how many of those muscles are actually the result of the steroids they take to fight their HIV?

And why does no one talk about it? Lloyd compared the silence to the experience of Holocaust survivors, who for many of the years following the concentration camps never spoke of what had happened. To speak it, they somehow felt, could bring it back. I think of my grandfather, who'd lost an uncle and three cousins in Auschwitz. I never remember hearing him talk about it. I'd never have even known it had happened at all if it weren't for my mother. I was a generation removed from the Holocaust, just as I felt removed from AIDS.

Except the analogy stops there. The camps can't reach across the intervening years and grab me by the throat the way the plague still has the power to do. Even though I'd only been tested three months before, I went again for another test just last week. Maybe I'm being overly cautious, as I've been relatively risk-free: handjobs and massages weren't exactly high on the list of unsafe behavior. But I did it anyway. For Brent in some ways as much as myself.

"Was that my cell phone?" I suddenly ask, yanking it from my pocket.

"Calm down, sweetheart." Shane makes a face. "It's just the DJ."

I check just to be sure. No call. I slip the phone back into my pocket.

"What's got you such a nervous Nell?" Shane asks. "What's Lloyd so worried about that you have to call him every hour on the hour?"

"I shouldn't say."

Shane licks my face. "I'll keep doing that until you do."

I grimace. "It's Eva. She—she hasn't shown up since threatening to kill herself a week ago. Apparently, her girlfriend dumped her and she was very distraught. He's planning on reporting her missing today."

"Such drama." Shane shivers. "Look, I *adore* Eva. But she's no dyke. Fag hags often go through such stages, thinking they're lesbians because they just want so much to be queer. They don't realize they already *are.*"

"Well, regardless, Lloyd's worried about her. She didn't even show up for Thanksgiving this week, and they had a whole house full of guests."

Shane smirks. "Poor li'l Lloyd must've run his li'l self ragged."

"Well," I concede, wishing it had been me, "Jeff went down to help."

"Ohoho!" Shane loves that, I can tell, and he milks it for all it's worth. "So our happy twosome spent the holiday together while you were down here with fifteen thousand men under the Florida sun. Maybe they built a fire and gave thanks in front of it."

"You're a brat, Shane. A total brat." I put my shoulder to him, my eyes suddenly meeting those of a hunky, sweaty guy with Mark McGrath highlights in his hair. "I'm sure they were far too busy with all their guests to be giving any thanks."

Okay, so I admit I'm a little jealous that Jeff and Lloyd spent Thanksgiving together. But I'm not going to let Lloyd know that. And I sure as hell am not going to admit it to Shane.

"Hey," Mark McGrath says. "Sup?"

"Sup with *you?*" I ask.

"Uh, Henry." Shane taps me on the shoulder. "I wasn't aware we had finished our conversation."

I turn back to face him. "Why don't you try dancing instead of talking, Shane? This is called the *dance* floor, after all."

"I just thought you might be interested in knowing who's staying at my apartment while I'm here."

I look up at him. "Who?"

"Eva," he tells me. "Sweetie, she's *fine.* She called me and said she needed to get away. I figured since I was coming here and my apartment would be empty . . ."

I'm stunned. "I can't believe you!"

He makes a face as if he doesn't get my outrage. *"What?"*

I stalk off the dance floor.

Shane follows. "Henry! Why are you so pissed?"

We're outside on the deck, where clusters of boys have gathered to talk and cruise each other. I spin on Shane. "I'm pissed because here's Lloyd all tied up in knots worrying about her—just as she wants him to be—and you're complicit in her scheme!"

"She just needed a place to get away! To clear her head!"

"Your head's the one that needs clearing." I'm pressing numbers again on my phone.

Damn. Lloyd's voice-mail again. Maybe he and Jeff are off giving thanks.

"Hey, it's me again. Eva's fine. Shane just told me she's at his place. Appears she just needed to get away and think. Call me."

I glare up at him.

Shane raises his eyebrows and crosses his arms over his chest. "So *you've* gone and changed your opinion of her, too. You used to think she was great. *Everybody's* against her. First Jeff, who turned Lloyd against her. Now Lloyd's turned *you* against her, too."

"Shut up, Shane."

He grabs my arm. It hurts. "Hey!" I protest.

"Don't you *ever* tell me to shut up!" he shouts. "Take it back."

"You are acting *so* childishly."

He pouts. "I don't know you anymore, Henry."

I sigh. I pull a deck chair over and sit down, patting the seat beside me for Shane to follow.

He reluctantly obliges.

"I'm sorry, Shane," I tell him.

He looks as if he might cry. "I was really hoping this would be a fun trip."

"It *is,*" I assure him. "I think I'm just getting a little tired of all this crisscrossing the country. You can't sustain it forever. Everybody drops out eventually."

Shane just shrugs.

"Don't you want something *more,* Shane? Ever since Brent's death, I've become very focused on what I want in my life. Next year I'll be *thirty.* I want a *relationship,* Shane. I want to love someone who loves me back. Brent *died* wanting that. I don't want to end up that way, too."

Shane looks at me evenly. "You don't think I understand, Henry? You don't think it's what *I* want, too?"

"Of *course* you want it. Everyone does. All these guys here with their drugs and their parties and their I-don't-care attitudes . . ." I try to smile genuinely. "You say you don't know me anymore, Shane. And do you know why you don't? Because I've *changed*. Changed for the *better*. You're the one who got me started escorting, but I was going about it all *wrong*. At first all I did was *take*. Now I'm getting very good at giving, and it's just as fulfilling. Even more so."

"Good for you," Shane says.

"It *is* good. Because I'm learning about *connection*. I never got the concept before. Which I'm sure is why I never found a lasting relationship. I'm only now learning how relationships *work*. The give and the take."

He looks a little perturbed. "I think you already knew how relationships worked, Henry."

"No, I didn't. You were *right* about Jeff and me, Shane. I was trapped in a one-way situation. It was all about *me* giving to *him*. So when you came along and showed me how I could get paid for actually *taking* from other people, being on the *receiving end* for a change, naturally I jumped right for it. But now I'm trying to integrate those two experiences, Shane. And it was *Lloyd* who helped me see how to do that."

"Uh-huh."

I smile, wanting to trust him, to take Shane into my confidence. I need a good friend, someone with whom I can talk about all this, who will really listen to what I have to say. I need a . . . *sister*.

"Shane," I say, taking his hands, "I think Lloyd and I are falling in love with each other. I think . . . we're going to make a relationship together."

"I think you're fucked," Shane says, shaking off my hands and standing up.

I follow him to my feet. *"What?"*

He lowers his face right into mine. "You'd really do that to Jeff, wouldn't you? Without the slightest qualm?" He snorts. "And you say *he* was the one insensitive to *you!*"

"Of *course* I feel qualms about it," I insist. "Of *course* I don't want us to hurt Jeff."

"Bullshit, Henry. You want to drive that stake right through Jeff's heart." He laughs derisively at me. "And you're even more fucked up if you think Lloyd's in love with you. You've said it to me a million times: Jeff and Lloyd are joined at the hip."

I stiffen. "That was before what happened between me and Lloyd."

"Well, bully for you, Bella Donna. But let me tell you something. I'm *so* pleased that you've finally figured out how to make a relationship work. I'm *so* thrilled that Lloyd taught you all you needed to know. But maybe you ought to try opening your eyes and looking around. Sometimes there are relationships going on right under your own nose that you don't even see."

I know he means himself. Him and me. Us. I let out a long sigh. "Shane, of course I value our friendship—"

"Listen, Henry," he says, cutting me off. "I need to apologize to you. Because I broke a promise we made to each other. That very first day, remember? In Grand Central Station in New York. We said we'd never lie to each other. That we'd always speak the truth. Remember?"

I say nothing, just look up into his big, wide blue eyes. He's crying.

"Well, I haven't always told you the truth," he says, his voice thick with emotion. "I've pretended it didn't hurt when you'd spend all night trying to find a husband and then settle for me when nobody else showed up. Nobody *better*. I've made believe that I didn't care when you'd make plans with me only to ditch them so you could spend time with Jeff, or your clients, or now Lloyd. I've tried to tell myself that I didn't need anything in return from you except your occasional presence, even after it was *me* who was there, night after night, when you were alone, or depressed about Brent, about your job, about the escorting. I tried to tell myself that so long as I was *aware* of the realities of the situation, so long as I knew what was going on, I'd be all right. That I wouldn't want *more*."

His eyes freeze on me.

"But I was *wrong*. I was lying to both you and to myself, Henry. I wasn't being honest, and for that, I'm sorry!"

He starts to sob. He puts his hands over his face and just bawls his eyes out. Maybe the chemicals spur him on, but it feels as if the dam has been cracking for a while and now the flood just can't be contained.

Have I really been so unaware? How could I not know about the depth of his feelings for me? How could I not have *seen*?

But I *did*. I *did* see it. I *did* know. That's the realization I have standing here. I knew all along. I knew that Shane cared about me, and that knowledge was sustaining. I had come to take Shane's feelings for granted; to acknowledge their truth would have been to risk losing them.

It strikes me just how similar to Jeff I've been, after all.

I try to put my arms around Shane, but he pulls away. "I came here to *dance*," he says, sniffling, wiping his eyes. "I haven't even brought out my laser guns yet. You go do what you want, Henry, but I'm gonna *dance!*"

He rushes off. But instead of heading back to the dance floor, he just finds a spot on the deck and begins moving on his own, a strange little ballet. He flashes his lasers, drawing attention to himself. He begins to sing, even as the tears are still dropping down his face. It's a little ditty to the tune of "My Favorite Things":

"Bullets and bumpers and yellow sunglasses,
doormen and barbacks with tight little asses,
tattoos and Diesels on ev-er-y queen,
these are all part of the gay circuit scene!"

A crowd begins forming around him. They hoot, laugh. Shane gets into it, spinning like a dervish with all eyes upon him, his voice getting louder and louder.

"Dealers and bouncers and homely fag-haggies,
uppers and downers in clear plastic baggies,
hot shorts and cock rings and all things obscene,
these are all part of the gay circuit scene!"

"You *go*, girl!" somebody yells.

He's at the top of his voice now, tapping each boy on the chest in rhythm with his song.

"Glow sticks and blow pops and loud metal whistles,
tearing your skin on unshaven back bristles,
K-holes and ODs becoming routine,
these are all part of the gay circuit scene!"

Shane flies dramatically from face to face, a crazy Maria Van Trapp on Ecstasy as she reaches the refrain.

"When my week bites,
when my life sucks,
when I feel so saaad
I simply retreat to the gay circuit scene,
and then I don't feeeeeel . . ."

He pauses. He speaks rather than sings the last word.

"Anything."

Everybody cheers. Shane doesn't acknowledge them. He just slumps off toward the dance floor without making eye contact with anyone. He manages to squeeze his way back into the crowd, where he dances in one spot, without conviction, without imagination, his energy depleted.

I follow him. I say not a word. I simply begin dancing by his side.

A Few Days Later,
A Café in Hartford, Connecticut

Jeff

"I always thought the American public wouldn't stand for it," Cynthia Cassell is saying, sipping her espresso across the table from me. "The candidate who received the majority of the popular vote being denied the presidency. I know that's the way the Constitution works, but still I thought people would be royally pissed off."

I have to agree I'm mystified by the lack of widespread outrage over the Supreme Court's declaration of George W. Bush the winner of the presidential election. "And all those uncounted votes," I say. "And the ballots that led people to vote for Buchanan. The polling places that disenfranchished hundreds of African-American voters. It's clear that Gore is the true, moral winner, but what's truth and morality got to do with politics?"

She laughs bitterly. "Sad but true." She leans back in her chair to look at me. "It wasn't always that way, you know. I'm old enough to remember a time when we actually thought politics could change the world. That we could make a difference using the ballot box."

"So what happened?" I ask, glancing down at my tape recorder to make sure it's still running.

"Oh, I'm not sure. Watergate. Reagan. And then the disappointments of Clinton." She smiles ruefully. "But I'm already missing that old adulterer. I think history will show he did an awful lot of good for us, though not much through any actual legislation or policy."

She's a wise old bird. Tall, thin, with frameless glasses and dyed-red hair down to her shoulders. She's run this café for years, and it's served as a kind of unofficial headquarters for the state's gay activism for almost three decades. Cynthia doesn't take to the streets or to the state capitol as often as she once did, but she still has her finger on the pulse. She knows what's real, what matters. I liked her immediately when we met, and was grateful she consented to be interviewed about the Robert Riley case.

"Riley's death was the shot in the arm we needed at the time," she says plainly. "Remember, we were still living in the age of Reagan and the first Bushwhacker. And AIDS had us all shell-shocked. The Catholic Church was being really assaultive at this time, with people like O'Connor down in New York and our own bishop here. There was a lot of fear, a lot of oppression. You had people really living very deep in their closets."

"The Riley case changed that?"

"You bet your watoosie it did. Some guy's bludgeoned to death in his own home, and the killers are kids from a Catholic school, and all these church leaders come out to say what good boys these two really are, with no mention of the dead fag. Well, that just rubbed a lot of us the wrong way."

"I can understand."

She sighs. "Of course, a lot of us said that if Robbie Riley had been some black drag queen from the North End of Hartford or some dyke on a motorcycle, nobody would've gotten quite so up in arms. But Riley was an upper-class white boy, and so we mobilized the upper-class white boys. That's where the power is—the clout—sad to say." She takes another sip of her espresso. "But you can't deny that when the white boys started coming out of their closets and attending rallies, writing and calling their legislators, opening up their wallets, things started to change. That's politics for you."

She smiles, leaning in over the table and lowering her voice. "Not to be disrespectful or anything, but Riley's death was the best thing that could've happened for gay politics in this state. Within a couple years we passed a gay rights bill, then a hate-crimes bill, then all sorts of AIDS bills. Now we're even talking marriage rights like they did up in Vermont."

I smile. "Let's hear it for my old home state."

"You got it, kiddo. We don't fool around here." She laughs out loud, waving over at someone across the room. "Of course, we weren't all that successful last year, but that's probably what you want to ask me about anyway, isn't it?"

I don't know what she means, but she goes right on talking before I can interject.

"We tried to protest, but it's like the Bush thing, you know? You just can't seem to get anybody outraged these days. We put together maybe fifty people to stand outside the courthouse with placards, but it did no good. Hey, no one from Riley's family showed up to say anything against it, so there wasn't much else we could do."

Gloria Santacroce's words are suddenly in my ears: *"I know the state prosecutor's office contacted us last year about something to do with the case. But of course, Mrs. Riley wasn't able to talk to him."*

I look across the table intently at Cynthia Cassell. I ask her carefully, "What exactly were you protesting against at the courthouse?"

She looks at me askance. "You mean you don't know? You said you wanted to talk to me about the Riley case. I thought it was about the kid getting parole!"

"Parole?" I ask, feeling like a total dumb-ass.

Cynthia laughs, shaking a finger at me. "You call yourself a reporter?"

"I might be a little rusty," I admit.

She lifts her eyebrows. "Well, in your defense, it's not like the papers covered it all that much. Not like they did when the case was going on. Anyway, the judge let one of Riley's killers out on parole."

I can barely contain my surprise. "Brian Murphy?"

"Yeah, Murphy. The white kid. The high school quarterback. Of course they'd give *him* preferential treatment over Ortiz."

"But I thought his sentence wasn't up for another few years."

She looks at me with dripping sarcasm. "Oh, but he'd been such a *model prisoner!* Remember, he'd gotten off with a much lighter sentence because he made some deal to talk. The charge against him was dropped from first-degree murder to manslaughter. That brought it down from a Class A felony to a Class B, which means his maximum sentence would be twenty years. The judge gave him fifteen, and he was eligible for parole after serving eighty-five percent of that. Well, guess what? That percentage was reached last year. They let him out the very day he became eligible."

Brian Murphy . . . free.

"Oh, he had them snookered right from the start," Cynthia's saying. "I remember how he cried in court, kept saying how sorry he was. And the judge believed him."

I look at her. "But you didn't?"

She shrugs. "He was sorry he got caught, sorry he was going to jail. You read his confession. These boys knew what they were doing. They came back to hit Riley again to make sure he was dead!"

I attempt some fast calculations in my mind. "How old would Brian be now?"

"Thirty-something, I imagine." She looks at me with deliberate eyes. "Maybe just thirty, actually. You *must* try to interview him. I'm *very* curious what he has to say after all this time."

"Any idea where he is?" I ask, not sure of the feeling that's taking hold of me.

"Nope. But his mother is still here in Hartford. She must know."

I have her address. I glance down at my notes. Mrs. Astrid Murphy. Brown Street, in the working-class South End of Hartford, one of the last white holdouts in a city becoming increasingly Puerto Rican and African-American. I look up again at Cynthia Cassell.

"You've been a tremendous help," I tell her.

"Just write a good piece. Say something new. We've heard it all before, you know. Tell us something we haven't heard already."

I promise I'll try.

Outside, the sky has darkened, threatening rain. It's cold and there's ice in the air. I dread the idea of winter. Summer seemed so fleeting this year that I hardly remember it. I get into my car and head through the city, past the gleaming skyscrapers of the Insurance Capital of the World. I know those buildings are deserted soon after five P.M., that downtown Hartford becomes a ghost town. The insurance workers all return to their safe, quiet suburbs, and only a few—Robert Riley once among them—ever venture back into the city after dark.

The only life that remains in Hartford is found in its outlying blue-collar neighborhoods, where, along Maple Avenue for instance, a few Italian *ristorantes* and bakeries still flourish. It's on a side street here that I locate Astrid Murphy's house, a two-family dwelling of red brick, its small, tidy yard enclosed by a chain-link fence.

What am I going to say to her? What am I hoping to find?

I park across the street and look up at the house. There's a car in the driveway, an old Chevy Nova. Surely not the same? It's parked under a frayed basketball net, where I imagine Brian Murphy once shot hoops. In an upstairs bedroom window there's an old Tot Finder decal, a guide for firefighters in the case of a blaze. I wonder if it had been Brian's room as a little boy.

Sitting there in the car, I recall Cynthia Cassell's words: "You call yourself a reporter?" I smile ruefully to myself. Lloyd has said to me he feels he should have recognized warning signs of Eva's mental illness earlier than he did. After all, he's a psychologist, and a good one. I understand his pique at himself: I'm one more professional not playing at the top of his game, too blinded by the proverbial forest to see the trees. I should have looked further in the indexes. A really good reporter would have. If I'd researched as thoroughly as I should have—looking up Robert Riley in each successive year right up to the present—I would've learned long ago that Brian Murphy had been released.

There are no coincidences, someone once told me. No coincidences. Maybe I wasn't supposed to find out about Murphy until now. Maybe Lloyd wasn't supposed to diagnose Eva earlier. If we had, what would be different? What might we have missed?

I pick up my folder from the passenger seat and flip through to the newspaper account of the sentencing. Cynthia Cassell was right: Brian Murphy did indeed receive mercy from the court, and his lawyers were quoted as saying they were "satisfied." Not so, gay activists, who complained that "Robert Riley is dead, while Brian Murphy will walk free while still a young man." There's a photograph of protesters outside the courthouse holding a banner. *NO JUSTICE, NO PEACE,* it reads.

Above it is a picture of Murphy, his head down, his shoulders hunched, his hands shackled behind his back.

My eyes scan the article for mention of his mother. I remember something about her speaking at the sentencing. Yes, here it is: "Please, Your Honor," she begged, "give my son a chance. I've had my problems. I turned to alcohol when I couldn't face them. I love my son; I tried very hard, but I guess I didn't do the job I should have. I wish I could take his punishment."

Dear God, how can I go up and ring this woman's doorbell?

But I know that the answer I seek is inside that house.

A dog begins barking from behind the door as soon as I walk up onto the front porch. There's a pumpkin on the steps, starting to rot, left over from Halloween a month ago. Cigarette butts are scattered here and there. A hanging plant is dried out and brown.

"Who are you?"

I turn. A woman has come around from the side of the yard. She's hauling a heavy trash barrel.

"My name's Jeff O'Brien." I pause. "I'm a reporter."

"Go away." Her voice is low and scarred, the result of decades of tobacco. She turns and drops the trash at the sidewalk.

The dog in the house is barking louder. I walk down the steps and approach the woman in the yard. "I'm very sorry to bother you. Are you Mrs. Murphy?"

She's light-skinned and fair, no eyebrows at all at first glance. Even her eyelashes are blond. Her hair is tied back in a short ponytail. The only makeup she wears is a slight pink lipstick. She's a small woman, with crystal blue eyes and an incredible mass of wrinkles. She looks to be seventy, but I don't think she's that old.

"Yes, I'm Astrid Murphy," she says. "But I don't want to talk to you."

She tries to walk past me toward the house, but I call after her. "Can you at least tell me how to get in touch with your son Brian?"

Astrid Murphy stops in her tracks. Without turning around she says, "You've got a better chance of finding him than me. After all, you're looking for him." She looks back at me over her shoulder. "I'm not."

"Mrs. Murphy," I plead, "I want to write an article that's fair." Cynthia Cassell's words suddenly come back to me. "Something new. Something we haven't heard already."

She turns to face me. She's wearing acid-washed blue jeans and a heavy black wool sweater that's starting to unravel around the neck.

"Something *new?*" she asks, taking a few steps in my direction. "Well, how about saying that we all got problems, that nobody got off from this thing with a good deal?"

"I believe that," I assure her.

She withdraws a lighter and a pack of Newports from her jeans pocket and lights up. Taking a deep drag, she lets the smoke out over her head. "Whaddya want to know?" she asks.

"When was the last time you saw Brian?"

"Six years ago."

"Six years? You mean, he didn't come to see you when he got out of prison?"

Her eyes are hard. "I assume he's reporting in to his parole officer every week, because I haven't heard any bitching from the court. But he hasn't come by here."

I look up again to the window with the Tot Finder decal. "Why is that, Mrs. Murphy? Why hasn't he come to see you?"

She sniffs. "Because prison turned him into something I don't understand. He wasn't my Brian anymore. He wasn't my son."

"I don't follow."

"I don't really care if you do or you don't." She takes another long drag on her cigarette. "Look, I did what I could. But at a very young age Brian saw his father hauled off to prison for all his gambling debts. He never forgot that. Who would? Then he watches as his father slowly drinks himself to death. Is it any wonder Brian's messed up? I couldn't do it alone, be both mother and father. Is it any wonder that Brian's— *messed up?* Become this—*thing?* He's not the son I knew!"

I watch as she throws her cigarette to the sidewalk and grinds it out with her toe.

"It's not just the murder that you're talking about, is it, Mrs. Murphy?" I ask her softly.

"Go on," she says. "I said I don't want to talk to you."

She starts walking back up the steps to the house.

"Mrs. Murphy," I call after her. "Just one other thing."

She stops, but once more she doesn't turn around.

"Will you just tell me where Brian was born?" I swallow nervously. "Have you always lived here in Hartford?"

Astrid Murphy turns to look at me with hard eyes. "What has that got to do with anything?"

"Please," I say. "Will you tell me?"

"We used to live in Illinois. Lake Bluff. That's where Brian was born."

She turns away from me, opening the door to her house. A large black Doberman jumps up on her. She speaks some reassuring words to it, easing it back inside. Then she closes the door.

Lake Bluff, Illinois . . .

Dear God, what am I thinking?

Maybe what I've known ever since Cynthia Cassell told me Brian Murphy had been paroled.

Maybe what I've known for even longer than that, somewhere down deep.

Back in my car I peer again at the newspaper photograph of Brian Murphy, lifting it close to my eyes as I study his image. Just a collection of black and gray dots really. What can a bunch of dots tell me? And anyway, he's looking down, his face turned away. Even if I thought there was a resemblance, how could I really tell?

It's just a collection of dots.

The Next Day, Nirvana

Lloyd

"I just talked with Shane," Henry reports, switching off his cell phone. "He said Eva left Boston a couple hours ago."

"Then she should be here shortly," I say.

I settle down on the couch. This has to be it. The end. I can't enable her behavior any longer. I need to sit down with her, find a way out. Thankfully, our last guest left an hour ago; the house is empty. I have no idea how Eva will react, and I'm grateful that Henry is here to hang in the background. I push my head back into the cushions and close my eyes.

Sadness overwhelms me. This had been my dream, my hope for a new life. I wanted so much for Nirvana to be the transformation of my grief over Javitz, a way back to living and interacting with the world. I had such plans, such hopes, such visualizations of life here. Now I feel as I did a year ago: alone and adrift, without any mooring, any direction, any destination.

This morning we watched as the first snowfall of the season danced off the bay. A light, pretty dusting that made me think of this time last year, of all the excitement we had felt, Eva and I together. By noon the snow had turned to rain, and now only a messy slush remains on the front sidewalk. I feel so terribly sad.

I can't think past this imminent encounter with Eva. What lies beyond is uncertain. Will she buy me out and keep Nirvana as her own? Will we both sell and recoup our costs, maybe even make a tidy little profit? The Provincetown market is white-hot, after all, and we've fixed the place up nicely. But then where will I go? Back to renting? Will I buy something else? Will I even remain in Provincetown?

And then there's Jeff to consider. How will this impact us?

"A penny for your thoughts," Henry's saying.

I open my eyes. He's sitting on the hassock in front of me, our knees nearly touching.

"They're hardly worth even that much," I tell him, managing a smile. "They're just a bunch of neurons colliding at random, not making much sense."

Henry puts his hands on my thighs, leaning in to kiss me lightly on the lips. "I know you're wondering what's to become of all this."

I nod. *All this.* I look past Henry to take in all the work we've put into this house. The paint. The new windows. The new floors. The artwork. The paintings. The statues of Buddha. I realize that despite my struggles with Eva, I've come to consider this place home. Even with all the work, I enjoy the comings and goings of the guests. It's been a fascinating parade of humanity in and out of these walls. Some were hell, I can't deny that, but most have been interesting and respectful, leaving the guest house a better place by their presence here. I think of the older gay couple from Toronto, together fifty-two years, and how we sat out on the front porch talking until midnight. I think of the student from Namibia, sharing with me the story of her coming out as we sat across from each other at the dining room table. I think of the straight couple who, embarking on a drive across the country, chose Provincetown as their starting point, situated as it was at the very point where the land ends—or begins, depending on your viewpoint. They sent me postcards from various stops along their route: Niagara Falls, Chicago, St. Louis, the Grand Canyon. They've become my friends "Sid and Gerri." I've made so many friends in the past year.

"You don't want to give it up, do you, Lloyd?"

I sigh. "No, I guess I don't. But I just don't know how I can go on. I can't do it with Eva, but neither would I want to do it alone."

He smiles at me. "Maybe you won't have to."

I shrug. "Jeff's made it clear he isn't interested in running a guest house."

Henry's back stiffens. "I didn't mean Jeff."

I look over at him. "Henry . . ."

He stands up. "I was thinking," he says, "of leaving my job. I'm not happy there. After they screwed me on that promotion, I feel all I owe them is two weeks' notice." He turns to face me. "I could work here, if you'd hire me."

"Henry . . ."

"I could do whatever was needed. Work the front desk. Do the laundry. Keep up the grounds. I could share your vision of this place, Lloyd." He kneels down in front of me, his hands on my thighs. "Your *dream*. I really could."

He looks so earnest kneeling there in front of me. So sincere. So willing to give his entire self to me, if only I'd ask. My heart breaks for him.

"Henry," I say as gently as I can, "I think you ought to follow your *own* dream."

He blinks a couple of times. "My own dream?"

I nod. "Whatever that is. My dream isn't your dream."

"But it could be."

"Eva once said the same thing." I smile kindly at him. "Henry, do you think that maybe, just maybe, you have a tendency to get caught up in the dreams of others?"

He bristles a little. "I was just trying to tell you how I feel about you."

I pat the place beside me on the couch. He sits, looking over at me with wide, vulnerable eyes. How dear he is. Why *didn't* Jeff ever fall in love with him?

Maybe for the same reason I never did. There's somebody else. And there always has been. Only one man for Jeff; only one man for me.

"You are going to make somebody an amazing husband," I tell him. "You have so much to give, Henry."

He smiles weakly. "But it's not going to be you, right? That's what you're trying to tell me."

I sigh. "Right now, I can't think past this confrontation with Eva. But if I try, if I force myself to, I know there's another issue I have to finally face when all this is over. Something I've not fully faced or completely dealt with. Not since Javitz died."

He nods. He knows. "Your relationship with Jeff," he says.

"Yes," I agree. "I have to figure out where we're supposed to be in each other's lives. What this past year has been all about. What we were supposed to learn."

Henry closes his eyes and leans his head back into the cushions of the couch. "I've always known that you and Jeff had something special. I think in my heart, down deep, I've always believed that the two of you were meant to be together." He opens his eyes and I can see they're moist. "I guess I just hoped against hope . . ."

I take his hand. "First with Jeff, then with me. Can you see a pattern, Henry?"

One tear escapes. Just one. "I tried to be more honest with you," he says thickly. "I was never honest with Jeff."

"He does love you, you know," I tell him, "very much."

That's when the tears come. He puts his head down on my shoulder and just starts to bawl like a baby. It's good for him. I pat his hair.

"He was the best friend I ever had," Henry sobs. "Next to you."

"Maybe you ought to tell him that," I suggest.

"I've allowed myself to forget all the good, concentrating only on the bad."

I pat his hair. "Maybe you *needed* to do that for a while."

"Jeff *was* there for me. He gave me courage. He taught me to believe in myself."

"All he did was point out the strength that was already there."

Henry wipes his eyes. "That image you described, of Jeff combing Javitz's hair and singing to him—I keep thinking about it."

I nod. "And do you know that on the night of Brent's overdose, he sat up with you nearly all night? He stroked your hair, too. You should have seen the concern on his face."

Henry sniffles. "Do you think it's too late for me to make up with him?"

"I don't think it's ever too late, Henry. You ought to call him and—"

Just then I notice headlights sweeping past the front windows into the driveway. Eva's back. I hear her car door slam shut.

Henry's on his feet, wiping his eyes. "I'll just go into the back room," he says. "If you need me, I'm here."

"Are you okay?"

He nods. "Thanks, Lloyd. Thanks for being my friend."

I smile. He disappears into the back just as the doorknob starts to turn. I pick up a magazine from the coffee table and begin thumbing through it.

Eva says nothing. She comes inside, carefully removing her boots so she won't track slush all over the front hallway. Then she heads upstairs to her room. I wait for fifteen minutes, keeping watch for her. But she doesn't return. It would be so like her to try to thwart any confrontation by hiding out in her room. I stand, prepared to walk upstairs and knock at her door. But just as I do so, I spy her coming down the stairs. She's carrying two suitcases.

"Excuse me, Eva, but I think we need to talk."

"I suppose we do." She sets the suitcases beside the front door and faces me calmly. "But I'm on my way to Candi's. I'll be staying there from now on. Don't worry. I won't neglect my duties here. I'll be here to do whatever needs to be done. But I see we don't have any guests scheduled until the weekend."

"Candi's?" I ask. "So you've reconciled."

"Yes, we have."

I fold my arms over my chest. "Did you tell *her* where you were all week?"

"No. Not at first."

I shake my head. "Don't you think disappearing like that was completely irresponsible of you? I was ready to call the police and file a missing person report."

"I regret if I caused you any worry." Her voice is even, emotionless. "You might not believe that, Lloyd, but it's true. I'm sorry."

"Eva," I tell her, "I can't go on like this."

She stiffens. "Neither can I."

"We need to discuss terms," I say.

"I'm happy to do whatever it takes, Lloyd." Her voice remains calm and without a trace of passion. "You can buy me out or I'll buy you out. Whatever works. Just so that we can get this whole thing over with."

She seems so hard. *This whole thing.* As much as I know it's the right thing to do, her lack of emotion over the shattering of our dream distresses me. Had everything really been so insincere?

"Well," I suggest, "maybe we can call Ty and ask him how we can go about—"

"Not Ty," she says quickly, efficiently. "I have my own attorney now, right here in town. To be honest, I don't think I'd feel very comfortable working with Ty at this point."

I guess I can understand that. "Eva," I say, unable to keep up this facade of efficiency, "I am filled with tremendous sadness that it has come to this."

Finally, a spark of emotion behind her eyes. "Do you think I'm *not?*" she asks. She sighs, running her hands across her short-cropped hair. The cardigan sweater she's wearing parts to reveal a low-cut red blouse. Funny how she's stopped trying to conceal her breasts, how she seems to have lost any self-consciousness about them.

"Look, Lloyd," she explains. "I am doing my best not to resort to any emotional tricks. I suppose that means I'm coming off indifferent. It's not how I feel."

I just look at her.

"Do you know why Candi took me back? Because I'm in *therapy,* Lloyd. When I was in Boston, I found someone on my own. Someone I like. Not someone you recommended, not someone Candi wanted me to see. Someone I found all by myself. And she's *good*, Lloyd. She's very good."

"I—I'm glad."

She takes a step toward me. "The other day on the breakwater you hurled some pretty powerful things at me. And you were *right*, Lloyd. I've been taking a good, long, hard look at myself, and I haven't liked the woman I see. The woman I've been for much of my life." She doesn't cry, and somehow, without her tears, her emotion seems more believable, more *trustworthy*.

"I'm sorry, Lloyd. I'm ashamed of many things that I did. I convinced myself that deleting Jeff's E-mails to you was merely a way of protecting you from being hurt. The same was true for locking you in your room. But I see now they were merely the acts of a desperate, sad, pitiful woman. I am truly, truly sorry for all the grief I caused you."

She lets out a long sigh and turns, as if there's nothing more to say, as if she'd just pick up her suitcases and leave. But she stops and looks back at me, seeming galvanized to speak.

"You always talk about sharing your truth, Lloyd," she says, her voice steady, even strong. "Well, here's mine. I've been a scared, lost, insecure little girl whose father was not the great god she has long tried to believe. No, not a god. Not at all." Her voice catches, but she continues. "So I grew up a scared, lost, insecure little girl—but one who believed that such things as compassion, self-sacrifice, commitment, and loyalty might ward against any future loneliness."

She laughs, a little bitterly.

"Why I should have thought so seems strange now. I was compassionate and committed and loyal to my father, and then to Steven, but still they left me, each in their turn. Did I get carried away at times? Did I allow myself to go overboard? Did I indulge in daydreams and fantasies? Yes, I did, and I'm sorry for all that. You don't know how sorry."

"Eva, I—"

"Let me finish. You're always the one talking at me, telling me the way things are. Maybe for once I have something to say on my own." Her eyes fasten on mine. "You were the one to tell me, in no uncertain terms, that we were *not* lovers. That I mustn't delude myself into thinking that we were. You would make that point very clear, Lloyd—and then you'd allow me to sit at your bedside rubbing your feet after a long day of climbing ladders and fixing the roof. You'd let me hold you and cook for you and take you for long walks on the beach. When Jeff or Henry or another friend came to visit, you'd keep me at arm's length, insisting that it was for my own good—but then, when they were gone, when you felt alone and full of your grief, you'd come to *me* with your thoughts, to seek *my* counsel or find solace in *my* words. Oh, how often you would assert our great differences—that I was a *straight* woman and you a *gay* man—but then you'd take comfort in our sameness, sitting there half the night in my arms on my couch in New York, talking about grief, and love, and the human condition."

She closes her eyes.

"No, we were not lovers. Wherever would I get such an idea?"

I just look at her. There are tears in her eyes now. But they aren't any tears I recognize. They aren't noisy or dramatic. They're genuine. They're not manipulative. They ask for no consolation.

"I will bear my responsibility as a scared, lost, insecure little girl, who did some terrible things," she tells me. "But might you consider your own accountability, for whatever it's worth? I don't need you to, nor am I even asking you to do so. It's just a suggestion, Lloyd. Take it or leave it."

She bends down and retrieves her suitcases. "I'll be back by the weekend. If any unexpected guests arrive, call me at Candi's."

There's nothing I can say at that moment. I just let her go. I hear her start the engine of her car. Henry comes out of the back room and stands behind me, placing his hand on my shoulder.

"How'd it go?" he asks.

"I'm not sure," I tell him. "I think . . . I think I just want to be alone."

Whether Henry feels hurt, I can't tell. He just nods, and I gently touch his cheek. He squeezes my hand.

All I want at that moment is Javitz. If only he were here . . . God, how often have I wished that over the course of the past year. I know I said it's time we started trying to figure things out on our own, to stop lamenting the fact that Javitz isn't here to do it for us. But I can't. I need Javitz to help me make sense of what Eva said. Have I really been as complicit as she described? Where do her issues end and mine begin?

In my room, I dig under my bed for the Javitz video. I need to see it again, to hear his voice, to see his face, to magically transcend time and once again be the young boy with a thick head of hair out on the deck goofing around with Javitz and Jeff. I feel mushy and foolish, as if Barbra Streisand should be on the sound track singing "The Way We Were." "Was it really all so simple then?" Or has time rewritten all the lines? However those lyrics went, that's how I feel. That life was once so easily understood, so uncomplicated—even if, in truth, life has always been complicated, that even as we cavorted on the deck that glorious summer day, we were struggling with complexities and ambiguities now forgotten, obscured by the giddy shimmer of memory.

I pop in the video and settle back into the pillows of my bed to watch. Several seconds tick by, and the screen remains black. I'm puzzled. "It should be playing by now," I murmur to myself. Then I laugh, realizing I must have forgotten to rewind it the last time I watched it. I hunt around on the side table for the remote. It must have fallen to the floor, maybe under the bed. I lean over, pushing around books and videos and my bottle of lube. A couple of dust bunnies scamper off across the floor. Where is the damn thing?

All at once I hear a crackle from the video screen. I look up. An image is forming there. There's *something else* on the tape—something beyond the point I've always assumed to be the end.

It shivers into view. My mouth falls open as I watch in wonder.

The Next Day,
The Beach in the East End

Jeff

Once, years ago, I met an old man on this beach. A painter who taught me a little lesson about life. About how precious it is, how mysterious. How it can sneak around from behind and surprise you, catch up with you and make you rethink everything you've ever believed. "After living on the same beach for thirty years," the old painter told me, "watching the seasons come and the seasons go, watching the gulls eat the sand crabs and the cats eat the gulls, there's only one thing I don't believe in anymore." His rheumy old eyes tried to focus on mine. "And that's *co-incidence*."

It was no coincidence that I'd met that old painter that day, just when I needed him most, and no coincidence that I've come to this same place again today. Somehow I *knew* to come here, out along the beach at low tide, strewn with seaweed, the sky sharp and blue. There's a bite to the wind, a promise of winter. They're predicting more snow this week. How fast winter has come around again.

I knew somehow I'd find him here. He's walking ahead of me, his hands thrust deep into the pockets of the leather coat I'd bought him, his backpack slung over his shoulder. It's no coincidence that I knew to come here, just as it had been no random meeting that night on the dance floor last New Year's Eve. There was *purpose* in my discovery of Anthony, in his finding of me, in the love that developed between us.

He turns, as if expecting me.

We say nothing at first. He still looks the same. Why would I think he'd look any different? He still has that glow to his skin, a tan that hasn't faded. His eyes are still soft and blue, wide and entreating. He has the same majestic taper to his torso, the same broad shoulders and the same gait to his walk. But still, he's different. As much as I hoped he wouldn't be, he is.

"I can tell by your face that you know the truth," he says at last.

I struggle to find my voice. "I only know facts. What I don't know are feelings, Brian."

He makes no reaction to hearing me call him by his real name. He offers neither confirmation nor denial, but there's no point, really. The truth is now plain. He's no roommate of Robert Riley, no lover or son of a lover. He's the man who killed Robert Riley. Or rather, the boy.

"What is it you want to know?" he asks at last.

"Tell me why you took Anthony Sabe's name."

He doesn't respond right away. He just gazes back over the sea, the waves crashing only a few inches from his feet.

"I'm not sure," he says finally. "Maybe because I wanted him to live."

I watch as he slips off his backpack and unzips the front pouch. He withdraws a folded sheet of yellow legal paper and hands it to me.

"What is this?" I ask.

"Read it."

I open it. It's a handwritten letter, dated November 30, 1994. Almost exactly six years ago. It's written in scrawled blue ink that has smudged in places. The paper is crinkled, a sign of being well read, and it's signed "Anthony." I know without inquiry that its author is Anthony Sabe— the *real* Anthony Sabe, not the boy who lived with me all those months, but Anthony Sabe, the lover of Robert Riley, who'd died of AIDS. And it was written only about a month before his death.

Dear Brian,

I've read your letter over and over again. I have it beside me, where I can see it. Thank you for it.

You have your whole life ahead of you, Brian. Someday you will be free and I hope you will remember all I've told you. Don't set limitations on yourself, or on those you love, because you're always going to surpass them. Don't let others tell you how or what you're supposed to be. Be true to yourself and to nobody else. Be who you are.

*There are not enough words to describe how we are to be fully
human, Brian. Remember that, and you will always be free.*

Anthony

I look up at him. I recognize the words. He had spoken them to me,
that first day, on Ninth Avenue, when my heart had first melted toward
him. I know right away they're words he's memorized, words he lives
by, words he repeats to himself every day.

"I wrote to him from prison," Brian Murphy explains, looking again
out over the waves. "I wrote to him to ask his forgiveness. For killing
Robert. For all I'd done that night." His voice tightens. "That horrible
night."

"And . . . he did? He forgave you?"

"Yes. *He forgave me.*" The tears are silently running down his
cheeks. "We wrote back and forth for a few months." His voice trails
off. "Then he died, too."

I try to focus my gaze on him but find it difficult. I've known the
truth ever since my trip to Hartford, but now, facing him, hearing him
speak it is devastating. His confession keeps coming back to me. *"I
tackled him to the ground. I punched him in the head and told him to
shut up."*

"Anthony Sabe forgave you," I repeat, more to myself than to him.

He looks at me boldly. "Is that such a radical notion for you, Jeff?
Yes, he forgave me for killing his lover. For taking the one man he'd ever
loved, the one man he'd hoped to spend the rest of his life with, the one
man who should have been there, taking care of him as he grew sick and
died." His jaw quivers as the tears come harder and faster. *"He forgave
me.* And he left me these words, the words that finally gave me the
courage to face who I am, *what* I am, and why I did what I did."

I can't say anything.

"And you can tell Mrs. Riley he forgave her, too."

He takes the letter from my hand and replaces it in his backpack.

"It was always here, Jeff," he says, a little bitterly. "You could have
found it anytime. Just unzipped my backpack while I slept."

I've started to cry, too. "Please. You've got to understand that I only
wanted to find out the truth because I cared about you."

He shrugs. "Maybe, in the beginning. But I became a story to you.
An investigation that got your blood pumping again after so long."

"No, Anth—no." I can't talk. I can't make words.

He looks at me with hard eyes. "Aren't you pleased with yourself? You took my challenge and you met it. You're still the same old good reporter you've always been. Isn't that what you wanted? You finally know the truth."

"No," I say. "I don't know the truth. There's still so much I don't know."

"What details are left outstanding?" he asks, a sarcastic, angry kid I don't recognize. "What more do you still want to know?"

"Please," I say, trying to take his hands, but he pulls back.

"*Twelve years*, Jeff. Twelve years I sat in prison. Do you know how *long* that is? What were you doing for those twelve years, Jeff? It encompasses your whole time with Lloyd, doesn't it? In those twelve years, you met Javitz, you loved him, and he died. All the while I sat in prison."

I just stare at him, unable to speak.

"And yet it's no time at all, really, not when you figure Robert's never coming back. But it was long enough for me to think about why I was there. Why my youth had been taken from me. No—why I'd thrown it away. Why I had no family, no true friends."

He picks up a stone and tosses it out onto the waves. "And I came to accept the fact that what they'd implied about me in court was true. I was homosexual. I was acting out my repressed feelings when I went with Frankie and the others down to the Chez Est to beat up gay guys."

I seize a thought. "It was *Frankie* who was the ringleader. *He* was the instigator."

"If you need to believe that, Jeff, go ahead." He smiles sadly. "Sure, Frankie was the one we all looked up to. He was the coolest. But I can't back off from my own responsibility. I was there. I could've said no. I could've tried to stop it. But it was me who tackled Riley. I got him down on the ground so Frankie could hit him with the log. And not just Riley, either, Jeff. There were other guys I tackled, punched, beat up. *Gay* guys, Jeff. Like you." He pauses. "Like me."

It's almost too much to listen to. I make a sound in my throat and turn away.

"Sitting there in prison, I thought over and over again about how Frankie had gone upstairs with Riley, and I couldn't deny what had been going through my mind as they were up there. That I *wished it was me*. That I wished it had been *me* who Riley had asked to go upstairs with him. I knew what happened up there. Frankie later tried to make it seem as if Riley had just made a pass, but I knew there was more. Frankie was hiding his own truth, though I doubt he admits it, even now. But the moment I acknowledged to myself that I wished it had been *me* that Riley took upstairs, everything became clear."

I look at him. "How did you ever . . . I mean . . . how could you . . . in prison?"

He shrugs. "It's surprising what you can find in the prison library. I began reading articles. Watching television. Remember that degree I told you I got? I got it in prison. See, I was determined not to sink to the depths that I saw all around me. I tried to isolate from the bad stuff as best I could. I learned to defend myself. I *had* to, Jeff. I was *sixteen* when I was locked up. *Sixteen.*" He pauses, looking at me. "Fresh meat. Chicken."

I make another sound in my throat.

He looks down at his feet, scuffing his shoes in the sand. "I worked out at the prison gym, for hours at a time every single day. I made myself *strong*. I got involved in none of the bullshit of prison life." He looks up at me. "See, I was *remaking* myself, Jeff. I was focused on one thing and one thing only: on getting *out*. I literally counted down the days until I could be free, until I could restart my life. I made a calendar, little boxes representing all four thousand-plus days of my confinement, and every day I'd check them off, one by one. Finally it got so that I'd checked off more boxes than were left, and I still remember crossing off the last one. That's when I knew Brian Murphy was gone, and that Anthony Sabe lived."

"It was your parole officer," I manage to say. "That's where you disappeared to once a week."

He nods. "Very good, Jeff. Yes, I reported in once a week to the parole board in Hartford. I'd sleep the night in the bus station. I never missed one appointment. I was determined to finally get a clean slate. And this fall I was finally free. The year was up. I'd done my time. The whole thing was over."

"But you had to travel so far," I say. "First from New York, then from Boston. Why did you go so far away when you had to check in once a week in Connecticut?"

He lifts his eyebrows. "Didn't you talk to any of the gay activists in the case, Jeff?"

My face betrays that I have.

"I thought so. Then I'm sure you found out how they protested my release. Surely you read the things they said about me, that I should have gotten the same sentence that Frankie got, but that the judge went easy on me because I was a privileged white boy. They hate me, Jeff. No, there was no way I could have stayed in Connecticut."

"But your mother . . ."

Only for a second does any surprise register on his face. Then he smiles. "Well, very, *very* good, Jeff. I *am* impressed. You managed to talk with my mother. That will be a great addition to your story." He laughs. "Well, then you know I was hardly privileged, and you can maybe also figure out the *other* reason I didn't want to stay in Connecticut. My mother has no use for a gay son. She said I must have been raped in prison and brainwashed. She said she'd rather have a murderer for a son than a queer. Yes, she actually said those words."

Astrid Murphy's face is in front of me. *"Is it any wonder Brian's messed up? Become this—thing?"*

He's looking at me. "My mother always contended that Riley simply got what he deserved, trying to pick up two underage boys."

I put my hands to the sides of my head, staggered by the onslaught of information. I feel weak, as if the wind that whips down the beach will simply knock me over face first into the sand.

The images begin flooding through my mind: Anthony—*Brian*—in New Orleans, in Montreal, in Palm Springs, in my arms, in my bed, looking over my shoulder wistfully at my drawer full of gay trinkets and mementos.

Sitting there across from me that first morning at the Chelsea bistro, excited about blueberry pancakes and the glitter on the face of the waiter.

"So what do you find so fascinationg about gay culture?"

"Everything. I never imagined there was so much going on."

And then on the monorail at Disney World, his pit stains showing on his red shirt, which he'd insisted on wearing *so that he could be identified as gay.*

"Jeff, I mean it. I owe all of this to you. And I don't just mean you paying for my plane ticket. I mean, all of it. My whole life. My whole gay life."

I'm overcome. "Did you *ever* plan on confiding in me?"

He looks away. "I thought maybe . . . maybe after it was all over. When I didn't have to report to the parole board anymore. When I was finally free."

"If you had trusted me earlier . . ."

He spins on me. "Why should I have trusted you, Jeff? Any of you? Those shouts from the gay activists standing outside the courthouse still ring in my ears. And you and Henry and Brent—don't you remember what you called Matthew Shepard's killers? Fucking self-repressed, self-loathing closet cases." His eyes are blazing. "You called them *scum*. Brent said they should have been killed the same way they killed Matthew. Beaten and tied to a fence and left to die in the cold."

"But we disagreed with him," I defend myself. "Henry and I both."

He closes his eyes. "Don't you see, Jeff? A part of me felt Brent was *right*. That's what was so bizarre about all of it. I *agreed* with him. I *should've* been put to death! Or rather, Brian Murphy should have." He opens his eyes. "You see, I had become somebody new. I was *gay*. And a *part* of all the gay people around me. The tribe. The extended family you taught me about. I was *part* of something for the first time in my life. I loved you all. Even Brent."

"If you had only told me—"

"You still don't get it, Jeff. Part of me was *glad* you felt the way you did. It was the way I wished I could be, self-righteously hating gay bashers. That way I would really, truly be gay, *really* be a part of all of you. To tell you about my past would have allowed Brian Murphy to live again. And you wouldn't have liked Brian Murphy very much."

"You don't know that."

"Come on, Jeff. I remember what you said." He looks at me. "I'll quote you. *'The bottom line is, they killed one of us. I suppose I wouldn't have been sorry to see them fry.'* " He narrows his eyes, studying my reaction. "Isn't that it, Jeff? Isn't that what you said?"

My words, back at me. I feel almost as if I might faint. "Yes," I admit. "That's what I said."

"And do you still feel the same way?" He draws closer to me. I can smell the soap on his skin, the leather of his coat. "Be honest with me, Jeff. Do you still feel the same way?"

New images begin assaulting me.

Mrs. Riley in her chair, staring out into her garden and calling her dead son's name.

Cynthia Cassell sitting across from me: "Some guy's bludgeoned to death in his own home, and the killers are kids from a Catholic school, and all these church leaders come out to say what good boys these two really are, with no mention of the dead fag. Well, that just rubbed a lot of us the wrong way."

Brian sitting there reading a *Far Side* comic book while Ortiz went with Riley upstairs. *"We were hesitant about ripping the guy off because we thought he was kind of cool. But since we were already there, we decided to go ahead with it."*

My eyes flicker over to the man standing in front of me, the man whose body I've explored every inch with my tongue, who once sang a silly love song to me in a moment of spontaneous joy.

"Frankie told me to tape his mouth and I did. I got blood on my jean jacket as I was doing it. Frankie picked up the log and hit him one more time in the head. The guy shook and made a noise. While we were driving away we talked about if the guy was dead or not. We decided to turn around and make sure."

"Well, Jeff?" he asks. "The last time you saw me, you insisted that no matter what, you *did* love me. Knowing what you know now, do you still feel the same?"

I look at him. "I don't know," I say honestly.

He smiles. "If you had said anything else, I wouldn't have believed you." He looks away. "There was a time when I allowed myself to dream. To imagine that I might have a life with you. That you could love me the way you love Lloyd, that the two of us could build a life together, a home."

I take a step closer to him. "I *did* care—I *do* . . ."

"If nothing else, Jeff," he implores, "please be honest with me."

I can't speak.

"What I want," he says, "what I think everyone wants, is what I've seen between you and Lloyd. Two people trying to work out a life together. Struggling and accommodating and making *dreams* actually happen."

"You'll find it someday," I manage to say, my voice cracking.

He shakes his head. "I'm not so sure. I don't think it's possible for me, with you or anyone else." He smiles tightly. "Why should it be? Why should I have what I took away from Robert and Anthony?"

I have no reply for that.

"Good-bye, Jeff," he says softly.

"Where are you going?" I ask. "Will you remain in Provincetown?"

He smiles, looking up at the sky. "I can go anywhere now," he tells me.

I watch him walk off down the beach until he's nothing more than a tiny speck, the waves eager to lick away his footsteps, leaving no sign, no trace, that he was ever here.

A Week Later,
Boston, The Westin Hotel

Henry

I know he makes his way through here every evening on his way home, and I'm counting on his adherence to routine. Sure, he might've had an appointment, or stopped off for dinner, but I trust that I'll see him. *If it's meant to be,* Lloyd said, *he'll be there.* And I believe strongly it's meant to be.

See, I want to surprise him. I want to be standing here with this big array of balloons, looking like some geek from the Publishers Clearing House Sweepstakes waiting to surprise the big-money winner. But there's no cash prize tucked inside my pocket, just the thirty balloons I hold in my right hand. The yellow ones are emblazoned with *HAPPY BIRTHDAY;* the pink ones read, *YOU LOOK MAH-VELOUS.*

I check my watch. It's a quarter after six. He usually passes through here between six-fifteen and six-thirty. I find a spot near the escalator and stand with my balloons. People passing me either smile or completely avoid my eyes. That's what happens when you let yourself look like a fool.

Did I mention I'm wearing a clown suit? And a putty nose? And an enormous wide-brimmed pink hat? Well, I am.

Finally, I spot him. I honk the horn that's strapped to my belt.

"Shane!" I call. "Happy Birthday!"

He approaches me warily.

"Happy Birthday to you!" I sing. "Happy Birthday to you! Happy Birthday dear Shaaaaaaaane! Happy Birthday to you!!!"

His face reddens. Do you know how delightful it is to see Shane embarrassed by *someone else's* antics for a change?

"Henry?" he asks, peering in at me past the red nose and white makeup. "Is that you?"

"In the clown flesh!" I say, honking my horn again. I thrust the balloons at him. "Take 'em, sweetheart! They're yours!"

He just looks up at them in disbelief. Several passersby stop to wish him happy birthday.

"And many moooooooore!" I sing.

Shane looks down at me with a crooked smile on his face, folding his arms over his chest.

"Henry," he says, "today is *not* my birthday. My birthday was *months* ago."

I grin. "Figured that would be the case. The odds were stacked against it being today. Actually, about three-hundred-sixty-four to one that I'd get it wrong." I draw in close to him. "But I've known you almost a year now and I never knew the actual date. You never told me and I never asked." I pause, my voice going serious. "I'm sorry about that."

Shane's eyes suddenly grow moist. "Henry. Why did you do this?"

I place my putty nose against his. "Because friends celebrate each other's birthdays. And because I figured I'd missed yours. So I wanted to celebrate it tonight."

He's staggered. He can't speak. Some kid walking by with earphones hoots, "Hey, happy B-day, dude!"

Shane gives a little laugh. "Henry, I'm . . . overwhelmed."

"See?" I slap my knee with my free hand, delighted my idea has worked so well. "You're not the only one who can come up with a gimmick." I grin, my big clown mouth stretching across my face. "Got you to notice me, didn't I?"

He's shaking his head, his eyes locked on to mine. "You went to all this trouble . . . just because . . ."

I touch his face with my polka-dotted clown mitt. "Because I thought maybe you'd give me another chance."

A mischievous smile slips across his face. "Wanta go back to my place and fool around?"

"Yeah," I tell him. "Right after I make you a fabulous birthday dinner."

"Well," he says, easing back into his cocky old self again, "make sure you scrape that paint off your face. I'm not getting pancake on *my* tongue."

"You got it, buckaroo. I'll run back home, take a quick shower, and pick up the wine and the groceries. Give me half an hour. Forty minutes, tops."

Shane twinkles, heading toward the escalator. "The clock's ticking," he says.

"Hey!" I call. "These are *yours.*"

I hand him the balloons. He takes them and then impulsively leans forward, kissing me on the mouth. "Hell," he says, laughing. "A little pancake never hurt anyone."

I'm still laughing when I head back out through the mall and into the skywalk.

That's when I spot Jeff coming toward me.

I could, of course, just let him pass. He'll never know it's me under the clown suit. I've gotten so accustomed to dodging Jeff whenever I see him that it almost comes automatically now.

I'll just let him pass by. I'll be late to Shane's if I dawdle, anyway.

But I can't. I can't let him just walk by me. If I'd been planning for days how to make things right with Shane, I've been thinking as much about Jeff. About the friendship I treasured so much and then pushed away.

I once asked all of you not to judge him, to hear him out, to see him in his entirety. I asked you to give him a chance, but I did exactly the opposite. For the past few days I've been thinking about it all. About the way we often blame other people for the very things we do ourselves. About how much I've missed Jeff, whether I've allowed myself to admit it or not.

"Jeff," I say.

He appears startled, glancing over at the funny-looking clown with big, floppy feet calling his name.

"It's me," I say. "Henry."

He approaches me, a smile on his face. "Dare I ask? A client with a Bozo fetish?"

I laugh. "No. I just surprised Shane with balloons. For his birthday."

"That was sweet of you."

I shrug. "I'm trying." I pause significantly. "How have you been, Jeff?"

His eyes wander away. "Well, it's kind of hard to say."

"Look, Jeff, I know we've been distant. I know we've had some harsh words between us. But I also know you've been really struggling about your feelings for Lloyd and Anthony. I know it's not been an easy time."

He raises his eyebrows. "You're right. Easy it hasn't been."

"I just want you to know . . . that I care. About you, I mean. And if you ever want to get together and talk—"

Jeff smiles. "Henry, are you suggesting we might be friends again?"

I look at him. *Yes.* Yes, I am. I am indeed suggesting we be friends. *Sisters,* the way we once were, or claimed ourselves to be. For the first time, I feel as if I can honestly, truly be *friends* with Jeff. I'm suddenly hit with a freight train of memories, from that first night on the dance floor to working out with him in the gym to him telling me that I have so much to offer and to stop selling myself short. I had blocked out all that was good, refusing to remember it. I was *terrified* of it, really. Terrified of remembering that it was Jeff who was the first person in my life to tell me I could be anything I wanted to be.

"Jeff, I was wrong," I blurt. "You *can* be a good friend. I'm sorry I said what I did."

He shakes his head. "No, you were right, Henry. I haven't always been the best friend I could have been."

I look him deep in the eyes. "Well, maybe we can both do better from now on. I want to *really* be friends with you, Jeff, with all that real friendship is supposed to mean." I hesitate, knowing how guarded he can be, but I decide to plunge on. "I know how you took care of Javitz, how you were there for him. How awesome that must have been. You were there for him in a way that defines what friendship is all about. What an honor that must have been. For both of you."

Jeff seems moved by this little speech. I see the moisture well in his eyes.

"That's what I want, too, Jeff. I want us to be real with each other. I know you think you've shared stuff with me, confided in me, but you've always been so guarded, Jeff. You've held back when it got too deep. You wouldn't admit when you felt vulnerable, when you felt weak."

"You're right," he admits. "I've drawn a line and lived pretty insistently behind it."

"Why, Jeff? Because you didn't trust me?"

He can't seem to hold back the tears. "It was never about that, buddy. Never about trust. I've trusted you more than I have anyone since Javitz."

"Then what was it?"

He's crying now. *Jeff is actually crying.*

"I thought you wouldn't like me if I were weak," he manages to say. "If I wasn't the hero, the mentor, the know-it-all."

"Oh, Jeff . . ."

I put my arms around him, wrapping his torso in my puffy sleeves and polka-dotted clown mitt hands.

"You've taught me so much," I tell him. "Now let me use it."

He pulls back a little to look me in the eyes. "Javitz always said eventually the student teaches the teacher."

"You've been an excellent teacher. Now be my friend."

He gives me a smile. "I'm sorry, Henry. Sorry for everything."

"Jeff, there's no reason to apologize. I've been caught up in my own struggle, my own drama. I let myself forget how you've been there for me."

He's shaking his head. "I wasn't always as sensitive as I could have been."

"As if any of us are." I smile wryly. "Why do you think I'm trying to make things right with Shane?"

Jeff is clearly touched. "Henry, I would *love* to be friends with you again. I've missed you so much, buddy."

We hug. "I want to be the kind of friend Javitz was," I tell him. "I know I can never replace him, but I want it honest like that. Real. Where you *know* things about each other. Where you trust each other completely."

"You know an awful lot about me, Henry," Jeff says. "Sometimes more than I know myself."

It means so much to hear him say that. "Thank you Jeff," I tell him. "Thank you."

He smiles. The smile bubbles up into laughter as he takes a step back from me. "Henry," he says, "as poignant as all of this is, you do realize that it's very difficult not to crack up looking at you standing there dressed like Ronald McDonald."

I laugh. "And if I start to blubber, I'll look like one of those crying-clown velvet paintings my aunts have hanging on their walls."

Jeff looks over at me and lifts one of my mitts to his lips. "I love you, buddy."

"I love you," I reply.

"You want to go dancing this week?"

I beam. "Yeah. I so *totally* want to go dancing."

"Alex Lauterstein is spinning at Machine on Thursday," he tells me.

"Alex Lauterstein? The hunkiest DJ on the entire planet?"

"The very same."

"Well, *of course* we have to be there," I say, grinning.

Jeff grins back. "And bring Shane," he tells me.

Shane. I realize I have to hurry. "I'm making him dinner. I have to go. . . ."

Jeff nods. "Don't keep Shane waiting. You never know what he'll do. Drop a bucket of water on your head or zap you with a stun gun."

"I'll call you tomorrow," I promise.

We embrace again. I must make quite the sight. Big old gay clown kissing all these boys in the middle of rush hour. Jeff keeps laughing as he looks back to wave as we continue in opposite directions. I'm grinning so hard myself that my painted cheeks start to hurt.

If it's meant to be, Lloyd promised, *it'll happen.*

It was meant to be.

Christmas Day, Boston

Lloyd

We chopped down the tree together, just like old times, a tall, fragrant blue spruce with some of its cones still intact. We hauled it back into the city on top of my car and then up the three flights to Jeff's apartment, where we secured it into the stand only to find its branches were much longer and heavier on one side, making it look squat, like a fat lady curtsying. Once, after we'd gotten all the ornaments attached to her body, Miss Lucy (as we dubbed the tree) toppled over, and we came running back into the room to the sound of glass breaking and aluminum beads rolling across the floor. We simply laughed, righted the poor old girl, and tied her to the wall.

Out had come the gifts: a pile for Jeff, a pile for me, a pile for Mr. Tompkins. When he was a kitten, Mr. Tompkins would climb up inside the Christmas tree, meowing through the tinsel. Now the best he can do is sit underneath beside his pile of gifts, idly knocking low-hanging ornaments with his paw. It's a game that quickly bores him, however, and with a heavy sigh, he curls up back on the couch and falls asleep.

"He seems so much more content these days," Jeff observes. "He hasn't taken off anybody's finger in *weeks.*"

I smile smugly. "Maybe he's just glad to have me back around."

Jeff wraps his arms around my waist. "He's not the only one."

We kiss. We've just returned from a day at Jeff's sister's house, where we dressed as Santa and Mrs. Claus and surprised little Jeffy with a sackful of gifts. The kid looked up shrewdly at Mrs. Claus and instantly identified her as Jeff under the wig and red lipstick. "Hey, Unca Jeff," he said. "Are you a big old *drag queen?*" We all just cracked up.

It's been a lovely day. Even Jeff's mom gave me a hug and a kiss, not to mention a gift (a flannel shirt, a size too big). I placed a call to my parents in Iowa, promising we'd visit soon. Yes, *we*. Jeff and I. Maybe in February. Jeff even got on the phone and wished them all a happy holiday. My dad said it seemed maybe I was "settling down." I said I just might be, at that.

Tonight we've planned a little gathering with Henry and Shane. Henry actually brought Shane home with him for Hanukkah, and last night he spent Christmas Eve with Shane and his mother in Portsmouth, New Hampshire. They've been together almost constantly since Henry cooked that birthday dinner. "The pasta was a little soggy," Henry admitted to me, "but everything else was tasty and firm."

It's good to see him happy and focused. Whether he and Shane will be able to make something work between them remains to be seen. Henry's been pretty fixated on muscle-boy types for a long time, and Shane shows no inclination to head to the gym. "If it's meant to happen," I've told Henry, with him finishing my sentence: "It will."

"Lloyd," Jeff says now, "before they get here, I thought we might want to open these gifts." He reaches far behind the tree and withdraws two small boxes wrapped in red cellophane, both topped with white satin bows.

"Who are they from?" I ask, but even as the words came out of my mouth, I know.

"They're from Eva," Jeff replies.

Eva. She hasn't been far from my thoughts all day. I know she's back at Nirvana, she and Candi, taking care of our houseful of guests. Two days ago, she came to me and told me she'd decided to sell me her share in Nirvana. "This isn't easy," she admitted. "But the work I need to be doing right now doesn't involve running a guest house."

"And what *is* the work you need to be doing?" I asked her.

She just smiled. "I'm finding that out, little by little, every day."

It was, in truth, what I'd been hoping for. I didn't want to lose Nirvana. There was no way the two of us could go on together, but I'd come to love the guest house and my work there. Yet is it even feasible? Could I possibly afford to buy her out? What might she ask as a price? Could this be her strategy—one last manipulation to get what she really wants? If she demands an amount she knows I can't pay, she could then buy *me* out, and keep the place all to herself. Maybe sell it later for an enormous profit.

I remember looking at her as she told me of her decision. She seemed so different. For the first time in months, I felt inclined to trust her words, not second-guess her motives. Part of it's simply knowing she's in therapy, working on her stuff—the "work she needs to be doing." Part of it's Candi: underneath her tough exterior, she's a good woman, loyal—and introspective, too, if she was the force behind Eva's finally seeing a therapist. In fact, we've all spent so much time debating whether or not Eva is really a lesbian that we've overlooked the real significance of the relationship. It's the first time in her life that Eva has formed a bond with another woman. That's progress. That's breaking out of the pathology. No matter what she turns out to be, no matter the truth of her relationship with Candi, she's turned some kind of corner.

But there's yet another reason Eva seems different to me. I've had time to digest what she said, to live with it. It *does* take two to tango, and I can see quite plainly now my own part in the dance. "Darling," Javitz used to say, "the first step toward enlightenment is recognizing our own accountability."

"Eva," I said to her, "I want you to know that I'm sorry, too."

She looked at me.

"For everything and anything," I added.

"Thank you, Lloyd," she said simply.

I look down now at the gifts in Jeff's hands. "How did you get these?" I ask.

"She gave them to Shane, who brought them by."

I look up into Jeff's eyes. "I have to admit I'm a little scared to open it."

He smiles. "I'll go first." He tears off the cellophane and opens the small cardboard box. He lifts out a chrome-framed photograph, taken a year ago in the snow: Jeff and I with our arms around each other's shoulders. I can hear Eva's voice: *"Say, 'If you please, pass the cheese!' "* We look a little pained staring into her lens, but also infinitely younger—evidence of just how much you go through in the course of one year.

"Open yours, Lloyd," Jeff says.

I brace myself. Will it be another expensive gift? An intimate item of Steven's? But even as I peel the cellophane wrapping from the box, I know it won't be. I let out a little sound when I recognize it. It's the little wooden Buddha we found under the couch at Nirvana so long ago. How often I'd wondered where he went. He's painstakingly painted, smiling serenely.

"Oh, Jeff," I say, sitting down on the couch, the Buddha staring up at me.

He looks down at my gift. "Did she paint that? Do it herself?"

I keep looking at the Buddha, and he keeps looking at me. "Yes," I say. "I'm sure she did."

Jeff sits down beside me. "Call her, Lloyd," he urges.

I sigh. I reach over and pick up the phone, pressing in the numbers for Nirvana. I have no idea what I'll say: *Thanks? Merry Christmas? Let's rethink everything?*

I get the machine. "Eva," I say, "I just wanted to tell you that the Buddha is lovely. It's—just wonderful. Thank you. It means—a great deal." I realize I'm crying. I can't even say Merry Christmas. I hang up the phone.

Jeff takes me in his arms.

Jeff

"It's okay," I tell Lloyd. "Go ahead and cry."

"I think she finally gets it," he says, wiping his nose. "And finally, I do, too."

I hope so, but I remain just a tiny bit suspicious. True, my heart has softened toward Eva. Her gift to me was symbolic, I think, recognizing—even honoring—the relationship between Lloyd and me. She would never have given such a gift a year ago. And I can't deny that I remain grateful for the help she extended to Anthony. But at what cost, I still wonder? Is she now as entangled in Anthony's life as she once was in Lloyd's? Is that why she can talk of selling Nirvana? Has she found a new male host body off of which to leech?

Okay, I know that sounds way hard. And I know Eva has been making a great show of her newfound lesbianism. I'm just *cautious;* that's all. Maybe a little cynical. It's in my nature to be cynical—as you've probably detected by now. It's just hard for me to believe that Eva Horner can ever *give* without demanding *more* in exchange.

"What's been most difficult for me," Lloyd is saying, "has been realizing just how *unaware* I was of my *own* part in all this. I always think I'm so self-aware, so conscious."

Now *that* much I agree with. It's not just Eva who bears responsibility for their breakup. For breakup is what it was, just as the split between Anthony and me was a breakup. And I know damn well that I shoulder *my* share of the responsibility for that.

Anthony. I just can't bring myself to call him Brian. Brian Murphy remains seventeen years old in my mind, a villainous jock, the kind I myself knew in high school, the kind I was only too glad to see caught and punished, sent away for life. Anthony Sabe was another person: just turned thirty, a boy-man without a cruel thought in his head, a gentle soul who'd somehow survived living among wolves. Lloyd told me this morning that Anthony's little cottage in Provincetown is now empty. Where has he gone?

Just as I'm sure Eva has never been far from Lloyd's thoughts these past few days, so too has Anthony always been close at hand for me. And just as Lloyd struggles with his own accountability, I've wrestled with my own. If I *had* trusted Anthony, allowed him to tell me the truth in his own time, might things have been different? Might he still be here?

But if he were, would Lloyd and I have put up this Christmas tree together? Would we now be nestled together on this couch, Mr. Tompkins purring between us?

And, in truth, Anthony's question still resonates for me without a satisfactory answer: *"Knowing what you know, do you still feel the same for me?"*

Do I really love so conditionally? I lean back into the cushions of the couch, suddenly overtaken by sadness. How had it been that Javitz had been able to love without conditions?

Lloyd's looking at me. He can read my thoughts. But you know that by now.

"We've made Javitz into a god," he tells me, "when he was a man. Just like us."

I sigh. "Javitz wouldn't have made a mess of things like we have. Anthony, Eva, Henry . . . and ourselves, Lloyd. We still don't know what we are to each other."

"Of course we know, Jeff." He smiles. "We know very well what we are to each other. We love each other. We are living our lives together— as crazy as those lives sometimes are."

I think of Anthony's words: *"What I want is what I've seen between you and Lloyd. Two people trying to work out a life together. Struggling and accommodating and making dreams actually happen."*

Lloyd runs a hand through my hair. "I think we've been too hard on ourselves at times, Jeff. Look, we fuck up. We're sometimes stubborn and insensitive. But generally we do the best we can. We want to do the right thing. When we mess up, we try to put things right."

I shrug. "Maybe you ought to ask Anthony if he feels I put things right."

out process, but let
remember. Process
ou make mistakes
n you move on to
re I'm going with
an *if* but a *when*—
process. You make

off dreamily past

mistakes," he says
two other people
takes around me.

just the pot talk-
maybe you *don't*
g with you, shar-
ing passion. Like
But still, there are
very difficult for
ther, closing your

, thick hair. "As
ate the family we
unique value of
found that one
ther. Sometimes I
is or that drama.
Cherish what you
is what we all,
have been extra-
has it ever kept

res.
lets out one of
the dick dock
do you shut this

, shaking my head. "You

thinking.
ad of yours?"
He reaches down into his
He extracts a video.

sure . . ."
him, Jeff. *Hear* him. This
He pauses. "But there's
g I didn't know was on

es on the TV. And there's
he deck. Wonder of won-
se in paroxyms of grief. I
again. How young we all
Did Lloyd ever really have

ore," Lloyd assures me be-
corded it after we went to

avitz flickers back onto the
n, looking directly into the
gasp, pulling back a little.
aught me, who'd loved me,
e is: all big brown eyes and
.

voice that greeted us every
out how to work this damn
s Super-8." He laughs, that
arbage disposal.

f to bed," Javitz is saying.
n you'll see this. Maybe to-
He takes a drag on his ciga-
were talking tonight about
t. But we *do* get onto these
them to death or until one of
"

He laughs once more.

"Anyway, *process*. I said a lot of things tonight a
me just add one more. Something I want you to
means making mistakes. That's the whole point.
and you learn and you do your best to fix them, th
make more mistakes." His eyes twinkle. "Get wh
this? Sure, you do. When I get sick—because it's not
you *will* make mistakes. That's how it goes. That's
mistakes and you fix them and you move on."

He inhales again on his cigarette, his eyes lookin
the camera.

"I don't want you wasting time worrying over
firmly. "Listen to me when I tell you this. There aren
in the whole entire world I'd ever trust to make m
You two are my heart and my soul."

I feel the tears come.

"But you know all that." He sighs. "I suppose it'
ing. But there's something else, darlings. Something
know." He seems to hesitate before continuing. "Be
ing my life with you, has given me great and abi
tonight. Like so many nights." His voice thickens. "
times, after such moments of passion, when it can b
me to watch the two of you stagger off to bed tog
door behind you, while I go back to my room, alone.

Lloyd squeezes my hand.

"You see?" Javitz runs his hand through his lon
much as I treasure our friendship, as much as I celeb
have created, as much as I believe in the worth and t
what the three of us mean to each other, I have nev
man in my life the way the two of you have found tog
watch the two of you spin your wheels, caught up in t
I want to bop your heads together. It's all so fleeting.
have together. It is *precious*. So goddamn *precious*.
each one of us, ultimately searches for in this life. Yo
ordinarily generous in allowing me into your lives. B
you from going deeper between yourselves? I wonder.

He exhales smoke, momentarily obscuring his feat

"And maybe I'm just stoned and a little horny." H
his long, audacious sighs. "Guess I'll be heading out
now." He cackles, leaning in toward the camera. "Ho
damn thing off?"

Then blackness.

He's gone.

We sit there in complete silence for several minutes. I wipe the tears off my face with the sleeve of my sweater.

"He forgives me for not being there," I finally manage to say. "*He forgives me. He already knew we'd make mistakes.*"

"You *were* there, Jeff." Lloyd puts his arm around me. "And you have continued to be there. We've both spent too much time imagining Javitz laughing at our attempts to carry on. But he hasn't been laughing. We've made our mistakes and we've learned and we've gone on." He smiles. "I venture to think Javitz has actually been pretty proud of us."

I think of Henry. "You've taught me so much," he said. "Now let me use it."

"Maybe," I say, "maybe you're right. Maybe I *have* managed, somehow amid all the craziness, to pass on what Javitz taught. Maybe I haven't been such a fraud after all."

"I think that's right, Cat. I think you've done a pretty good job."

I look at him. "Then why has it been so hard for the two of us to come together?"

Lloyd sighs. "I think we fell back into an old pattern. You and I never had much experience at just being a couple. There was always Javitz. He was right. As wonderful and enriching as our relationship with him was, Javitz was also our buffer. Our protection against our own intimacy ever getting too deep."

I look back at the darkened television screen. "He wanted so much what we had," I say softly. "And he died without ever finding it."

Lloyd nods his head. "And I think once Javitz was gone, you and I didn't know quite what to do with each other. How to be together. How to *be*, period. So we drifted apart."

I smile wanly. "It makes me think of parents who lose a child. You'd think it would draw them closer, but it often ends up driving them apart."

"Exactly," Lloyd says. "And we never had any role models. There aren't a lot of examples of relationships outside the heterosexual norm that we could follow. So, when we reconnected, without even thinking about it, we began setting up the old triangular structure, the only one we knew. I brought in Eva and you brought in Anthony. Because we somehow believed that we needed a third person from which to bounce—or deflect—our intimacy with each other."

I cover my face with my hands. He's right. He's dead-on right.

"I don't want to be afraid of making commitments anymore," Lloyd says. "You and I—we have our work cut out for us."

"I'm willing to give it a shot," I tell him.

He takes my hands. "We make mistakes, we learn, and we move on to make more."

"Does there ever come a time when the mistakes stop?" I ask, looking at him. "Or at least, become fewer and fewer?"

Lloyd smiles at me. "I think they already have."

My eyes find his. "I love you, Lloyd."

"I love you, Jeff. I never want to spend a Christmas without you."

We kiss.

"Let's watch the video again," I say.

Lloyd hits REWIND on the remote. We sit through it once more in each other's arms.

"I don't ever want to stop missing him," I say when it's all over.

Lloyd smiles. "I don't think that's possible."

The doorbell rings. It's Shane and Henry. They're bearing gifts. Ahead of them trots Clara, all pop-eyed at the sight of Mr. Tompkins, who could easily make two of her. They study each other for a moment, then decide on bemused tolerance as the best strategy for coexistence.

"We could take a lesson from them, huh, Jeff?" Shane asks quietly as Henry and Lloyd head into the kitchen.

"Are you suggesting that *you and I* might be friends, *too,* Shane?"

"Sure," he says. "Want to shake on it?"

I level my eyes at him. "If you have anything in your palm or up your sleeve, buddy boy, I'm sticking you ass-first on top of the tree in place of the star."

Shane grins broadly. "No more gimmicks from me, Jeffy-poo. Cross my heart." He holds out his hands to show he's clean. "Ah, the hell with a handshake." He wraps his long arms around me. It's a real hug. I hug him back.

"You see what I was saying about the Christmas spirit, Henry?" Lloyd says as they come out of the kitchen. "You never know what miracles it may bring about."

They've made some hot cider spiked with rum. Shane lifts a glass to propose a toast. "God bless us, everyone!" he says. "Except Miss Izzy, who I still haven't forgiven for Halloween."

All in all, it's a very good night.

New Year's Eve, Provincetown

Henry

"Everybody had it wrong last New Year's," I'm insisting. "That wasn't the *real* start to the twenty-first century. *This* year is."

Jeff's zipping up his leather jacket to just under his chin. He gives me one of his looks, all eyes and attitude. "Okay, Henry, and the significance of that little factoid *is* . . . ?"

Shane pats my shoulder. "Henry just likes to keep the record straight." He snorts. "So to speak."

"I suspect," Lloyd says, pulling on his gloves, "that Henry actually has a point he wants to make here."

"*Thank you,*" I say, folding my arms over my chest. "The point seems obvious to me. We all thought we were starting new lives last year, just in time for the new millennium. Such perfect synchronicity— or so we thought. Then we went and fucked everything up."

I look around the room at the three of them. Nobody disagrees. How could they?

"But *this* is the new millennium! Starting *tonight!* We can start *all over* and do things better this time. Think about it, you guys. How many second chances do we get in life?"

There are nods all around. I feel pretty pleased with myself. Henry Weiner puts it all in perspective yet again.

I button up my coat and wrap a scarf around my neck. It's cold outside. One by one we head out into the icy wind that's whipping in from the bay. Of course, we could be in Miami tonight—Shane had originally bought tickets and everything—but I've got a feeling that traipsing around the country isn't going to be as easy as it once was. I've got some new responsibilities now, starting with a full house of guests at Nirvana, which means we have to get up very early to cook our special New Year's breakfast for everybody. "Just until midnight," Lloyd told us all. "That's as late as we're staying out."

Yes, you guessed it: I'm working with Lloyd now. Nirvana general manager and resident sex worker. That second part isn't official, of course, but I've already begun planning a series of sacred-sex workshops that Lloyd will advertise on Nirvana's Web site. I'm flying out to San Francisco next week to go through the training seminars; I'm thinking also of getting my license as a massage therapist. It's a whole new life, a whole new career—one that I'm *good* at, one that I love—so much different from sitting in my cubicle shuffling papers.

Of course, my parents freaked when I told them I'd quit my job, but I'm not living my life for them. Not anymore. The only person I'm living my life for now is *me*. Maybe the money won't be as good, but I've learned over this past year that it's not what you get in life that makes you happy, it's what you *give*. I know that sounds hokey, a tired old bromide, but it's true. I think most people, if asked to make a choice between being happy or being rich, would choose happy.

And maybe—just maybe—I can have both. The happy *and* the rich. We'll see. Hank just set up a brand-new Web site, and in one week it's gotten almost a thousand hits. *A thousand!*

So things look good. Check in with me in a couple of months. I'll let you know.

Oh, and have you noticed? None of us is twisted tonight. Nobody's rolling. Now, don't draw too many conclusions from that. It's not like we've sworn off drugs or that we're turning into moralistic prigs—I mean, there's nothing like one little bump of X to occasionally break the ice—but tonight, we all decided we wanted to play sober. Sure, the fact that we have to get up early in the morning has something to do with it, but we all agreed that this time we wanted to enter the new year with a clear and conscious mind.

"You *do* know what tonight is, don't you?" Shane is suddenly whispering in my ear. "I mean *besides* the real start of the new millennium."

"No, what?" I ask, blinking my eyes as I look over at him.

He pouts. "Well, if you don't remember . . ."

I look over at Jeff and wink. He winks back, letting me know he's arranged for everything. We've reached the center of town now, walking up the red carpet to the Crown and Anchor. Suddenly an overhead spotlight swings down, catching Shane in its glare.

"What the . . . ?" Shane gasps.

Two hunky barechested boys in leopard-print sarongs brave the cold to hurry down the carpet toward Shane, each bearing a dozen red roses. They kiss him and fuss over him before thrusting the roses into his hands and hurrying back inside.

"Happy anniversary," I tell Shane.

"You *did* remember," he says.

Okay, so I know some of you may be skeptical. You're thinking it will never work between Shane and me. You're thinking that a guy so into how he looks (me) would never date a guy who doesn't give a shit (Shane). While I'll admit I haven't given up hope that I'll get Shane to the gym, I'll tell you this much: one more thing I learned this year is that it's what's *inside* that counts. One more soggy old cliché, I suppose, but it's true nonetheless.

Look, I've been searching for *years* for a husband who would be devoted, constant, insightful—one who would make me laugh and, yes, make my dick hard. On every point, Shane qualifies. So I'm giving it a shot. Wish us luck, okay? If it works out between us, it gives hope to every guy out there, every guy who was once like me, standing on the sidelines, letting the world pass him by. No more of that. Henry Weiner's *living* his life.

I kiss Shane in the spotlight. Big and sloppy, the roses wedged between us.

That's when I hear the shouting.

"Perverts!" I hear. "Abominations!"

Lloyd

Jeff and I turn quickly. Across the street, watching Henry and Shane kiss, two guys and a girl stand shouting. They're late teens, maybe early twenties, and obviously drunk.

Jeff reacts. If I wasn't holding his hand, he'd have been across the street and at their throats. "This is *our* space, you fuckheads!" he yells. "Get your sorry asses out of here!"

"Jeff, don't," I plead. "It will only make things worse—"

One of the guys is defiant. He takes a few steps toward Jeff. "The Bible says homos are an abomination!"

Jeff breaks free of my grip and gets right up in his face. "Abomination! My, my, such a big word for such a little boy." He stabs the guy's chest with his finger. "But your grammar's wrong, junior. 'Homos' is plural, 'abomination' is singular. Your sentence doesn't make sense, and neither does your Bible."

"Faggot," the guy snarls.

I see Jeff's hand pull back to slug him. I'm immediately behind him, restraining him. The guy's friends are pulling him back, too. "Go on," I tell them. "Get out of here. What's the point in starting fights in the street?"

They see the wisdom of my words as a group of gay men gathers, lining the street, asking what's going on.

"Nothing," I assure them as the three punks hurry off down the street.

Henry and Shane flank Jeff. "You okay?" Henry asks.

"My Sir Galahad!" Shane gushes, kissing Jeff on the cheek.

I look at him. "Cat, you didn't need to mirror their behavior."

He sighs. "I know. It was dumb. It was just totally instinctive."

"Well, you got *me* hard," Shane says.

"You go ahead, you two," Jeff says. "I just want to calm down out here a minute."

"You sure?" Henry asks.

Jeff nods, looking over at me. I know what's going through his head. I know who he's thinking about.

After Shane and Henry have gone into the bar, I put my arms around Jeff and look into his eyes. "There's always somebody waiting to jump at us," he says to me. "Always something there to hit us over the head."

"Forget about them, Jeff."

"Like I ever could."

I look him deep in the eyes. "You need to stop blaming yourself about Anthony," I tell him. "You did what you did."

He looks up at the dark sky. Frost appears in the air as he speaks. "These idiots were just like he was," he says. "That's what he looked like, standing there harassing fags. He probably once used the same words." He sighs, resting his forehead against mine. "How dare they come after us *here?* In Provincetown? They've got the whole goddamn *world* to come after us. This is *our* space."

"Try to let it go, Jeff," I tell him. "They're not worth the trouble."

He smiles. "What would I do without you?"

"Probably get your face broken by a couple of drunken straight boys."

"Then you'd better stick around."

"I promise."

It's easier than I thought, making promises like that. Letting go of my fear of commitment wasn't the big effort I always thought it would be. Living with the fear was far more difficult. Do you have any idea how much work, how much energy, is needed to live with fear? I think Nirvana showed me that despite all my yakking about not wanting to "settle down," I really did. I wanted to find a place to be grounded, to make room for others and for myself, to become the person I really am. And that's not a person who defines himself by any fear.

"You okay to go inside now?" I ask Jeff.

He nods. We follow Shane and Henry into the club. It's already packed. I see there's some entertainment in progress, a drag queen dressed as Connie Francis commanding a little stage.

"Where the boys are," she lip syncs, *"someone waits for me . . . "* The crowd of shirtless boys on the dance floor are applauding and whistling.

Ahead of us I spot two familar faces: Drake and Ty, arms linked around each other. From the look of their glistening skin, they've been dancing a while.

"Hey," I call. "I didn't know you were coming to town."

Ty and I exchange quick kisses. I smile at Drake.

"It was completely last-minute," Ty says. "I was planning on calling you."

"Blame me," Drake says. "I talked him into it."

"We *did* call the guest house," Ty adds, "but you were booked. I talked to some guy name Hank . . . ?"

I smile. "Don't worry about it. It's just good to see you, that's all." I notice their arms are still interlocked. *"Both* of you," I add significantly.

We all smile. Jeff kisses each of them. I have to suppress a little grin, thinking of him and Drake together. Jeff notices and nudges me.

"Ladies and gentlemen," a top-hatted emcee is suddenly announcing from the stage, "for tonight's final performance, we bring you a very special duet. Together for the first time anywhere: Mr. George Michael and Miss Mae West!"

I look over at Jeff. Could it be . . . ?

Ty's mouth drops open.

Onto the little stage saunters Eva, one arm akimbo, the other pushing at her hair. But she's a different Mae this time: instead of the long, padded Victorian garb, she's wearing a black leather miniskirt, red go-go boots, and a polka-dotted bikini top. Only the wig is the same, and the voice.

420   *William J. Mann*

"Ohhhhhhh," she purrs. "I want your *sex.*"

Now from the other side of the stage bounds a very convincing George Michael, complete with sunglasses, stubble, leather jacket, guitar, and tight blue jeans. He swings his ass at the audience. I'm about to think, *Nice butt,* when I realize it's Candi.

"*Yes, it would be nice,*" George sings to Mae, "*if I could touch your body . . .*"

Mae follows up with the next line: "*Not everybody—ohhhh—has a body like meeee.*"

She shakes her breasts at the audiences. The boys whoop. And so it goes.

Thankfully, it's brief—the crowd is itching to get back to dancing—and George and Mae leave the stage amidst hoots and whistles.

I watch Eva blow a kiss to the crowd. How she loves the applause. We're scheduled to talk tomorrow. Finally, I'll know what she wants as a buy-out price. I'll learn if I'm meant to continue here with Nirvana or find yet another path somewhere else. Henry's convinced it's all going to work out: "It's *meant* to be, Lloyd; I can tell."

But I'm not so sure. I spot Eva and Candi on the side of the dance floor, accepting well-wishes from their fans.

"Jeff, I'll be right back," I tell him. He nods.

Eva spots me as I approach. "You caught our little act," she says.

"Yes," I tell her. "You were terrific." I look at Candi. "Both of you."

Candi smiles. "Thanks. I'm glad you liked it."

"In fact," I tell her, "you kind of turned me on."

She laughs. "Now, that's the ultimate compliment to any drag king." She looks at me kindly. Maybe she understands a little better now, I think. She's the one who motivated Eva into seeking therapy, after all. I can only imagine what they've been through together, what triggered Candi's insistence that Eva seek help; but maybe, now that they've been together a while, she understands my experience a little better. "Thank you, Lloyd," Candi says. "I appreciate the compliment."

We exchange smiles. Candi heads over through the crowd to fetch their coats, leaving Eva and me together. There's a moment of awkwardness. We look at each other and smile uncomfortably. "Not staying till midnight?" I ask.

"No," Eva says. "We have friends coming by."

I feel a little wistful, and I think she does, too. How far apart we've grown in the space of one year. How different, how separate are our lives.

"Eva," I tell her, "I want you to know that I'm glad—I'm proud of you—that you're doing the hard work that you are. Maybe at some point we can find a way to be friends again."

I see her eyes glisten. "Thank you, Lloyd. And I hope you know that I want only the best for you in the new year. No matter what happens between us, I want you to know that."

I stiffen. *No matter what happens?* Is she preparing me for what she has to tell me tomorrow?

Somehow, I think, she senses my apprehension. "Lloyd," she says all at once, "I want you to have Nirvana."

"Yes," I say. "I appreciate that. I guess I'm just wondering about the terms. . . ."

"Those *are* the terms, Lloyd," she says simply.

I blink. I'm not sure what she means.

She smiles. "Do you remember once how you said that life is about balance? That it's not always about what a thing is worth on paper? About not being attached?"

I'm still wary, not following her.

"I'm trying to find balance, to make things right, in so many areas of my life." She looks at me. "That's why I want you to have Nirvana. No terms. Just have it."

I'm stunned. "You mean, without any payment . . . ?"

"Oh, you've already paid, many times over." She laughs. "I guess there does need to be some exchange of money. They usually quitclaim things for a dollar, don't they?"

"A—*dollar* . . . ?"

"I think that's how it's done."

I look at her. "Eva, I'm not sure I can accept such a—a gift—"

"Please. Don't see it as a gift. See it for what it is. Something that I *need* to do."

"I don't understand."

"Listen to me, Lloyd. This is the only way I know to set things right. Let's not make a big deal about this to anybody. Let's just do it." She smiles sadly. "Yes, I do hope someday we can find a way of being friends again. But I still have a lot of work to do. I'm no saint, Lloyd. I wish I could say this comes from the sheer goodness of my heart, that I'm a new woman, totally free of all my issues, perfectly realized, completely cured. But that's not the case. A part of me wants to cling on to Nirvana, cling on to you, kick and scream and cry and make life miserable—because that's how I've always done things. I'm trying to find a way of breaking that pattern. This is a way to do that." She sighs. "I'm not making any of these decisions easily. But each time I make them, they do become less difficult."

I'm still staggered. "I—I don't know what to say."

"Then don't say anything. We'll talk tomorrow, make it all official."

So that's it. That's the end of our story together. I wish I could tell you more. I wish I could tell you what's really going on inside Eva's head—what prompted such impressive generosity, what kind of work she's doing—but I can't.

And I realize, standing here, that I'll *never* know more than I know right now. We came into each other's lives, our paths crossed, we served as catalysts for change for each other, but now it's over. I'll never know the source of Eva's pain, whether the abuse I suspect was real, or if there was something else, something I can never know. I'll never understand all her motivations, all the reasons she did what she did, what was true and what was false. That's the way it is with most people who come into our lives, isn't it? We only ever learn so much. In the end, I'm left only with what she's taught me; I only know what I've learned. I only know that this past year with her has been perhaps the most important of my life. The little Buddha is hardly her only gift to me.

Candi's returned with their coats. Impulsively I hug her, and then Eva as well. "Happy New Year," I tell both of them.

"You too, Lloyd." She pauses, withdrawing something from the pocket of her coat. "Oh, Candi, will you wait just a minute? I have to deliver this."

I watch her. She shoulders her way out onto the dance floor toward Jeff.

Jeff

Eva's heading this way. She gestures to me. I lift my eyebrows. She mouths the words: "I have something for you."

I follow her off to a spot out near the pool so we can talk. "What's going on?" I ask, looking around for Lloyd, but I can't spot him.

Eva hands me a small sealed envelope. My name is written on the front. I recognize the handwriting.

"Where—how . . . ?" I stutter.

Eva's looking up at me. "He sent it to me in a Christmas card. He asked that I give it to you tonight. He was insistent that you get it on New Year's Eve."

I stare down at it, then move my eyes over to her. "Where is he?"

She shakes her head. "I don't know, Jeff. I'm being honest with you. The postmark was from Texas. But he said he was moving on."

"And you haven't asked?"

"No," she tells me. "If he chooses to tell me where he is, that's up to him."

I study her. "You gave him money, didn't you? That's how he can afford to travel."

"He needs to be able to find himself," she says softly.

I make a little laugh in disbelief. "And you've asked for nothing in return? He's just free to—to *go?*"

Eva's eyes find mine. They're not the eyes I remember. Lloyd's told me she's been doing work, that she's trying to change, and I haven't entirely trusted it. But maybe I should. These eyes are very different from the ones I remember.

"Anthony has a chance to remake himself, to start over," she says.

"And you want to help him to do that."

She nods. "Don't you see? It's what I always tried to do, but was never successful. I don't know what Anthony's running from, but I know he's tired of running. I saw myself in Anthony. I saw someone who wanted to recreate his life, to begin again. It's what inspired me to look at myself." She pauses. "I want Anthony to succeed where I failed."

I study her some more. She's being sincere. I'm certain of it. Finally, I look into her eyes and see truth reflected back to me. I've been the one person she's never been able to fool, and it's *honesty* that I see at long last in her eyes and hear in her words.

"Maybe," I tell her, "maybe you haven't failed at that."

She gives me a small, hopeful smile. "We'll see," she says.

I embrace her. "Thank you for this," I tell her.

"Happy New Year, Jeff."

Then she's gone.

I open the note. I stand with it under a dim light, being jostled by guys too twisted to notice as they head into the men's room. I pay them no mind. The note is simple:

Jeff,

> *One year ago tonight I met you, and my life changed. I want you to know how much the past year meant to me. How much you meant, and all you gave to me. You will always be family to me.*
>   *No, more than family.*

With love,
Anthony

I look up into the crowd on the dance floor.
No, more than family.
More than the way family is defined by straights.
You can't describe it because there aren't words. You don't set limitations, because you're always surpassing them. You don't let others tell you how you're supposed to be. You're true to yourself and nobody else. You're just who you are.
"We're just who we are," I whisper, looking into the crowd.

I think of those idiots out on the street, calling us abominations. What do they know about us? What do any of those who look in from the outside know about our hearts and our minds and our souls?

We're good people. The music is mixing into a song about loving one another. Isn't that what all the songs are about? Love: finding new love, getting over love. Love, love, love. Too often have we believed the old lie that says we're bad, we're perverted, we're abominations. But those who spread the lie don't know. They don't know how we love, how we hurt, how we live.

I look out into the sea of sweaty men in front of me and I think of those gay men who recoil from this, from *any* embrace of our subculture—the ones who don't like femmy guys or show-tune queens, who turn up their noses at leathermen or circuit parties or Bette Davis imitations or anything that's simply "too gay." They carp over all that's bad, while acknowledging little of what's good. I think of the critics, forever standing on the outside, forever observing, never participating, never a part of anything. I think of how strenuously they object to being part of the gay tribe—*any* gay tribe—and I remember how desperately Anthony wanted the very thing they reject: to be *a part of us.*

I wish that I could paint a more complete picture of Anthony for you. All those disparate pieces, all those intriguing snippets of his life: that home in Hartford, that basketball hoop, the girlfriends and the football team, the years in prison, the thoughts he must have had late at night staring at the ceiling of his cell, the yearning that led him to me. I wonder how often people come into our lives who impact us greatly and yet remain unknown to us.

Henry's right: I want to be fully present, fully revealed, to the people in my life. But Anthony will have to remain an unfinished person. I'm sorry about that. I can do no more now than let him go.

"Jeff!"

I turn. It's Eliot and Oscar, and behind them come Billy and Adam. The extended family.

Anthony once called them cousins.

There are hugs all around, and Eliot holds me out by the shoulders to look at me. "Girl, it has been a long time!" he gushes. "Where have you *been?*"

"And you never told us you were a writer!" Adam says. "I saw your picture accompanying some article in some magazine, and I said, 'I know him!' I was so *proud!*"

I laugh. Yes, I submitted an article to *The Advocate,* and yes, they published it: a short piece, part of something longer, something still growing, about finding one's soul in the middle of three hundred gay men on a dance floor.

"So maybe you'll write a book someday," Oscar chimes in.

"Yeah. Maybe I will."

"A gay book?" Eliot asks. "Like the great gay American novel?"

I shrug. "I can only hope. But yeah, it'll be gay. I'll definitely be a gay author."

They all hoot, pulling me out onto the dance floor.

"I've missed you guys," I say, falling into their embrace. "I'm so glad you're here."

I spot Lloyd and Henry and Shane, waving them over as we all move out to dance. "This is my partner," I say, introducing them to Lloyd. They all coo over him, sizing him up and down appreciatively. "And you know my two very best friends in the world, Henry and Shane."

Hugs and kisses, lots of hands on chests and grabbing of butts. So maybe the cousins have done a couple bumps of X. But for me at least, the love survives the chemicals. For the moment I feel total bliss. The music mixes into Amber's "Above the Clouds," and I get a little emotional.

"I just want you to know," I say, surprised at how choked up I am, "how very happy I am being with all of you here tonight." I look over at

Henry and Shane and then back at Lloyd, taking his hand. "You are my family. If the past year has taught me anything, it's that. And how important family is."

Lloyd kisses me. "That's very sweet, Cat."

I look off into the crowd on the dance floor. I see Javitz dancing there. He's never far away, thank God.

"Seriously," I say. "I think sometimes we don't appreciate just how much we all mean to each other."

"True, true," Shane agrees.

"And what friendship really means. And how much—"

"Jeff." Henry's suddenly in my face. "We all love you, too. But you're forgetting one thing."

I look at him.

Henry smiles. "No talking on the dance floor."

Everybody laughs. Especially me. I throw my arms around Henry, then Shane, and finally Lloyd. *"We're flying above the clouds,"* I sing out.

"So beautiful and clear," Lloyd sings back.

You see, this is my moment. Someday, when they look back and write about these times, I will be able to say that *I was here*. I danced every dance and knew the words to every song.

I wrap my arms around Lloyd.

I can see everything from here.